MW01181136

Beyond the Knoll

Ginger Cucolo

Allen House Publishing

Cover Image by Mackie Cucolo
Inside sketches by Ginger Cucolo

Published by

Allen House Publishing
2013

www.allenhouseprinting.com

For those who understand…
I may not be good at voices,
but imagination is a whole 'nuther thing.

TABLE OF CONTENTS

Chapter 1
Letters in Time

I looked around my room knowing my new life was better than I ever could have imagined. I glanced over at my luggage, realizing I didn't have too much time before I had to depart, but in my hand was a letter from Ma that just arrived. I looked down at it knowing her words were written before my most recent letter, and most critical, was sent to her. I opened her letter, filled with apprehension about the future.

December 29, 1851

Dearest Allie,

I am stunned at reading your last letter. I believe you to stretch your imagination of my feelings a little too much because of your desperation for this current situation. Whether my feelings are true or not, Brody and I are heading to America. Mr. Farraday would not hear of me going alone, and Brody has spoken often about coming to America to increase business contacts. Mr. Farraday himself would come with us if Patrick had not just returned. Patrick is not well, and Anne Haddock has moved back in to help take care of him. I support Mr. Farraday staying here for Patrick, and since Brody and I have been through so much together, I accepted their offer. We sail on March 12, and will be on a clipper ship like the Seagull, so hopefully we will be with you in the Spring.

When you talk to Captain, please tell him of our pending arrival and we will be willing to help him any way we can.

Your loving Ma

As I finished Ma's letter, I stood up and went to my dresser where I kept a wooden box for my keepsakes. I opened it, looked in, and took out a stack of letters. I sat down at my desk and looked out the window thinking about tomorrow. I sat there, knowing that as I read through the letters I stir memories of years gone by.

Every time I do this, I smile a little, and cry a little, but I needed to do this simply to remember. I had my journal I could read through, but the letters were words from the people I loved and some of my dearest memories. I didn't want to forget these people; I wanted to have them alive and fresh in my memory. I gently untied the ribbon that surrounded the letters and kept them together. I turned the stack over and began to read the letters of the years past.

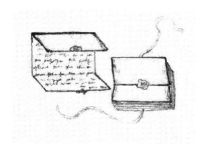

I copied my own letters in the hopes I could remember what I had written before. That was the excuse I used, but I think I copied them to make sure they were more perfect. I wanted Brody to see them and be amazed I had written everything so neatly and correctly. I wanted him to know his mother had done a wonderful job teaching me, and I was continuing my lessons.

I began with one of my very first letters to Ma…

March 5, 1848
Dear Ma,
We had the grandest party for my 14th Birthday! Rufina made small cakes for each of the guests, and it was lovely. Captain gave me two more scarves you would love. One of them is light blue like the sky in the spring, and the other one is an

ivory color that will go with just about anything. Rufina gave me some more bathing salts for she knows how I love them. We invited all of my friends from school, even the ones that are not so kind to me. There is one girl by the name of Irene Butterfield who has lived here all of her life and has a group of girls that follow her around like goslings. They came to my party, but spent most of their time across the room watching, as if we were embarrassing them. I didn't care, though, because it was my party. My first one at that!

I was so exhausted that night. I went to sleep reading your last letter. I'm glad you heard from Uncle Brennan. It sounds exciting that he is in California. I can't believe they found gold! Many people here are talking about closing their shops and heading west. I hope he is able to find some gold and maybe send you some of the takings. Maybe you and Da can come over sooner than expected!

How is Da? You didn't say anything about him in your last letter. Have you seen him? How is Mr. Farraday? And Brody? I miss everyone so much. I am repeatedly reminded of my good fortune with every day that goes by. Please let me know if my letters upset you, for I would never want to hurt your feelings. I tell you because I don't want you to feel left out. Even though we are separated, I feel much closer to all of you and want to hear about everyone and everything. I hope you do, too.

Captain leaves in two weeks for his journey back to Ireland. I can't wait for you to meet him! You will love him. He is kind and generous and doesn't care that I am Catholic! He lets Rufina and I go to Mass. Of course, we now go with Mr. Bruno since he and Rufina are courting. It is very cute. They won't say anything, but I can tell they really like one another. He brings her special things from his bakery, and she takes him food whenever she can. They discuss issues like Da, Mr. Farraday and Patrick used to do. They are currently caught up in something happening in Italy called the Statuto Albertino. While I don't follow everything they say, I like watching Mr. Bruno agree with Rufina and her lively conversations with him. He sits there and shakes his head 'yes' almost all of the time and doesn't seem to have to say anything because she is doing all of the talking. That seems to be enough for both of them!

It will be very different with the Captain gone. I will miss him, but will look forward to hearing from you and your opinion of him.

Write back and let me know about Da.

From your loving daughter,

Allie

April 30, 1848

Dear Ma,

I am writing to you because my patience has never been a virtue. I am keeping a diary with the hope that I can remember each day and share them with you in the future. I hope you are in good health. I worry about you and Da and what might be happening. I understand my imagination gets the best of me, but I don't know how to stop it. Therefore, the diary helps me put my thoughts down and keep me busy.

I actually like writing. My words may only entertain me, but my teacher thinks I have quite a way with words and I should continue with my journal and expressing myself.

By now, I can only hope you have met the Captain and you are happy I am his ward. No one could be any luckier than me. I am so anxious to hear what you think. I can only guess Brody went with you, and you both stayed at Mr. Leeds. Isn't his home wonderful? And Betsy, isn't she wonderful? I am comforted in thinking you stayed with him, and were able to experience such a soft bed, and enjoyed such a wonderful bath. I smile as I think about it, knowing it is wonderful. I wish you could live like that, Ma, always. Maybe when Da and Mr. Farraday get out, you can have a life like that here in America.

I told you about a most unpleasant girl last time I wrote, Irene Butterfield. She is not at all unpleasant to adults, or the friends she has chosen, but to many of us she is quite wretched. She makes fun of my accent and of my friend's hair or clothing. Fortunately, we all wear the same uniforms to school, but at parties, she can be quite rude at times. The other day a friend of mine, by the name of Vivian Arnold, she is my best friend, spilled some punch at a party. Irene called her clumsy and gawky. Vivian is tall and not too sure of how to act because of her height. She is even taller than many of the boys our age. I think she is beautiful and is so interesting. She has a love of Latin and is quite accomplished at it. Irene is mean spirited and sometimes I wish the schoolmaster would give her a good spanking. It takes everything I have to hold my tongue. The Captain tells me I must hold it and will be glad in the end, but that does not help my distress at the moment she is bothering us. Rufina tells me the quickest comebacks, but I dare not use any of them for fear I might be the one that gets the punishment. She says, All are not saints who go to church.

Please write as soon as you can.

From your loving daughter,

Allie

I thought about Irene and how she tormented Vivian and me during our time in school. I still didn't like her, but I had such an attraction to her brother. He didn't seem at all like her. Funny how I could like him, and not his family. I looked back down at the papers and continued with Ma's words.

June 29, 1848

Dearest Allie,

I can only hope I am making the right choice. What I do know is you are not here in Ireland. People continue to die. It is still a struggle to get by, but I feel fortunate the Brumleys still allow me to work for them. Brody continues to help Father Donovan and is able to stay in touch with his father. I have not been able to see Mr. Farraday as much as when you were here. Brody is teaching me to read and write, and this is my first letter I have written completely, myself. What do you think? He gets frustrated with me at times, but I don't blame him. This is quite hard to do. I am glad you are starting at a much younger age. Think of everything you will know! It pleases me greatly to know you will have many more advantages in life than your Da or me. Do not stop telling me about your days because I appreciate every morsel you tell me.

I will write more, soon.

Your loving Ma

August 2, 1848

Dear Ma,

Captain arrived home yesterday and gave me your letter. You thought he was a nice man? Of all the things! I thought he would have made more of an impression on you. I am glad you had a good gut feeling about him, because you are right, he really is a good, nice person. He told Rufina and me last night he has decided he will no longer be making trips to Ireland. The Kate will continue bringing immigrants to America, but he is buying another ship, called a Clipper. He feels he needs to stay closer to home and not be gone for so much time, which Rufina agrees with. He told me I could help him name the new ship. What do you think? What should we call her?

You didn't say anything about Da, again. That worries me. Is he all right? Captain said you told him you had not been able to see him, yet. Must I write Brody for information? Please let me know what you have heard.

You said in your letter Brody is working with Father Donovan. Does he see Mary when he goes to the church or helps around town? Is he still interested in her? And what about Finola? I know you must have met her when you traveled to Galway. What did you think of her? Did they spend time together?

I was a little disappointed you didn't speak of Mr. Leeds or Betsy, more. Do not misunderstand me, I am grateful for any words you write to me, but I yearn to hear anything about you and home.

I do not know why I feel so disgruntled. I have no

reason to be so, so forgive me. I am most grateful for your sacrifices and willingness to let me share a life so far away from you.

I will close now and write again when I am in a lighter mood.

From your loving daughter,
Allie

October 14, 1848
Dear Ma,

Can you believe a year has gone by? I cannot, and am amazed how quickly time has flown. Of course, the Captain has me so involved in so many different activities it helps pass the time.

The Kate should be back in Galway now and ready for her departure. It is the first time the Captain has not been on her and is quite anxious. He trusts everyone on her, but he says anything can happen and it is his responsibility, ultimately. I wish you and Da were going to be on her. I heard about an Irish revolt in Tipperary and wondered if you knew of anyone involved. I hope the British were not too cruel to the Irish involved. I'm sure they will put them in the already overcrowded workhouses.

Speaking of, how is Da? Any word on him, yet? And Mr. Farraday? And Brody? He has not written to me this entire year. I wish he would.

Captain and Rufina have been keeping me informed of news in Ireland, and other places. They say it is best for me to be informed. I have heard about France and the King abdicating, only to have Napoleon Bonaparte become King. Such upheaval! The French continue to be in a mess, too!

Here in New York, cholera has broken out everywhere. They have closed our school in the hopes of curtailing it, but many of my friends and their families have become sick. I only know of three people that have died from it, but many are sick. Rufina is very protective of me and limits my time outside of home. This has not stopped her from going out. She and Mr. Bruno have decided to get married, in March or April. They are hoping to do it when the Captain is here. He is planning a trip on his new Clipper ship, the Seagull. Had I told you the name before? We wracked our minds for a name that would fit this wonderful new ship which is long and narrow with sails that whip like clouds in the sky. It made me think of a seagull and the Captain agreed! She is to be much faster than the Kate is, and he is going to use her for trade along the eastern shore of America. He says it will keep him closer to home. I hope so.

Write soon.

From you loving daughter,

Allie

It was strange to think this year went by so quickly. As I read the letters, I thought about so many things I had left out. I knew I had written more in my diaries, and I thought I had written more in my letters to Ma, but as I looked back over them, I realized I hadn't. I wondered what had kept me from including so much more about my life because, I am sure Ma would have wanted to know. One day, I would try and tell her everything, especially about my letters from Mr. Leeds and my relationships here. There was so much to tell her. I did not want her to feel as though she was left out of my life.

December 17, 1848

Dearest Allie,

Brody and I just read your letter, and he promises to write and tell you about this past year. Mr. Farraday is supposed to get out of his workhouse in the next 6 months and we are hoping this is true. Brody has been trying to contact many of his previous business associates and see if there is any hope for his father's return to business. It does look promising, but it might mean he needs to move to England and I wouldn't quite know what to do without both of them. I do still have the Brumleys, but, well, you know my feelings about them.

Forgive me for not writing of your Da. I think I am reluctant to write you about him when I have had no news. Until now I have heard nothing, and it was only through my own hopes I remained positive. We have word he was moved to a workhouse called, Ballinrobe. This workhouse is in County Mayo, which is good. I am hoping to travel there in the next couple of months when the Brumleys are planning a trip to England and will be gone for two months. I am hoping they will allow me some time off. I will tell Da you ask about him constantly and are concerned that he is okay. I will also tell him you are looking forward to our coming to America. It will be good to tell him of your good fortune, he will be so relieved, I promise you! I'm sure he misses you as much as I do!

Your loving Ma

December 23, 1848

Dear Ma,

I am writing as the snow falls outside and the fires burn warmly inside. It is another year, but we are purposefully not decorating as much as last year. Many more have died from cholera, and both the Captain and Rufina have felt sickly. Angelo helps me take care of them as much as he can. I do not think they have cholera because they do not have the same symptoms as many of the ones we have heard about. I am doing my best to cook and clean so Rufina does not think she needs to do it all of the time, but I don't mind. As I look out the window in my bedroom, I am further reminded how lucky I am to be inside a warm house with people who care for me.

I have not seen Vivian in about a month. I hope she is all right and her family is well. I look forward to the day when we can go back to school. I enjoy the company of many and actually take pleasure in the subjects and I am doing well in Latin and writing. I am enthralled in literature and am often so deeply absorbed my teacher has to call out my name to get my attention! I hope you are able to read, now. Has Brody allowed you to read any of their books? Mrs. Farraday had such wonderful taste in literature, and I was reminded of her as recently as yesterday when I heard the news of Emily Bronte's passing. What a sad day and what a loss for future prose! Her sister's book, Jane Eyre is such a wonderful book, and I hear Emily has one that just came out called, Wuthering Heights. I look forward to reading it.

I will pray the Brumleys are agreeable to your time off. Surely they will not require you to work while they are away? I would not put it past them, so I pray they are more thoughtful about you and your situation.

I am sorry this is such a short letter, but I must get back to the Captain and Rufina. Have a blessed Christmas.

From you loving daughter,
Allie

December 23, 1848
Dear Allie,

I have been a cad for not having written to you sooner. I have no excuse, but I am always glad to hear from you through your mother's letters. Your life seems quite enjoyable and it sounds as though going to America was the right thing for you to do.

Your mother misses you daily, and we do speak of you often. She is working hard for the Brumleys, but you know how little they respect her and her loyalty. We are hoping she is able to travel to see your father, and I will try to go with her if it is possible.

We had a very nice time in April at Mr. Leeds. It is always good to see him, and being able to see Captain Kiper was a delight. He seems quite taken with you and excited about being able to be a part of you education and experience in America. We have not heard from your Uncle Brennan, which has been quite a disappointment for your mother. However, it is with great fortune that Captain Kiper stepped in and accepted you as his own. I'm sure you will learn many exciting things under his tutelage.

My father sends you his best and continues to ask about your well-being. He is doing as well as can be expected, and we are hoping he is to be released in the next six months. I am not sure what the future holds, but I want him to be able to feel valued again and be free whether it is here in Ireland, Britain, or America. Many of his past contacts have offered their assistance, and I am doing what I can to ensure his success.

We have not heard from Patrick. We still assume he is in Australia and doing well. Father wishes we could find him and let him know of his release and that maybe we could all be together again. I am still quite cautious of contacting him and would not want to jeopardize Father's release. Hopefully, in the future, we can find him and be together.

Father has asked your mother to come with us wherever we go for he does not want to leave her alone. She is concerned about your father and her position with the Brumleys. Father is quite partial to your mother and only wants what is best for her, but she has not made a decision, yet. Please do not tell her of my indiscretion in telling you, I would not want her to carry any more guilt than she already carries. I think she would still call father Mr. Farraday if he did not insist otherwise!

I am pleased to hear of your studies and your activities. I know you are enjoying such a wide variety of activities, especially horseback riding. You are probably the best rider, or at least the most determined. I miss riding the most and hope to ride again one day, myself. Mother would be so excited to know you are continuing with your studies.

I will do my best to write again without so much time passing.

Respectfully,
Brody

Well, it was about time, I thought! I wonder why it took Brody so long to write to me? I guess his life has moved on and I was more of a bother than a thought. I had gone through so much in this past year and I truly did not think he had seemed concerned or even cared. I guess it doesn't matter. Rufina used to tell me it must matter if I ask her why he wouldn't write to me. She said I wouldn't bring it up at all if it truly didn't matter. She just doesn't know our history. I don't really care, I just wonder.

Back to Ma…

January 29, 1849

Dear Ma,

We are back in school! Vivian is fine physically, too, but she lost a sister from cholera. The school lost four girls in total and we had a prayer service for them the day school reopened. It was quite sad because the school is so small, you know everyone. Irene is back and hasn't changed. She is still unkind and rude to Vivian and me. I am trying to ignore her. Vivian and I have changed our seats to the opposite side of the room, hoping we can stay away from Irene as much as possible.

Captain and Rufina are fine now, too, and Captain is preparing for his first voyage on the Seagull. He plans to leave in February for Charleston, South Carolina, on the southern part of the east coast of America. He is hoping to trade in coffee and might go to a place called Guatemala. He has relatives that have written to him who are German and settled there to grow coffee. Americans seem to like coffee more than tea, even though Rufina still makes tea for me.

Rufina and Angelo plan to marry in April. After Rufina felt better, Angelo became ill and his business suffered from it being closed. They say they can wait to marry. They haven't decided where they are going to live. Angelo has some rooms above his bakery, and of course, Rufina has a room on a floor at Captain's, which he says they can have the whole floor if she would like to stay. Boy! Wouldn't we have a house full? I would rather Rufina stay here. I like Angelo, and Rufina is always such a busy bee running around and taking care of everyone. She exhausts me at times just watching her!

Can't wait to hear from you and hear if the Brumleys allowed you to visit Da.

From your loving daughter,
Allie

February 12, 1849
Dearest Allie,

I am writing to you on the eve of my trip to England with the Brumleys. They have decided to take me with them, and I am disappointed I am not able to go and see your father during the time they are gone. My trip to see him will have to wait because we are to be gone for six weeks. Mrs. Brumley says I am required to take care of her as her personal maid. Brody is old enough to be on his own, and I really have no other reason not to go. I will be able to collect quite a bit of payment on this trip, so maybe it is a good thing after all.

Thorne's release is ever so promising, (yes, I call him Thorne, now) and there are two constables working on his release. They say there is so much overcrowding, they would be glad to get rid of many of the prisoners. I wish that were the case at your father's workhouse. Right now, the word is Ballinrobe is one of the worst workhouses. Thorne tells me he is willing to go to Ballinrobe and try to gain Da's release as soon as he gets out. I know he can do it and I will look forward to that when we get back from our trip.

I hope Captain Kiper and Rufina are feeling much better now and you are back in school. I look forward to hearing from you and will write again when we have returned. Maybe I will have word of Da!

Your loving Ma

April 2, 1849
Dear Ma,

I am hoping your trip to England was acceptable, even if that meant you had to attend to Mrs. Brumley all of the time. I know she must be a constant source of anxiety, but hopefully you were able to see parts of England that were pleasant, and she allowed you to see some places on your own. Were you able to see the palace? I don't' have much interest in going to England, but since you were there, maybe there was something good that came of your trip.

Since you should be home, now, maybe you have been able to visit Da. Is that so? Please write to me as soon as you can. I want to hear from him and hear what he says about me being in America. He probably has something witty to say.

Captain has been worried about his family and friends in Germany. He tells me of the upheaval their country has been involved with and the revolution. Many have immigrated to Guatemala. Had I told you that? He should be back from his first voyage on the Seagull. He has written and said a life changing event happened to him in Charleston, South Carolina, and he will tell us all about it when he gets home. He also said this ship is much faster than the Kate, and he is glad he purchased her.

I anxiously await word from you.
From your loving daughter,
Allie

May 15, 1849
Dear Allie,

This is not a letter I would ever want to write you. The message is difficult to reveal for I know what anguish it will bring you. Your mother made it to your father's workhouse, and was able to see him. However, you father was quite ill and died shortly after her arrival.

My father was released from his workhouse the week before, and we were both able to travel with her to Ballinrobe.

Father and I were not able to see your father, but your mother was by his bedside when he drew his last breath. We were not able to bring his body back to Knock. The workhouse buried him in their graveyard, and we placed a small marker on his grave. Father promised your mother that one day he would come here with her and bring him home to be buried by Moira and Quinlan.

We have just returned from this journey and your mother asked me to write to you so you know of his passing. She is doing as well as can be expected. Father and I are here for her, and father has spoken to the Brumleys asking them for a few more days off for her to be able to grieve. She is quite strong, and Father is amazed at her resiliency and focus. She wants to get back to work at the Brumleys as soon as possible. Does that surprise you? I think not, she has always been motivated by duty and responsibility, and you would be very proud of her.

I know she is concerned about your reaction and emotional state. She will gather her thoughts and write to you soon. My deepest sympathy goes to you. Your father was a good soul who we shall all miss.

Respectfully,
Brody

I wept as I read over this letter. Brody's words bring back so many memories of Ireland and our families, and all the families that had family member's die. I miss Da, and I miss Moira and Quinlan, and Mrs. Farraday, too. I miss Ireland, even with its horrible situation. I miss the land and the temperament of the people. I miss the gaiety that was once so abundant in our family, and our neighbors. With Captain missing, my heart tugs at what has been lost and can never be recaptured.

I grabbed a handkerchief and dabbed my eyes and wiped my nose, then laid my head in my hands. I put the letters down for a moment and cried. I had a lot to do in the days ahead. Many of it unknown, but I did have the strength of loved ones still alive. I took a deep breath in and raised my head, looking back towards the window and at the sky. The openness of it gives me hope of all that is possible.

I had my memories and wanted to always cherish them. I picked up the letters, knowing I wanted to finish them before I left on my journey.

July 9, 1849
Dear Ma,

I am crushed beyond belief. I have just read Brody's letter and am in distress. Da? Da is gone? I never even considered it a possibility since Mr. Farraday was doing so well. What are the particulars? What did he say? Were you able to let him know where I was? What did he die of?

Captain is allowing me to stay home from school today because of the news. I don't think I could stand seeing Irene and having her treat me most unkindly today. I know that "A silent mouth is melodious," but I'm not sure I could hold my tongue today. Captain is leaving me alone, but Rufina is hovering over me like a mother hen. She says we must go to church right away and say a prayer for Da. I will, I promise, but today I want to sit and cry. I want to envision Da, and I am having difficulty doing so, but I will persevere. I must remember him!

There seems to be so much unrest in the world, and we did hear of Ballinrobe and all that died. We also heard of more uprisings in Germany, and of the French in Italy. I'm sure Captain and Rufina are worried about their loved ones, but they are allowing me to be self-absorbed today, which is good because my mind is on nothing else.

Please tell Brody I know his letter must have been difficult to write, but I appreciate his words and am glad he took the time. Had he not, I would have been worried more so because of the news from Ballinrobe. I am glad he and Mr. Farraday are there for you, you know Da would be grateful.

I pray you are in good health and as strong as I remember. I'm sure Da would want you to be that way. I wish I was home, and together we could comfort one another. Please know I stretch out my arms to you and hold you in my dreams, wanting to catch any tear you might shed for Da.

From your loving daughter,
Allie

May 21, 1849
My Dearest Allie,

My heart weeps for your father, but I knew he was not doing well. How could he? Ballinrobe was a dreadful place with too many people who were sick, and the workhouse was not well kept and the stench was overwhelming. They say over ninety people died within the same week as your father. The Lord blessed me by allowing me to see him before he passed. He was so pleased to hear of your arrival in America, and told me to tell you, "It is a long road that has no turning." He loved you dearly and was very proud of you. As he was dying, he told me a most beloved thing, "My Wife, A tender shoulder to rest upon. A patient ear to sound upon. A soft caress I depend upon. A loving heart to rely upon. All these things I find in you, My only lover and My best friend." Not his own words, for this is an Irish saying, but he spoke it so tenderly. I held his hand and laid my head upon his chest, and he took his last breath.

He is in a much better place now and God will take care of him, and he can watch over us with Moira and Quinlan. As I look up to the sky I am comforted by the thought of their looking over us. I hope you can feel this way, too. Allie, he was so sick and poorly. He was quite thin, in pain, and I would not wish that on anyone. Please allow yourself to remember him in the fondest of ways and be soothed by knowing where he is. Ask Rufina to take you to church and say a prayer for him, and to light a candle, too.

I believe Brody told you about Thorne being released. We are ever so grateful for that, especially since he and Brody went with me to Ballinrobe. I do not know what I would have done without them. They have been such an important part of these difficult times. Brody has grown and matured into a wonderful young man, and has the best of characteristics from both his mother and father. I will miss them if they move to England. I think it will be best for Thorne and Brody, but I am torn. Thorne has invited me to go, but I find it most inappropriate at the moment, and would not want to devalue the memory of your father. Mac was too important to me. I have a good position with the Brumleys and would hate to lose my employment. It is a lot to think about. If you have any thoughts, I would treasure knowing them. I respect what you have to say, so do not be silent at this moment when your ma would welcome your guidance.

Your loving Ma

August 5, 1849
Dear Ma,

Rufina, Angelo, and I have just come back from St. Patrick's Cathedral. I say a prayer every time for Da, and I have added you in my daily prayers. There are quite a lot of people who need prayers, and while I do not think God might particularly listen to me, I feel better by praying for them.

Captain has had quite an awakening since his last voyage. I won't go into the specifics, but he has opened his heart again. This time it is for the brown skinned people, the Negro. He witnessed shocking atrocities and can barely sleep at times. Rufina has been worried about him, and she and Angelo have moved back into the house because she feels she can take better care of him if she is in the house with us. He is supposed to make another voyage in the next week, but Rufina has asked him to postpone it until the spring. I am not sure what he will do.

I have read your letter over and over again, and have put much thought into your situation. While I am deeply grieved by Da's death, neither he nor I would ever want you to be alone. Mr. Farraday and Brody only speak the kindest words of you. I know you, and know you probably will not allow yourself to be considered of their stature. Remember what we have all been through, and that they have never treated you or Da like their tenants and they have been through such an ordeal themselves. Do not deprive yourself of living a better life.

From your loving daughter,
Allie

August 5, 1849
Dear Brody,

I am writing to you in the hopes you can convince Ma to go with you and your father to England. I think you are the best person to sway her your way for she respects your judgment. I would appreciate your consideration of her. Her being alone and left to work for the Brumleys without any support would weigh heavily on my mind.

Please give my best to your father.
Respectfully,
Allie

December 15, 1849
Dear Ma,

I have not heard from you or Brody, and am ever so concerned about your happiness. Another year has come and gone, and I have grown anxious over many things. Perhaps I am just melancholy. The Captain continues his personal disgust of slavery, and I support him completely, but worry about his safety. This year marks the passing of Da, and many in the artistic world – Anne Bronte and Edgar Allen Poe, Chopin and Strauss. Rufina reminds me to be strong and thankful, and we continue to go to church and pray for those we worry about. We have added President Taylor to our list since there is unrest in America, and Rufina says he will need it.

We are on break from our school, and this is the first time I am grateful to take a break. Vivian will not be coming back. Her parents want her to be a governess for a family in Philadelphia, and she will be teaching their children and helping rear them. She is all right with the thought of being a governess. I think she can do so much more, but she feels as though this is what she is supposed to do. She promises to stay in touch, but I have been told that many times, and end up losing the ones I wish to stay in touch with.

I hope you are not alone this season, and not working for the Brumleys anymore!

From your loving daughter,
Allie

January 2, 1850
Dear Allie,

I sit at my desk in our home in London, England as I write you this letter. I have once again allowed too much time to pass, but we have been totally consumed with moving and with father's renewal of business associates. It goes quite well and the British have once again welcomed us into their world. We are close to Westminster Cathedral. This is not the Abby where the royal family is buried, but a Catholic church. Father has returned to his devotion of the Catholic Church and much of it has to do with the influence of your mother.

I took to heart your request at convincing her to join us here in London. As you can imagine, she has quite a stubborn streak, and no amount of my persuading swayed her one bit. Even father could not get her to move. She finds it difficult to change her status and move on. Father understands. He writes to her at least once a week, and promises to visit every month. He is not giving up, just yet!

She continues to work for the Brumleys, and steadfastly believes they might get their come-uppance still. Word is out the tide is turning for the Irish. We will not hold our breath, but as you can imagine, the hope for a successful potato crop is the New Year's wish. We shall all hope for the best!

Mr. Leeds wrote and told us about the new venture Captain Kiper has taken for slaves and their circumstances. I would be quite interested in learning about his deeds. It sounds quite admirable.

Respectfully,
Brody

February 22, 1850
Dear Ma,

Brody has just written me and told me of his father's attempt to get you to London. You must be blarmy! Can there be a sensible reason for your loss of reason? I think not. You choose the Brumley's over a new life in London? I would ask that you explain yourself, and yet, I am almost certain I understand why. It is not just Da's passing, but also your inability to see yourself as more than a work horse. While I realize I will not change your mind, I am begging you to remain open about a life outside of Knock.

I have spoken to Captain about you since he says the two of you correspond at times. I have asked him to impress upon you the value of yourself. You are a person of character and love and should be happy in life. I have told him my opinion of the Brumleys and the way they treat you. Pay heed to his opinion.

While Captain works against slavery, Rufina has chosen to support the Women's Movement. If anything, I have been placed in a socially conscious household. Through Rufina, I have received some of my best opinions for Vivian, but she still holds steadfastly to her role as a governess. I am supportive of her, but I feel she has so much more to offer. At least she is teaching her children, and hopefully they will learn to love the subjects that she did so well in.

Irene has decided I am a blot as a student. She says I need to take more time to learn more of sewing and manners. I listen, but enjoy literature, writing, and languages so much more. Captain and Rufina say I am fine and they are glad I have a mind of my own, but I must realize there is always a place and time for differences. I have still held my tongue, but it remains a difficult thing for me to do.

From you loving daughter,
Allie

I smiled and looked out the window, remembering this letter and the time where I had no idea of Ma's true intentions. I read on, knowing what was to come of all of it, now.

February 23, 1850
Dear Brody,

I am at a loss for mother! Her self-absorption is not ego but self-esteem. And even then, it is not her belief in herself, but her value of herself. Do you not agree? How could such a wonderful person not value their self more? I believe she would not feel this way if she were brought up in another class system. I hate the class system, and understand the Captain's strong feelings for the injustice of Negroes here in America.

His new ship takes him to a place in America called Charleston, South Carolina. He has decided to trade in coffee, and gets the coffee from a country called Guatemala. On one journey to Charleston, he was unloading his coffee when he heard anguished crying from across the dock area. He left his ship to see what the raucousness was about and came across a sale of Negroes. He inquired as to the goings on, but was pushed aside by those involved in the sale. He was horrified at the scene. He said they were pulling families' apart and selling family members to different people. Mothers, fathers, and children were crying. Pulling at their new owners to let them go. He was appalled and sickened at the situation. He could do nothing at the moment, but knew he could not live with himself if he did nothing.

Since his time back at home, he has questioned many who he believes are sympathetic to the cause. There are quite a few abolitionists who have given him guidance as to their mission. He believes he can use his new ship to help in the cause. The Seagull is fast and sleek and should be a perfect ship to help him in this risky undertaking.

I would be glad to help him, but he says it is too dangerous for me to know too much. However, I am quite sneaky in my ways and find out more than he believes I know. Please do not tell, for I am sincerely interested in helping, too. I will be safe.

Vivian, my best friend, is enjoying being a governess. While she could be doing so much more, she chooses, and is happy, to be doing this. Irene says it is her place and I should be hoping for something as good, but I do not respond to her suggestions. Her implying that doing the same as her would be good for me is such a reproach to me.

There is so much out there in the world, I can't imagine being limited by anyone or anything. I guess I have your mother to thank for that! She introduced me to a completely new world in literature, and being in America, especially New York, has shown me the possibilities are endless.

I suppose you are enjoying London as much as I enjoy New York. I am sure your father is grateful for your help during this time. Will you be traveling back to Ireland with him? Tell him I appreciate his regard for Ma and staying in touch with her.

I look forward to hearing from you.

Respectfully,

Allie

March 25, 1850

Dear Allie,

Father and I have traveled back to Knock and we have seen your mother. Her mind has not changed, and she is determined to remain in Ireland. She says her situation at the Brumleys is much better since they are now spending more time in London. We will have to find them and interact with them socially. It would be interesting to hear what they have to say now that we are in London, too.

We enjoyed seeing her and she was quite attentive and

sincere to us. Father brought her small gifts and two dresses from London. Your mother said she could not accept them, but father left them in her trunk before we left. He did not want her to feel as though it was charity. When we left, she did ask us to come back, so we will definitely continue to write and visit.

County Mayo is hoping for a much better year. The crops are on schedule and men in the pubs are optimistic. Father says business is opening up again, and with health concerns going down and crops growing again, maybe Ireland is beyond the worst of times.

I was able to see Mary. Do you remember her? Her family is doing fine and they are staying in the area. She has begun spinning and selling her yarn to tailors. Isn't that what Moira used to do?

You have not spoken of your studies, or more so, if you are reading. I hope you have many books available to you whether through school, Captain Kiper, or the library. I hear your city has opened a library, which I hope is a reference for many enjoyable books, and gives you the ability to research more. We have a collection at the British Museum here and father encourages me to go daily to read newspapers from around the world and see what is new. I am researching possible new contacts for him, including those in America. It seems as though the population is going west.

Which reminds me, have you heard from your Uncle Brennan? I forgot to inquire about him when we visited your mother. I would be interested in his thoughts on the west. I admire his courage in setting out alone and facing dangers and situations where you have no idea what is to happen. I am not sure I could undertake such an adventure.

I hope you have kept a written record of your adventures because I believe you will be glad you have done so one day. Just your voyage to America was one to be remembered. You are quite brave yourself, Allie.

Respectfully,
Brody

May 5, 1850

Dear Brody,

It is quite remarkable to me that my Uncle Brennan is seen as courageous by you. I felt abandoned by him, but Captain tells me I must not feel this way towards him. He says I would not be a part of his life if Uncle Brennan had taken me away. He is right, of course, but I was disappointed. I think Ma probably was, too. Who knew my fortune would be so lucky? Not everyone has turned out this way. There are many here who are orphans and in workhouses, or in a section of town called, Five Points. I think it is called that because of streets coming together in this section. You may have heard of it in writings of Charles Dickens. He said, "This is the place: these narrow ways diverging to the right and left, and reeking everywhere with dirt and filth. Such lives as are led here, bear the same fruit here as elsewhere. The coarse and bloated faces at the doors have counterparts at home and all the wide world over. Debauchery has made the very houses prematurely old. See how the rotten beams are tumbling down, and how the patched and broken windows seem to scowl dimly, like eyes that have been hurt in drunken frays. Many of these pigs live here. Do they ever wonder why their masters walk upright in lieu of going on all-fours? And why they talk instead of grunting?" I could be living there, but someone, somewhere, is blessing me and I feel it is my duty to repay the good fortune. I have no idea how, but Rufina says I must finish school first and then I may allow my destiny to be determined.

I have been writing my daily thoughts and activities down in a journal. I enjoy writing and have continued reading. Captain is very thoughtful and tries to buy me books he thinks I will enjoy, which normally means Rufina has told him of ones I have been talking about. I remind him we do have a library, and will gladly go and read the books they have. He goes with me sometimes and it is an enjoyable outing for us both.

My latest interest is a very long poem by Henry Wadsworth Longfellow. He is an American writer, and this is a fairly new published work. Have you ever heard of him? This is titled, Evangeline. I was so enthralled as I read it, the Library was closing, and the Librarian stood over me clearing her throat repeatedly. I picked it up as if I was leaving and went between two bookshelves and plopped down on the floor to finish it. It is such a lovely, but tragic story, and the story so completely consumed me. I heard the huge doors being pulled to and locked. I dropped the book and ran to the doors as the librarian gave me a most displeased look. I ran right past her and out the doors! If you get the chance, it is a story about survival, adversity, strength, and love. I even think they have a tree connected to this story. Remember your mother's story of the mulberry tree? That is a most precious memory to me.

I am gladdened by the fact your father and you are continuing to visit mother. Hopefully she will come around. I know she would enjoy London and maybe even thrive in a new environment. Captain says he continues to stay in contact with her, also, and they have discussed her coming here. While I would love for her to be here with me, I know it would be very difficult for her to leave Ireland. At least England is much closer! I have not heard from her lately, so I appreciate your correspondence to me.

Respectfully,
Allie

I had not thought about Uncle Brennan in such a long time. I wondered what had become of him? I read about the Gold Strike in the penny papers and the New York Tribune, and things do not seem to be going very well for many of the miners. Strange we haven't heard from him.

May 6, 1850
Dear Ma,
Brody has informed me of his visit with his father. Did you ever try the dresses on? I'm sure he has wonderful taste and the dresses are probably quite nice. Wouldn't it be wonderful to

go somewhere in them and enjoy yourself? I think London would be a very suitable place for you to wear them!

Captain has been quite busy here with his many responsibilities. With both ships working, he has quite a demanding schedule. Also, he has been restoring this house and adding what he calls a safe room. It is not very large, but this hole in the ground is being constructed under the kitchen table. Isn't that queer? I have enjoyed watching him, Rufina, and Bruno do this work. We are not to tell anyone, but surely telling you will not jeopardize their work. What do you think it could be? It will be interesting to see when it is all finished, and I will let you know.

School is almost done for the year. There is a dance at the end of school, and if you can believe, Irene's older brother asked me to go with him. He does not seem at all to be like his sister. I dare not tell him of my thoughts regarding her, but I do not know how he could not know. Rufina say boys do not always see what is obvious, and I should accept his sincerity. He is quite good looking, and many of the girls at school have affection for him. I do not know him very well, but the school is a safe place for us to socialize says Rufina. Captain is not too sure, but Rufina has promised to be there as a chaperone. We picked out a fetching new dress, and I am going to wear my hair in a different style which I hope will be pleasing.

Too bad we cannot wear our new clothes together. Mother and daughter in new dresses, wouldn't that be delightful! I could try to style your hair in a new way, too! Is it still long? Have you changed it since we last saw one another?

Take care of yourself.
From your loving daughter,
Allie

July 20, 1850
Dear Allie,

It seems as though I am the one that brings you unfortunate news. However, this story looks as if it is going to have a happier ending. Father went back to Knock in June after Mrs. Knapp wrote him a letter to tell him of your mother's illness. She has been in poor health and did not let father or me know. Supposedly, she was sick when we last visited, but kept it from us. Father made it to her as quickly as he could and stayed with her until she was feeling better. He has convinced her to come home with him and I am expecting them any day now. I have prepared a room on our main floor where she can rest and be comfortable. Father was passionate in his request to me to find a midwife who can watch over her and help her regain her strength. I have done so and we will be glad when she is here and we can help her with her recovery.

In your last letter, you spoke of Evangeline and your peaked interest in its story. I have read the poem and smile at the thought of your scurrying through the library to finish it in one sitting. Mother would have enjoyed this poem. Father planted a mulberry tree in our back yard in memory of her. He and I have fond memories also of that tree and the knoll it sat upon. It seems like it was so long ago, does it not? It would be nice to go back in the future and sit below its branches once again.

I sensed a feeling of resentment in my telling you of my admiration of your Uncle Brennan. Forgive me for my callousness. I should have known it would ruffle your feathers. I always seem to be able to do that, don't I? It makes me laugh, but I didn't mean it in that way. You haven't changed very much. The same Allie I remember, so next time I will try to think before I write.

Your mother should be here soon and we will take very good care of her. She has done that for all of us, and now we can repay her. If anything, she will get a good rest and be able find her strength again. Do not worry, if you can.

Respectfully,
Brody

September 30, 1850

Dear Ma,

I was alarmed at Brody's letter this past time and of your illness. You push yourself too hard and do not take care of yourself! I see that in the Captain, too, and have to force him to stop at times. Please take care of yourself. I am pleased to hear Mr. Farraday has whisked you out of Knock and brought you to London. If anything, you are being taken care of now and can enjoy a lifestyle you are not accustomed to. Try to accept the help, even though I am sure it will be difficult for you. I think it is best. Even Captain says it is best, and he says to tell you he will write soon.

I do not know what news you received while in Ireland, but Brody told me he keeps up with world news for his father in London. The man that was the President here died in July. The new one is named Millard Fillmore. Rufina says we are to add him to our prayers. I continue to pray for you and will add extra words for you in the hopes you allow the Farradays to take care of you.

Captain told me quite a bit about his reason for the new hole under the kitchen table. I understand it now and will one day explain it to you. I think you would appreciate its purpose and understand its meaning. He has also been concerned about Germany, but says he can only change that for which he is able.

We were able to see a German opera by Richard Wagner called, Lohengrin. Neither he, Angelo, nor I particularly liked it, but Rufina loved it. It was my first opera. I don't know if you would like it or not. Hopefully we will go together one day and you can share your opinions of it with me. I would like that. We also went to a concert by the famous singer, Jenny Lind. What a triumph! She is such a gifted and remarkable woman. They call her the Swedish Nightingale. Before we went, I couldn't imagine why, but after hearing her, I wish, I wish I could sing. She was inspirational. Rufina has not stopped singing since. Bruno loves her to be this way, but I think I could do without it all of the time! Fortunately they are back in their place above his bakery. She is working with him, and they are thinking about opening another one, or enlarging this one. She likes to be busy, so this will be good for her. I still see her every day, she stops by Captain's house, or I go to the bakery. I like doing that because Bruno always gives me a warm cookie. I like the shortbread ones the best. He makes them especially for me he tells me. When you come to America, we will go and get a shortbread cookie.

Rest and allow yourself to be tended after.

From your loving daughter,

Allie

December 15, 1850

Dear Brody,

I haven't heard from you or mother and am most dismayed I suppose you have both chosen to leave me in suspense, but am hopeful it is because of encouraging things taking place, not negative. You have been the bearer of bad news in the past, and I presume you would do the same again if the situation warranted. Captain Kiper says I shouldn't be sullen about it, even though he has not heard a word from Ma, either. I can tell he is a little concerned, but he would never let me know.

He carries quite a lot on his shoulders. I pray this letter not be placed in the wrong hands, for the very reading of it would put his life in jeopardy. Please do not tell anyone for the exact same reason. Captain Kiper is part of a group of people that takes slaves from the southern states in America and helps them escape to the north. He uses the Seagull, and hides as many as he can in her hull where there is a hidden hold. So far he has not been caught, but there is always the risk of it happening. He has had two voyages this year, and hopes to continue doing this to help as many Negroes as he can.

The import of coffee is his ruse and cover for him. I guess it is not just a ruse for he sells the coffee and imports it as before. This is a secret network of people, and I am hoping you will keep his secret, including not telling Ma. This would worry her greatly. When I am finished with school this May, I hope to help him all of the time. He does not know of my wishes, but I plan to ask him after Christmas day.

Captain and I had a wonderful ride the other day. I do enjoy horseback riding, and I find it very comforting. He was thrown once because he didn't know his horse very well, but jumped right back on. Rufina and Angelo have no interest in learning how to ride, which is difficult for me to understand. How could anyone not love it? Have you been able to ride again? As we were returning to the stables, a soft, slow snow began to fall. The flakes were enormous, looking the size of mints that Angelo makes. I love the snow during the holidays. We stay inside quite a bit, with a fire burning and are able to do more reading. It is quite peaceful.

Please encourage Ma to write. Or would you help her if she were not feeling well? I just need to hear from her, and hear that she is safe.

Respectfully,
Allie

December 15, 1850
Dear Allie,

I have good news! Your mother has recovered and is doing splendidly. She has run our midwife, Mrs. Haddock, from the house! Well, she did not actually run her from the house. Your mother started feeling better in October and Mrs. Haddock started feeling ill. Your mother fell right in to her usual paces of taking care of everyone, including Mrs. Haddock. Father told her repeatedly we could get help for Mrs. Haddock, but your mother insisted on taking care of her since Mrs.

Haddock had taken care of her. Your mother is definitely back to her old ways! And neither father nor I can persuade her any better than before. She and Mrs. Haddock became fast friends, and after her illness subsided she moved back home, but stays in touch with your mother. They meet at the market at times and catch up with each other. Father enjoys your mother's determination.

She has new clothes, and is able to spend more time on herself. She spends quite a bit of time reading and trying to improve herself, so we must not shame her for that. I am proud of her, as is father. I wish you could see her. I do believe you would be surprised and happy for her.

We have gone out a few times, and if you will believe, have been in the same social circles as the Brumleys. Can you imagine your mother? Father stands by her proudly, as do I. Your mother shrinks from embarrassment, but we hold her elbows and move along. At first no one else knew the situation, nor should they, but I must admit Mrs. Brumley has made it difficult. She is a gossip, and while your mother remains kind and considerate, Mrs. Brumley is the epitome of boorish behavior. Maybe she and your Irene are kin?

We all wish you could be with your mother this holiday. London is a sparkling city full of festive decorations and historical buildings. Father is reading Charles Dickens, A Christmas Carol, on Christmas Eve to a small group of friends. Mr. Dickens is a friend of fathers, and he had originally said he would be reading his story, but he has had to change his plans. Your mother is quite taken with some of his writings, and is enamored with him, I believe. I think it is more of his notoriety than him in actuality. I will ask him of this Five Corners you spoke of and hear his thoughts on the situation.

By the time you receive this letter, it will be a new year for all of us. Maybe this year will bring less anxiety and more happiness for each of us.

Respectfully,
Brody

January 4, 1851
Dear Allie,

It is a new year and I have not been able to keep up with the time. So much has happened, and while I know Brody has written you about much of it, I want you to hear it from me.

First of all, I am fine and have recovered from a most

frustrating illness. I am not sure if I would have left Ireland at all if it were not for Thorne and Brody. If it were not for the two of them, I am not sure I would be alive today. I was exhausted and ill with a high fever, not allowing myself to stop. Needless to say, the Brumleys were not considerate of my situation until they thought they might get sick from me. Brody said I should have allowed myself to get too close to one of them. Nevertheless, Thorne spoke to them giving them notice of my resignation. He left, and I never went back. He then made arrangements for me to come to London, and here I am.

Their home is lovely. Smaller than their estate in Knock, but their own home once again. Thorne and Brody have taken the time to find things that make it look as if they had lived there for years. You would love it. They have shelves and shelves of books, and fireplaces in almost every room. I feel as though I am a kept woman. They do not treat me that way and there is no reason for me to think that way, I just can't seem to wake up to the reality of it. I have the best time with Thorne and Brody and enjoy every moment I am with them. You do understand that it does not mean I did not love your father. I still love him dearly, and keep him in my prayers.

Do you think the Brumleys will hold their tongue? I truly doubt the Mrs. will, especially when I call her by her first name...Ivy! Kate, take a breath. Now, I will have to let it go, because it is quite unkind for me to even discuss it.

Write to me with your thought. I shall wait for your response before deciding on anything.

Your loving Ma

February 8, 1851
Dear Brody,

Finally! You have left me worried for months! Did you not think I would be worried sick? I have never been very patient and both of you should know this! I will however forgive you since you letter was most encouraging. I am calmed.

How very gratifying to know mother is out and about

and no longer working for the Brumleys. I want to come to London just to give Mrs. Brumley my piece of mind! I will try to send Ma my opinion of the matter and see if it makes any difference. I hope you do not mind, I shared your letter with Captain. He was worried about Ma, too, and now feels relieved to know she has recovered from her illness. He asked many questions, but I suggested he write to her directly. Your father has done so much for mother. I am eternally grateful.

Captain leaves at the end of this month for another trip to Guatemala, and then stopping in Charleston and other towns on his way back to New York. He continues his missions and is involving me more. We have just come back from a trip. I was able to travel on the Seagull for the first extended time since my voyage to America. This one was much more acceptable and pleasant, even though it was quite cold. We went north to Boston, Massachusetts and saw many things I have been reading about. It was a delightful trip. Rufina came with us to cook, and she even enjoyed the trip. I think she was too worried about me to allow me to come alone! I loved Boston, and told the Captain I would enjoy traveling with him more if the sailing was calm as this trip. It snowed often and the days were short, but Captain and I were together with Rufina again and it was like our first times together. The trip will be a good memory.

If I think about that, it makes me rather sad. I guess mother and I are starting a completely new set of memories without one another. You are lucky to have her there with you. Forgive me, you are lucky to have your father there, too. You will all have good memories together.

Respectfully,
Allie

March 15 1851
Dear Ma,

It is honorable for you to think of Da, but he would not want you to be left alone and unhappy. Being with the Farradays is like being with family, so please do not allow others to bother you with thinking ill of you.

Captain is gone on another voyage to Guatemala. It is turning out to be a profitable decision. Captain has created quite a good relationship with the Germans who live there and are farming coffee. I am glad I get to see him more. He has taken me on a voyage where I actually enjoyed the trip. Can you believe that would be true? I wasn't sure I would ever get on a ship again, but the Seagull is such a sleek and fast moving ship. I hope he will teach me how to sail her one day. I will have to cut my hair and dress like a boy, but what fun it would be! Do not worry, he says there is no thought that he would allow me to sail her. At least not yet!

I have been waiting more than six months to tell you of a friendship I have. Remember Irene? And her brother? Well, Irene has not come around to accepting me, yet, but her brother, Jonathan Butterfield has. Doesn't his name sound wonderful? He has Da's name, so it must be an indication of irrefutable association. Remember Captain's ship? She had your name, and now Jonathan has Da's. I am so excited about his visits. Rufina is not too sure, yet, but she helps me get ready every time. I get quite thrilled when he asks me to go somewhere. This week he is taking me to his home for dinner. Actually Captain is going with us, but Jonathan has promised to pick us up. I am nervous about this meeting because I have never met his parents. I have seen them at school functions, but Jonathan never introduced me, and you know Irene never wanted me to meet them, so I am nervous. Did I say that already?

Here we both are with a different life. Isn't it unexpected? You know Mr. Farraday, and Brody, and should have absolutely no qualms about staying with their family. Won't Patrick be excited? I'm sure he would be delighted, too.

This May I shall finish my schooling! I am proud of myself for completing this part of my education and am not sure what the future holds. But for now, I shall wait eagerly for your letter and the news it will surely carry!

From your loving daughter,
Allie

June 2, 1851

Dear Allie,

I sat there smiling as I read your letter, and didn't move an inch except to turn your pages! I know you are about to be quite upset with me, but I moved in with my dear friend, Ann Haddock, shortly after my last letter to you. She was the woman who Brody hired to nurse me back to health. Thorne pays for my lodging because I asked him to help me. He does not want me to work, and I must admit the women in our social group do not work outside of the home, and so I accept his kindness of payment so I might be able to think better and feel better about the situation.

My dear friends, Ann Haddock and Clara Fallon are being ever so supportive of my situation. Clara lost her husband, Captain Fallon, at the British Garrison of New Zealand during the Flagstaff War. Thorne is kind enough to include them in many of our social gatherings. Clara is a very kind and generous person who shows me strength through her own actions, but in quiet and respectful ways. She, Thorne, and I enjoy one another's company and all share an accepting sense of loss. However, she was born and reared in a higher social status than I, but she would never treat me any differently than she does now. She is accepting like Thorne.

I am not sure if I am able to live a life like this. Will I always doubt myself? If my life was to only be with the Farradays, I think I would be all right, but to be in social groups with the likes of the Brumleys is very difficult, and they do not make it any easier.

Brody is in Galway visiting Mr. Leeds and taking care of business for Thorne. I am glad you have feelings for someone, because Brody and Finola have been corresponding with one another, and he jumped at the chance to go to Galway. She is a nice young woman, and I think she is good for him. I know Mr. Leeds likes her and her family, and is excited Brody is interested in her. Brody has no shortness of young ladies who are interested in him. He is handsome and the perfect height and build. What I think is so charming is his truly courteous ways. I state I am glad you have found a beau because I always felt you had a fondness for Brody, something very special and private, and I didn't want you to be upset if you were besotted with him. Now that it is out in the open, Thorne and I can relax and not worry. I will be glad to hear about your meeting Jonathan's family. I can understand why you would be nervous, but I'm sure they will grow to be very fond of you.

Thorne, Brody, Clara, and I have all gone to the Great Exhibition here in London. It is a fantastic site! We were there for its opening and I was able to glimpse Queen Victoria. She came in with her family as cannons went off and the crowd cheered. It took my breath away at how spectacular all of it was. The exhibition hall is one enormous glass structure with sparkling lights shining so brightly. If you can believe, it is so large they have placed full size trees inside! You would find such pleasure in seeing all of this. I thought of you constantly as we viewed all of the exhibits.

By now you have finished school and hopefully are enjoying your summer. Let me know what you and the Captain have planned for the Fall.

Your loving Ma

I stopped and took a breath, remembering my complete indignation at the slightest hint of my caring for Brody in the way Ma described. I looked back over my own letters and see nothing that would even hint of such a thought! Maybe she was projecting her own wishes on to me. I liked Jonathan, I thought – Jonathan!

August 14, 1851
Dear Ma,

What in the world would make you think I fancied Brody? I don't see him like that. Do you not remember how we squabbled, or how angry he used to make me? Japers! Brody? I think not! Absolutely do not think that! I do not know if Finola is right for him, but if she is whom he wants, then he would know best. I must scold Mr. Leeds, for in all of his letters, he has not hinted at the coming together of these two, either.

I am baffled at your decision to move out of Mr. Farraday's home. Captain says it would be best for me not to fret over your decision, because it is ultimately up to you. He reminds me we want what is best for you in the end, but I am still fretting as I write this letter.

I have read of the Great Exhibition and dreamt of seeing it. Captain and I discussed coming to London, but are aware of our responsibilities here. Save any memorabilia from the exhibition so that I might see it in the year to come. I am sure it will be a wonderful memory for you.

Let me tell you of Jonathan. When I last wrote, Captain and I were going to his house to meet his parents. Rufina was itching to go, and told me she wanted to be a fly on the wall! I wish she had been. I would have loved for her to see and hear all that went on! Jonathan picked us up in their carriage and brought us to their home. It is a lovely, huge, stone mansion with a rounded entrance drive that lends itself room for many a buggy along its road. There are two stone lions that sit atop two pillars and watch over their home. It is rather cold looking and fits his family's personality perfectly. Jonathan is the only considerate person in the lot! A butler brought us in to their home, and into a humongous open entryway whose ceiling went two floors up. The stairs split in the middle and rounded up the walls to the second floor. The butler then took us in to a side room that had formal loveseats, a piano, a desk, and a very large fireplace with a dog that lay on the ground in front of it without even moving! I wasn't sure if he was dead or not! Jonathan was polite to us and kept us involved in conversation until the rest of his family came in. When his parents and a younger sister came in I jumped up having felt my heart leap from my chest. Captain handled it perfectly. I felt as though my tongue was swollen and I couldn't talk. When Irene came in, my tongue relaxed, but my anger took over.

She had a look of disdain on her that never subsided the

entire time. It was as if Captain and I were two stray dogs in her house, and uninvited at that! Jonathan never made us feel that way, but Irene never stopped. Her family was quite aloof during the meal and social time. The lions in the front of the house were a perfect representation of the way they acted. Jonathan's father is a Banker, which should mean nothing, except they seem to act as though they were above us in culture because Captain only has a fleet of two ships! Captain never allowed them to bother him, and he remained gentlemanly the entire time. When Jonathan took us home, he apologized, but I was disappointed in his seeming inability to stand up to his parents. He never said a word as they made sly remarks. We had our first row after that, but have made up since. I understand his position a little better now.

Before this event, we had only seen each other about five times. We had gone to the school dance, and then to the library two times. He doesn't particularly like that. We met at Angelo's bakery once and he walked me home, and then he met me at school once and walked me home. Rufina says I should not think Jonathan would not be seeing anyone else, or that I should not. She has warned me of his family's reputation and she knows it would be difficult for him to go against them. She wants me to find someone who wants me, and likes me the way I am. Isn't that like a mother? She is such a worry wart!

Well, I have gone on and on. We still see each other, and have professed our love for one another! I find him very acceptable, but we are not able to be together as much as we would like. Jonathan is going to college to be a banker like his father, and I am helping Captain with his ships. Captain says there is still time for me and not to rush into anything, yet. You know how good I am at waiting! Fortunately, there is quite a bit for Captain and me to do, so time passes quickly.

From your loving daughter,
Allie

September 2, 1851

Dear Allie,

I am not sure when I wrote to you last, so I cannot remember what I have told you. Your mother has kept me informed of the past few months. It sounds as though your life is full and you are happy with your situation. I am attending Oxford and working with Father. I have been consumed with school and our business. We have even been able to expand our relations with ships traveling to Australia. We are hoping to find Patrick and bring him home to London, but we have not received word from him in years

I have been to Galway a few times since I last wrote. Mr. Leeds says he is always glad to hear from you, and Betsy enjoys it, too, of course. Her son is a good boy, and says he is looking forward to working with his father in a mill. At six! I am sure Mr. Leeds keeps you informed of her family.

On my previous trip to Galway, I was informed of the horrible condition of the ships that took immigrants to Ireland. They are calling them Death Ships. I had heard this before, but am appalled at the actual representation that is shown now, and the facts behind them. You are quite a lucky young girl, Allie. It is appalling to think of the situation that occurred. Father has become quite strict in his acceptance of contracts. I can understand the Captain's persistence in trying to improve the black people's situation. It should be improved. Your story of his witnessing has been deeply rooted in my thoughts. It is a worthy cause.

There is word here about a much awaited book called, The Whale. It is to be published here soon in England. It is written by Herman Melville, and is to be a stupendous sea story. I am looking forward to it. I have read two of his other works, Typee and Omoo. They are about the South Seas, a place I have never been but hope to encounter in my lifetime. It sounds like a different time and place from Ireland or England.

Respectfully,

Brody

November 19, 1851

Dear Brody,

Rufina and I are preparing for Thanksgiving. This is an American holiday, which started in recognition of Pilgrims finding success here in their new world. I have read about it, and this is our first time to celebrate it. Rufina is cooperating with me because she enjoys cooking and the family being together. Captain should be home in the next couple of days and we should have a wonderful day together. We will probably be feeding more than just us, but I am pleased each time we do such a thing because it means we have helped someone

You did not speak of your complete trip to Galway. For example, you did not speak of Finola. How is Finola? Mother tells me you visit her when you go to Galway, so I am surprised you have not mentioned her before. Mr. Leeds has not either. I find it queer you would not say something about her in your letters to me.

I will assume Mother has told you of Jonathan. He is the son of a Banker and is quite smitten with me. He goes to Columbia. It was previously known as King's College, which was established in 1754 for King George II. He comes from a very smart family who is accomplished in their fields and has quite a large amount of property to show for it. I do not get to see him as much as I like, but every time he has time off, he makes an effort to see me. We have picnics and go horseback riding. Captain likes him and thinks he is good for me.

How ironic that you bring up Herman Melville's book, The Whale. It has just come out here, but titled, Moby Dick. Captain is a friend with Mr. Melville's family who are merchants here in New York. I read his book, Typee, but have not read the following one. There does not seem to be much fuss about it here.

If you would like a good read, please take the time to find and read, Uncle Tom's Cabin, by a woman named Harriett Beecher Stowe. It is a good characterization of the situation Captain has witnessed, and for what is happening in America.

We have read her work before in her articles she wrote for papers, and look forward to her published book. It should be quite captivating.

We have a newspaper here now called, The New York Times. We have our normal penny papers, and the New York Herald. Two major papers, publishing a new one every day to disseminate the news. I cannot imagine, but hope they will be able to keep their promise. They have writers from everywhere. Since the railroads have expanded and the telegraph system has been instituted, I guess they can get information constantly. Isn't that remarkable? I will look forward to reading one of them every day and finding out what is happening all over the world.

I cannot close without telling you of two authors who died this year. They remind me of our lives before. Did you hear of the passing of Mary Shelley and James Fenimore Cooper? Remember his books? I wonder if Uncle Brennan has encountered such activities? Surely he has seen some of the wilderness as described by James Audubon. I heard he died, also. Jonathan's family has some of his prints in their home. They are astonishingly detailed. The Butterfield's say Mr. Audubon gave them the prints they have in their study. They have enough money to purchase whatever they like, and their friends are of very high stature, like the Brumleys.

Respectfully,
Allie

December 20, 1851
Dear Allie,

We are preparing for another Christmas, but this one will be very special. Patrick has contacted us and is taking a ship from Australia to England. The ship is supposed to arrive by Christmas, so father, your mother, and I are all excited about his arrival. This year, Mr. Dickens has promised to read his story to our gathering. Your mother is starting to feel more comfortable and has planned a wonderful meal and decorated superbly. She is finding a place for herself amidst all of the social turmoil. She is doing some sewing for other women and has received some very good reviews from women who are impressed by her designs. She also helps Mrs. Haddock with her nursing. Your mother has a wonderful sensitivity for those struggling in the poor areas of London. She volunteers there and has a special connection with many of the people. She says she would try not to work, but I truly do not believe it is in her blood.

Did you hear that James Fenimore Cooper died? Were you ever able to finish his series? I can still hear Mother reading to us, and see her sitting up against the mulberry tree on the knoll with her head slightly cocked and shifting as she reads his book.

We will keep you informed of Patrick and our Christmas,

Respectfully,

Brody

November 23, 1851

Dear Ma,

As we get closer to Christmas day, we are still waiting to hear from Captain. We are desperate to hear something. His ship was supposed to arrive at the end of November, and days came and went and we heard nothing. Then, today, we hear his ship has been seized, and he was taken. We have no word. I would have written you sooner, but I didn't want you to worry. Yes, Ma, worry. I know your secret. Let me explain...

I have been so wracked with worry; I went through the Captain's letters trying to find anything that would help me help him. As I rifled through his letters, I came across those you had written to him. I apologize, but I read them. How could this have happened? No wonder you are not comfortable in the Farraday home. You are in love with Captain! Why would you not have told me? Or maybe, do you even know yourself? You tell him some of your most personal thoughts, and your concern for him shows in your begging of him to be safe. I had no idea! As I think back I am amazed I did not notice it any sooner. It was right in front of me. The more I think of his concerns of you and his questions about you, the more I realize what was happening. Maybe you both don't know it, but it's there. You both love one another.

I will let you know as soon as we get definite word on Captain. The Kate is docked now, and Skully has offered to help others and me in case we need to use her to go to South Carolina. Once we find out what is happening, I promise to let you know.

From your loving daughter,
Allie

I wondered if Ma had any inkling that she was starting to care for Captain? Not one of her letters to me allowed for such a hint, but the letters I read of hers that were written to him are more than enough to beg sincere caring and concern. They flirt and speak of each other's interests without ever really saying what seems so obvious in trying not to. It is almost embarrassing to read their letters knowing what they feel, and yet what they have never said.

January 14, 1852
Dear Ma,
This will be my last letter for a while. We have received word from people who know of Captain and his circumstances. It seems the Seagull was brought back to Charleston after an informant told of her secret hold and that slaves were more than likely being hidden there. Captain had seven Negroes with him, and fought for them to be allowed to leave. The Fugitive Slave Act, which the United States Congress passed last year, requires escaped slaves to be returned to their owners if the owners so wish. Because of Captain's resistance, he has been held in Charleston and we do not know what he is being charged with. We do not know of the whereabouts of the Seagull, nor of the seaman with Captain.

I will be safe. Skully is taking me and five other people with his crew to Charleston to see if we can gain his release. In this group of five, we have a lawyer, a representative, two merchants, and a freed slave who is willing to risk her freedom for the Captain. She says he is worth the risk so others might go free in the future. I feel prepared and ready for this journey. Rufina is staying here to take care of Captain's home, and promises to keep any mail or correspondence I receive.

Please do not worry. I feel as though I am meant for this. I am keeping a journal now not only for myself, but for posterity. Jonathan is very supportive and has come to tell me goodbye. He says he would like to marry me when I come back, but he wants me to have the Captain here for me. He is considerate, is he not? He will be a good man. He has one more year of school, and then will work for his father here in New York. I am glad he is supportive of this because I could not be so fond of him if he were not.

Give my love to Mr. Farraday and Brody, and especially to yourself.

From you loving daughter,
Allie

December 29, 1851
My dearest Allie,

I am flabbergasted at reading your last letter. I believe you to stretch your imagination of my feelings a little too much because of your desperation for this current situation. Whether they are true or not, Brody and I are heading to America. Thorne would not hear of me going alone, and Brody has spoken often about coming to America to increase their business contacts. Thorne himself would come if Patrick had just not returned. Patrick is not well, and Anne Haddock has moved back in to help take care of him. I support Thorne staying here for Patrick, and since Brody and I have been through so much together, I accept their offer. We will set sail on March 29. We will be on a clipper ship like the Seagull, so hopefully we will be with you in a month or so from now.

If you talk to Captain, please tell him of our pending arrival and we will be willing to help in any way we can.

Your loving Ma

As I finished reading the last letter, I am reminded of how fast the time does pass. We leave tomorrow for our trip to Charleston. I am excited about sailing and seeing the ocean again and knowing we are going to get Captain and hopefully continue our venture of freeing as many Negroes as possible. I am particularly interested in sharing time with Nella. She was torn away from her husband and son over four years ago and has not seen them since. She escaped a year and a half ago, and has been lucky enough to remain here in New York. I am sure she has many a story to tell, and I hope my venture with this entire group will help me to understand this conflict better.

I go to sleep with the letters in my hands. I have taken the satin ribbon and tied them together so they are always in order and safe. I hold them symbolically to my heart, thinking about the ones I love and hoping I will see them when we return. Ma and Brody, Rufina and Angelo, and hopefully the Captain will be here, too.

CHAPTER 2
JOURNEY ON THE SEAGULL

I am awake before Rufina is moving this morning, which is quite a rarity. She hears my shuffling, and jumps up to put on her robe and heads down stairs. She is once again talking as fast as rain drops sliding down a tin roof, and I smile knowing I will miss this constant chattering.

She made pancakes, one of my favorites, and as I sit down, she continued her talking.

"You must send word. Do you hear, Allie? As soon as you get anything, please telegraph us and let us know. Angelo and I will be worried sick the entire time, and I cannot stand the thought of something happening to both of you. Do not be a hero now, do you understand? You let Skully or the other ones with you take the chances. Do you understand?"

"Yes, of course, Rufina. They have all handled themselves in situations like this before, so I will be watching and learning."

"You say that," she said, "but I know you and you will get your little nose stuck in there and I will have to come down there and get you out of jail myself! Do you think those southerners want a mad Italian woman to come in there screaming and pushing her way around?"

We both laughed at the thought of it, and I took this opportunity to change the subject.

"Rufina, when Ma and Brody come, put Ma in my room and Brody can stay in the room across from yours. Don't you think?"

"Do not be worried about them. I will take care of them and make sure they are all right," she said. "It will be good for them to be here and for me to have someone else to worry over."

"Yes, I know, but Ma is about the same when it comes to wanting to take care of people, so don't you both go driving each other blarmy"

"An Italian woman blarmy? I think not! Now maybe

bonta, but not blarmy!"

We laughed again and there was a knock on the back door. Rufina walked through the laundry area to get to the door and opened it. It was Skully,

"Are ya gonna let that young whipper snapper go, or do I have to come in and take her me self?"

"Hold on, she's finishing her breakfast. You probably don't have enough for her to eat on the Kate, so I want to fill her belly before you go off and starve her!"

Skully humphed, and turned from the door. "Come on Allie," he yelled, "The others are already there and ready ta go."

"I'll be right there!" I yelled, and stuffed in two more bites as I stood up to go.

Rufina grabbed my bags and went with me to the door.

"Yer gonna say geh-bye to her right here!" Skully said as he held out his stiff arm to Rufina, "I'm not gonna have you gettin' everyone riled up on the Kate. Anyway, you'll embarrass the poor girl if you come down there and act like she's never been alone."

I gave Rufina a big hug. "Rufina, give Angelo a hug for me and I will send word as soon as we can."

"And don't you go worryin' if you don't hear anythin' soon. We might be too busy to send word!"

Skully grabbed my two bags and turned towards the street, walking off without me.

I waved to Rufina as I scuttled to catch up with Skully. She waved back as she walked to the gate to watch us go. I looked back one more time as we started up the ramp. I waved hoping Rufina would see me. I knew she needed to see me wave one more time for her own comfort.

Skully led me up the ramp and took my things to the Captain's cabin.

"Skully? Where are the others staying?" I asked him.

"Down below in the open hold, but I didn't think you would want to stay down there."

"I can't stay up here if they are all down there! Give me my things and I will carry them down to the others. Are they already settled?"

"They're down there and ready to sail."

"Then that's settled, I'll take my bags down and thank them for coming."

Skully placed the bags next to me and went out the door. I looked around for a second and thought of the Captain. I hoped he was all right. It would be good to have him here and telling us what to do, but it was up to us to make things right and continue this mission. I picked up my bags and headed out the door and down the stairs to join the others.

After dinner, we must have sat there for hours. Skully came in to let us know he was going to bed and was changing shifts. We all thanked him for letting us know and continued our discussion. I found it fascinating. Nella kept right up with the men and they seemed to sincerely take in her words and give them the same value as their own. I'm sure she appreciated it. I don't know what I was expecting, but watching and listening was definitely a learning experience for me.

It must have been the middle of the night when we finally broke up. I stood up and gathered the few remaining cups on the table, when Nella said, "I'll do that, Miss."

"Please, call me Allie."

"If you wish, Miss."

"I mean it, Nella. If we are all working for the same thing, it's the least you can do for me. Anyway, I am the youngest and least experienced here. I want to learn from your experience. I am fascinated."

"My life is far from fascinating, Miss. In fact, it is one no one should have to live through." She said.

I looked around and the men had already retired. Only a few hours were left in the night.

"Will you tell me about it anyway?" I inquired.

"Sometime. Sometime I'll tell you about my people, about my family." She said, "But right now we need to get our sleep so we can continue our planning tomorrow. Any chance we get to sleep we should take because you never know when you have no time to sleep."

We walked back towards our racks and crawled under the covers. We were in a separate area from the men, but we could hear them talking. I was glad because the talking lulled me to sleep.

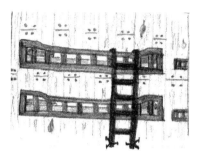

I don't even remember falling asleep when I was awakened abruptly. I had fallen on the floor, and Nella was standing over me, trying to help me up.

"You all right, missy?" She asked.

"I am." I said groggily trying to adjust to my spot. "I must have had a bad dream, or been shifted off the rack by the boat swaying. Has it been rough?"

"Not at all," She said. "Smooth as a canoe on a glassy lake."

"You must be Irish! Such a way with words!"

She laughed as I crawled back into the rack.

"I'm fine, really. Go back to bed, and let's get whatever few winks we have left for the night." I pulled the cover up towards my waist and turned towards the hull, hoping I had convinced her I was fine. I lay there embarrassed for a bit, but eventually slipped back to sleep.

The group must have let me sleep, because when I woke up, Nella was gone. Her items neatly folded on her rack. I stood up and joined them in the mess. They were already discussing their plans, when Mr. Marshall, the Representative, saw me walk in.

"Good morning, Miss Kiper. Nella tells us you had a rough few hours of sleep. We hope you don't mind we let you sleep it off?" He asked.

"No, I'm appreciative of your kindness. Have I missed very much?" I asked.

"Only talk," he said, "we have much more to cover and you are more than welcome to join in."

"Thank you." I said, and picked up some tea and toast and sat down next to Mr. Barnes, one of the merchants.

The morning was spent going over any facts we had about the Captain and the situation. It was odd, he was a father to me, but to each of these people sitting at the table around me, he was a man on a mission. I loved it! It was a completely different connection with this man. It was an adventure, and they weren't looking at me as if I was a schoolgirl or his daughter, we were in this adventure together. I was ready for this excitement!

I thought of Brody for a moment, and then shook my head as if I needed to get him out of my mind. Why would I be thinking of him at this time? Probably because it was an adventure, and I'd not had a true one since my journey to America and he was part of that memory. It must be that, or the thought of him and Ma coming to America. They were on an adventure, too. Goodness!

I focused back on the conversation at hand, and they started getting up from the table.

"Let's take a break for a while, and possibly gather upstairs in a bit for more discussion," said Mr. Cotton, the lawyer.

I remained at the table and Mr. Barnes, the fabric merchant, noticed me before he left the room.

"You are a young one to be involved in such a serious situation. Don't you think?" He asked.

"I can't imagine doing anything else, but this right now." I told him. "Captain's done so much for me. Anyway, if I was just sitting at home, I would be so worried I wouldn't be able to sleep at night. I'm not very good at waiting."

"I can understand that." He said. "Some of our friends here are not very good at it either. Take Nella, she has the most to lose. If she were captured, they would surely take her back into slavery. She has taken repeated chances for years. She believes in this mission and it is through her devotion and commitment we have become a part of her convictions."

"Were you for slavery, before?"

"No, no, no, none of us were, but she made us take the next step. To be an activist changes people's opinion of you, and many people cannot handle the pressure of standing by their beliefs. Oh, many may want to, but stepping out there on your own is too much for some people."

"But this is the right thing to do!"

"Maybe it is a good thing for you to be here. You have the youth and the innocence to not know any better." He laughed and put his hand on my back. We went out the door and headed to the outer deck.

I hated to be thought of as too young. None of these people knew what I had been through. They hadn't all seen their family members die, or hordes of people starving or all alone with no place to go. I looked at the lot of them and tried to think about their past. They all knew one another, so I probably wouldn't hear about their stories. I would have to ask Captain about them once we found him.

I sat up on deck with my coat, hat and gloves on and looked towards the coastline on our starboard side. I could see horses running along the grassy shore. I must write about this, I thought to myself. The horses look so free. I sat there and stared at the horses wishing I had paper and pencil to write down my thoughts. Sometimes I forget my thoughts and the feelings I have if I wait too long to write it down.

While I sat there mesmerized, Nella came up to me and sat beside me.

"What are you thinkin' about, Miss?

I released one of my arms from under my chin and pointed towards the shore.

"Do you see the shoreline? There are horses running free. It is a beautiful site."

Nella looked out towards the horizon and we sat there

quietly for a moment.

"What do you see?" I asked.

"I see strength and energy with natural entitlements. They are free because they know no difference. It is their right and natural instinct."

"You're rather poetic, Nella. Do you ever take the time to write down your thoughts?"

"I started when I was younger, but never finished learning how to write, or I never had the time. I want to free slaves."

"Have you ever wanted to learn?"

"Yes, but I want to free people more. That's what I want to do."

"We have time on this trip, would you like me to help you? I'd like to if you will let me."

"Maybe," she said "maybe. I don't want anyone to know."

"I don't think they would care."

"Maybe not, but they are all educated people and it makes me uncomfortable."

"With everything you've done for the cause? You inspire them all. Why would they think any less of you? They might be willing to help."

"Maybe, but can we keep it our secret for now?"

"Yes, Nella, I will keep your secret."

We sat there and watched the horizon pass by. We remained silent for maybe an hour or so until Mr. Cotton called us together, up top. The group gathered and agreed being outside when the sun was out was a pleasurable place to meet.

"How about we bring a table up here for future planning?" Mr. Cotton said.

"That's a wonderful idea," said Mr. Marshall. "I'd rather be outside if it's not too cold, and have the fresh air. Maybe it will help us with our thoughts."

"Unless we end up daydreaming!" Nella said as she looked at me.

They all laughed and I blushed at the thought of not staying as attentive as they all were.

Mr. Barnes must have felt for me and said, "Maybe we need someone who has idealistic thoughts that can inspire the rest of us when we are consumed with our plans. Did you bring any books with you, Miss Kiper?"

"Oh, indeed I did!"

"Well then, if you choose, might you share your books with us and grant us the pleasure of some readings? I think that would be an enjoyable escape for us during our voyage."

"Of course! I would love to read to you. I would find great delight in reading to you!"

"Then tonight we shall be your subjects and enjoy your recitations."

"But what shall I read?' I asked.

"Whatever you choose," said Mr. Marshall.

"Yes, whatever you choose," agreed Mr. Cotton.

He then brought the focus back to the group and to the finances of our journey.

The discussion lasted another couple of hours before we headed off to dinner. I began to feel anxious about what I would read to the group. I had brought a collection of poems, and a Charles Dickens's novel, *David Copperfield*. I also had Jane Austen's, *Pride and Prejudice*, but figured this would be too romantic a novel for the men, at least for the first story to read. I decided on a sea story I thought would be entertaining for them. I relaxed a little when I had made my decision and finished eating.

We cleaned the area of our dishes, took a break, and then gathered back by the table for the evening. The men had pulled the chair away from the table and they sat there with a grog and chatting amongst themselves until I was in my chair and ready to read to them.

They quieted down when they saw me open my book and pull the lantern closer to me. It was actually a perfect moment. The glow of the lanterns and the appeal of the audience helped me to resolve any issue I might have had about my reading. They were ready and eagerly awaiting my words.

"I've chosen *The Rime of the Ancient Mariner* by Samuel Taylor Coleridge, if that is all right?"

"Of course," said Mr. Barnes, "That would be wonderful!"

I smiled and opened the book slowly. I was a little nervous, but was comforted by the environment and the support of the people around me. It reminded me of Mrs. Farraday and her enjoyment of reading to us years ago. I smiled and took a deep breath in, and then began the story.

"It is an ancient Mariner,
And he stoppeth one of three.
'By thy long grey beard and glittering eye,
Now wherefore stopp'st thou me?

"The Bridegroom's doors are opened wide,
And I am next of kin;
The guests are met, the feast is set:
May'st hear the merry din.'

"He holds him with his skinny hand,
'There was a ship,' quoth he.
'Hold off! unhand me, grey-beard loon!'
Eftsoons his hand dropt he.

"He holds him with his glittering eye--
The Wedding-Guest stood still,
And listens like a three years' child:
The Mariner hath his will.

"The Wedding-Guest sat on a stone:
He cannot choose but hear;
And thus spake on that ancient man,
The bright-eyed Mariner.

"The ship was cheered, the harbour cleared,
Merrily did we drop
Below the kirk, below the hill,
Below the lighthouse top.

"The Sun came up upon the left,
Out of the sea came he!
And he shone bright, and on the right
Went down into the sea.

"Higher and higher every day,
Till over the mast at noon--'
The Wedding-Guest here beat his breast,
For he heard the loud bassoon."

I stopped for a moment and looked up from my book. All eyes were on me and listening intently. I sat back in the chair and continued on with the poem, looking up and down as the natural breaks of the verse allowed. I tried not to bore, so I raised and lowered my voice as needed for emphasis. I finished the poem with all alert.

"Farewell, farewell! but this I tell
To thee, thou Wedding-Guest!
He prayeth well, who loveth well
Both man and bird and beast.

"He prayeth best, who loveth best
All things both great and small;
For the dear God who loveth us,
He made and loveth all.

"The Mariner, whose eye is bright,
Whose beard with age is hoar,
Is gone: and now the Wedding-Guest
Turned from the bridegroom's door.

"He went like one that hath been stunned,
And is of sense forlorn:
A sadder and a wiser man,
He rose the morrow morn."

I slowly closed the book before looking up again, but when I did they were all still sitting quietly.

Mr. Cox sat forward in his chair and said, "You must continue entertaining us like this, Miss Kiper. You have a wonderful voice and your intonation lends to a most pleasing way with words. Doesn't it everyone?"

Everyone was kind enough to agree, and Mr. Barnes asked, "Will you consider reading to us every evening?"

"I would like that!" I said.

We all rose from our chairs and placed them back under the table. Each of them thanked me for the reading and headed out the door. Nella and I followed last and walked to our birth.

As we undressed, she said, "That's what I would like to do."

"What?" I asked.

"I want to be able to read to my son. I can

tell a story and entertain, but I want to be able to read to him, and show him how to read. Will you show me how to read?"

"Of course." I said. "Let's start the first free moment we have. All right?"

"Aah, the first free moment. Words can have funny meanings, but, yes, thank you, Miss Kiper."

"Allie, remember?"

"I don't mean to be disrespectful, but the same way you call the men by their formal names, I must call you by yours. It's just the way I was brought up."

"But I'm younger than you, Nella, I should be calling you by your formal name. What is your last name?"

"Well, I was born as Anella Still, in New Jersey, and my husband's name is James Turner."

"So do you go by Still or Turner?"

"Turner. My brother is a leading abolitionist, and I didn't really know of my birth family until recently. I love my husband and want to keep his name. I was one of eighteen children."

"Eighteen children! Japers! Your poor mother."

"I know it. She must have been quite a woman. I only have one child, and the sorrow that comes with being separated from him is more than I can handle, so having eighteen separated must be overwhelming."

We crawled into our rack as she continued telling me of her family.

"Pa split us up to other family members and we were separated over the years. Some of us were sent to family in the Caribbean, and that's where I ended up. I met James there and we were married and had our son, Jim. Oh, he's a fine boy, with good bone structure and smart, too. He's quick to learn, and strong. It's a good thing. His life won't be an easy one."

"If you were living in the Caribbean, how did you come to be a slave?"

"They take you from there, too. We just happened to be in the wrong place at the wrong time."

"Why don't you go back?"

"Because they need me here. Slaves need anyone who is willing to make them free, and I still have a husband and family, somewhere. They need me to help. I can't rest until I have my son. I know what slave traders and plantation owners do to Negroes and I can barely sleep at night. There aren't enough hours in the day."

"I'm sorry, Mrs. Turner."

She laughed and said, "Now what are you doin' that for?"

"If we are to be called by our formal names, then you are, too"

"No, Missy, it doesn't work that way."

"It does for me."

She snickered and suggested we go to sleep. I lied there thinking about my thought earlier of no one having been through what I had in Ireland. I was wrong, absolutely wrong. Nella had been through horrible circumstances, and what was worse, hers was not over. Would it ever be?

That night I had another nightmare, but Nella jumped up to check on me. She always seemed to be right there. She had the rack above me. I never heard her move, and yet I knew she had to be getting in and out.

The next morning, as we were getting ready to go to breakfast, she asked me, "Miss, what are dreaming about to wake you so badly?"

"I don't do well on ships. I came from Ireland and my journey was not a pleasant one."

"Were the seas rough?"

"Not just that, I was alone and I was confined to an empty dark room in the bottom of the ship. I spent most of the journey sick and scared."

"Where were your parents?"

"My father was in a workhouse, my sister and brother were dead, and my mother stayed to work and help my father, but he died also."

"So, it was just your mom?"

"Well, and another boy that was part of the family, his name is Brody."

"And Kerry, who is Kerry?"

"How did you know about her?"

"You say her name and Brody's name during your dreams."

"I do what?"

"You say both of their names at night when you dream."

I was taken aback at the thought of saying

anyone's names out loud when I had no control. Why would I do that? "I, I…"

She took my arm and headed towards the mess, "It's all right," she said, "We don't have to talk about it."

As we breezed down the coastline, the weeks passed quickly. I worked with Nella any chance we had, and at night, I would read to the group. We learned about each other as the days passed and the reading sessions were so very enjoyable. They loved David Copperfield and often called each other by names from the book as they jested with one another.

The day before we were to land in Charleston, I was lying on the open deck and looking up towards the sky.

"What are you thinking about?" Nella asked.

"Well, Mrs. Turner," she smiled at me as I explained my thoughts. "I am looking at the clouds, and reciting a poem by a poet, William Wordsworth, to myself. Silly isn't it?"

"That depends, will you tell me the poem?"

"Oh, you don't want to hear it. Let's talk about our arrival tomorrow."

"Really, I want to hear it."

"All right, it's called *I Wandered Lonely as a Cloud.*"

She smiled, laid down on her side, and listened to me recite the poem.

"I wandered lonely as a cloud
That floats on high o'er vales and hills,
When all at once I saw a crowd,
A host, of golden daffodils,
Beside the lake, beneath the trees
Fluttering and dancing in the breeze.

"Continuous as the stars that shine
And twinkle on the Milky Way,
They stretched in never-ending line
Along the margin of a bay:
Ten thousand saw I at a glance
Tossing their heads in sprightly dance."

She looked up at the clouds, like me, as I finished the poem.

"The waves beside them danced, but they
Out-did the sparkling waves in glee: -
A poet could not but be gay
In such a jocund company:
I gazed -and gazed -but little thought
What wealth the show to me had brought.

"For oft, when on my couch I lie
In vacant or in pensive mood,
They flash upon that inward eye
Which is the bliss of solitude;
And then my heart with pleasure fills
And dances with the daffodils."

"Isn't that lovely?" I asked her, still staring upwards toward the sky.

"How do you think of such things? When I look up at the sky, I only see clouds and blue behind it."

"How can you not?" I asked her. "How can you not think of anything else but how alive they are?"

"I guess that's why you do so well at writing. You have a special way with your imagination."

Mr. Marshall overheard my recitation and said, "You really do have a romantic way of looking at things, Miss Kiper. This world we live in can be a very harsh world. I hope you don't ever lose your ability to see things the way you do."

I sat up as he finished his sentence. "I'm sorry, I didn't know you were standing there."

"Don't be sorry, I enjoyed hearing you recite the poem. I hadn't heard it and it is an amusing way to look at clouds."

We all looked back up at the sky, and Mr. Marshall said, "We're about to meet again down below, would you like to join us?"

Nella and I nodded and followed Mr. Marshall down below. Everyone was already there and waiting for us to begin our final discussion. As we discussed the next day's actions, I began to get nervous. Because of my accent and youth, I was to play a necessary part in our plan. We had to be very careful with Nella. She was to stay on board with Skully. She wasn't happy with this, but she knew she was knowledgeable about the situation and would know what to do if everything fell through.

Our basic plan was this, Mr. Cotton, Mr. Marshall, and a sailor were to try the court system and see if they could find and free the Captain. Mr. Barnes, Mr. Cox, me, and a sailor were to try to find out what we could by talking to people on the street. We split the money we had between the two groups, knowing we might have to use all of it if needed to free him. If Mr. Cotton and Mr. Marshall failed, it was up to us to lay the groundwork for his ultimate release. That's where I would play more of a part. I was to wear one of my pretty dresses.

I was restless through the night, and Nella sang to me as we lied in our racks. She must have known I was anxious. I liked her songs. They were quite different from what I was used to, but they were comforting. I didn't sleep very much, and when I woke up the next morning, we were in Charleston.

Nella was already up with Skully. I walked over to them and stood by Skully looking at this town I had heard so much about.

"Are you all right this mornin', Allie?" Skully asked me.

"I am, but I'm a little apprehensive." I told him.

"As you should be," said Nella "they can be awful unforgivin' to those who go against them."

"That's what's on my mind. How will I know who to trust?" I asked.

"Follow the lead of Mr. Barnes and Mr. Cox." Said Nella "But don't look too scared, they'll smell it."

"Humph!" snorted Skully, "She'll be just fine. Follow your instincts." He said.

"I'll try." I said and Skully called to Nella to help him with a mast. She needed to look as though she was part of the crew, and she was doing a good job. Now, I just needed to do mine.

Mr. Cox called to me as he went down to the mess, "We

must get something into our stomachs." He said as he motioned me to come down below.

Mr. Cotton joined the rest of us a few minutes later and asked if we were all ready for the day. "The ship will be our checkpoint. We'll send our sailor back during the day to give word on our progress. If there is an emergency, remember, Skully or Nella will change the flag on the ship, and the other group should immediately come back to the ship. Does everyone understand?"

We all nodded and finished our breakfast. I wasn't able to eat much, but did finish a piece of toast. I brushed the crumbs from my dress and stood up with the men as we headed up and out onto the deck. Mr. Cotton and Mr. Marshall left the ship first.

I paced the deck until Mr. Barnes took my hand and in a softened voice told me. "It's okay, Miss Kiper, everything is going to be okay. We're going to pull this off."

I took a deep breath in and tried to stand there, calmly next to him. We pretended to be looking through some paperwork, and all turned to one another to discuss our final moment before leaving the ship.

Mr. Barnes said, "All right, let's go." And we turned and walked down the ramp.

I glanced back up towards Skully who winked at me as I walked away. I didn't see Nella, but Skully kept his eye on me until we were beyond the pier and out of his sight. I was looking back and forth and trying to fall into place as naturally as possible but I couldn't help but be tense.

Mr. Barnes grabbed my wrist and pulled me into a doorway, Mr. Cox was right behind. "Allie!" He hadn't called me that before! "Allie! You must relax. If you look as though something is wrong, you'll give us away. We must act as if we are visiting or doing business here. Remember if anyone asks, you are traveling with us."

I shook my head in acceptance and tried to breathe deeply. I knew how important this undertaking was for Captain, and that's what I needed to focus on, but when I focused on it, I became more nervous. I needed to pull myself together.

I looked down, then up again at both men and said, "Let's go."

They looked at each other and the three of us stepped back out on to the street and continued down the street.

I tried to take my mind off the mission, and looked at the houses as we walked. Most were wooden houses, two stories with large trees and ivy growing freely. In the trees was a grayish, tangled something that I had never seen before. Here we were in February, and it was chilly, but not bitter cold. When the sun was out, it was cool, but quite nice. The houses had shutters, and some houses had them closed while others had them open and we could see inside. It was a quaint city, charming in a different way than I had seen in America before.

I followed the men and listened as they questioned different people around the market area. The information they received took us back to the wharf area and to a slave sale that was to occur in thirty minutes. I was thrilled to be able to see this in person. This is what Captain had talked about and what everyone said bolstered their dislike of slavery. We gathered at the sight and Mr. Barnes and Mr. Cox casually talked to people and walked around.

I stood back and took in the scene. It was an energetic crowd with people dressed nicely and chatting. Men, women and children were all there. It reminded me of a gathering at school or a crowd before a concert in New York. I wondered how this could be so bad?

As soon as my thoughts wandered, my eyes caught a line of Negroes being pulled towards the wooden platform. They were tied together, men, women, and children. A man untied one of the boys, maybe he was twelve, and took him up to the stage. The boy looked nervous as he stood there waiting.

Someone in the crowd yelled for the sale to start, and the rest of the crowd cheered. I grimaced at the thought of this poor boy having to stand up there by himself and be gawked at. The boy looked down at the line of Negroes and I saw a man and a woman pulling the ropes reaching towards him. They couldn't get free and one of the men holding them pulled out a belt and hit him with it. I was appalled. Mr. Barnes and Mr. Cox saw this and looked back at me to see my reaction. Mr. Cox walked over to me and stood with me.

"It hasn't even started, yet." He said.

I looked up at him in disbelief, and heard someone ringing a bell and yelling at the crowd. They were beginning. I looked back at the platform. The man standing with the boy pushed him and shoved him making him turn around, hold out his arms, and open his mouth. People were yelling dollar amounts at the stage and acting jovial as if they were picking out livestock for their farm.

When the final highest amount was reached, the boy was pushed towards the man who won him. The man, who must have been his father, was pulled up on stage next and the process was repeated. Another man bought him. Yet another man bought the woman, and when she was pushed to this third winner, she was screaming and crying and pulling towards her son. It was such a humiliating and awful site I began to feel sick to my stomach.

Mr. Barnes came over, "Are you all right, Miss Kiper?"

"No, I'm really not. I'm so sorry. I didn't think I would react in this way. I feel sick. I must get back to the ship. Please! I can't stand seeing this anymore."

"All right," he said, and motioned for the sailor to come back and check on me. "We'll do some more searching, and come back and check on you this afternoon. I know how harsh this is, but try to remember our reason for being here."

I couldn't say a word. I followed the sailor back to the ship and went down below. I sat at the mess table with my head in my hands on top of the table. I was in shock. Captain told me how much this had affected him, and I read about and heard about it from others, but to see this degrading experience in person was more than I could handle. I wasn't sure if I could go on.

Nella came in and put her hand on my back. "Missy? You all right? Skully said you came back without the other men.

What happened?"

I didn't speak. I kept my head down, and moved it from left to right.

"Talk to me." Nella said, "What happened?"

I pushed myself up from the table and walked to the corner, still in shock. I turned back towards Nella. "Your family! I just saw what happened to you and your family. I am shaken to the core of my being." I grabbed Nella's hands and squeezed them as hard as I could. "It just isn't fair! It is too cruel for me to think about. How can you live through that?"

She dropped my hands and took a hold of my shoulders, firmly. "This is why we do what we do. Don't you feel anger for the situation?

Fairness has nothing to do with their belief, justice is what we want. Take your feelings, now, and use them to create strength in your actions. Don't ever lose what you feel now, for this will make you stronger in the long run."

I dropped my head down, and she took my chin in her hands.

"Do you understand?" she asked.

I shook my head up and down to say, yes, but I wasn't sure I could do it. She hadn't let go of my chin, yet, and she asked, "Can you do it? Can you continue with our mission? This is a calling and you have to believe and be strong about it." She gripped my chin harder and asked again, "Can you do it?"

I looked in her eyes and said, "I'll try."

"Give yourself some time, today. It's a big step and you have the heart, see if your mind will go along."

She left me in the mess, and must have gone to the outer deck. I walked out and went to my rack to lie down. Skully came down and knocked on our doorway, "Missy, it's a harsh world out there, try not to let it get ya down." He patted my leg, and went back out.

I stayed there all afternoon, not able to shake myself out of the shock I was in. I thought of Ma and wondered what she would be telling me right now. I thought of Captain, and knew he needed help, but didn't know if I could actually do it. I hated myself for even considering not being able to do this. What was wrong with me? I had come this far, and hadn't made it past the first day of our mission. The men were right, I wasn't just young, I was naively innocent. I had lived through hardships, but had taken a romantic view of the world. Who was it just yesterday that said, "I hope you don't ever lose your ability to see things the way you do?" I think it was Mr. Marshall. Japers! What was I expecting? I could hear everyone going to the mess for dinner. I was hoping they forgot I was here. I was too embarrassed to face any of them.

After dinner, there was a knock on our opening, "Allie? It's Mr. Barnes and the rest of us. Might you allow us to come in and check on you?"

I sat up in my rack and watched them file in. Mr. Marshall spoke first, "What you saw today was horrible, and the shock of seeing it the first time can be very upsetting."

"We all understand," said Mr. Cox, "we don't blame you for feeling this way."

"But I've let you all down. I couldn't even carry through with the very first day." I told them.

"And that's all right," said Mr. Cotton, "better now than in the middle of something more important. This is part our fault, too. While you never get used to this, you do learn to acknowledge what you see and suppress the anger and disgust you feel for it and make those feelings the impetuous for your future actions."

"That's what Mrs. Turner told me earlier. I just don't know if I can do it. You all seem to be so dedicated and sure of what you are doing. I believe, and agree with it, I just don't know if I have the stomach for it."

"It is intense. You are right." Said Mr. Barnes, "But the outcome for the Negro much outweighs our sacrifice. We each have a threshold of tolerance, for ourselves and for others, and we can each tell you a different story of what that threshold might be. So, do not think we are judging you on your inability to handle the situation. What we do know is we trust Captain Kiper, and if he trusted you enough to tell you of his position, then he sees something in you. Something you might not know you have. Something deep inside. Take the night, and see if you can find that something he saw in you."

They each acknowledged me before they stepped out. Nella stayed in with me.

"Here, eat some of this." She handed me a baguette and some tea. "The tea may not be hot anymore, but you can at least use it to wash down the bread. Do you feel any better?"

"They're just being kind. I still feel embarrassed."

"Well, you must get over that. We don't have time to dwell on being ashamed. We have people to help. There is never too much time once you're in the midst of your plans. Things move quickly."

"It's not a matter of understanding, or agreeing with what we're doing, it's something else. I don't know how to explain it."

"We all come from different backgrounds, and have different points of view. I can't put it in to words like Mr. Barnes or Mr. Cotton, but I can tell you from the way I see it."

I scooted over on my bunk and motioned for her to sit down, asking her to tell me without having to ask her.

"People talk about havin' their heart ripped out, and it's true. Not literally, but emotionally. And what's worse, it just doesn't happen one time, but over and over again. I thought I would never get over the first time when my son and husband were separated from me. It is like they sliced you open and pulled out your heart! I have not healed from that one, yet. I no longer cry. Anger has taken its place. You worry, but that gets you nowhere. You realize you won't ever see the ones you love again, unless you take the steps to change things.

"At the plantation where I was a slave, we picked cotton. Cotton, cotton, cotton, all of the time. Your fingers bleed, your back aches somethin' terrible, your head pounds, and your skin blackens. Your eyeballs feel as though they're goin' to pop right out of your head! And it's not just you, it's people of all ages; old, young, pregnant, and dyin'. Most owners don't even care. They need that cotton picked and you better do your job. I looked around and saw my future. The old ladies were near crippled, and that was if they had done their job. If they hadn't they had an ear cut off, or punished with no food or unable to talk to anyone. The men broken in spirit and in body. If they didn't do their job or stood up against the foreman, they were beaten 'til their back was raw, or worse. That's what you see as your future. There is none, it's pointless.

"If you have anythin' left, you talk of leavin', of escapin' this cruel world. The problem there is, if anyone overhears you, you might get beaten, or hung, or shot, or traded again. Even your own people turn you in. But I understand that, 'cause they think they'll get better treatment if they tell. You have to be very careful who you talk to. And then if you get away, you'd rather die than get caught because they don't care what they do to you, they want to make an example out of you, so you're life gets worse."

"Stop it Nella, I can't stand to hear anymore!"

"If you're gonna be a part of this — you have to hear it! We need you to understand what you'll see, what you'll hear! It's not pretty, it's not romantic, it's life! It's life for thousands of Negroes. What hope do they have unless people like us give them hope? It's worth my life. My life against anyone I can help be free. If I don't do it, who is to help my son? Maybe someday, someone will do the same for him. Don't you see? We have to do this!"

"Don't you hate the South and everyone in it?"

"You want to, but there are good people, too. People who live here but don't agree with what is goin' on, and we have to be grateful for them. Without them, we wouldn't have any help down here. Not every Southerner or even every landowner is evil. There are some very kind ones who are good to their slaves. There are even slaves who want to stay with their owners because they are good to them."

"It doesn't sound like it."

"Well, there are some good ones and they are the ones that help us, and who will help us turn this situation around. We all have a different purpose. I help find the slaves who want to be free and help them escape. They call me a conductor. I talk to them and let them know it's all right and they're doin' the right thing, but that there are costs, and their life may be one of them. Mr. Cotton handles the legal side of it, Mr. Marshall tried to change the laws and talks to white people to try and get them to understand the situation. Mr. Barnes and Mr. Cox can travel and talk to people as they do business. This way landowners don't know they are helpin' the Underground Railroad. Do you see that we all play a part? Your Captain helped transport slaves to freedom. He has a most important part, and is one of the most dangerous parts of our plan. He is called one of the Stationmasters. He not only helps hide slaves in his ship and house, he helps transport them. We need him, and right now, he needs you. We all need him to get him out of this tight spot.

"Here are some of the key things. When someone escapes, they're called passengers or cargo. If a conductor tells them where to go and sets up an escape plan for them, the passengers then get a ticket, even though it's not an actual ticket, that's what we call it. Then the Stationmaster places them in a home or station, and that home is carrying passengers or cargo. The secret password for all traveling is, A Friend with Friends. You DO NOT ever use that and give it away because there are people out there who try and act like they want to help, but they are really trying to grab runaway slaves and get rewards for their return, or they sell them for the money.

"I tell you all of these awful things, not to scare you, but to make you aware. If I can get you to realize the seriousness of our jobs and how important it is even though there are ugly parts of it and serious consequences, maybe you can work through your feelings and accept the challenge. Mr. Barnes was right. We should have been tellin' you this all along. We have now wasted your time and ours by not havin' made you aware."

"Don't take this on yourselves, it is my problem. I wasn't ready to see it myself, even though I thought I was. I wanted to help because it is the right thing to do, and I somehow allowed myself to be naïve about the whole thing."

Nella stood up and started preparing for bed.

"Nella, did anything happen today I should know about?"

"No, neither group was able to do anythin'. They didn't find out where Captain Kiper is, or who was involved with confiscating his ship. Oh, Mr. Barnes and Mr. Cox did find the Seagull, but they didn't try to board her. Mr. Cotton and Mr. Marshall will try that tomorrow."

"Thank you," I said.

Nella slipped into her rack as I slipped out. I needed some fresh air. It was a little chilly, but it felt good for the moment.

"Get down below and get yar wrap!" barked Skully.

"I will if I get chilled, Skully. I promise." I told him.

"That's all we need is for you to get sick. I wouldn't ever hear the end of it from Rufina! I can just hear her now!"

"You're right." I told him and snuck back down to get my coat. The least I could do was try not to get sick.

I walked to the port side and looked out over the open water. There were other ships anchored out there, and noises coming from those ships, but it was calm. There were a few clouds in the sky, but they moved along nicely so I could see the stars. I wondered what Johnathan was doing. I wondered why I hadn't really thought about him very much. I knew I should be thinking of him, especially if I was going to marry him. I wondered where we would live. In his parent's home? In Captains? In our own home? As I was wondering, I felt a hand on my shoulder. I turned around and saw Mr. Barnes.

"Thinking about today?" he asked.

"No, I was thinking about someone." I told him.

"He must be important if he is taking priority over everything you witnessed today." He said.

"That's just the thing, I was wondering why I haven't been thinking about him more? I think he has the intention to marry me once we return, and I thought that's what I wanted, too, but shouldn't I be thinking about him more often if that were the case?" I asked him.

"I don't know, everyone is different, but your love of

literature and your slant on life leads me to believe that whomever you love would come to mind quite naturally."

"What do you mean?"

"As you look at things, you would think of them. For example, as you look out over the stars, or as you walk along the street, or as you dream, even as you face difficulty." He said.

I looked back out over the side and thought for a moment about what he said.

"You're in no rush right now, you have time to think about him and whether or not it is a relationship you want to have." He told me.

"Of course, forgive me, we are here for a very important reason, and I did not mean to be thinking of myself, when I should be pulling myself together and helping each of you."

"You know, I am a plantation owner here in the south."

"No, I did not know that."

"Well, I am, and I struggled with the entire economic situation in my business and personally."

"You have slaves?"

"Yes, I do. I have up to 30 slaves at any one time."

"Do Nella and the others know?"

"Definitely. It is through my plantation we are able to move slaves to freedom. I have freed my slaves, but they continue to stay and work to help others. I allow them to be a part of my business and they profit from their own work."

"Do other people know?"

"Absolutely not. Only the few we can trust. I have two nieces and a nephew who live on the property and manage it for me. From the outside, you would never know what we are doing. We have to keep it that way to help. We regularly try to buy families together so they are not split, and I try to buy older slaves so they may enjoy the last years of their life. There are many places they can go once we get them to the North. It's getting them there that is our biggest difficulty. However, if you were to come and visit and you didn't know, you would think we are like any other plantation."

"So why do you not live there?"

"I run my business in New York and Boston. I have two mills that make fabric."

"I don't completely understand. You need the cotton that slave labor produces, so why are you against slavery? That is the main excuse I have heard from literature, and Captain"

"You're right. Free labor only benefits me financially, and many people truly believe this justifies the means, but does it? We founded this country on freedom. We left England and other countries to be free, so how do you justify enslaving someone else? I am still able to get by without taking someone else's freedom, so I choose to help all men be free. As much as it is financially profitable for me, it is not just."

"All of you have so much at stake in this entire process. Nella took the time to explain it to me, and to tell me what each of your positions are for this mission. I understand the words you all say, intellectually, and I hear you, but understanding it and actually doing something are two different things. I hope you all know I want to help, I just don't know if I can." I looked at him feeling so ashamed of my weakness.

"You are not the only one to ever feel this way, and you won't be the last. Maybe time will help you with your decision. Whatever you choose, and whether you know it or not, the road you take will forever be altered." He looked out over the water, looked me in the eye, and then turned to go down below.

CHAPTER 3
CORA IT IS

I looked back out over the water and heard a commotion on the starboard side. I walked that way and noticed a group of men coming out of a pub. I could hear them talking and hid behind the mast so they wouldn't see me. They were talking about the Seagull and how she was to be put up for sale next week. They talked about how fine she was and pushed each other, jesting, and saying how each of them was going to have her and what they would use her for. The last man said he wasn't going to be using her for helping slaves escape, and they all laughed.

The man next to him asked, "What happened to the slaves he had with him, anyway?"

I stepped to the edge of the ship, moving towards them as they walked by. I strained to hear what they said. The group split up and the two that remained were talking and stopped for a moment.

"They kept them all in the jail, waiting for their owners to reclaim them." Said one of the men.

"Were they all claimed?" Asked another.

"No, they were resold a few days later, at a profit I might add for the agents who captured the ship. The ol' jailor probably got a cut, too."

"Is the ship bein' watched?"

"I only think they have one man on duty.

She's a fine ship to not be manned more closely."

"What would you think about goin' over to check her out?"

"I'd say a mighty fine idea."

I watched them head down the dock and I assumed towards the Seagull. I looked around hoping to see Skully to tell him what I had just heard. I frantically looked around, but saw no one. I was in a quandary. If I took the time to go get someone, I might miss whatever they decided to do, but if I went ahead, I could watch them and then tell Skully or one of the others when I returned. Maybe I could make up for my weakness today!

I scrambled down the ramp and onto the dock. I tried to stay far enough back so as to stay out of their sight. The dock took a turn at the end, and I watched them follow the turn and slip out of site for a moment. I slowly went up to the turn, and looked around the corner. There was a ship at the corner, so I was able to hide behind some of its ropes and anchor chain. I saw them about three ships down, and waited for them to go up the Seagull's ramp. They were talking as they went up, and I could hear another man's voice talking with them, but couldn't hear clear enough to make out what they were saying.

Whatever they told him, worked. They were allowed on her deck. I walked over and surveyed the area trying to find the best place for me to stand. They were far enough onto her deck so that they could not see me standing at her stern, behind her tie down rope. I stood there hoping to hear something, anything that would help me find the Captain.

It sounded like there were three men up on deck. They were talking about the pub they had just come from, and their latest voyage, and where they'd been in the past couple of months, nothing in particular. Then one of the men asked about the Seagull.

"How long have you been standin' watch?" He asked

"Oh, I've got the nighttime watch. I get relieved in the mornings."

"Must get pretty boring, standing up here and doing nothing," Said the other man.

"Yeh, but I get paid for it and it's not very hard to do."

"What do you do the whole time?" Asked the first man.

"Just sit up here and make sure no one steals the ship."

"Yeh, you can't have that now, can you?" Asked the second man. "How about a drink? We could sit up here with you and have a drink?"

"Oh, I don't know about that. Can't leave my post, you know?"

"Of course not, how about we go down below and see

if we can find some whiskey? We'll bring some to you. That way you don't have to leave the deck?"

"I guess so." He said.

The two men headed down to the galley to see if there was any liquor. I slipped out from beyond the ropes and starting walking towards the ramp. The man on the deck saw me as I was heading to the ramp. I wanted to get to him before the other men came back. I looked up at him, as I heard the other men yell at the man above. I stopped in my tracks.

"Hey, where's the lantern down here? We can't see what we're doing? Come down here and show us!"

The man up top looked at me and waved his arm as if shewing me away. He paid no more attention to me as he turned to go down towards the galley.

I yelled, "Wait! Wait!" but he was gone before I could stop him. I ran up the ramp and looked down towards the galley. At the same time I heard a thump, and saw the man slump down to the ground. I wasn't sure what had happened, but I knew I would be in trouble if the men saw me. I turned and ran towards the ramp, but one of the men was right on my heels. I was barely to the ramp when he caught the back of my coat.

"Hey…hey…hey, Missy! And what have we here?" He pulled me around and we looked face to face. He yelled down to his friend, "Hey, Robert, come take a look at what I found!"

I tried to pull away, but he had too firm a grip on my coat, both front and back, now. His friend came up the steps slowly and looked over at me.

"Well! What a prize! Where'd you find her?"

"After you knocked the guy out, I saw her up the stairs awatchin' us. Didn't think we wanted her to get away after seeing that"

"I really didn't see it." I said. "I won't say anything. Let me go!"

"What are you doin' up here, anyway?" The man named Robert asked.

"I know the man who owns this ship, and I didn't want you to take it or hurt it." I told him.

"Hmm. You know him, and you know this ship?" He asked.

I didn't answer because I didn't know where he was going with his train of thought.

"What do you think Willy? Should we take the ship, or take the girl? Or both?"

"Yeah, let's take both!" Willy said.

"Where do you come from? What's that accent? Are you British?" Robert asked.

"I'm Irish!" I said.

"Hmmm, and where are you staying while you're here?" He asked again.

"Right down the way, on another ship."

"Why do they have a girl watching this ship? Don't you have any men on board?"

"Of course we do, but I was the only one on deck that overheard you talking about the Seagull, so I followed you."

"You didn't go get anyone else?"

"No! I didn't need anyone else to find out what you were doing."

"Suppose you didn't expect to get caught?

Well, what do we do with ya' now?"

"You let me go and forget about taking this ship. It's not yours, and they'll find you, anyway."

"We could be long gone before they even knew it was gone. They say this is a fast one, she sails faster than most."

"She does, but the three of us can't do it. You'd be crazy to take her out with just us. We'd flounder for sure, and then you two would be the laughing stock of the city."

"She's made a point Robert. We need more than just us to sail her."

"I suppose so, so we're back to deciding what we're gonna do with her." Robert said.

"If you leave the Seagull alone, I won't tell a soul if you let me go."

"Yeah, and we are to believe that? Then we would be the laughing stock of the city. You're going with us and we'll decide what to do with you later."

"What about the guy down there? What happens when he wakes up?" Will asked.

"I'll go tie him up and by the time the next guy comes, we'll be long gone. He won't remember what we looked like. I'll pour some bourbon on him and they'll think he was drinking and deserted his post. They won't believe a thing he says. You stay up here with her, Willy. Don't let her go. I'll be right back."

The man named Robert headed back down

to the galley and Willy stayed with me. I tried to pull away again, but his hold was firm.

"Stop your squirmin'!" He said. "We're not going to hurt you, just take you with us."

"But my friends will know I'm not in my rack." I knew this not to be true. Nella had probably noticed I went up on deck, and Mr. Barnes knew he left me on deck to think. They probably wouldn't notice me gone until tomorrow morning. I was in a fine mess. What was I to do?

Robert came back up and said, "Let' go, we'll take her to our boarding house, and decide what to do with her tomorrow."

They shoved me along, and while I hoped we would pass someone I could yell to, I knew it was late and no one would be out. We went in the back way to the boarding house and up the stairs to their rooms.

"Willy, we're gonna have to all stay in the same room so as to watch her over the night." Robert said.

"Yeah, well, who's taking the first shift?" Will asked.

"You are! Here's a blanket for you." Robert said and then looked at me, "What's your name, anyway?"

I didn't answer him because I didn't want him to know my name.

"Fine, have it your way!" Robert barked at me, "Willy, you sit against the door so she can't get out. Wake me in a couple of hours, you hear?"

"Got it, Robert. I'll be right here, watching her like a hawk." Willy said.

Robert fell fast asleep and I took my coat off and

bundled it up to put it under my head. I lay there and thought about the mess I was in. I would have to wait until tomorrow to see what was going to happen and what I needed to do to get out of this predicament. Hopefully, Nella would wake up early and alert everyone.

I knew I couldn't sleep and I lay there trying to look as if I were asleep. Fortunately, I heard Willy fall asleep against the door. Both men were snoring. I shifted and made some noise, seeing if that would rouse them from their slumber. It didn't so I knew I had a chance to look around and see what I could find.

I slipped out from under the blanket and went over to the window. I looked out seeing if anyone was there. There wasn't, so I looked around to check out the surroundings. There were businesses across the street, which lifted my spirits. That meant people would be coming and going tomorrow and maybe I could motion to someone.

I just happened to try the window, when I realized it shifted slightly. Might they have left it unlocked? Maybe I could open it and slip out. My mind raced as I tried to look straight down to see what was below, but as engrossed as I was at the moment, I had not heard Robert get up and come over to me.

"What do you think you're doing?" He barked. "Willy! Is this your way of watching her? So much for watching her like a hawk! Get back over there and lay down! I'll not have you escaping under my watch."

Robert was determined to not let me go, and he stayed up the rest of the night. Rather than lying down I chose to sit up against the wall and try to stay awake. The night got the better of me, and I dozed off only to be woken up in the early morning by Robert waking Willy.

"Willy. Willy!" Robert snapped. "Go downstairs and get us some breakfast. Bring her something, too. We can't have her fainting on us later from lack of food or sleep."

"Yeah, yeah, all right," said Willy, "I'm going."

He gathered himself up and stretched to get his blood flowing, and then he opened the door and headed out. Robert was staring at me and making me very uncomfortable.

"Are you going to tell me your name this morning, or do I have to make one up for you? Maybe that's what I should be doing anyway." Robert said.

I didn't move. I didn't say a thing, I just sat there and stared back at him, trying to be defiant and show strength. I didn't want him to think I was scared of him even though I was. He walked over to me and bent down, taking my chin in his hand.

"Let's get a good look at this face." Robert forced my head from side to side. "Get up and let me have a good look at you!"

I stood up slowly and stood there in front of him

"Hmmm. Turn around. Go ahead, turn around!"

I tried to do what he said, but I didn't want to obey him.

"Hold your arms out and turn around again!"

He put his hands at my waist and forced me to turn. He then took his hands and went up and down my sides feeling my figure. I didn't like him doing that, so I jerked away from him

"I'm not going to do anything to you, Lassy. Hah! You little Irish peasant!"

That infuriated me so I jumped towards him with my arms up to lash out at him. He grabbed both arms and threw me down on the ground.

"Stay there until I decide what to do with you!" He roared. "Are all Irish as spirited as you?"

I was furious but could do nothing. He was too strong for me and I knew it. I sat there fuming. Will finally came back and brought us something to eat. He threw some bread at me and told me to eat it. How reminiscent. I had been in this position before. Where were Brady, Brody, and Brudy, my little rat friends? I smiled thinking about them.

"We have something else to worry about," said Willy. "The Landlady knows we have someone else up here and she wants to know when we're going to pay her for our visitor."

"Fine, fine, I'll take care of it." Robert told him, "Does she know anything about who it is?"

"She alluded to the fact we brought a female guest up

here, but she didn't say anything more than that. I think she's more interested in getting paid for the guest, than who it is."

"We'll have to pay her then for our little guest." Robert and Willy looked over at me and laughed.

"Let's eat." Robert said and they sat down at the table towards the window. When they were done, Robert leaned back in his chair and looked over at me. "I tried to get a name out of her again, but haven't had any luck. Can you think of something, Willy?"

"We could slap her around." Willy said.

"We could, but I think she's a defiant little thing. She has some strong Irish blood in her with the spirit to prove it. She showed me some of that spirit when you were gone." Robert told him.

Willy stood up and walked over to me. He knelt down, reached toward me and said, "Do I get to see some of that spirit?"

But as soon as he had said that I slapped him!

"Whoah, you're right, she does have some defiance and spirit in her doesn't she!" Willy said.

Robert laughed at loud, and Willy stepped back from me. He went back over to their table and sat back down.

"How are we going to tame this one?" Willy asked.

"We're gonna have to find a way." Robert said. "We're stuck with her for a while until we figure out what to do with her. I think I need to go out and see what the word is on the ship. Maybe they've found the sailor by now and others are talking about it."

"That sounds good. Do you want me to go with you? We won't be taking her out will we?"

"No, no. You need to stay here with her, but do you think you can stay awake and make sure she doesn't leave?" Robert asked him.

"Yeah, yeah, I'll keep her here with me. Who knows, maybe we'll become friends."

They both laughed and looked. Their look and Willy's comment made me ill at ease. What did he mean by that?

Robert left and reminded Willy not to let me out of his sight. Willy looked over at me again with the same disturbing look. I was standing against the wall and I bent down to grab my coat and hold it in front of me as if it were going to protect me from him.

Willy locked the door and went to the window to look out. "Guess it's just you and me for the day, what would you like to do?" He said as he walked towards me.

"Stay away from me!" I told him as he came closer. "I mean it!"

"And just what are you going to do if I don't?"

"Scream as loud as I can, do you want that?"

"I don't care if you do." He said as he grabbed my coat away from me and pulled me towards him. He was trying to kiss my neck and hold my arms down at the same time.

I screamed and fought at the same time, trying to get away. He forced me over on the bed and threw me down. I continued to scream and fight him as he ripped the top of my blouse and continued his horrible assault on me.

Finally a woman came to the door and banged on it, shouting at the same time. "Is everything all right in there? What's going on?"

Willy quickly placed his hand over my mouth to keep me from screaming. I struggled but he overpowered me and pinned me down, still holding his hand over my mouth.

"Everything's fine!" he yelled back, "We're just having a little fun."

"Doesn't sound like fun to me! I won't have this type of stuff going on in my place!" She told him. "Now quiet down or I'll kick you out!"

"Yeah, yeah, we'll quiet down. We don't want to be kicked out, now do we honey?" Willy said, looking down at me.

I tried to mumble, "Help me! Please!" But his hand over my mouth muffled the words and she went back down the stairs without helping me.

"See what your yellin' gets us?" He said, and he pulled me from the bed and threw me back to my spot on the wall.

"Fine. Keep your Irish spirit to yourself, for now. We'll have a lot more time together."

Willy left me against the wall and went back over to the table to sit down. He glanced out the window and then sat down. He pulled something out of his pocket and began playing with them. It looked like two square things that he kept throwing. I eventually felt comfortable enough to sit back down on the floor against the wall, and watched him off and on all afternoon.

"What is that you keep throwing?" I finally asked.

"What do you care? It's keeping me from being bored to death." He said.

"I just want to know what those things are you keep throwing." I didn't want him mad at me when Robert came back. I knew I needed to be on their good side, rather than their bad side. "Well? What are they?"

"It's called Hazard, and it's a game you play with die. See these two die? Each of them is called dice, and they have numbers on them. You throw them and people bet on what numbers will roll out. Come over here, I'll show you."

I stood there for a moment and he said, "Come on, I won't do anything to you. Come on!"

I walked over to him and he showed me the dice.

"Here. See the numbers on each side? It has black dots that stand for the numbers one through six. Do you see?"

I shook my head, yes, and he handed them to me.

"Now you shake them in your hand, then you throw them on a table or floor and they roll till they stop. Try it."

I held them in my hand, but didn't move them.

"Here!"

He grabbed my hand and forced me to shake the dice and then he motioned my hand to throw it out.

I followed his motion and let go of the dice as he showed me.

"See? Now let's say I said your next roll was going to be a two and a six. You might say something different, and then you'd roll the die. If one of us were correct, we'd win whatever the wager was."

"What's a wager?"

"That's how much you're betting for. Do you understand?"

"I guess so." I told him.

"All right then let's try it for a while. I'll bet the next roll will be a one and a four."

"And what are we supposed to wager?" I asked him.

"You don't. We don't have anything to wager, we're just playing to pass the time. Now go ahead and roll."

"Don't I get to guess some numbers?"

"Go ahead then, guess."

"All right, I'll say a three and a three. Can I do that?"

"Sure. Now roll!"

I rolled the die and neither of us rolled the correct numbers. We continued on like this until Robert returned. We were sounding familiar when Robert walked in.

"And what's going on here?" he asked.

"I'm showing her how to play Hazard," said Willy.

Robert walked over to us and grabbed the die out of my hand. "Well you won't be playing it anymore, ya hear? Let's not go getting too friendly with her. She's our ticket to riches. Got it?"

Willy nodded and asked, "So what happened today? Any word out there about the girl, or the ship?"

"Plenty," said Robert, "They're looking for her, and for the men who attacked the sailor on the Seagull."

"They didn't recognize you?" Willy asked.

"Fortunately not. They say the sailor can't remember a thing, but they're hoping he regains his memory soon."

"What are they saying about me?" I asked.

"You don't need to know, but what we do need is to is get out of here. I talked to the Landlady and she knows we'll be heading out tomorrow."

"For where?" I asked. I thought about Skully, the Captain and everyone on the Kate. Surely they would find me before we left. Surely they would be looking for me!

"New Orleans. There's a real fine place there that is looking for you." Robert said.

Willy looked puzzled and I was bewildered.

"What do you mean they're looking for me? Who?" I asked him.

"Your name is Cora." Robert said.

"No it's not, it's Allie Kiper!" I told him.

"Hah! Now you tell me! Well I think it's Cora, and that's what we're naming you!"

"Why Cora?" asked Willy.

Robert reached into his pocket and pulled out a piece of paper. Willy read over it and then handed it to me snickering.

I looked down at it and read:

FIFTY DOLLARS REWARD

Ran away from the possessor, three months ago,
a quintroon girl, named Cora,
about twenty-five years of age,
white, and brown reddish hair,
a cut on her upper lip; has a scar on her forehead about five
feet five inches high;
she passes for free;
talks French, Italian, Dutch, English, and Spanish.
Mathew Blatchen.
Lower side of St. Mary's Market. —N. O.
Picayune.

"But this isn't me!" I screeched, "And you know it! I don't speak all of those languages, and my hair isn't red, and I'm not twenty-five, and I have my two front teeth! You'll never pull this off! Never!"

"Aah, but we will, and we'll get the reward for bringing you in."

Willy laughed, and Robert grabbed the paper back, folded it again and placed it in his pocket. This is our ticket to a new life. He looked at Willy and said, "Willy, we are now bounty hunters for escaped slaves. How does that sound?"

"Sounds like we have come across the perfect first runaway!"

I was furious at their consideration of this wild scenario, and I sat back against the wall and steamed to myself, wondering what was I going to do to get away from these two monsters. I kept slamming my head back against the wall and Robert came over to me and bent down in front of me.

"Stop that incessant banging, Cora!" He pushed my head, and both he and Willy started cackling.

They were reveling in their new found idea, and their naming me Cora.

Cora! Of all things, Cora. Just like Cora of Last of the Mohicans. At least I had something to connect her to and think of, but where is my Hawkeye? Here I go again, I thought to myself, I am making my life a story from a book, when in all actuality I need to focus on the actual happenings. I was in my own mess and there was no Hawkeye to help me out of it.

Willy brought up our dinner, and they invited me to sit at the table with me. I didn't want to so I took my food and sat back down against the wall. I was going between hating them and trying to make them like me. I didn't know which way to play it, but I knew I wanted to eat as far away from them as possible.

They ate, and I overheard Robert asking Willy about my torn blouse. He also told Willy that the Landlady mentioned some yelling coming from the room. Willy made light of it by saying I was trying to escape and my Irish spirit was rising up. They both laughed and Robert accepted his explanation. I just shook my head and continued eating.

We finished our meal and I lay down to rest for the night. I bunched my coat up again to lay my head on it, and I pulled the blanket over me. I started thinking about home. Not New York, but Ireland. Here I was lying on the floor and thinking about Ireland. I remember all too well spending the better part of my youth on the floor at night. I thought of our home and of Da and Moira and Quinlan. How very sad that they are not alive and able to be with Ma.

I then thought about Mr. Farraday and Brody. Brody, with his strong family ties and enjoyment of his mother's words. Of his horseback riding, and the way he looked in his riding clothes, and the new clothes Mr. Leeds gave him. He really was handsome. A kind and gentle person, whether he bugged me at times or not. I fell asleep thinking of him and wondering what he looked like now.

Robert woke me up before it was light outside. "We have to go! Get yourself up and put your coat on?"

"Where are we going?" I asked groggily.

"Just get up and let's go! Willy, get her moving and I'll take care of the landlady."

Willy pulled me up and shoved my coat towards me. As I was putting it on, he grabbed their bags and organized them at the door. I didn't have anything else with me, so I just stood there watching.

"Come on, now. Pick up one of these bags and let's get moving!" He growled.

He pushed me towards the back stairs and down we went and out onto the street. I glanced around trying to get the attention of anyone, but there was no one out. I heard someone coming and hoped to get their attention as soon as they came out the door, but it was Robert. My heart dropped and I let out a sigh.

"Thinking about talking to someone, were you?" Robert asked.

I said nothing and waited for one of them to tell me what to do. My mind was racing with thoughts of the Captain, and Skully, now. What were my new friends on the ship going to do about me missing? Weren't they out there looking for me? Where were they? I knew Skully would be pushing to find me. What could I do to help them find me? I hurriedly racked my brain to come up with something to give them a clue. The only thing I came up with was to drop my scarf. I still had it in my coat pocket, and needed to drop it without either of the men seeing me do it. I put my hand in my pocket and felt the scarf. I looked at both men and they were gathering the bags and getting ready to walk down the street. I looked around to see where I should drop it and figured I needed to drop it here. Right here, where we stayed the night.

"Follow us!" Robert barked, and I looked around, too scared to drop it, yet.

"Come on!" He barked again.

I knew if I didn't drop it now I might lose my chance, so I let go of it as we were walking, and saying, "All right! I'm coming."

They didn't say anything about it, so maybe I had been successful. Maybe Skully or Mr. Barnes would find it and figure something out. Maybe I was like the story of Hansel and Gretel, and they would follow my path. That's what I needed…they needed to follow my path!

I lost track of the days as we traveled to New Orleans. Robert had Willy steal two horses and I rode with Robert as Willy carried the bags on his horse. Along the way we picked up one of Willy's cousins. He was another hanger-on, but Robert seemed to accept him as someone who could do some of his dirty work. Robert was the leader and the most educated of the three. I didn't know his story, but he must have come from a learned family. He knew a lot about the world and how to come off as being a businessman, at least when he wanted to. He was arrogant at times, and both Willy and his cousin, Tom, followed his direction.

Robert and Willy were average size men, both strong and in good health. Tom was a scrawny man and rather simple minded. He didn't mind doing the manual labor on the trip; carrying the bags, stealing things, knocking people out if needed, or manhandling people to get what Robert wanted. A lot of that went on.

We spent most of our nights out in the open. On the nights we were able to be inside, we were with members of one of their families, or with friends. They told people I was a runaway slave, and with the paper Robert had, it seemed everyone believed him. I tried telling people along the way, but most just laughed or turned from me without hearing my story. I couldn't believe anyone would believe him over me if they could hear my accent. Why would a slave have an Irish accent?

Robert realized he'd have to come up with a story about my accent. He decided I was trying to act like I was someone important. Kind of lawdy daw, I guess, and my talking like this was only a ruse. He reminded people that if he did not return me to my rightful owner, charges would be brought against whoever kept me. It worked.

Most nights we were cold, and either Tom or I had to get the firewood, build the fire, and get it going. I tried escaping quite a few times, but each time I tried, they caught me and brought me back. Once I made it to a farmhouse, and the family took me in, but when Robert showed up with the paper, they had to let me go. I think the family from the farm was the only ones that took the time to hear my case. Even the man of the house thought it strange a runaway slave would have an Irish accent.

I don't think I had one night of good sleep.

Tom tried to force himself on me at least three times, and Willy once more, so I had to sleep with one eye open. I was worried every night one of them would try something, again. I did my best to stay as close to Robert as possible. At least he hadn't tried anything, yet, and he scolded the others each time they did try something. I was filthy, and tired, and looking the part of a runaway slave by the time we made it to New Orleans.

Not one day had gone by I had not thought about the Captain. I wondered if they had found him and if he was back in New York, or looking for me. I realized after we left, no one would have any idea where I really was or who I was with. I felt completely alone and had submitted myself to this fate. What other choice did I have? I had tried to fight. I had tried to get along. Nothing worked and I felt as if I had to surrender. Maybe Robert wouldn't sell me after all, or turn me in and get the reward. Maybe he would allow me to go along as his cook or lackey. If I could just remain with him, maybe I could gain his trust and get away later. That's what I would work towards, gaining his trust and getting away later.

In New Orleans, we stayed at another boarding house. Robert kept me in his room and told the Landlord I was his little sister. Willy and Tom stayed in their room. Robert labeling me his little sister encouraged me. Maybe he would not be going through with his original plan. I was also glad I would be in his room rather than the other two. At least I could get some much wanted sleep, even if that did mean I was going to be on the floor. I was used to it again and just the floor would have no bearing on my ability to sleep. I had lots of practice sleeping like this.

They rotated watch over me the next few days. I was much tougher now and used to fighting my way out of their clutches, so my fear of them had slightly subsided. I was still disgusted by them and their lack of respect for me as a person. I was just a thing to them. I had truly lucked out with thwarting their advances, but that didn't mean they didn't berate me and show a total lack of consideration for me.

They didn't have to be with me all of the time, which was good. Robert had a room which could be locked from the outside, and we were on the third flight up, so jumping out of the window was out of the question. I would have to be patient, make sure they trusted me, and then take my chances. Anyway, if Robert was thinking about other plans for me, I didn't need to make him mad right now.

I had no idea what the plans were, and Robert and the other two didn't talk business in front of me anymore. About the fourth day in New Orleans, Robert bought me a new dress.

"Here is something I bought for you today." He said.

"I was told it was the style. I had no idea what your size was so I picked out a lady that looked like your size and asked her which size would be best to buy for my little sister."

"It looks like it will fit fine," I told him.

It was a light pink or peach colored dress. I hated the color, but the dress was in a pique fabric, I think, which was a nice lightweight fabric. It was a thinner fabric made of what felt like cotton. It had satin trim on the seams. I had no idea what day it was, but the days were warmer now and if summer were on the way, this would be a nice weight for the warmer months.

"There's a woman coming up here to take you to a bath and fix you up. I need you to look nice, like my sister would look." He said.

His statement of my looking like his sister once again encouraged me. Maybe he really wasn't going to sell me like he said for so long. Maybe he was going to use me for something else. Whatever the reason, I was looking forward to a bath and getting out of these clothes and into something else. I was revolted with the clothes I had on right now, and I was reminded of the other time I hated my clothes and just wanted to throw them away. I sure could wear out some clothes, I thought.

I no longer looked in the mirror because I hated the sight of myself. My hair was once again disheveled and tangled, and my skin had a permanent tinge of dirt. My dress was torn in places and had lost the look of its once attractive appearance. I looked like the people I had left in Ireland; those poor, homeless and downtrodden people, left alone to die and be forgotten. However, I had some spark of hope with Robert calling me his sister, and bringing me this new dress. Maybe I had something to look forward to.

I looked out the window as I waited for the lady to come and get me. I glanced up at the sky and leaned my head against the frame, closing my eyes and feeling the warmth of the sun against my face. Leaving my head against the frame, I turned slightly to rest against the frame with my back, leaving my eyes closed. How I wanted to be somewhere else. How I wanted to be back in New York, and with Captain and Rufina again.

The keys jingling at the door broke my moment of thought and I opened my eyes and stood up waiting for whoever was at the door. It was Robert with a Negro girl.

"Come on!" He said, and I followed him and the girl as he motioned me to come.

No one said anything and we went down a flight of stairs and in to another room which had a bath in it.

"Now, scrub her down real good, and fix her up real nice." He said.

"Yes sir." Said the young girl.

She had to be younger than me, and much frailer. She was in a dress with a tightly pulled scarf around her head.

"Get undressed, Miss, we got to git you fixed up good." She said.

"Do you know why?" I asked her.

"No Ma'am, I just do what I'm told."

"What's your name? Mine is Allie."

"Mine is Matilda."

"Matilda? That's a pretty name."

"We can't be talkin', Miss. I don't want to git in trouble. Let's just git this done."

I finished taking off my clothes and slipped in to the bath. It wasn't that hot, but it felt good to slip down under the water. Matilda scrubbed my body and washed my hair. She was hurrying so, I thought she might take my skin off.

"Not so hard, please?" I asked her.

"We've got to git you good and clean, now let me get finished with you." She spouted.

"That's the second time you've brought that up. Why?"

"Cause that's what I'm getting' paid to do."

"Matilda, are you a slave?"

"Yes'um"

"We're you taken from your family?"

"Yes'um."

"Me, too. These men I'm with took me from Charleston. I was with a group of people helping slaves escape to the North."

"Stop it right now!" She forcefully whispered. "Right now! I can't git in to no trouble, ya hear?"

"I hear, but I've been taken, too. Can you help me?"

"No Ma'am. I'm sorry, but I can't. I don't have no one, and I'm sickly. Do you know how long a sickly slave lasts? I'm worth nothin' to them unless I'm workin', and that's all I got."

"Is there anyone else I can talk to?"

Just then there was a banging on the door. "Are you finished in there?" Robert yelled.

"No, sir." Matilda said.

"Well, hurry it up! You want to get paid, don't you?"

"Yes, sir." She said, and with a force that came out of nowhere, she started moving me about as if she were three of her in that little body. She was moving me with a purpose. She pulled me out of the tub, dried me off, and started putting my clothes on.

First it was the drawers, and then the stay. She pulled it so tight I thought I wouldn't be able to breathe. It felt like it had bones or metal pieces in it that cinched my ribs and waist. She then pulled a petticoat over my head and down to my waist. I had never had so many pieces to put on. She then pushed me down on a seat and lifted each foot up to slip on stockings and then button up the boots. Last but not least was the dress itself. It was a little too small, but she slipped me into it like sausage in the skin, and buttoned up the back.

There was no full-length mirror so I had no idea how I looked. That didn't seem to bother her, though, for she was focused on my hair and getting it fixed. She towel dried it and then took her brush and pulled it through my hair as if I was a horse ready for show.

"Matilda, please!" I begged her.

"Sorry, Miss. Mr. Man wants you ready and out of here."

Mr. Man. I smiled to myself thinking he had

no name, just Mr. Man. That was fitting. No Robert, or Mr. Thistle, but Mr. Man.

She finally brushed the tangles out of my hair, or what hair was left, and brushed it to the back. She puffed it softly around my ears and then rolled my hair up the back so it was neatly in a roll around the bottom of my head. It was neatly done and I could see myself in the dresser mirror as she finished putting powder on my face. I felt like a doll that was being dressed up for playtime.

Before I could say anything, she went over to the door

and knocked, saying, "She's ready."

Robert unlocked the door and opened it to see her work. I was still sitting when he barked, "Get up! Let me see what you look like."

I stood up and turned towards him. "Nice, very nice. I'm going to have to keep you away from Willy and Tom for sure, now." He said.

I cringed at the thought of my looks attracting the two of them and felt cheapened by his comments.

"Back upstairs!" he barked again, and I slid past Matilda and up the stairs.

As I was cresting the last two steps of the third floor stairs, Willy stepped out of his doorway. "Tom, come look at this! She's all cleaned up and pretty like."

Tom stuck his head out of the doorway and they were both unrelenting with their dreadful comments as I passed their doorway going to mine.

Willy grabbed me as I passed him. "Guess

this makes you think you're still too good for us, don't it?"

I didn't comment on his statement, but jerked away and continued walking towards my door. Will and Tom laughed and went back in their room, but left their door open. I waited outside the door for Robert to come and open it.

"Tomorrow's a whole new day for all of us." Robert stated to me as he opened the door.

"What do you mean?" I asked him.

"You'll just have to wait and see." He said. "Tonight I want you to take that dress off and lay it across the chair. I don't want it wrinkled and looking bad. Do you hear? And don't you go messing you hair up, either. I'm not going to pay to have you fixed up again. I'll bring you some dinner, later. Put on these clothes to sleep in tonight."

He threw the clothes towards me and went out the door again locking it behind him. I picked up the clothes he threw at me and looked at them. They were his underclothes. Clean, but nonetheless a horrid thought. I cringed thinking about putting them on, and threw them down on the floor wishing I had something else to put on.

I walked away from the clothes, towards the window, and caught a glimpse of myself in the mirror. I stopped and turned towards the mirror looking at the dress. If I didn't think of me being in the dress in this dreadful color, it wasn't that bad. It was the pink pique with satin trim. The bodice was fitted below my waist and came down to a point in the front. The neckline was a V shape with a sheer fabric that covered the opening of the V. The sleeves flared out slightly at the wrists and the skirt flared out on the petticoat.

I looked much more mature than I ever had before. The dresses Captain had bought me were always nice, but they were for a schoolgirl. This dress was for a woman, and I looked the part. The tight stay lifted my breasts and brought in my waist. I turned around and felt the sway of the petticoat and the skirt as I turned. The tightness of the stay was starting to wear on me, and I was looking forward to getting out of all of this soon.

However, getting out of it meant I had to get into Robert's under garments. What a revolting, vile thought. As quick as that thought came to me, another one popped in to my head. I had on undergarments! Maybe I could sleep in the layers Matilda put me in? I wouldn't be getting this dress wrinkled, so what would it matter to Robert?

I reflected on the layers she had pulled me into, and remembered a distressing thought. To get to those layers, there were dozens of tiny, little buttons to undo. Who was going to undo those buttons? I reached back to feel the buttons, and see what my range was in being able to undo them. There was no way I was going to be able to undo those buttons myself. Who was I going to get to help? I was dismayed at my choices, and sat down wondering what I was going to do.

Willy brought me dinner and plopped it down on the table. "We'll be out late tonight." He said. "You better get some sleep. Come tomorrow, you'll be wishing me and Tom were taking care of you!" He laughed and walked out the door.

I ran to the door banging on it. "Willy! Willy!" I yelled.

"Please! Come back! I need to ask you something!"

"Oh, now you want me to come back, do you? What do you want?" He asked.

"Matilda. Could you ask Matilda to come up here and help me get undressed?"

"If you need some help getting undressed, I can help you with that." He snickered as he said it.

"No, no, forget it. I'll just have to sleep in this dress. Robert won't like it, but that's what I'll do." I told him hoping to make him think about Robert rather than me. I stepped away from the door as if I was resolved with answering my own request.

"I'll talk to Robert, but if he wants me to undress you, I'll be right back."

He had that strange snicker in his voice again and I dreaded the thought of his coming back. Surely Robert wouldn't let me get hurt tonight. Whatever his plans were, surely he wouldn't want me looking as though I had been in a fight.

My fears were quelled when I heard Robert

opening the door. "Guess this is two person job." Robert said.

I was uneasy with his comment and the thought that he was going to be undressing me.

"Turn around and let's get this off." He said. He took my shoulders in his hands and forced me around.

I was silent as he started unbuttoning my dress. My eyes were closed and I don't think I took a breath the entire time he fingered the buttons. He was clumsy but the job was done. He took a finger and slowly ran it across my upper back.

"Looks like this skin has never seen the light of day?" He said.

I twirled around and reached behind me to hold the back together.

"I'm not going to do anything to you." He said. "Not a thing. We have tomorrow to think about, and I need you looking nice."

"What's..."

"You'll find out tomorrow." He said, and went back to the door. "I'll be in late." Locking the door behind him, I was once again alone in the room.

I slipped out of the dress and laid it on the chair. I had completely forgotten about needing help with the stay, so I kept it on rather than asking for more help. If I were worried about someone unbuttoning the dress, unbuttoning the stay would be much worse. I was going to have to sleep in it the best I could. Sitting was quite uncomfortable in it, so standing up or laying down flat was the most comfortable.

I went to my spot on the floorboards and lied down. It was difficult getting there, but after a plop to the floor, I was down and stretched out. Being on my back was best for my hair, too.

I looked at the pattern of the boards as they made up the ceiling and it reminded me of being on the Kate during my voyage to America. I counted the boards until the light was taken from them. There remained only the shadows of the things or people outside that the lights reflected from. They moved almost eerily across the ceiling and danced in their own way. I thought of clouds and the poem by William Wordsworth, again. Last time I had recited it, I was with Nella on the Seagull.

I thought of those last few days of being on the ship and arriving in Charleston. I thought about my inability to accept and be part of the agents' plans. What were they all doing? I wondered. What were they all doing?

I then thought about Ma and Brody. Surely they were in America, now. Either Ma was taking care of Rufina, or Rufina was taking care of her. I smiled as I thought of both of them. I wondered if Captain was back home, and if he and Ma had realized they were in love? I hoped they had. It would be nice to think of the two of them together and helping one another. I know Ma would feel the way we do about slavery. She would be much better at accepting it and going through with the agents' plans.

I took a deep breath and sighed knowing I had ultimately disappointed everyone. I knew they could go on without me, and probably did, but I hated to think I was just an extra body. An extra body that was of no help, just extra.

As I lied there, I was quite uncomfortable. I tried squirming to move my ribs and get some extra breathing space in the stay, but there was none to be had. I was going to have to make the best of the night with this bone hard stay around me.

I thought about Jonathan and wondered what he was doing? Word would have traveled back by now about me. Maybe he had met Ma and Brody. I wondered what they thought of him? Maybe they would all be working together to find me. That would be wonderful. I would love for Jonathan to rescue me, and then we could go on with our lives.

Our lives. Our lives were so different. He was from a wealthy family whose grandparents had come over years before. He knew nothing but wealth and high society. He seemed sincere enough about me, but could we make that leap? Could he? My life had been so different. At least Rufina and Captain understood. We shared so much in our little threesome. They accepted me. We were such an odd trio, but it worked somehow.

My thoughts went back to Ireland. I remember such a poor Ireland; so much pain and struggle, so many losses. There were only a few people left that I had any connection with from my past. There was Mr. Leeds and Betsy. There was Mr. Farraday and Patrick. And, of course, there was Ma and Brody.

Thank heavens I read through my letters before I left. The years that those letters covered had gone by quickly but the words in them are constant reminders of my past and of the ones I love. There were some good memories of Ireland and I hoped I would never forget them. For some reason I lived. For some reason...

CHAPTER 4
BELLE TERRE

The keys in the door awakened me. I opened my eyes and realized the sun was up. I sat up on my elbows as far as the stay would allow.

Robert walked in and asked, "Did you sleep? I hope so, you've got a big day today."

"Did you stay out all night?" I asked him.

"I sure did and it was worth every penny."

"Gambling?"

"Yes. And I hope to do it again tonight." He said. "But right now, we've got to get you up and ready to go out."

"Go out? You're going to let me go out?" I asked him.

"Yes I am. We have something to take you to. Now, come on, let's get up and get ready."

He helped me to work my way up with my stiff torso, and then I stood there with the blanket around me waiting for him to turn around.

"After all this time, you're still modest around me!" He said, snorting. "I'll turn around and you get that dress on. I imagine we've got to re-button all those buttons! Seems like a lot of trouble to me."

He turned and I went over to the chair and picked up the dress. I stepped in to it and slid my arms into the sleeves and then pulled the dress up and situated it on my shoulders, hips, and waist.

I pulled the fabric towards the back and said,

"All right, I'm ready. Will you please button the back?"

"Gladly! We need to get you out there in the world today."

I was almost gleeful at the thought of being out and about. I didn't know what was in store for me, but I was looking forward to being out in the sun and walking around. I hadn't seen very much of New Orleans, and I was hoping to get a glimpse of some of the ships and the waterfront area.

Willy and Tom came to the door and knocked loudly.

"We're ready whenever you are!" They laughed.

"Need any help in there?"

"We're coming out in just a few minutes," said Robert. "Do you think you two buffoons could wait? Go on downstairs and wait for us there."

They laughed as they headed down the stairs and obeyed Roberts's orders.

"Now here's what I want you to do today," said Robert, "you get out there and show your pretty self in a very proud and ladylike way. Got it? Show everyone what you have and be proud, stand tall, and show off your shape."

That was a very strange request, I thought.

Show off my shape! It sounded as if he was trying to sell me on the street.

"I will not prostitute myself!" I barked at him.

"No, no, of course, you wouldn't. Who said anything about that? I just want you to show yourself in the best light, all right?"

I didn't answer. I just followed him out the door. I didn't want to make him angry after he had bought me this dress and was calling me his sister. I didn't need to make him mad and have him change his mind.

Willy and Tom were waiting for us outside. We stepped out onto the street and Robert said, "You walk between them."

I looked at the two men and moved over to stand between them. Willy took my arm as if not to let me run away, and we followed Robert as he walked down the street. We walked to a market and looked around the merchant's areas. There was fresh fruit and vegetables. There were live chickens, and pigs, and other livestock. There were loaves of bread, and reams of fabric. There were flowers, and cheese, jams and jellies. There was fish and meat, and…oh, no!

"No!" I said, and tried to jerk my arm from Willy.

Robert overheard me and spun around walking right up to me. "Don't you dare try anything! You ruined our chance of getting that ship, now we're gonna get our due!"

He pulled a piece of paper from his pocket and shoved it in my face. I read it in shock.

"I don't even know what a Quintroon girl is!" I barked at him. "But I suppose it doesn't matter!"

Bright Quintroon Girl
For sale to settle debts, named, Cora
white, clear skin and flowing hair.
Passes as free.
Eighteen to nineteen years old.
Reads, writes, sews and cooks.
Five feet four inches.
Full set of teeth, strong limbs, shapely form.
Robert Thistle.

Robert forced his hand over my mouth and closer to my face. "You stay quiet and go along with this or we'll make your life more miserable. I won't be there to protect you from Willy or Tom tonight if that's what you want!"

I couldn't think of anything worse at the minute and nodded to him in acknowledgement. I would keep my mouth shut. Robert slowly took his hand away and motioned to Willy, who still had a grip on me, to follow him. We walked around the merchants on the outside of the area. As we did, I noticed a group of Negroes tied together, and standing close to a platform.

My heart sank. Any hope I had of being a sister rather than a thing, disappeared immediately. I now knew why he bought the dress, and why he had Matilda wash and dress me and fix my hair. And why he wouldn't let Willy or Tom hurt me. He needed me to be perfect for his distorted plan. I was going to bring him money and I had to look my best to get the best price.

As I looked around the crowd that was beginning to assemble, I saw the piece of paper posted around the area. I was humiliated and embarrassed. I didn't want to look up any more because I did not want to see anyone's faces, or maybe I did not want them to see mine.

The sale started and it was just as awful as the last one I had seen, but this time I had no supportive person with me, I had nowhere else to go. I couldn't go to the ship and hide. I had to wait my time, and this time it seemed as though it was moving bitterly slow.

I heard every cry and scream the human beings that were being sold let out. I heard the taunts and hollers from the crowd, and the demanding roars of the barker and trader. I heard the snap of whips and the crack of belts on those that fought the process. This was no good. I was ashamed to be a human being at this moment, knowing we were really all one. It was just a matter of who was in control.

As the line grew shorter, Robert came over to me and grabbed my chin and in my face again. "You get up there and get me my money! Do you here? Otherwise you're Willy's. You got it? Show them how pretty you can be!"

Pretty?! What a horrible adjective to use for this instance. I felt anything but pretty, and hated the fact he used that word for this moment.

"Hold your head up, too! Stand tall, Cora!" Robert sneered.

Something happened when he called me Cora. It infuriated me. He made up this name to fit his plan. Willy pushed me towards the platform. I felt like I was being pushed to a scaffold, and the steps leading to it were the precursor to a beheading. I looked up at the barker and out towards the crowd. I could see their mouth's moving and the excitement in their gestures, but it was all in slow motion and my brain wasn't assimilating all of the pieces. Willy pushed again, and I was up on the stage.

I turned to go back down but the Barker pulled me towards him at the same time I heard Robert yelling to Willy, "Get her up there, Willy!"

I tried jerking away, but I couldn't get free. This seemed to excite the crowd and the Barker, so I stood there as still as I could so as not to encourage any more of this humiliating exhibition. Another man read through the paper Robert had written about this imaginary me.

Someone from the crowd yelled, "Turn her around!" And others yelled in agreement.

The man holding me took me by my waist and turned me around. He ran his hands down my sides to show my figure, and the other man said, "Now that speaks for itself!"

He twirled me back around front and lifted my chin, turning it from side to side. "White as can be! You'd never know the difference!"

Men started yelling out numbers, and I felt like piranhas were taking bites out of me with each amount yelled. They started with fifty dollars, but quickly the numbers went up to four hundred, then five hundred. Six hundred, then seven, and up. There was such excitement in the crowd. The auctioneer had to tell them to slow down so he could hear each bid. When the amount slowed down at one hundred eleven, they twirled me around again to see my backside, and then back to the front again, this time holding my arms out for all to see my front.

The bidding was now down to two men, and the increments had shrunk to tens. Eleven hundred and ten, eleven hundred and twenty. Could I take anymore? Eleven hundred and thirty. Japers, please! I thought. I just wanted the whole process over and to be able to get off the stage. Eleven hundred and forty!

The auctioneer sounded as if it was over. "I have eleven hundred and forty! Will there be eleven hundred and fifty? Eleven hundred and fifty? Going once, going twice! Thank heavens, I thought, it's over. Sold! For eleven hundred and forty dollars! Give the man his woman."

His woman, his property. That's what it's come down to, somebody's woman, not even Cora anymore. They manhandled me down the stairs and to the crowd of Negroes that had been sold. They bundled us together and as each owner paid what was due, he took his winnings. We peeled off to different people, and I was placed with two other slaves who were led to two horses and a wagon.

We stepped up in the wagon and were pushed together with the other items he had bought from the market. I looked towards the other wagons and saw some Negroes tied together with rope, some shackled, and some loose like us. I wondered what the difference was and why.

No one spoke or barely looked at each other for our long ride to wherever we were going. The man that bought us didn't even speak to us. He was focused on the road in front of him, and kept the horses moving.

We moved along the road as if there was no end. If you took away the unpleasant act that had occurred this morning, or the situation we were all currently in, one might look around at the trees and the flowers that were so brilliantly blooming. It must be Spring I thought to myself and looked around at the countryside and the splendor of nature. There were these white blossoms or vines with flowers on them that hung from the trees. They were everywhere and their beauty looked so natural and free.

We were definitely heading away from New Orleans, but I didn't know which direction. I should have been paying attention to the road in case I needed to know how to get away. I began looking around more and trying to think back of the road we followed before here. How can I be so absentminded, I thought? I always let my mind wander and I miss things I should not have.

As the man made the horses turn, I looked in front of them and saw a huge gate and entry for a private road. It had an abundance of flowered bushes that edged the entry making it most welcoming.

I overheard one of the Negroes say to the other, "This is that sugar plantation Joe told us about. He was right."

I looked around for any fields but didn't see any. I only saw beautiful green grass and trees lining this private road. The trees had large trunks and huge leaves that were shiny and glossy looking. Its flowers were huge white blossoms. The fragrance from all of this was overwhelming. It was as if I was in Betsy's bath. Here in this fresh air. How wonderful I thought! I took a deep breath in, and must have let the air out most noisily.

"Look at Miss Uppity here. She's enjoyin' the smells." One of them said, and then they both laughed.

"Can you believe its fragrance?" I said.

"Believe its fragrance?" The other man said. "This is hard time working in a sugar plantation.

"You've got another thing coming."

"What do you mean?" I asked

They both laughed and looked away from me shaking their heads. I really didn't know what to expect, but I could hope for the best, couldn't I? If I was to live amongst the flowers and trees and this beautiful landscape, then I was going to try and make the best of it.

I looked ahead of the horses and saw a huge white house coming into focus through the branches that hung over the road. We turned away from its location and headed down another road. I looked back towards it and saw a beautiful two story home with pillars all the way around the house. I wondered why we were going away from it if that was where we were going to stay.

I leaned towards the man sitting next to me and said, "Why are we going this way if the house is over there?"

"Because you're a slave, Miss Uppity! You don't get to sleep in the Master's house!"

They both snorted at my apparent ignorance, and faced away from me again. I followed their head direction and looked beyond the horses in our new direction. We slowly left the area that was full of trees and flowers and crossed a rather weedy, mirky wetland and then back out onto fields. This must be the sugar fields.

I looked left and right and saw fields stretching everywhere. I also saw people working in the fields, handling horses and wagons, and watching over huge pots of something. No one looked our way, but continued with their work. Most were Negroes. I saw two men on horseback that were white, but everyone else was dark skinned. There must have been thirty to forty people that I could see.

The two men with me talked to one another as we came across this sight. I couldn't hear them and I was careful not to bother them. I didn't need to aggravate them or give them more ammunition to mock me. I was ignorant of the situation and it was going to take a lot of learning on my part to understand all of this. I was feeling quite apprehensive about what was unfolding and decided watching and listening would be the best thing for me to do right now.

We came up on some wooden shacks and the man who bought us pulled up to the larger of the buildings. A woman hurried over to the back of the wagon and started taking things out.

"Now the three of you get on down from there, and help Letty take what she needs out of this wagon." The man who drove us said.

"Did you have a good trip Mr. Williams?" The woman he called, Letty, asked.

"Indeed we did, Letty. I wasn't even going for these two, but I couldn't pass 'em up. It's a good thing, because this Quintroon here took me to my limit. Mr. Patout (pronounced Pah-tew) is gonna be awful glad we were able to get her. She's the main reason he called me to New Orleans."

"Did Mr. Patout come back with you?"

"No. He said he and Genevieve would be returning tomorrow or the next day."

Letty stopped us from taking anything else from the wagon, and said, "These things here, Mr. Williams, go to the main house. Nane'll know what to do with them."

"All right then. Will you find a place for these three, and I'll be back to tell them what their jobs are before dinner? "

"Yes, sir, Mr. Williams." Letty said quite compliantly.

She stood there watching the wagon head back to the main house, and then turned back to us.

"Where am I gonna put you three? What's your names?"

I stood there silently and the man that sat next to me on the wagon spoke up first. "My name is Jim," he said, "Jim Archer."

"And you, what is your name?" Letty asked the other man.

"Ben." He said.

"Yes, go on, Ben, Ben what?" She prompted him.

"Ben Field"

"Not much on words, are we?" She then looked at me and said, "Now you, I know your name. We knew about you before you got here. You're sleepin' with some of the younger women, Cora. Come on, I'll show you where your goin'"

"The name is Allie, Allie ..."

And before I could get the rest of my name out, the two men who rode with me huffed, and the one said, "She means Uppity, her name is Miss Uppity."

They laughed but Letty shot them a stern look and they stopped there. "You two stay here while I show C-or-a her cot." She motioned for them to stay and then for me to follow her.

We walked down five cottages or shacks and stepped into the fifth one.

"This is where you'll be stayin." She said. She threw some clothes at me and said, "Here's what you'll be wearing. Now take off those fancy clothes and get in to this. You won't be needin' that dress here."

She turned towards the door, and then back towards me, "I'll be back for you in a bit. Get ready and wait here. Don't try anything or one of the field hands will give you a welcome you ain't never wanted." And out the door she went.

I stood there, slightly numb, trying to take in the scene

and my new quarters. I looked around and saw wood and dirt. I had visions of Ireland in my mind, and wondered how I could have brought myself back to a place like this. The walls were poorly built with wooden slats. I didn't see any shutters, but only open windows and an open door. There was no door to close for privacy, and I was thinking about having to change my clothes with nothing to obscure my nakedness.

I glanced down, behind me, and looked at the cot that was to be my bed. It was a wooden frame with slats across the center. It had straw on the slats and then fabric laid across the straw. I sat down on it, feeling the crunchiness of the straw as I sat down. The three other beds were the same as mine, but one had a cradle next to it and by the fireplace in the room. There was a pot hanging on a rack, of sorts. If it weren't for the warmth of the temperature and the different aroma of this place, I would have thought I was back in Ireland.

I picked up the clothes Letty had given me and looked through them. I had some undergarments, a thin petty coat, and a very common dress. She had also left me some flat shoes that were almost boot-like. This would do, I thought, and changed my clothes waiting for Letty to come back and get me.

As I waited I could hear people working from all directions. I heard talking and laughing. I heard singing and the whirl of machinery. I heard horses snorting and someone shouting every now and then. It wasn't often, but I could tell he was serious and was trying to get people to keep working. I wanted to go to the door and look out, but I was leery of doing anything but sit here on my bed.

It wasn't long before Letty came back and told me to follow her.

As we walked back to the bigger house, Letty told me, "You listen to Mr. Williams and do what he says. If you do that you should be all right."

I nodded and followed her into the house. It was a large open area with four tables and a bigger fireplace. This one had shutters and a door for the front, and back. Mr. Williams was waiting by the back door leaning on the frame. The other two men were already there and sitting at one of the tables. He told me to sit next to them, and puffed on his cigar a few times before continuing. I hated cigars and had no fond memories of their aroma. At least the windows and the door were open, and there was a breeze through the house.

"I'm Mr. Williams, and I'm the Foreman of this sugar plantation. I make the rules, and you live by them. You two men will be working in the fields. Work starts early and goes until the overseer says you stop. You might get two hours during the day for a break, but don't ask for it, he'll decide if you deserve it. The Negroes you're living with will help you get started. You help the ones you're living with, and they'll help you. You eat with them and you sleep with them. Don't expect anything and you won't be disappointed.

"Life isn't so bad here, unless you make it so. You do your work and we give you everything you need to live; food, clothing and a roof over your head. Mr. Patout is a very nice man, but he doesn't have to worry about your running away. I do, and I don't like it. If you do something against him, your overseer, or me there will be consequences. You just ask around and the other ones will tell you what happens to someone who tries to escape or is too hard to handle. You might as well make the best of it because you could have a lot worse. Cora, you're to be working in the main house, with Mr. Patout's daughter. When he…"

There was yelling going on in the fields, and Letty ran into the room.

"Mr. Williams! Albert's getting' a whoopin'! Come quick!"

"You three stay here!" He said and out the door he went.

We all sat there a moment listening to the raucous, and then Jim and Ben stood up to go to the doorway and look out. "Can't see nuthin', but he's probably getting' a good one."

"What do you mean?" I asked, as I stood up and turned towards the two men.

"You heard the man, if you don't follow the rules, you

get justice," said Jim.

We could hear Mr. Williams coming back our way and Jim and Ben scurried back to our bench and sat down again. We listened as Mr. Williams gave a stern talking to a man.

"I'm not gonna tell you again, Lott. You better have good reason to take the whip to someone, and just because he was speaking in his own language doesn't mean you get to beat him." Mr. Williams told him.

"I don't like him speaking when I can't understand him. It's just not right. What if he were to be plannin' something, we should know about."

"In the middle of the field? With you riding right by him? Whether it was in his own language or ours, I don't think he'd do that."

"You're too easy on them, Harry. They're goin' to take all of this away from you one day, and I'll be there tellin' you so."

"Maybe you will, but until then, I'm still your boss and you won't be whipping anyone without a better reason. You don't get any more chances. I mean it! I'm tired of you making things worse. I've got some new ones in here that I'm talking to and I don't want to have to bother with you right now. We're trying to keep our labor force, Jones, not lose them. Punishment doesn't always work, got it?"

We didn't hear him answer, but Mr. Williams walked back into the place where we were all waiting. He continued right on with his explanation of what I was to be doing.

"Where was I?" Mr. Williams asked. "Oh, yes, Cora, you're to be working in the main house with Mr. Patout's daughter, Genevieve. They are not here right now, but still in New Orleans. When they get back, Mr. Patout will talk to you about what he wants you to do specifically. Until then, you will be helping Nane with whatever she wants you to do in the main house. You will go there in the morning. All three of you have tonight to rest, and then you are expected to be ready in the morning. It comes bright and early. Any questions you have, ask Letty. All right, Letty?"

"Yes, sir, Mr. Williams."

Mr. Williams walked out the door and Letty turned her attentions to us. "You two follow me. Cora you stay here until I come back. You're to help me with things in here. We've got a weddin' tonight."

Ooh, a wedding! How much fun! The only wedding I have ever been to was Rufina and Angelo's, and it was marvelous. Everyone was happy. I thought about their wedding, Captain, and their friends.

Letty came back in, "They're out there chopping wood for tonight. You come on in here with me and help with the cookin'."

She handed me a basket full of potatoes, "You peel these and then put them in this pot." How ironic, back to potatoes!

I did as she told me to do, and after a while, she asked me, "What's your story, anyway? Somethin' just doesn't fit."

"You wouldn't believe me if I told you."

"It doesn't matter no how." She said. "You're here and you belong to Mr. Patout. Of all the places you could've been taken to, you lucked out comin' here. Most of us accept bein' here, and he's had a hard time of it."

"Why do you say so?" I asked.

"He had a beautiful wife who died last year, and he he's had a hard time getting' over her death. It's sad, very sad that a man should be so broken after losing a wife. And he's got that adorable little girl, Genevieve, who reminds him of Mrs. Patout, daily."

"Does she look like her?"

"She does, and her mannerisms are like her, too. She has a lively spirit, but is gentle."

"What am I to do with her?"

"You'll have to wait and let Mr. Patout tell you what he wants. She stays with Nane most of the time, now, but she's starting to be of school age."

"Who is Nane? Does Nane teach her any subjects?"

"Nane does the cookin', housekeepin', and a little

storytellin'…what do you mean does she teach her any subject? It's against the law for slaves to have any schoolin'. That way they keep us ignorant, or so they think."

Ben stepped in the doorway with his arms full of wood. "Where do you want this wood, Miss Letty?" asked Ben.

"Right in here. See that pile over here that's low? That's where I need it to be stacked."

She kept talking to me, "Yep, we can't get no schoolin'. Of course, some of us have already had some schoolin', but we can't let anyone know. Mr. Patout probably wouldn't care, but it's not him we're worried about."

The stack of wood fell over, and Letty yelled, "Now look what you've done. Start that over and get it lined up nicely. We got a weddin' to celebrate tonight! Once you're done stacking that wood, get on back out there and turn that pig!"

We finished preparing the meal, which must have been enough for one hundred people. There was pork, and potatoes, red beans and rice, cabbage, and biscuits. We laid out cloth on two of the tables, and scooted all of the tables back so there was more open room by the fireplace.

Letty handed me a broom and said, "This is my gift to the couple."

I looked at it with a puzzled look.

"It's not for sweepin', it's traditional. They jump over it, together, before they're announced as husband and wife." She said. "Go place it over there by the wood stack. I'll hand it to Preacher Tim during the ceremony."

I placed it by the wood stack, and then Letty walked outside and rang a bell. A huge bell that was as loud as anything I had ever heard.

"Everyone will be comin' in from the fields, now. It won't be too long before this room is full of happy people."

Letty said.

I stirred the pots Letty and I had prepared, and watched as the room began to fill over the next hour or so. There must be fifty people I thought to myself as Letty greeted many of them. She would point me out to a few of them as she chatted with them, but I did not actually meet anyone new. Jim and Ben watched from the other side of the room, but I did notice they spoke with a few people off and on.

Letty organized the group and quieted them down as she pulled the bride and groom forward. The preacher was already at his position by the fireplace, as Letty placed the groom in his spot, and the bride in hers. The preacher had a long jacket on with a white shirt. It didn't look new, but he looked the part as he stood there officiating in front of everyone. The groom was in a nice pair of pants and a shirt, while the bride was actually wearing a fine dress that fit her nicely. None of it was fancy, but it was quite charming.

The bride stood next to the groom, and they both faced the preacher. She looked about my age and he looked about ten years older. They stood there facing the preacher but not holding hands. They were barely touching one another. I don't even think they glanced at one another.

The preacher spoke personally about the couple and their love for one another. He spoke on the special circumstances of slave life, and said:

The Spirit of the Sovereign LORD is on me, because the LORD has anointed me to preach good news to the poor. He has sent me to bind up the brokenhearted, to proclaim freedom for the captives and release from darkness for the prisoners, Instead of their shame my people will receive a double portion, and instead of disgrace they will rejoice in their inheritance; and so they will inherit a double portion in their land, and everlasting joy will be theirs. For I, the LORD, love justice; I hate robbery and iniquity. In my faithfulness I will reward them and make an everlasting covenant with them. Their descendants will be known among the nations and their offspring among the peoples. All who see them will acknowledge that they are a people the LORD has blessed.

Throughout the service men and women would chime in saying, "Amen," or "Praise the Lord." It was an interactive type of feeling, as if everyone held stake in the happiness of this couple and the blessing the preacher was placing upon them. They sang songs and raised their arms and swayed to the music, but not dancing. They were entranced in the preacher's words in body and soul.

He brought it all together stating there was a bigger purpose in life and that our physical beings on this earth were not all that mattered. There was a bigger purpose.

Therefore, I urge you, brothers, in view of God's mercy, to offer your bodies as living sacrifices, holy and pleasing to God—this is your spiritual act of worship. Do not conform any longer to the pattern of this world, but be transformed by the renewing of your mind. Then you will be able to test and approve what God's will is—his good, pleasing and perfect will. For by the grace given me I say to every one of you: Do not think of yourself more highly than you ought, but rather think of yourself with sober judgment, in accordance with the measure of faith God has given you.

Just as each of us has one body with many members, and these members do not all have the same function, so in Christ we who are many from one body, and each member belongs to all the others. We have different gifts, according to the grace given us. If a man's gift is prophesying, let him use it in proportion to his faith. If it is serving, let him serve; if it is teaching, let him teach; if it is encouraging, let him encourage; if it is contributing to the needs of others, let him give generously; if it is leadership, let him govern diligently; if it is showing mercy, let him do it cheerfully.

He ended by stating:

Love never fails. But where there are prophecies, they will cease; where there are tongues, they will be stilled; where there is knowledge, it will pass away. For we know in part and we prophesy in part, but when perfection comes, the imperfect disappears. When I was a child, I talked like a child, I thought like a child, I reasoned like a child. When I became a man, I put childish ways behind me. Now we see but a poor reflection as in a mirror; then we shall see face to face. Now I know in part; then I shall know fully, even as I am fully known. And now these three remain: faith, hope and love. But the greatest of these is love.

I stood there with spoon in hand as I watched this blessing, the words the preacher spoke were not that different, but the whole feeling and acceptance of the service was different. They finished the service by taking hands and jumping over the broom Letty had made for them. In their excitement, the bride giggled and the groom jumped too high. Everyone clapped and the two of them kissed, hastily, and then faced the audience. They were now married and everyone cheered and went up to hug them.

Letty motioned to me to start the food line and I jumped back behind the table to place the spoons and other utensils in their proper places. Everyone was joyous. There was talking, and laughing, and singing. It was a most pleasant time. I smiled at the people walking through the line, but I received no responses. It was as if I wasn't even there. They weren't rude to me, that wasn't it, I just wasn't there.

I looked towards the front door, and noticed two white men standing there and watching. They were only talking to each other, they didn't mingle with the Negroes. I don't know what I was expecting, but there was a special feeling throughout the room. I wasn't a part of it, but I could feel it. I was definitely the outsider, but I wasn't afraid, I was just different.

Here was this group of people, all having shared the same circumstances, and were pulled together because of those circumstances. I wasn't a part of that group and it was obvious. I could tell many were not approaching me because of their wariness of the way I looked. At least that's what I felt. I was like the two men standing at the door, and yet, I didn't fit in with them either.

I watched the festivities for quite a while. Letty came over and told me I could go to bed anytime I wanted to, she would take care of the food. I thanked her and wandered back over to the house I was to stay in. I felt someone following me while I walked and I turned around to see the two white men coming my way. It made me feel very uncomfortable, so I slipped in to the house as quickly as possible. I didn't hear them come to the door, but the thought of it worried me enough to stay in my clothes and I lied down on my bed without taking them off.

I pulled the covers up over me and lay there listening to the music and the noises of the party. The music was so different from the church music I had heard, or the music Jenny Lind sang at her concert, or the songs from Ireland. This music had its own type of depth and feeling. It spoke volumes in its tone and manner. The songs from Ireland did the same, but they were different, and yet so much the same in their story telling. It was easy to fall asleep listening to such joyfulness.

It was still dark when I heard the bell clanging loudly. I woke up and looked around. The other women in my shack were getting up and talking. The baby was still asleep, and the woman closest to her was fixing her own bed. I had slept through the night without hearing one of them come in. I started to get up and follow their actions even though I had no idea what we were doing and whether it was nighttime or morning. One of the women went over to the stove and poured some water in and asked another to go get some wood, the fire was dying down.

"Can I help?" I asked.

"Sit there, you're no good to us." The woman at the fireplace said.

The other woman brought some firewood in and I sat on my bed, waiting for instructions. After she put the wood next to the fire, she came over to me and sat down next to me.

"I'm Anna. I think you're a goin' to the main house today. You better get sometin' to eat and then get on over to

Letty. She'll tell you how to git there."

"Thanks." I said.

"That's Henrietta at the fire, and then that's Lucy. Her baby's name is, Angus. He's a precious little baby. N'er seems to cry or be upset."

Lucy made a feint gesture of waving in acknowledgment as she tended to Angus on his waking up.

"She's got to nurse him before we head out," said Anna. "We all work in the field, and Lucy carries him on her back most the time. Sometimes we help, but he likes his Momma the best."

"Stop that, Anna, you know that's a lie!" Said Lucy.

"Sho'nuff is not" said Anna, and they both laughed.

"All of you get over here and get your grits. We've got to be movin'," said Henrietta. "you saw what Mr. Lott did to Albert yesterday. He's gonna kill one of us yet!"

"She's right." Said Anna, and she motioned for me to come over to the fire. She handed me a bowl and a spoon. I held it out for Henrietta who plopped some white looking, rough textured something in it.

"That there's grits." She said. "Eat it. It'll keep your belly full for a while."

I took a bite thinking it might be an oatmeal texture, but it wasn't. It startled my taste buds but I dared not show any ungratefulness at the risk of alienating myself more. I ate it all and followed Anna to the water bucket where we rinsed out our bowl and placed it back by the fire. As we were doing that, I watched Henrietta place a hunk of meat in another pot of water and cover it. It was for dinner she told me, and I didn't ask what it was.

I watched Lucy tie a wrap around her and pick up her baby. She put Angus in the cloth and shifted him around to her back. He lay there nice and neat against her back, not making a noise. Anna grabbed my hand and pulled me out the door.

"See that cart over there?" asked Anna. "Go there and Letty will tell you what to do."

I shook my head yes and before I knew it, they were gone and off to the fields. I looked over at the cart, and saw

Letty looking my way and I supposed she was waiting for me. I ran to her as she stood there with her hands on her hips.

"Are we gonna have to wait on you every mornin'?" She asked.

"No, no, Letty." I told her as I crawled up in the cart.

There was an older woman in the cart already, and she introduced herself to me. "I'm Elizabeth. I work at the big house too."

"That's Cora, Elizabeth. She's to work with Genevieve when they get back. Nane already knows." Letty told her.

"Good, good." Elizabeth said.

"And Cora, that's Isum. He'll be driving you back and forth each day."

The man driving the cart, Isum, nodded and stepped up onto the carriage seat behind the horse. He looked back at Letty and she waved us on. Elizabeth took no time in telling me about herself and everything else she could on our trip to the main house. She went on and on about her upbringing in Africa and how she was a princess there. Her father was the ruler of their tribe, but other people who didn't like him took her and sold her to get revenge on him. I asked her if that meant other Africans sold her, and she said yes. She started swaying and humming and before I knew it, she was singing words I didn't understand.

Isum looked back at me and said, "Don't worry about her. That's a song from her long, long past. Sometimes she slips into another time period. She'll be all right."

I nodded and we listened to Elizabeth sing her song and hum the rest of the way. She was still going when we arrived. A Negro woman stepped out of the house and walked over to us. Isum gave a signal to her with a nod of his head, and she approached Elizabeth first.

"Elizabeth! Elizabeth! You're at the house now, come on in and let's get to work."

I stepped down from the cart, and moved aside for the woman to help Elizabeth down from the cart. She motioned for me to follow as she continued talking to Elizabeth and guiding her in. By the time we stepped in to the kitchen, Elizabeth seemed to be all right and was telling the woman who I was.

"Yes, oh yes. I know who Miss Cora is, and if she hasn't already figured it out, my name is Nane." She said as she looked at me. "I run the household and the house servants so this is where you'll come every morning. Elizabeth and I live back around that way behind the house, so I can be close to Mr. Patout and Miss

Genevieve."

Elizabeth started getting out pots and pans, and mixing utensils. "What are you doin' Elizabeth? There ain't nobody here today but the four of us. Don't need nothin' extra made." Nane told here

"Come on, let's show Cora the house."

"I'm gonna stay right here, if that's all right with you?" said Isum.

"Don't need you know how, right now." Nane said.

Nane, Elizabeth and I walked around the house. She showed me every room and gave quaint anecdotes for each room. Elizabeth would chime in and agree. It was sweet. They obviously loved the Patouts and being in the house. I hadn't quite figured out Elizabeth's role in all of this, but I'm sure Nane would tell me about her at another time.

The downstairs area was for storage. Everything from food rations to antiques was down below. The upper floors were the living area. Nane said there was a lot of room, but the two of them, that is, Mr. Patout and Genevieve, really only used five rooms.

We lingered a little longer in Genevieve's room since that's what I needed to know about. She showed me Genevieve's favorite things. There was a beautiful doll that her mother had given her. Nane said she loved it but would never touch it. She was afraid something might happen to it like it had to her mother.

Nane showed us the doors to Mr. Patout's room, but didn't think it proper for her to show me. He had a study off to the side of his room. Genevieve had a similar room off of her bedroom, but she used it as a playroom. They had lovely things.

Everything had much more adornment than I was ever used to, Nane said it was Mrs. Patout's taste and she was delicate and charismatic, like the décor.

We went back downstairs and back in to the kitchen. Isum was peeling peas when we walked in, and he barely looked up at us. He kept on peeling. Elizabeth sat down next to him, and told me to sit next to her. She handed me some pea pods and started her own pile.

"Now Nane already washed these peas." Elizabeth said, "But here's what you do. Pinch off the stem with your fingernail, like this, and then you pull the string down the length of the green pod. Then it will pop open. Next, you push out the peas with your thumb, and then start on the next one."

I smiled and picked up my first pea pod to shell. Elizabeth corrected me a few times, but I generally understood it. I sat there and listened to them talk as I shelled the peas. We spent more time talking than shelling, but it was a good thing for me because I learned a lot from all of them talking to one another.

They told me about Mrs. Patout and her illness. She was pregnant with another child, but lost the baby, Nane said. Right after that, she contracted a fever they were never able to control. The Doctor told Mr. Patout she had an infection from the birth. But Nane said she thought her heart was broken so much from her loss, she never regained her strength. It was very sad for all of us.

She was a gentle and kind lady, they all said, who loved flowers and took an interest in all of them. They said Mr. Patout had not recovered being over her death and was still having a hard time with it. Genevieve was sad, too, but she had Mrs. Patouts kindness and her lively spirit, they said.

Nane fixed us lunch and I helped her clean up after we were finished. I enjoyed the morning and my time with them. It didn't seem so bad listening to their stories and learning from them. After lunch, Nane took Elizabeth to their shack and had her lay down for a while, telling her she needed to rest. Elizabeth squabbled for a moment, but when her head hit the cot, she was out and fast asleep.

Nane and I went back in the house and she took out some silver pieces. She handed me a rag and some polish, and assumed I knew what to do with it. I followed her lead and copied her actions, polishing piece after piece. There must have been fifteen pieces and everything from candelabras to bowls. Isum was no longer in the kitchen with us and I had no idea where he had gone, but with Nane and I being the only ones in the kitchen she told me about Elizabeth.

"Elizabeth has been here as long as the Patouts." Nane said. "Mrs. Patout purchased her and her two sons when they first got here, which has been close to ten years. She's like family to them, and when she started getting ill in the head, Mrs. Patout would not hear of anyone getting rid of her or not taking care of her. She always worked in the house, and when I came along, I started under her. I've been here eight years, and have no problem letting Elizabeth come and go as she always did. None of us do. One of the last things Mrs. Patout told her husband was to always take care of Elizabeth, and he has obeyed her wishes. Ooooh! He loved that woman!

"We're lucky, ya' know? There aren't too many slave owners who care about their people. I was sold from an awful man who took his turns with his women, and who split up families so they wouldn't join against him. That's what happened to me. He split up my family and I's don't know where they are. They might still be in Alabama, I don't know.

"I had me a little girl. She'd be about ten now. I'm hopin' she's not still with that man, because I don't want him taking his way with her. It makes me sick to think about it, so I don't, think about it, that is. I sure do think about her, though, and I see Genevieve and just love on that baby. She needs that love since she don't have her Momma now, either."

"Are Elizabeth's boys still here?"

"Ooh, yes, but they're not boys anymore. I think Dan is twenty-three and Louis is twenty-one. They're strong young men who help out in the field. You saw one of them last night, Dan. He married pretty Bay Lee. They are now, Mr. and Mrs. Dan Swett. At least to us. The white folks won't accept our marriages. Bay's parents and brother and sister live here, too. They are Juba and Rema Lee, and then Beau and Rosa.

"Juba Lee! Ain't that too much! He said he had an African name, but no one understood it, so his last master's wife said he was always happy so he should be called Juba Lee! He fits it, too. Maybe you remember them from last night?"

"I'm sorry, I really don't. I only remember Letty and the two men I came in with." I told her.

"I guess so. It was a festive night and there was a lot going on. I saw you helping with the food. That's the best thing you can do here is help. You're not gonna be well accepted 'causin' you're so white n all. No one's gonna trust you 'til you earn their trust. You're gonna get it bad from both sides. The whites ain't gonna want ya because ya got some black in ya' and the blacks ain't gonna want ya 'cause you got the white in ya."

"But that's not the way it is." I said. "I don't have any black in me that I know of. I'm from Ireland, of all places, and I just arrived here myself over three years ago."

"It don't matter to no one, now. Someone sold you as a slave and your stuck. Just like the rest of us. You're not the only one. I've heard of other white women in the same position as you, but you're all stuck. Might as well make the best of it. At least you're at a place that won't treat you bad. It's just fine livin' here."

Just fine, I thought. Hmmm. I really didn't want to have to live my life just fine. My life story was no easy ride, but theirs is worse, and I guessed I shouldn't complain about my life.

"When you go back today, it will just be you and Isum.

Elizabeth was only there last night for the wedding, and Letty had her stay there so she could watch her late into the night. I think she enjoyed the wedding."

"I enjoyed it, too." I said.

"Good. Now let's put all this silver back in its place and change the water in the flower vases. Can you wander through the house and pick up any vase you see? One at a time though. We don't want to drop any of their crystal."

"Of course, not, I'll be very careful."

We put up the silver and I walked out into the dining room where the first vase stood in the middle of the buffet, reflecting off a mirror that hung behind it. I looked at myself in the mirror, and realized my hair was coming down from being up, only the day before.

Was that honestly just yesterday, I thought?

What a change! That nasty, nasty man, Robert. I am glad I am away from him and his two cronies. The last few months had been a seesaw for me and I didn't know how to catch up with the changes that had occurred. I was horrible one minute, and then all right the next. I guess the answer was living through all of it and sustaining my faith. That's what Ma had done and she made it.

Nane looked through the door and said, "Stuck in the mirror? Try to pry yourself away and bring that vase in here."

"I'm sorry, I was looking at my hair and thinking about the past few days, and my Ma, and…"

"It can be rather overwhelming, can't it? You have to rise above it, or it will get the best of you."

"That's something my Ma would say. She lived on beyond all her heartache."

"And so will you. I can tell."

Nane took the vase from me and handed me the flowers. She washed out the vase, washed the bottom of the flower stalks, and then refilled the vase, and placed the flowers back in. She sent me back out in to the house and we went through this same ritual for seven vases.

"That's a lot of flowers." I said.

"Yes, but the Mrs. would have wanted them around her house, and fresh, daily. She loved that." Nane said as her thoughts turned to Elizabeth. "I checked on Elizabeth about an hour ago, and she was sitting and looking out the window. Will you go and tell her to come in? You're about to leave and it's getting dark."

I found Elizabeth who was still sitting and looking out the window. She was humming again, and I broke her train of thought to ask her to come with me.

She looked at me very blankly, so I said, "Elizabeth, it's Cora. Remember me?"

What had I just done? I had just called myself Cora. The transformation was beginning.

I led Elizabeth in to the kitchen and Isum was there waiting for me. "We can head back any time you like." Isum said.

"Why don't you all go on?" said Nane. "I'll see you in the mornin' Cora. You can fix your hair here in my house if you like. I know there's no mirror where you're livin'."

I thanked her, and Isum and I walked out to the cart. I climbed in the back and settled in. Nane was standing at the kitchen door with Elizabeth, and they both waved as we took off. Isum and I waved, too, and we headed back down the road to our houses.

When we arrived, I thanked Isum and stepped out of the cart and headed towards our house. Letty came out and asked me if I wanted to get some bread for the others and take it back to our house. I followed her to that house to get the bread. She had made about ten loaves today, and handed me one for the house.

"See you in the morning." Letty said, and I headed back.

No one had returned from the fields, so I placed the bread down by the fireplace, and checked the pot. The big chunk of meat must have been ham, so I stirred it hoping to help in even the smallest of ways. I laid the plates and stoked the fire, adding some logs. I didn't eat because I didn't want the others to think I was selfish. They hadn't come when I fell asleep against the wall waiting for them.

Anna woke me up and said, "Did you do this?"

I shook my head yes and stood up.

"That was nice of you." She said and showed the others when they came in.

Henrietta didn't say anything, but picked up her bowl and started eating. Anna shrugged her shoulders and went over to Lucy to help her. Angus was asleep and Lucy laid him in his crib. She plopped down on her bed after putting him down.

"Lucy?" asked Anna, "You've gotta eat something. You have to keep up your strength for Angus. He'll need that extra for your nursing."

"I'm too tired to eat." Lucy said.

"Come on, Lucy, Cora and I will help you."

Anna motioned for me to get a bowl for her, and she helped Lucy sit up slightly so she could feed her some of the broth and meat. She ate a little, and then Anna gave up and let her rest.

She came over to me, and asked, "Have you eaten, yet?"

I told her no, so we took our bowls, pulled off a chunk of bread and started eating. We ate silently. Henrietta was finished and lying down. Lucy and Angus were out, so Anna and I finished our food and lay down on our own beds.

There was no singing or talking tonight. It was so quiet you could hear the crickets outside. I thought about the day and everything Nane told me. I thought about the Patouts and hoped to meet them tomorrow. I figured tomorrow would be a good day, and even with some anticipation. I wasn't sure what to expect, but I wanted to be my best.

Be my best? Be my best, for the man that bought me? Hmmm. That was a denial of thought. Why would I want to look my best, or even care about it when I was only a commodity to this man? I was torn between the awful, total fabrication of my situation, and the gratitude Nane and others seemed to have for this man. Is it a good thing that someone owns me, or is it a good thing that I am owned by a good man? And, is he a good man if he owns people? I didn't know how to feel or how to act, but Ma treated the Brumleys kindly, so surely I could do the same and give this man an opportunity to put right my situation. My guess is he doesn't even know my situation.

The next day started bright and early like the day before. This morning, Henrietta fixed biscuits for all of us. She didn't speak to me, but I noticed she really didn't speak to any of us. Angus was a little fussier this morning, and Anna told her it was because she's not eating right. Lucy didn't pay too much attention to her, but I noticed Anna put an extra biscuit in her pocket, and motioned her head towards Lucy. I nodded yes, and they went out the door. They left before me, and came back after me. It was an awful hard existence.

I put myself together as best I could then walked down to Letty. Isum was waiting on me.

Letty handed me a doll. "This is for Genevieve. I made it myself for her. Surely she can play with this one without worrying about her dyin'."

I took the doll and held it in my lap as Isum took off. It was a little overcast this morning, and I was hoping it wouldn't rain. I was afraid maybe the rain would hold the

Patout's up and they wouldn't make it in today if the weather was too bad. We pulled up to the main house, and Nane was outside looking at the exact same thing.

"Don't want no storm today," She said, "We need our baby Genevieve to get home and be safe."

"Uh-huh, we sho' do," chimed Elizabeth who was standing behind Nane.

"Cora you come on in, and Isum, you better go put the

horse and cart up today in case they was to git stuck out in the rain," said Nane.

"I do believe you're right, Nane," said Isum, "I's um a gonna do that right now."

He called the horse, Dizzy, and pulled it along towards the shed behind the house.

"Why is she named Dizzy?" I asked Nane.

"Because she goes crazy when the weather gits bad," answered Elizabeth before Nane said a thing.

"Now come on, you two, let's get inside," said Elizabeth.

"I forgot," I said, "Letty gave me this doll she made and said it was for Genevieve."

"Ooh, isn't that a precious little thing," said Elizabeth.

"Yes," said Nane, "and for a precious little girl. She'll play with this one, I bet! We'll give it to her when they get here and get settled. Don't you think?"

"Yes, I do! That's what we'll do!" said Elizabeth.

They were a good team, and Nane treated Elizabeth quite well. I don't think Elizabeth had any idea that something was wrong with her at times. She fit in just fine and Nane made sure. And, they both were accepting of me. Maybe some of the others would come around once they saw how Nane and Elizabeth treated me, and Isum and Letty, oh, and Anna. Well, maybe I wasn't going to be around here too long. Maybe if Mr. Patout hears my story, he'll figure something out to help me.

Mr. Williams knocked at the kitchen door and then walked in.

"You're here already?" asked Nane. "Is Mr. Patout with you? I wasn't expecting you this early."

"No, no, when I went back yesterday, we finished our business early and I helped him to get ready to come back today, but I left before dawn this morning hoping to beat him here. He probably won't get Genevieve up until mid-morning."

"Have they been visitin' with anyone? Or has it just been business?" Nane asked.

"Now you know that's not any of your business," said

Mr. Williams. "Mr. Patout, and who he visits with or not, is up to him."

"Yes, yes," said Elizabeth, "but did he *visit* with anyone or not?"

I really didn't know what they were talking about and so I just sat at the table and listened. There was something both of them wanted to hear. As we were waiting on his answer, Isum walked in.

"Isum, did you put Dizzy and the cart in the shed?" asked Williams.

"Yes, sir."

"Did they *visit* with anyone or not?" asked Elizabeth with a stronger tone, and not letting Mr. Williams get out of this one.

"Yes, they did." He said.

"And is it who we think?" asked Nane.

"Yes it is, now let's get this house ready for their return, which should be mid-afternoon. I'm going to go and check the fields and the machinery. Can you all be ready by this afternoon?" asked Mr. Williams.

"Of course we can!" said Nane.

Robert went over to his horse and leaped back on, and turned down the road. Nane watched him ride away, and then turned back to us.

"Now what do you think about that?" Nane said.

"I don't like it, one bit. Not one bit!" said Elizabeth.

"You women have got to stop puttin' your nose where you're not supposed to. You heard Mr. Williams, it's none of your business what he does," Said Isum.

They didn't pay attention to what he said at all, and continued with their train of thought.

"At least he won't be bringing her back today," said Nane.

Elizabeth humphed and I broke in to ask, "I'm sorry, but whom are you talking about? Is there someone *bad* in the family?"

"Not yet, and we're hopin' there never will be," said

Elizabeth.

"There's a woman in New Orleans that is after Mr. Patout. She knows what he has and what a good catch he would be for her. She needs someone to push around and get her claws in to, and he lets her."

"Oh, I see. Is he fond of her?" I asked.

"Well it sure sounds that way," said Nane.

"I don't think he's seein' her as much as she's seein' him!" Elizabeth said and they both laughed.

Isum shook his head and reminded them they should stop talking about the Master of the house that way. "Whether he marries her or not is his business." He told them.

They stopped their talking about it and we spent the morning working around the house. We had lunch, and then returned to our work. By mid- afternoon, the clouds had gone away, and the sun was back out.

"Now this is the way our baby little Genevieve should be welcomed home." Nane said as she stood outside the kitchen door.

She brought her stool and told us she would be sitting out there until she saw them coming down the road. Elizabeth and I followed suit and brought out stools and sat with her. Isum was out back working in the shed.

As we sat out there and waited, Elizabeth started singing some of her songs. I didn't understand any of her words, but she sat on her stool, swayed, and sang.

"That's one of hers from her tribal days," said Nane. "Elizabeth, why don't you sing Cora the one called, Move Members Move?"

She didn't say a word or even acknowledge Nane, but she broke right in to song. Nane started clapping in rhythm, and I just sat there, feeling awkward. I wasn't sure if I should start clapping and join in or just listen. I chose to listen, and noticed some dust moving down the road, and then a horse and carriage breaking from the overhang of the trees.

"I think they're here!" I told them as I stood up.

CHAPTER 5
MEETING GENVEIEVE

Nane and Elizabeth immediately stopped singing and gathered their stools and went inside. We all straightened our clothes, and Nane called us together in the kitchen. Isum had heard the carriage and came to join us. We all looked at one another and Nane walked out of the kitchen and into the main part of the house, and we all followed. I was nervous and anxious.

We walked out through the front doorway and stood there in line, waiting for them to get out. Isum walked beyond us and went to their carriage. He held the horse as they stepped out.

Mr. Patout stepped out, and then Genevieve. She saw Nane and ran straight to her jumping up on her and hugging her. They swirled around a few times, and then Elizabeth was telling them she wanted a hug, too. Nane didn't let go, but Genevieve let go of her grasp long enough to reach over and give Elizabeth a hug. She didn't really look at me, so I stood there waiting for my cue.

Mr. Patout walked up to us, and cordially greeted Nane and Elizabeth, telling them he was glad to be home.

He looked at me next, and said, "Welcome to Belle Terre." He said. "I'm sure Nane has shown you the house. Let me get settled in, and then you and I shall have a talk. Nane, why don't you take Genevieve and Cora for a little bit, and then show her to the living room where she can wait for me?"

Nane nodded, and she and Elizabeth held her hands and walked her inside. Isum took the bags out of the carriage and placed them by the steps, then walked the horse and carriage to the back of the house. I followed Nane, Elizabeth, and Genevieve inside and into the kitchen.

No one introduced me to Genevieve, yet. I watched the other three interact and stood there waiting for someone to say something. It never occurred, so I continued watching. Nane had a very motherly way with Genevieve. She offered her food or drink, and hugged her and played with her asking her all about their trip to New Orleans, if they bought anything, and what she did.

I remembered the doll Letty had made for her, but didn't say anything because I didn't want to step on Nane's toes. I figured she remembered and was waiting, but she still hadn't given her the doll by the time she took us in to the living room and we were waiting on Mr. Patout.

He came in shortly, and asked if I had met Genevieve, yet. I said no, and he introduced us. She remained next to Nane, but did look at me. I said, hello, but there was no response.

"She's just bein' shy," said Nane, "she'll warm up to ya."

Mr. Patout told Nane they could go on, and he would be spending some time talking to me. They left the room, and it was just Mr. Patout and me standing there.

"Why don't we sit down, Cora?" And he motioned towards the sofa for me, as he sat down in a tall back, upright chair.

As we sat, Mr. Williams came in, "Excuse me Mr. Patout, I'll be in the shed with Isum if you need anything."

"Thank you, Harris. We're fine right now. I'll talk to you later." He told him.

He waited a moment for Mr. Williams to leave, and then turned his attention back to me. I was sitting up straight and at attention, nervous about the situation.

"No one's going to hurt you, Cora. You may relax."

He said it, but it didn't change my feelings, yet. I still sat up and forward on the sofa with my feet flat on the ground and my hands at my knees.

"What has Nane or the others told you about Belle Terre, and why you are here?" He asked me.

I stared at him for a moment, not knowing what to say. They've told me a whole bunch, I thought, but what could I say or not?

"Did they tell you about Genevieve?"

"Yes!" I said, thinking that's what we would start with. I would let him guide my comments. "They showed me her room, and her favorite things. And they told me what she likes to do."

"Good, and did they tell you what I would like for you to do with Genevieve?"

"They said you would like for me to be her teacher, is that correct?"

"Yes, that's correct. She is old enough now to start school, and we live so far away from any school, I thought it best to bring the teacher to her. I know there are schools in New Orleans and elsewhere I could send her to, but that would mean we would be separated and I don't want to do that. Can you understand?"

I nodded yes, and he carried on.

"Did they tell you about Mrs. Patout?" He stood up and turned his back to me as he continued, "I'm sure they did. We all miss her terribly. It was such a shock to lose her, and because of that I don't want Genevieve to ever be very far from me." He turned back towards me and adjusted his clothes as if trying to force himself to not be upset. He gathered his composure and sat back down.

"I'd like someone to be with her, teach her, and travel with us if needed. That's why I wanted you. You seem to fit the requirements. The information sheet about you stated you knew various languages and were educated."

"Yes, sir, but that wasn't true." I told him. "I only speak English. I'm of Irish decent and immigrated here to America a few years ago."

"But the paper said you were a Quintroon? That would make you one sixteenth African and the other parts European. Do you have no African blood in you?"

I thought for a moment wondering why it would matter. Why should you own anyone whether they were a different skin color or not. Why was this no different than the difference in religion in Ireland? Should I say something, or would I be jeopardizing my own situation by stating my thoughts? I held my tongue as Captain and Rufina used to tell me, that there might be a better time and place.

"No, Sir, I was born in Ireland and didn't come to America until I was thirteen. I was stolen, kidnapped in Charleston, with the intent to sell me to make money." I told him with my head bowed. I didn't want to sound angry or combative, just sadly truthful.

"Is this true?" He asked. "The men that kidnapped you, stole you and sold you as slave? Do you remember their names?"

"I do. I shall never forget them." I told him.

"Make sure and give Mr. Williams their names, and we will follow up with that. Until then, I am in a quandary. I have paid for you and expected to have a teacher for my daughter. She is the one I am thinking of, and I truly do not want to start my search over. You are here until your situation is sorted out. Agreed?"

I nodded, once.

"If you do not speak any other languages, then what subjects might you be able to teach Genevieve?" He asked.

"My favorite thing is literature. I can gladly teach her to read and write, and I will try my best to have her help me with French. I would love to learn how to speak something besides English."

"Literature, reading and writing would be quite acceptable, but you are not here to have her teach you. If you learn on the side, that is all right, but do not take time away from her lessons for your own."

"Yes, sir, I understand." I told him.

"Then why don't you spend the next couple of days with Nane and Genevieve, and let her warm up to you. She will grow accustomed to you, and allow you to begin her lessons."

"Yes, sir."

"That will be all today. We'll see how the next couple of days go."

"Sir, may I ask you something?"

"Yes, Cora, what is it?"

"What day is it?"

"It is Tuesday." He said.

"No sir, I mean the month and the day."

"Oh, don't you know? Have you lost track of that much time?"

"Yes, sir, the men who took me never let me know what day or month it was." I told him.

"It's the fifteenth of May. What do you last remember?"

"I believe it was the middle of January. Is it really May?"

"I'm afraid so. Guess there's no making up for lost time, is there?"

"No, sir."

I stood up and excused myself from his presence. I walked back in to the kitchen and Nane, Elizabeth, and Genevieve were in the kitchen squeezing lemons. Elizabeth accidentally squirted some lemon in her eye and reacted to it, while the other two started laughing.

"Looks like you are having fun!" I said to them.

"We are, if we can keep it out of our eyes," said Elizabeth. The other two laughed again, and I sat down and joined them for an extra hand at juicing the lemons.

Nane took the juice once we were finished and put it in a big steel pot. She put water in it and added some brownish looking sugar.

"Is that sugar from this land?" I asked Nane.

"It is." She said. "All that hard work and it dissolves into nothing almost immediately. Can't seem to understand how that balances out."

"It's because it makes it taste so much better," said Genevieve, as she licked her lips.

"Uh huh, you're right," said Elizabeth. "That lemonade would taste too sour without that wonderful sugar!"

Nane stirred the lemonade pot, and let Genevieve taste it. Nane accepted her approval and asked her if she wanted some. Genevieve said yes, but that she didn't like it hot.

"Let's take out a pitcher full and set it aside so you will have it for dinner without it bein' hot? How about that?" She asked Genevieve, who happily agreed.

Later on, Nane served them dinner, while Elizabeth, Isum and I waited in the kitchen. When they were done, Nane told Isum we could go on back, so he went and prepared Dizzy . Nane took me in to see Genevieve and I told her goodnight. She didn't say anything, but her father told her to say goodnight and she obeyed. Nane then took me out to Isum and the cart, and we headed back to our shack.

The next week I followed Nane around and helped out where needed. I didn't try to push myself on Genevieve, thinking it was better for her to come around herself. On the eighth day, we were sitting out back and Genevieve was running around with a butterfly net, trying to catch the pretty butterflies.

We were enjoying one another and Elizabeth was telling tales, when Nane asked, "Do you have any stories, Cora?"

"I wouldn't be Irish if I didn't." I told her.

"Well then, why don't we hear one of yours, if it's suitable for all ears?" She said.

"Let me think of one, for there are many to choose from."

I thought for a moment and then remembered one that they might like. I readied myself into character and began my tale. Genevieve was still catching butterflies as I started, but soon she was taken by my story and my acting it out. In full Irish character, I began.

Once upon a time there were two farmers, named Hudden and Dudden. The brothers were lucky to have many sheep, and cows, and land, and yet they weren't happy. On a farm next to them lived a man by the name of Donald O'Neary. He lived very poorly and only had one cow. Her name was Daisy. She rarely gave him enough milk for butter or to drink.

In spite of their own wealth, Hudden and Dudden were jealous of Donald and schemed for days wondering how they could get his cow from him. Why they would want Daisy, poor thing, we'll never know because she was really just a bag of bones. Their scheming included getting rid of Donald, and all they could think of doing was getting rid of Daisy.

Genvieve stopped her butterfly catching and came and sat on Nane, listening to my story.

Hudden and Dudden decided to go through with their horrible plan, and crept over to Donald O'Neary's house, and then in to his barn where Daisy stood not knowing what was about to happen. Whatever they did must have worked, for when Donald came in to check on her, she was only able to give him one last lick.

Donald was distraught over the loss of Daisy, but knew he had to make the best of it. The next day he decided to take her hide into town. He placed pennies in many different spots in her hide and threw it over his shoulder and took her in to town. He walked into the best tavern in town and threw the hide over the seat next to him.

"Some whisky, please, the best." He said to the innkeeper.

The innkeeper gave him a strange look and Donald asked him if it was the way he looked that made him cautious of payment. He took Daisy's hide and shook it. Out popped a penny. The innkeeper was taken aback, and leaned forward in interest.

"Are you willing to sell that cowhide?" He asked

"No, no, I don't plan on parting with something of such good fortune." Donald told him.

"I'll give you gold for that hide?" The innkeeper told him.

Donald hit the hide another whack and out jumped a second penny. "I'll not be getting' rid of this. How would I pay my way?"

The innkeeper kept at him until he sold the hide for lots of gold. He took his winnings and went over to his neighbors. He asked to borrow their scales. Hudden and Dudden scratched their heads, wondering where Donald had gotten all of his money, but they lent him their scales.

Before Hudden handed over the scales, he put a pat of butter on the bottom, thinking himself quite tricky. Donald took the scales home and weighed his gold. When he returned the scales, one piece was left on it, being stuck to the butter pat.

Hudden thought himself ever so clever and showed Dudden the gold piece that Donald had left. They thought they were smarter than O'Neary, and so they decided to pay him a visit and find out how he had gotten his gold, but O'Neary was ready for them.

"Aye! You two thought you had broken me when you took care of ol' Daisy, but I am appreciative of your actions. Hides are quite valuable and I knew I could get her weight in gold by selling her in town. See? You've done me a favor!" He told them.

Hudden and Dudden stood there for a moment, and then Hudden came up with a bright idea, and motioned for Dudden to take leave with him.

"Have a good evening, Donald O'Neary," Hudden told him, and he and Dudden walked out the door and back to their property.

Hudden and Dudden decided they would be the richest brothers in Ireland, and piled every hide they had, from all of the cows they owned onto their cart. Their horse even had a hard time pulling the cart from the weight of the hides.

They came to the town and set up their cart next to the market. They laid out some of their hides, and even walked around the market holding the hides out for all to see. Both men yelled out, "Hides for sell! Hides for sell!!"

A man walked over to Dudden and asked him how much his hides were, and Dudden told him, "they are worth their weight in gold" proudly. The man told him he should not have come out for something so expensive. And back he went into his house.

They yelled again, "Hides for sell! Hides for sell!" and a merchant came over and asked them how much their hides were. "Their weight in gold!" they replied again, but the merchant said they must have been playing with him because they were only hides. And back to his own cart he went.

They tried again, "Hides for sell! Hides for sell!!" and another man came over and asked the same thing as the others. When they replied as before, the man called for the Sheriff!

"These are vagrants who must be part of a group of men who trick people into believing their hides are valuable. Stop them! He yelled!"

Hudden and Dudden were taken by the Sheriff and required to pay a stiff penalty for trying to take advantage of people. When the Sheriff released them, men were waiting to chase them from the town. They ran all the way home, seething at the thought that Donald O'Neary had tricked them.

They decided to go over to his house and tell them a

piece of their minds. When Donald saw them, he acted surprised and asked them if they had been robbed. They told him their story and angrily accused him of taking advantage of them, but he knew better and asked them, "did you not see the gold pieces yourself? I got them from Daisy's hide. I did not deceive you."

They were not to be taken again, so they ran home and came back with a meal sack. They forced Donald O'Neary into the sack. They tied a pole through the knots, and decided to take him to the nearby lake and dump him in it. That would show him.

They walked and walked, but were already tired from their day. The road to the lake was dusty and they were dirty and thirsty. On the way they passed a tavern, and decided to go in and get something to eat and drink.

They dumped the sack with Donald in it and told him not to move. Donald stayed still until enough time had passed. He then began talking to himself, but loud enough for a walker nearby to hear him.

"You can't force me to take her, you can't! I'm telling you I won't! Take her back I'm telling you!

A man who was walking a herd of cattle by came over to him and kicked the sack. Donald stopped talking and asked who was there. The man told him he overheard him talking and wondered what he was talking about.

"It's the Princess. The King wants me to marry her, but I do not want to. Oh, she's beautiful enough, and has jewels all over her gown, but it would not be right for me to marry her."

The man asked if he could have her, and told him he would like that. Donald told him he seemed kind enough, and if he would untie the cord around the sack, he would surely let him have her.

The man untied the sack and let Donald out. Donald helped the man get in, and re-tied the cords. He told him not to move or make a noise, and eventually he would see the princess.

The man told him to take his cattle for trade, and Donald took his new herd home.

When Hudden and Dudden were finished eating and drinking, they came out and picked up the sack. They both thought it was heavier, but figured they were tired from the day. When they got to the lake, they plopped the sack in and yelled to the lake that Donald would not be tricking them *anymore!*

They were pleased with themselves and headed back home. On their way home they went by Donald O'Neary's place thinking it was theirs now. Low and behold, there was Donald watching over his cows!

"What are you doing here?" Hudden and Dudden asked Donald.

"The lake is known as the land of promise. Had you not heard that? It's true! Look at my cattle!" Donald told them.

Hudden and Dudden were shocked at what they saw and begged Donald to tell them his secret. Donald told them it wasn't his secret, but the secret of the lake and it wasn't his to own. It was there for all. I don't wish to keep the luck all to myself, there is plenty for all.

Hudden and Dudden thanked him and headed back towards the lake, full of excitement. They looked out over the lake and the reflection of the clouds above made it look like cattle in the water. They both were happy jumping up and down, and then both jumped into the lake never to be seen again. Never.

As for the man, Donald O'Neary, he had enough cattle for the rest of his life.

I finished the story and Genevieve was still sitting there waiting for more.

"That's all," I told her, "the moral is it's not good to be greedy."

"I would say not!" said Elizabeth. "That Mr. O'Neary was a sly one wasn't he?"

"Sho' nuff!" said Nane. "We'll have to have Cora tell us stories more often, won't we?" She asked, but looking around at Genevieve still sitting on her.

Genevieve nodded, and that was the start of our relationship. Every day we grew closer and closer, and the stories I told and the books I read to her helped her soften her shyness towards me. The times that I read to her, she would sit on my lap and play like she was reading the pages.

By the time it was mid-summer, we were walking down to their pond and having picnics and reading under a huge oak tree. Around the pond there were wonderful old oak trees that looked like they could tell a story themselves. Once when Nane, Elizabeth, and Isum joined us, Elizabeth told us a wonderful story about one of the trees.

"Do you see that oak tree over there?" She asked us.

We all said, "yes."

"That tree has a story for us." She said.

"And what is that?" Nane asked her.

"It's a tree the Indians used as a sign to other Indians. Like A friend with friends for us."

The group quieted and I was stunned for a moment. I had never heard any of them mention that, even in the slightest. I didn't know they knew about the Underground Railroad. I noticed Nane looked at me, not sure about my thoughts on it, she tried changing the subject.

"Tell us more about the Indians, Elizabeth."

"See how the tree is split," she said, "They would use that as a directional tool for others so they knew which way to go."

I jumped in so they wouldn't think I knew anything. I wasn't ready, yet, to ask about it. "That is so interesting. Have you ever seen an Indian?"

"I have!" said Genevieve.

"You have not!" said Nane.

"I have, too! In New Orleans. They wear their costumes and everything." Genevieve said.

"My, my! Aren't you the world traveler!" Nane said. "I bet Cora has books about Indians she could show you."

"Do you?" Genevieve asked me.

"I could probably find something that would be about them and you would be interested in. I'll check through your father's library and see. How's that?"

We gathered our things and went back to the house. It was a long time before we ever spoke of anything connected to Elizabeth's statement, and it would be months before I let on I knew what they were talking about.

The next morning, I was looking through the library for a book Genevieve might be interested in, when Mr. Patout came in. "Bonjour, Cora, what's on the literary agenda for today?" He asked.

"I'm trying to find a good book for Genevieve about Indians, but I need one that is appropriate for her age. Do you have any suggestions?" I asked.

"Let me see," he said as he walked over to the shelves and started looking through their books. "I haven't gone through these books in ages. It's too bad too for there are some very good ones. Mrs. Patout tried to make our collection a very well rounded and complete library, but we never seemed to be able to completely get there! There was always one more book we needed to have."

We both smiled as he continued to look.

"Here's the section she started for Genevieve. I think some of it is young for her now, but you can look through it and see. We have *The Riddle Book, Ditties for Children, The Pearl,* and *Rollos' Travels.* Here's a grouping by Samuel Goodrich she liked. *There's Peter Parley's Method of Telling About Geography to Children, Peter Parley's Juvenile Tales*, oh, and I think this is about Indians, it's called *Peter Parley's Story of the Trapper.* Maybe this would be a good one."

"I don't know any of these, so I will enjoy reading them to her and hearing them for the first time myself."

"How is it going with Genevieve?"

"She is starting to grow accustomed to me,

and I think she likes my stories the best. I have tried to entertain her to win her over."

"When will you begin any studies?" He asked.

"I was going to start next week. I was thinking about using some of the *Mother Goose Nursery Rhymes*, but I don't see a book here for that. What should I do if there are books or materials that she needs?"

"Tell Mr. Williams and he can get them for you when he goes in to town."

"Mr. Patout, if I may inquire, have you heard anything from Captain Kiper?"

"No, is that the person who Mr. Williams was supposed

to send word to?"

"Yes," I told him, "I gave him the name and address and was hoping some word had returned."

"No, I'm afraid not. Mr. Williams is a very busy man, and he probably forgot. Why don't you remind him when you ask him to get the study materials for Genevieve?"

"Yes, sir, I will." I told him, but hated to have to ask Mr. Williams myself. He was our overseer and didn't always seem to like being asked to do something. I wished Mr. Patout would ask. It might get done quicker.

As I was walking out, Genevieve sleepily came in to the room in her nightgown and went over to her father. "Bonjour mon petit, avez-vous bien dormi ?" He told her.

"Bon, Pa-Pa," she told him.

"I hear Cora has been telling you some stories you have enjoyed, is this true?" He asked her.

"Oui, beaucoup!"

"Good then you should enjoy today. She has found a book that Ma-Ma bought for you years ago. Would you like that?"

"Oui." She said, but still quite tired.

"Would you like to go into the kitchen and see Nane? I bet she has some breakfast for you." I told her.

She nodded and slipped down off of her father's lap and walked over to me. I held out my hand and she took it. I smiled at her and then Mr. Patout, and then he smiled back. Genevieve waved at him as we left the room.

Nane gave the sleepy headed girl a hug and served her some breakfast. She asked us what we would be doing today, and I told them about the book Mr. Patout had shown me, and that we were going to read through it today.

"Is it about Indians?" Nane asked.

"I believe so, at least Mr. Patout thought it was. I have never read it, so it will be new to me, too. Would any of you like to join us," I asked Nane, Elizabeth, and Isum.

"I can't," said Nane, "but maybe Elizabeth and Isum can join you?"

"I can't either," said Isum, "Mr. Williams has work for me to do today."

"Well, what about you Elizabeth?" Nane asked her.

"If Nane doesn't need me in here, I would enjoy hearing the story."

"Then that's our group!" I said, "Where would you like to hear it, Genevieve?"

She shrugged her shoulders and pursed her lips.

"Now how is she supposed to understand what that means!" said Nane. "Where would you like to go and listen to her read this story, Miss Genevieve? You have the tree by the pond, you have your room upstairs, and you have the front or back porch, or the garden out front where your Ma-Ma used to love to go. How about that?"

Genevieve shrugged her shoulders again, but then she said, "Not the gardens, that's Ma-Ma's."

"All right then," tried Nane again, "how about the back porch and then I can hear some of it as she reads, too?"

"Yes, let's do that!" I said, "We can sit in the rockers, and we can bring out any extra stool we need for anyone else. Wouldn't that be fun?"

Genevieve nodded, and Nane took her upstairs to get dressed for the day. The back porch had a manual fan we could turn on as we read if we felt hot. That was a nice option for the house, since breezes didn't always flow through the house. The fans added a breeze when needed.

Isum helped Elizabeth and me arrange the chairs outside. It was still cool enough this morning, and the sun was not directly shining on us. Elizabeth offered to turn the fan, but I told her we probably didn't need it until later.

Isum bid us farewell and headed out to the field area with Dizzy.

"He loves that crazy horse!" said Elizabeth. "Guess that's more family than the rest of us!"

"I haven't seen her get crazy, yet." I told her.

"Oh, you will, one day. They'll come a storm and she'll be making all kinds of noise. Just you wait"

"Are you to talkin' about Dizzy, or me?" Nane said as she and Genevieve came out onto the porch.

"You know we're talking about that Dizzy of a horse. Isum's Dizzy horse," said Elizabeth.

"Well, he takes good care of her. We should all be that lucky!' Nane said. "Now where should our little Miss Genevieve sit?"

"Where would you like to sit Genevieve? I was thinking about sitting in the rocking chair." I told her.

Elizabeth chimed in and said, "And I'm gone sit in this rocking chair over here."

"Well, that leaves you a stool or the floor." Nane told her.

"The floor," said Genevieve, and she plopped down on her belly with her elbows supporting her head as she faced towards my rocker.

"I guess you're ready!" I told her, and I sat in the rocker and opened the book.

"I'll be in the kitchen and will listen as best I can." Nane told us as she headed back in.

I opened the book and began.

"I suppose you have heard of Lake Superior. It lies several hundred miles northwest of Boston. It is an immense sheet of water with many islands in it. The shores are in some parts wild and rocky, but the islands in summer are very green and beautiful.

This great lake is nearly surrounded by forests. There are no towns, and no white people there, but the woods are inhabited by wild beasts of various kinds, and tribes of Indians. The wild animals are deer, of which there are a great many. Moose, an animal as tall as a horse, with large branching horns, buffaloes which are as big as oxen, beavers larger than a cat, with very soft fur, of which hats are made. Besides these there are wolves, foxes, martens, otters, and other ..."

"What Happened to the Indians?" Asked Genevieve, "I thought you said there were Indians in this story?"

"Oh lord," said Elizabeth, "We might not make it through this story."

I laughed and said, "Let's keep going and see what they say about the Indians, all right?"

She nodded and I looked back down at the pages, happily seeing the word 'Indian' further down. Since I didn't know the story, I wasn't much help in being able to tell her something to hold her interest.

"creatures whose skins are valuable for the fur.

The Indians who live around Lake Superior, reside sometimes in one place and sometimes in another. Their houses or wigwams consist of skins supported by sticks, their shape being somewhat like that of a sugar loaf. These houses are very easily moved, and accordingly the Indians wander about from place to place as they see fit.

"The chief occupation of the Indian men is hunting. The women attend to matters about the house. The men sometimes use guns, and sometimes bows and arrows. Such is their strength and skill in the use of the bow that they will send an arrow quite through the body of a buffalo, and kill him dead. They eat the flesh of the animals they kill. Of some of the skins they make clothing; the rest they sell to white men who go to trade with them. Sometimes there are parties of white men who go up into the wild regions around Lake Superior for the purpose of catching ..."

I looked down at Genevieve and realized the story had captured her thoughts, at least for the moment. I went on through the story as she listened, sometimes she rolled over, but she was still intent on hearing the words. We were deep into the book when lunchtime came around, and Nane stepped out to tell us lunch was ready.

We talked about the story through lunch and then Nane suggested Genevieve take a nap. She wasn't very agreeable to it, but Nane insisted and she acquiesced. I promised her we would continue with the story later this afternoon.

No one had talked about the doll Letty had made for

her quite a while ago, and I found it in the pantry as I was helping Nane put things away. I pulled it out and presented it to Genevieve telling her she could take it with her if she liked and hold it during her nap. She seemed quite excited about it, and Nane told her how special it was since it was made by Letty. She was interested in looking at it as she and Nane headed upstairs for her nap.

When Nane came back downstairs, she took Elizabeth to their house and put her down, and then came back to the kitchen. Isum hadn't joined us for lunch today, and Elizabeth told me he was busy in the field. She said they were having problems with the machinery, and Isum knew how to separate the sugar and could manage going about it the old way until the machinery was up and running again.

"You seem to be doing better with Genevieve," said Nane.

"Yes, I think so." I told her. "Hopefully we can get started on actual school lessons next week. I want to make it interesting enough for her so she isn't frustrated."

"I think you can do that. She loves hearing stories, so maybe that could be an incentive for her to learn. She has to. We got to get that child educated so she doesn't fall behind. Mrs. Patout would have wanted that."

"I know." I told her, but was thinking about asking her something else, and I blurted it out. "Nane, I asked Mr. Williams to help me contact my adopted father, Captain Kiper and I haven't heard a word. What should I do?"

"Why would he contact him?" She asked.

"Mr. Patout told me to tell him his name and he told me he would contact him about my situation."

"Well, Mr. Patout would know then, but I can't really see Mr. Williams wantin' to get your message to that man any time soon." She said. "It wouldn't benefit them for you to leave."

"But I was kidnapped!" I said vigorously.

"Yes, and why were you stolen?" She asked. "It is all very suspicious."

I lowered my voice to a whisper, and told her the story of Captain Kiper and the other agents who were on the ship with me and what our mission was.

She put her finger to her mouth, and shushed me. She then walked to each doorway and check outside.

"Don't you say nothin' like that unless you know no one is listening!" She said emphatically, "Do you hear? We could all get in to trouble for your talking like that. You have to be careful who you trust, and I mean anyone!"

"But you can't mean other Negroes. Don't they want to be free, too?"

"Of course, but that doesn't mean they can't use you for their own circumstances, and they will. Some knows they get preferential treatment for telling on a Negro who's planning to run. If you're trying to get in touch with an agent, Mr. Williams might never contact him."

"But he doesn't know he's an agent!" I told her.

"Oh yes he might. Word gets around, you'll see. You can ask him if he's contacted him, but you might not be getting' the truth." She said. "Don't you tell no one 'bout what we just talked about."

"I won't, I won't." I answered her frustratingly. We moved on talking about other things as we worked in the kitchen.

When Genevieve woke up, Elizabeth wasn't awake, yet, so I suggested Genevieve and I make a swing and see if we could find a tree to put it up in. She thought that sounded like fun, so out we went to the shed in search of the items we needed to build the swing.

Isum was working in the shed, and told us he had been thinking about making her the same thing, and he even knew which tree it should hang from. He had already assembled a piece of wood and the cut rope, and went to the back of the shed to retrieve it. He came back up front and we all walked to the tree where he thought it would work best, out behind the house.

"This here's a pecan tree. See those nut looking shells

on the branches? They'll start falling between August and November, and we'll collect 'em for eatin'. Nane makes a mighty good pecan pie."

"I've never had a pecan pie." I told both of them.

"You've been missin' some might tasty stuff. She can also make pralines and cookies with 'em, too."

"What about the swing," asked Genevieve?

"That's what we're here for ain't it, Miss Genevieve? I'm gonna need some help with this one." Isum told her.

He threw the rope over a very sturdy branch and tied it to one end of the board, then repeated the gesture for the other side. He pushed down on it to check its strength, and then told her to come on over so he could get a feel for the correct height. It was a little too high off of the ground for her, so he lengthened the ropes and made it hang lower. She was able to sit on the board herself, now. He showed her how she should push off using her legs and then how to hold them up so she didn't drag them on the ground.

Tired of kicking off with her own feet, I offered to help. Genevieve loved the swing and squealed with glee as I pushed her higher and higher. Isum stayed there with us and enjoyed his handy work until Mr. Williams called him back to the shed. I told her to thank him because this was a wonderful, fun thing she could do now.

Elizabeth heard the fun, and came on out and joined us for the last few minutes of me pushing her. I was getting tired, even though she could have swung all day, I believe. She was disappointed in our stopping, but I reminded her we had a book we were reading, and fortunately, she was interested enough in the story to agree to break for it.

We went in and chose something to drink from Nane. Genevieve told Nane all about the swing and how much fun it was, and how high she went. She told Nane she could even swing herself, and Nane played along nicely acting very excited for her and her new found fun.

We asked Nane to join us as we headed back out to the porch, but she told us she wasn't able to join us. She said she'd listen when she could, and that the few parts she heard that morning sounded very good. We went back to our old spots, Elizabeth, Genevieve and I, and picked up where we left off.

Before I went home that evening, Mr. Williams came through the kitchen to talk to Nane, after having met with Mr. Patout. I was ever so anxious on hearing anything from Captain Kiper, and wanted to ask Mr. Williams about his ability to contact him. I let him finish speaking to Nane, and then I followed him outside.

"Excuse me, Mr. Williams?"

He stopped and turned towards me without saying anything.

"I was wondering if you had been able to contact Captain Kiper? Remember, he was the gentleman I gave you the address of who knows me and can prove this was a mistake."

"Cora, I haven't had time to contact him, or find out about your 'mistake' as you call it. I know Mr. Patout wants me to follow up with it, and I will once I get the chance, maybe, when we all go to New Orleans at the end of the week. I can get a telegraph to whatever city you said he was in. Remind me when we get to New Orleans." Mr. Williams said.

I had no idea about a trip to New Orleans, and so I asked him, "Am I to go with you to New Orleans?"

"I believe so, that's what Mr. Patout just told me. You will be going with Genevieve. He said you would be the best person to pick out the materials she needs for her lessons."

I tried asking Isum about the trip, but he hadn't heard anything about it. He said Mr. Patout would probably tell me about it tomorrow if it were true. We returned back to our living area, and I headed back to my shack. I was used to the others not being back, yet, so I continued helping with the dinner food so they wouldn't have to work more when they returned home. I don't know how they kept going. It was back breaking work and hot as can be.

I waited up late tonight hoping to ask Anna what she thought about my going to New Orleans, but they didn't come in until the middle of the night. And when they did, we were all called out by the fire. I wasn't sure why we were being beckoned, but as we gathered around the fire, I saw Anna, and went over to her.

"What's happening? Where has everyone been?" I asked her.

"It's Albert. He got caught speaking his language again." Anna said.

"So what's going…" she cut me off before I finished.

"Shhh, just be quiet." She said sternly, and we watched what happened next.

Mr. Lott had Albert tied up with his arms behind his back. He had Mr. Belcher force Albert down on his knees and they took a whip to him repeatedly. Mr. Lott was ranting and raving and carrying on something fierce about Albert and his not speaking in English and that Mr. Lott knew he was organizing something against Mr. Patout. The other man with them, Mr. Dixon kind of stood off to the side, but didn't do anything. No one in the crowd was saying anything to stand up for Albert. I didn't understand why someone did not do something.

The scene was more horrific than I had seen before and I almost said something myself, when Elizabeth's son, Dan spoke up. Mr. Lott and Mr. Belcher stopped their actions and the crowd was totally silent. Dan stepped forward and his wife, Bay, started crying and pulling on him to come back and be quiet, but Dan broke free and walked up to Mr. Lott telling him to let Albert go. He said he wasn't sparking any mutinous behavior. He was just speaking in a language he was accustomed to.

"He's getting' old, let the old man go!" Dan told him.

This infuriated Mr. Lott, and Mr. Belcher pushed Albert down on the ground and took to Dan. They tied up both his arms to opposite posts, and then spread his legs and tied them to the opposite posts so he could not protect himself. They cut off his shirt, and Mr. Lott told Mr. Belcher to split his nose. Mr. Belcher took out his knife and with one quick movement, split Dan's nose. Mr. Lott then told Mr. Belcher to give Dan twenty lashings.

"But!" Said Mr. Lott, "Is there anyone else that wants some of this? How about you, Bay?"

Dan started hollering at Bay to be quiet, and Letty went over to her and put her hand across her mouth and tried to subdue her so she wouldn't make any more noise.

"That's better!" Said Mr. Lott, and the lashings began.

I tried to turn away, but Henrietta forced me back around.

"You need to watch this!" She said.

When the excruciating demonstration was over, Mr. Belcher cut them both loose.

Mr. Lott turned toward the group and said, "Now you'll do what I say, or else, the next person will get it worse."

Bay ran over to Dan immediately, while everyone else stood there for a moment, waiting for Mr. Lott and Mr. Belcher to walk away. When they did, the crowd gathered around Dan and Albert and started helping them up. Dan's back was bleeding something terrible and he had lash marks across it. His nose was bleeding profusely so I pulled off my apron and wadded it up and handed it to him. Henrietta grabbed it from my hand and threw it down on the ground. I bent down and picked it up, looking at them as they now passed me walking towards Dan and Bay's shack.

Anna came up immediately and told me not to worry about her, it was just Henrietta's way. Anna then walked me back to the shack, and said we should all go to bed. I wanted to talk about what had just happened, but Anna said we couldn't talk now. We had to go to bed. It was best to be quiet.

I was disturbed the whole night, not sleeping much at all. When the bell rang in the morning for everyone to get up, there was an eerie silence amongst everyone.

"Don't you say a word to no one," said Henrietta, " 'specially when you get up to that main house. This ain't you're business, but if you tell, you'll make it yours."

CHAPTER 6
A TRIP TO NEW ORLEANS

I didn't understand, but I understood enough to know I shouldn't be asking Henrietta any questions, and I would wait until someone brought it up to me before I said anything. As the women left for the day, I walked to the door and saw both Albert and Jim going back out in to the field. Both injured and hurt, but nevertheless walking right back out as if nothing had happened.

No one said a word about the incident for more than three days. I was flabbergasted. Why wouldn't they talk about this inhumane treatment, I wondered? Why didn't I hear Mr. Williams or even Mr. Patout question Mr. Lott's actions? Why had they not called a doctor for Jim or Albert? Why had Elizabeth not said anything? I was full of questions, but didn't know whom I could ask or when to ask. I surely did not want to get someone else into trouble. Being kicked out of school back home for getting into trouble was one thing, but this was definitely a life or death situation.

I believe it was Thursday when Mr. Patout called me in to the living room.

"We are all going to New Orleans tomorrow," he told me, "that means you will be traveling with us. Look through the books in the library. I think it would be nice for you to read to us on our way there and back."

"Yes, sir."

"And take some of Genevieve's books, also. You will be able to buy her lessons when we are there, but she will need something she is familiar with. Do you have anything else to wear, but this one dress?" He asked.

"I have the one I was bought in." I told him, "It is wrinkled, but I think Nane will let me iron it if you like."

"That will be fine. We'll buy you something else when we are there. I wouldn't want you to feel unsightly when you are with us. Be ready by eight o'clock in the morning. We should be gone about a week."

"Yes, sir." I excused myself from the room, and went back to the kitchen to tell Nane.

She suggested I come very early in the morning and bring my other dress so I could iron it.

"Do you have anything to sleep in at night?" Nane asked me.

"No, I normally sleep in my undergarments." I told her.

"That won't do for this trip. You're more Elizabeth's or Letty's size. I'll see if one of them has a nightgown you could use."

Genevieve and I spent the day on and off looking at letters in books. I wanted her to start writing letters of the alphabet, but we would have to wait until we arrived in New Orleans and bought some paper and pencils especially for that. We spent some more time on the swing, and before we knew it, the day was over.

Isum drove me back home, and reminded me that tomorrow would be a very early day, but he would not be able to take me to the main house since Mr. Williams had him preparing the horse and carriage early. I was going to have to walk, so I needed to give myself enough time to get there.

"Leave as soon as you can after the bell rings," he told me

I prepared my dress for the next day before I lied down for the night. I wondered about the next day and the trip to New Orleans. I wondered if I would see Robert and either of the other two men. I hoped not. It would give them pleasure to see me being someone else's property, and knowing they made money off of me, even if it was incorrectly done so.

The morning bell rang and I quickly rose and straightened my bed. Anna told me to have as good a time as I could in New Orleans. She'd never been there but heard it was an exciting city. Neither Henrietta nor Lucy said anything and I grabbed my dress, hanging it over my arm, and then I set out without any breakfast.

I hurried down the road in the dark, not really able to see where I was stepping. The moon was covered, and the sun was not yet rising. I accidentally stepped in some puddles and the bottom of my dress became wet and my boots muddy. When I arrived at the main house, Nane was waiting for me in the kitchen.

"No one else is up, yet." She said, "So you have time to iron your dress, and have some biscuits and gravy I made for you."

"Thank you, Nane." I told her as she looked down at the dress I was wearing.

"What'd you do? Walk through the swamp to get here? You can't go to New Orleans with a dress and boots lookin' like that! Git undressed and let's clean the bottom of your dress and scrub those boots."

I slipped out of my work dress and handed it to Nane. I then sat down and untied my boots and took them outside the kitchen door.

"You leave them out there and get to ironing your other dress. I'll wash the hem of this dress and get to those boots after. Good thing you got here early!" Nane told me.

Nane had the ironing board out and the iron sitting on the stove already hot. I laid the dress out on the board, and started to place the iron on it, when Nane yelled out at me. "What are you doin'? Turn that dress inside out so you don't scorch it on the good side."

"I've never heard of that, but I don't have time."

"You have more time to do that than you do to make a new dress if you burn it!" She said, and was right.

I turned the dress inside out and began ironing the dress. I wasn't even thinking that I was in my undergarments, when Isum walked in.

"Whoah! No one told me there would be some naked ladies in here!" said Isum. Nane and I laughed.

"You know she's not naked Isum! We don't

have any time to worry about our modesty. Anyhow, you're an old man and shouldn't care about that stuff anymore, or at least with Cora, she's young enough to be your granddaughter," said Nane.

"Well 'um, I guess you're right, but what about her bein' white and all?"

We all looked at each other as soon as Isum was finished with his statement. He was right. But we were in such a hurry and fumbling so the thought of it at the moment was humorous, so when I laughed, they did, too.

Isum scraped and cleaned my boots for me, while Nane washed off the bottom of my dress. It was a concerted effort, which I appreciated greatly. I kept thanking them, knowing they didn't have to help at all.

As the sun started to rise, Elizabeth walked in and caught us in our prospective jobs, but with me still in my underwear. "And just what is goin' on here?" Elizabeth asked.

"We've got to get Cora ready for her trip." Nane looked at me and handed me my work dress. "Here. Iron the bottom of this dress and see if you can steam out the wetness. And don't forget to turn it inside out!"

"Whose dress is this?" Elizabeth was looking at my other dress I had just finished ironing.

"That's the dress I was wearing when Mr. Williams bought me." I told her.

"Well it's a mighty pretty one. It will go well in New Orleans. You'll have to tell us all about Mrs. Clarkson when you get back," said Elizabeth.

"Do you think I will be seeing her?" I asked.

"I sho' do!" We all laughed and I finished ironing the hem of my work dress until it was only damp.

"Nane, do you think this will do?" I asked her.

She came over and felt the bottom and said it should be okay. I turned the dress right side out and slipped it over my head. Isum was finished cleaning my boots for me and I put them on and tied the laces.

Nane put out some biscuits and some gravy on the table and we all sat down to eat.

I had only had one when Nane's service bell rang, and

she said to us before she walked out, "Guess Mr. Patout is up. I'll go check on him, you three finish up. Especially you, Cora. I'll find out what the morning schedule is."

As soon as Nane was out the door, Mr. Williams walked in. He grabbed some biscuits and gravy, but didn't sit down next to us. He stood in the kitchen, eating, waiting on Nane to get back. When she did, she told us Mr. Patout would be waiting on Genevieve a little bit and if she weren't up in thirty minutes, she would go and get her ready. She told me I could go with her to make sure I knew what they had packed.

I excused myself and went to the library where I pulled three books for the trip. I tried to choose some books I thought Mr. Patout would like, so I picked *Notre-Dame de Paris* by Victor Hugo and *The Three Musketeers* and *The Count of Monte Cristo* by Alexandre Dumas. I'm sure I would say names and places incorrectly, but I wanted to offer my consideration of his heritage as part of my readings.

I realized Genevieve might not enjoy these books thoroughly, so I brought *Ditties for Children*, *Rollos' Travels*, and *Peter Parley's Juvenile Tales*. I brought one more book, and selfishly for myself. I hoped Mr. Patout or Mr. Williams didn't see it, because I didn't want to get in trouble. This book was called, *The Book of a Thousand Nights and a Night*. I had read about it in the *New York Herald* some time ago and I thought it sounded very exciting.

Nane wrapped all of the books in a wrap and tied them up neatly. Isum had the horse and carriage ready in the front of the house. Nane placed the books on the seat facing away from the driver. She had also put together a lunch for our travels and placed the basket on the back of the carriage. I didn't know the man that was to drive us to New Orleans. I had seen him helping Isum sometimes, and then sometimes coming from the factory house, but I didn't know his name.

Nane had Genevieve ready and fed and waiting in the front. She was playing with some of the flowers and pulling petals off, one at a time. I asked Nane the name of the man who was driving us, and she told me his name was George.

"I think it is George Drum, but don't you go messin' with him. You keep your distance and stay with Mr. Patout. Let Mr. Williams take care of George."

I thought it odd, but I told her I would abide by her wishes. I waited out front with Genevieve until Mr. Patout and Mr. Williams came out. Mr. Williams shouted at Isum to get his horse, and they chatted a few moments until Isum brought his horse around. I followed Mr. Patout who called for Genevieve to get into the carriage. Both of them stepped into the seat that faces forward and I climbed in and sat opposite them. When

Mr. Williams was mounted and ready, Genevieve said goodbye to Nane, Elizabeth, and Isum and they waved back. We were off for our journey to New Orleans, and I was excited. I wondered what opportunities, if any, this trip would hold for me.

CHAPTER 7
DINNER AT MRS. CLARKSONS

    Mr. Patout asked me what books I had chosen. I opened the sack, hiding *The Book of a Thousand Nights and a Night*, at the bottom of the pile, and told him the ones I had. He seemed delighted at my choices and said his wife would have been delighted to hear of these. He asked Genevieve if she remembered *Notre-Dame de Paris*, but she didn't. He told her she would love it and asked me if I would read it to them. I told him I was glad to, and opened the book, placing the others back in the wrap and retying it to secure them.
    I opened the book and began the story.

    "Precisely three hundred and forty-eight years six months and nineteen days ago
    "Paris was awakened by the sound of the pealing of all the bells within the triple enclosing walls of the city, the University, and the town.
    "Yet the 6th of January, 1482, was not a day of which history has preserved the record. There was nothing of peculiar note in the event which set all the bells and the good people of Paris thus in motion from early dawn. It was neither an assault by Picards or Burgundians, nor a holy image carried in procession, nor a riot of the students in the vineyard of Laas, nor the entry into the city of "our most dread Lord the King," nor even a fine stringing up of thieves, male and female, at the Justice of Paris."

    Mr. Patout kindly interrupted and asked if he could correct me on my pronunciation. I told him I would appreciate it, so please do. He looked down at Genevieve and they both smiled. I continued.

    "Neither was it the unexpected arrival, so frequent in the fifteenth century, of some foreign ambassador with his beplumed and gold-laced

retinue. Scarce two days had elapsed since the last cavalcade of this description, that of the Flemish envoys charged with the mission to conclude the marriage between the Dauphin and Molly of Flanders, had made its entry into Paris, to the great annoyance of Monsieur the Cardinal of Bourbon, who, to please the King, had been obliged to extend a gracious reception to this boorish company of Flemish burgomasters, and entertain them in his Hôtel de Bourbon with a "most pleasant morality play, drollery, and farce," while a torrent of rain drenched the splendid tapestries at his door."

Genevieve snuggled up to her father and put her head against his arm. He lifted his arm so that her head lay against his side and his arm surrounded her. He placed his other hand on her head and stroked her hair. I stopped only for a moment to take in this tender moment and smile at the love they had for one another.

We stopped along the way to partake of lunch, in a lovely wooded area. I stepped out first and helped George lay out the blanket and food. Genevieve had fallen asleep along the way and Mr. Patout nudged her awake and they both stepped out of the carriage.

George and I stood to the side as Mr. Patout, Mr. Williams, and Genevieve ate. Genevieve asked me to come sit with her and eat, but I shook my head knowing it wouldn't be proper.

"Of course, Cora, please come and sit with us, and eat." Mr. Patout said.

I glanced at George, feeling very awkward that I was invited and not him, but Mr. Patout chimed in to him before the moment passed, and invited him to sit and eat. George and I sat there quietly while Mr. Patout and Mr. Williams talked about business in New Orleans. I overheard them talking about a meeting they were to have with a shipping company that would transport the sugar to the North.

I perked up knowing I had to get a message to the Captain somehow and ask him to pass it on to Captain Kiper.

This might be my only chance. I couldn't count on Mr. Williams to do it, but I would ask him again to help me send a message. One of these ways had to get through. Captain, my Ma, Rufina, they had to know where I was and that I was all right. Listen, Allie, and think!

We were finished eating, and Mr. Williams noticed my inattentiveness and had to call out my name to bring me back to the moment. I scurried up and helped put up the food and fold the blanket. George put the items on the back of the carriage, and readied the horse. Everyone retook his or her positions and off we went.

I began the story again, but was unable to finish when we approached the outskirts of New Orleans. Mr. Patout said he would tell me of the history of New Orleans and of the sites we were passing. I was thrilled and looked out the window at the landscape as we passed. He spoke of the trees and of the hanging vines. He spoke of architecture and neighborhoods. I told him I loved the hanging vines with the beautiful flowers that lined them.

"When Mr. Williams brought me to Belle Terre, the vines were filled with white flowers that are now gone. Do you know what they are?" I asked him.

"There are called wisteria, and they are a vine that wraps around wood, or grows up fence posts. I believe they bloom in March or April, I know there are also ones that have lavender flowers. If Mrs. Patout was here, she could tell you all about them. She loved the flora of this area. She knew so much, but I can barely remember."

"I wish I knew more," I said, "There are so many trees and flowers I know nothing about. What about the dried, grassy brush that hangs from the trees?"

"Mrs. Patout called it Spanish moss, and she said it had a story to it. Would you like to hear it?" He asked me.

I nodded, and he began the tale.

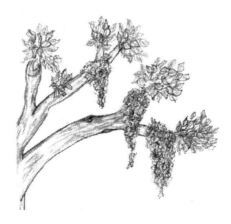

"*A Spanish soldier fell in love at first sight with an Indian chief's favorite daughter. Though the chieftain forbade the couple to see each other, the soldier kept meeting the maiden in secret. The Chief found out and ordered his braves to tie the Spaniard high up in the top of an ancient oak tree.*

"*The Spaniard had only to disavow his love to be freed, but he steadfastly refused. Guards were posted to keep anyone -- the chief's daughter above all -- from giving food or water to the poor Spaniard. The Spaniard grew weaker and weaker, but he still would not renounce his love for the girl.*

"*Near the end, the Chief tried to persuade him once more to stay away from his daughter. The Spaniard not only refused to disavow his love, but he told him his love would continue to grow even after death. When the Spaniard died, the chief kept the body tied up in the tree as a warning to any other would-be suitors. Before long, the Indians began to notice the Spaniard's beard continued to grow. The Indian maiden refused ever to take a husband -- unless the Spaniard's beard died and vanished from the tree.*

"*As the years went by, the beard only grew stronger and longer, covering trees far from the Indian maiden's village. Legend says that when the Spanish moss is gone, the Spaniard's love will have finally died with it.*"

"Mrs. Patout loved stories like that, and it is one of the reasons she loved this place." He tapered off and stared out the window, as we closed in on town.

The noise started to pick up from the city and he brought his attention back to us.

"I love the story, but so tragically sad. I remember one similar to that about the Mulberry Tree, in Ireland."

"We'll have to hear it one day. I know Mrs. Patout would have loved to hear it."

We sat there the rest of the trip quite melancholy. Fortunately we didn't have much further to go, and when we arrived at our lodging house, Mr. Patout pulled himself together and greeted the man from the house that met us when we pulled up. He took them inside and I stayed outside with George and Mr. Williams. We gathered their things, and ours, and they showed me another door for us to go inside.

How strange, but nothing surprised me anymore. George and I didn't speak. Not because we didn't want to, it seemed as though we shouldn't. We carried the things to the rooms assigned. I was staying with Genevieve, in a room connected to Mr. Patout's. George was in another part of the house, and Mr. Williams was staying in another room on the floor below. Mr. Williams told me to wait in this room for Genevieve and for further instructions from Mr. Patout.

I looked around the room and noticed what I assumed was my bed. It was shorter and closer to the ground than Genevieve's. Hers was nicely covered with extra pillows, while mine was plain, sufficient, but plain. It made me wonder how people could think of such things. How do they separate people? I remember wondering how people could separate others because of religious choices, and now they were doing it because of skin color. Well, not all, since my skin color was the same as theirs. None of it made any sense to me.

I put away all of Genevieve's things and then wandered over to the window and looked out. Genevieve and Mr. Patout came in and asked if I would like to go with them to purchase some school supplies for her. It's funny how he asks if I would like to go? Polite and considerate, but I really don't have a choice. The question is really a statement, disguised as politeness.

I joined them on the outing and we had a very nice time. We picked out spelling books, practice pads, easy reading books, pencils, erasers, sketching and art paper, paints, scissors, and string. It seemed to be fun for everyone, and Genevieve was already excited about playing with all of it. It took two bags to bring it all together, and Mr. Patout asked them to deliver it to the place where we were staying.

We walked back chatting about the selection of things and how we could use all of it for Genevieve. Normally I walked behind them, but as we walked back, Mr. Patout walked with me as Genevieve walked in between us. It was quite a pleasant time, and I think he was having lighter thoughts than the ones he had on our ride when he was thinking of his wife.

He allowed me to walk in the front entrance with him, and I looked up to see the name of the place. I hadn't paid any attention to it earlier, but paying attention has always been a problem of mine. My mind gets stuck on other things and I miss important details. The name of this establishment was, Bon Maison.

We stopped in front for a moment and Mr. Patout said, "This was the last place Mrs. Patout stayed when we were in New Orleans. She loved the French design and the layout of the rooms on the inside. We were looking for a house here in New Orleans, but I no longer need it without her."

As we walked past the front desk, a gentleman handed him a note. Mr. Patout stopped to read it, thanked the man, and then turned to us.

"We're going to dinner tonight at a friend of mine. We will all be going, so Cora, if you would please get Genevieve washed and presentable in her blue dress I would appreciate it. You may wear your nicer dress, and we shall all meet here in about an hour."

"Genevieve, won't that be fun?" I said to her.

"Who is it Pa-Pa? I don't want to go to Mrs. Clarkson's house. Is that where we're going? I don't like her. Please don't make us go? Cora and I can stay here in our room, can't we Cora?"

"But Genevieve, Mrs. Clarkson adores you and just wants you to like her. Is that so bad? I bet she will have a delicious dessert for us tonight. Won't you go for me? I would much rather have you there. I want you to try and like her, for me. Please?"

Genevieve was silent for a moment and then gave in to her Pa-Pa. "Yes, Pa-Pa, but do not leave me alone with her. She scares me."

"Oh Genevieve, do not be so cruel, she is a pleasant and fine person and we are invited as her guests. We will act appropriately."

We went to our separate room and Genevieve talked more about Mrs. Clarkson. She said she was a very nice lady in front of Pa-Pa and other adults, but she was cruel and mean to her servants. Once Genevieve saw her tie a girl to the sink in her kitchen and she left her there during the entire evening. Another time she caught Genevieve looking through her things in her room, and she grabbed her arm so tightly it hurt. She then bent down and talked to her with a horrible face and a totally different voice. She was crazed, Genevieve said. She was hurtful. Genevieve just didn't like her. I tried to reassure her I would be with her and protect her.

We washed her hands and face, and slipped on her pretty blue dress. I fixed her hair with a part on the left side and a ribbon on the right. I curled her hair under on pieces of fabric and asked her to leave them in until we were ready to go. I then washed my face and hands and put on my dress.

This dress had some bad memories tied to it, but I was not going to let them stand in the way of my making better ones and letting go of those. I fixed my hair, and we both waited until it was almost time to go. I then uncurled Genevieve's hair and we waited for Mr. Patout to come and get us.

He came through the door and doted on his daughter. He told her how pretty she looked and that she reminded him so of her mother. He was kind enough to compliment me, and then we headed out the door and down to the carriage. He greeted George, and then stepped in. I followed Genevieve and we were off to Mrs. Clarkson's house. I was slightly anxious, but Mr. Patout was reassuring to his daughter, which in turn calmed me down.

It was only about ten blocks away, and Mr. Patout and Genevieve stepped out, and then he turned for me to get out. This time he held his hand out to help me down. I allowed him to take it and I stepped down and we all walked to the house.

It was a huge house with three or four floors and a balcony for a porch on every one. The railing was metal in intricate designs and there were gaslights on each side of the entranceway and then on the corners of the house. We could hear the piano playing inside as we walked towards the door.

There was no need to knock because a gentleman opened the door as we approached and welcomed Mr. Patout by name. Mr. Patout returned the greeting and walked in handing him his hat. A woman walked down the stairs as we entered. She appeared to be the essence of perfection.

Her dress looked like satin with a fitted bodice and an open neckline that sat slightly beneath her shoulders. There were hand sewn floral patterns across her chest and at the bottom of the dress that must have had crinoline beneath it to make it stand out so. She had dark black hair that was full and long, but she had it twisted in the back to be pulled away from her face. It hung down the middle of her open back in a very soft manner. She walked and moved as if she was on a cloud, and her actions were more than welcoming for Mr. Patout.

She tried sweetly to welcome Genevieve, but she hid behind her father slightly, until he pulled her out and asked her to say hello. She nodded to me and asked her butler, Arthur, to show me to the back. Genevieve grabbed at me to stay, so I told her I would be back in the kitchen if she needed me at any time. I followed Arthur to the back and took my place to wait.

The evening must have gone nicely because the piano continued to play and Genevieve had not run back to get me at any time. George and I sat and ate with Arthur and Delores, in between their being needed at the dinner. I sat and listened rather than talking since I was the outsider. I seemed to get more information when I was quiet because they were more willing to speak. I needed to remember that in the future!

As the evening was winding down, Mr. Patout brought Genevieve into the kitchen and asked if I could go to the carriage with her and let her lie down. He would be there shortly and we could go home. George went and retrieved the carriage, pulled it around, and I picked up Genevieve and stepped into the carriage. She lied down next to me and put her head in my lap. She asked me to tell her a story of my childhood, but before I could get much out, she was fast asleep.

We were there a while, Genevieve asleep, George in the front seat, and me in the carriage, waiting for Mr. Patout. The music had stopped and while I thought he might be coming out. He didn't. I decided I would ask George some questions, since we were both waiting.

"George? Can you hear me?" I asked him, trying not to wake up Genevieve.

"Barely, but I can." He said.

"How long have you been with Mr. Patout?" I asked.

"About four years."

"Can you explain why no one has done anything about Albert or Jim? I don't understand"

"'Cause more will happen to them or anyone else that brings it up. It's just bad luck. None of us want to be treated like that. None of us."

"But what if Mr. Williams or Mr. Patout could do something about it? What if they fired Mr. Lott and Mr. Belcher? Wouldn't that be worth it?" I looked out the door to see if anyone was coming, yet.

"You think they's gonna take a Negroe's word over a white man's word?"

"But they have the scars to prove it!" I reminded him.

"No, no! That's not the way it works. It only gets worse for those that stand up. You have to do what the white man says to get along."

"That can't be right, always. And I don't think Mr. Patout would want anyone to be treated like that. I just can't believe he would."

I heard talking and glanced out the door. I saw Mrs. Clarkson drop her handkerchief, and Mr. Patout bent down to pick it up. Oh, she's good, I thought. She knows how to play the part and is definitely trying.

What was it Elizabeth said, "She's not sure he's seein' her, but she's seein' him!"

Yes that was it. Nane and Elizabeth were right. She was quite interested in him and trying very hard to win him over.

Mr. Patout stepped into the carriage as she waved her handkerchief goodbye. Her perfume was quite strong on him and its aroma wafted through the carriage as we road back to Bon Maison.

"Did you have a pleasant evening?" I asked him.

"I did, and yourself?" He asked.

I said, "yes," and then wondered how good of an evening it could be to sit in another room waiting on people at their beckon call. At least Arthur and Delores seemed courteous, and the food was delicious, so maybe I shouldn't judge the moment.

We arrived at Bon Maison and Mr. Patout stepped out first. He turned around and asked me to hand Genevieve to him. He said he would carry her. I did so, and then followed them both into the hotel. He brought her upstairs, and he was the one that undressed her and put her to bed. He kissed her on the forehead and stroked her head.

"Would you join me for a moment in the study, here?" He asked me, and pointed towards his suite.

There was a room between ours that allowed him to carry on business without it being in his bedroom. It was quite convenient for him while he was away from home.

"Yes, of course." I told him, but I was very uneasy for some reason.

I was not worried he would do anything improper; I was worried about what people would say. How would this look? To them I am a slave, and alone with him at night. I knew I shouldn't, but there was something in his voice that concerned me.

I stood as he began telling me of Mrs. Clarkson, and her desire to be more than just friends. He said he knew what people were saying, but he was more interested in the growth of Genevieve than of his own wishes. He asked me what I thought.

I told him I truly did not believe it was any of my business and that a man as accomplished as he, would know best for himself.

"But you've heard what Nane and Elizabeth and the others say, and you've spent enough time with Genevieve to get a feeling one way or the other. Is she missing anything in life that I cannot give her? Does she need another mother right now?"

I stood there staring at him. I had many things to say going through my head, but nothing willing to come out. Should I tell him of Genevieve's feelings towards this woman? Should I tell him of the woman's obvious tries at manipulating him?

"She is a very beautiful woman." I told him. That's all I could come up with? I had a chance, and that was it?

"I don't care that her appearance is beautiful. Would she be a good mother for my Genevieve?" He asked, again.

"I cannot be the judge of that, sir, you must make that decision."

He turned as if in a frustrated motion, as my mouth let loose.

"But Genevieve seems ever so happy just to be with you. And no one could love her more than Nane or Elizabeth. They treat her as their own. Even Isum, he had her swing all ready to put on the pecan tree before I ever asked him. They all adore her and only want the best for her, and I adore her personality and spirit and she seems to be fonder of me every day. I do not believe she needs another mother. We can show her and remind her constantly of the mother she did have and loved her dearly. No, No. I do not believe she needs another mother. She has women, good women all around her and she could not be getting better attention. Plus, I have seen you with her and you are very endearing and comforting. I think she is satisfied and for the moment does not need anyone else in her life."

He turned around smiling, "Well, once we get you going, there is an opinion hidden back there. I will have to remember that."

I probably turned red realizing I had gone beyond what I should have, but I seemed to have lucked out with his view of my opinion.

"What has Mr. Williams done for you in researching the man you asked him to find?" He asked me.

I had just spoken out of turn, and now, was I to do it again? Well, he was pleased with me at the moment, when else might I have this chance?

"No Sir," I said, knowing I must not make Mr. Williams look badly, "poor Mr. Williams has been so busy he has not had time to send a cable to Captain Kiper. I was hoping he could do so on this trip, if he was not otherwise engaged by you."

"Nonsense, he will have time this trip. Can you write it down for him, and if he does not get it done, just let me know?"

"Thank you, sir. Is there anything else I can do?"

"No, you've been quite helpful. I needed someone to talk to, and I appreciate your time."

He stood there for a moment, and then said, "Merci et la bonne nuit."

"Good night." I turned to go back to my room, but I remembered Jim and Albert. Mr. Patout would never want his people to be treated like this. Never, I believed. So I turned around and pushed my luck one more time.

"Yes, Cora." He said, almost knowing I had more to say.

"Sir, I find this very difficult to tell you, but I truly believe you would want to know."

"What is it?"

"Last week, I witnessed a most awful scene at the shacks. It was very late one night and I was already asleep when the field hands came in. Mr. Lott called everyone to the fire and he and Mr. Belcher commenced to beat Albert. Then Jim tried to take up for him and they slit his nose and beat him also. It was a horrific scene, but no one, not anyone has said a word and I have worried about the men and their slashes on their bodies."

I looked at him with an intense desire of wanting him to immediately fix things.

"Cora, I usually don't get involved with Mr. Williams work unless he thinks something should be done."

"Yes, I understand, but Mr. Williams doesn't know about this, either. He was not there, and no one has told him."

"Really? And what was it Albert did to cause his beating?"

I thought for a moment. What could anyone do that would cause a beating? Nothing justified what I saw.

"Mr. Lott said he was speaking in his native tongue and did it on purpose to cause an uprising against you. Then Jim took up for him saying he was only talking about the sugar stalks and the weather and not about anything improper. I've never heard anyone say a bad word about you. They are all very grateful for your consideration, and glad they're not at other plantations with owners that abuse their slaves."

"I'll speak to Mr. Williams about this tomorrow. You are right, though, I would never want such abuse to occur on my property. I will have Mr. Williams check this out."

"But please do not get Jim or Albert in trouble! I could not stand it if I was the reason for their punishment, and they are already leery of me because of my whiteness and accent. Please do not hurt them because of me! I beg you!"

"Cora...Cora! I won't. I trust Mr. Williams and he will look into it. Now, are you going to be able to sleep after all of this?"

"Yes, sir, I shall. Bonne nuit." I tried my very pathetic French to say good night.

"Bonne nuit à vous aussi, Cora."

We both smiled, and I went back in to our bedroom and closed the door quietly behind me. I checked on Genevieve who was still fast asleep. As I undressed, I thought about my conversation and tried to be happy that I had told him. I wanted him to fix it right away, but I should know that is not going to happen when we are so far away. I want them taken care of now, I thought, but I needed to let it go. I needed to be happy with the thought Mr. Patout would take care of it.

The next morning, Mr. Patout came in and woke me up and left Genevieve asleep.

"Get dressed and come in to the study." He said.

I had no idea what he was doing, but I rushed to change into my work dress and fix my hair. I slipped out the door as quietly as possible in to the study and joined him. He was having breakfast and asked me if I wanted anything. I knew I would be eating separately, so I declined his offer and stood there waiting for this demand.

"I've come up with a wonderful idea for you." He said. "I want you to write a note to your Captain, and I will give it to the Captain of the shipping company I am working with today. They are planning on going to New York as one of their stops, so he can take your note directly. How would that be?"

How would that be? I was jumping out of my skin with excitement! Thoughts running rampant in my head!

"I will write something right away. How long do I have? I will go now and put it down on paper. Will you wait? I'll hurry" I was too excited to stop buzzing around.

"Cora, you have time, so take your time and write what you like. Tell him where you are and what your situation is. If all you say is true, he must be very worried about you. I would be very worried if someone did that to Genevieve and I didn't know where she was."

"Thank you, sir, thank you!" I said as I went back to my room.

Genevieve was still asleep, but I looked through the items we purchased yesterday and pulled out some paper and pencil. I went over to the desk by the window, and cracked the shutter ever so slightly to get a little more light in. I took a deep breath in to begin my letter.

I looked at the paper, but I didn't even know what day it was. I ran back to the door, opened it, and stuck my face through it.

"Mr. Patout, sir, what is the date?"

He laughed saying, "You always seem to lose the date, don't you? It's July 3."

"Oh, tomorrow's a big day for America, isn't it?"

"Yes and we are going to have a wonderful time with fireworks and festivities. Now go write your Captain!"

I didn't say a thing, but shut the door and ran back to the table. As I sat down, Genevieve started to move and I wished she would be still for just fifteen more minutes.

Mr. Patout stuck his head through the door at the same time and said, "Cora, if Genevieve wakes up, send her to me until you finish."

I shook my head vigorously, being ever so grateful with each nod. I just might be able to get what I wanted down on this paper and out today. This was my day. Mr. Patout was better than anyone had said. I thought about that statement and then paused for a moment, if he were so good…why wouldn't he let me sail with the ship going to New York? I knew I couldn't bring up the topic after he had been so kind to offer my doing this. I really couldn't press my luck any more than this. Write! Allie, Write! I told myself. Stop thinking of other things that distract you!

July 3, 1853
Dear Captain,

I am alive and doing as well as can be expected. I am hoping beyond all hope you are home and safe, and Ma is with you. If she is, I only wish you both the best. You must share this letter with her since it is all I have to get a message to you. I was abducted while in Charleston, and brought to New Orleans by three men who sold me as a Quintroon.

I live on a sugar plantation called, Belle Terre, outside of New Orleans, as a slave. I do not know exactly where it is but it is about a half-day buggy ride from New Orleans. The owner's name is Mr. Bernard Patout, and he is allowing me to write this letter to you in the hopes of righting this wrong. I am in charge of helping his daughter learn to read and write. We are currently in New Orleans in a hotel called, Bon Maison. It is just off the wharf, and I can hear the familiar sound of the water and ships, and birds, and preparations for ventures on the sea. I wish I were home with you and Ma, and hearing these sounds with you.

This letter is coming to you on a ship Mr. Patout is using to transport his sugar. I do not know the Captain's name, but Mr. Patout says he trusts him to get this message to you, and so must I. I have also requested the overseer, Mr. Williams, to contact you, but I do not believe he has done so, yet. If so, maybe he can give more information as to my whereabouts.

Besides you and Ma, please give my love to Rufina and Angelo. I'm sure Rufina is out of her mind with worry! Tell Mr. Farraday, and let Jonathan know I am all right. I am sure he must be very worried and wondering when I will be coming back. If Brody is still there, please share this with him, also, since there are so many moments I think back to Ireland and our time together with his family.

With great affection,

Allie

I have finished without telling you something important! I go by the name of Cora! Please find me!

I folded the letter and thought about the stamp the Captain gave me years ago to seal my letters. I didn't have that, but I wrote Captain Kiper's name on the front, and hoped this would suffice. I looked over at Genevieve and realized she wasn't in her bed. I panicked for a moment running back to the door that was ajar to the study, and saw her sitting with her father. She was eating breakfast and seemed to be just fine. I must have been so engrossed in my writing, I didn't even hear her get up.

I knocked quietly and Mr. Patout told me to come on in. I handed him my letter and he took it and put it on his stack of papers. I stood there staring at it blindly and he reminded me he would take care of it and get it in the right hands for its journey.

I took another deep breath and realized I had to let go of it and hope for the best.

Mr. Patout was to be doing business all day, and so Genevieve and I decided to walk around the city. It would be just the two of us all day, and I told her we should enjoy the city and play today since we were here. She agreed, and we dressed her in her day dress and headed out.

It was a wonderful day, even with the hot and humid atmosphere. I felt free and alive, and Genevieve treated me as if I were her older sister. She didn't understand, yet, what slavery was or that her father was in the business of buying men for free labor. The thought of that sounded awful. If you looked at only the facts, that's what it was, but Mr. Patout seemed so much nicer. Why would he be a part of such an awful situation? By doing this, he must condone it. I didn't understand.

We walked up and down streets, passed beautiful homes and lovely churches. We even came across a cemetery, and Genevieve was curious to see the gravesites, so we stepped inside and walked through. Many of the plots were above ground tombs, and I had never seen that. There were crosses, and angels, and metal ironwork decorating the tombs, and the shadow of these decorations made the cemetery very eerie, even in the daytime.

Genevieve seemed to love the strangeness of it, but I was starting to feel it was inappropriate for us to be there. I took her by the hand and we started to walk out, when an elderly Negro lady stopped us.

"Looking for anyone in particular, young ones?" She asked. Her eyes seemed to go right through us. But Genevieve must not have noticed for she began to talk to this woman.

"Why are the graves so high?" She asked her.

"If you were to begin to dig, you would hit water. This city was built below the level of the sea."

"Are we floating?" Genevieve asked.

"No, not exactly, but you might think so the way the water rises up at times. Before they raised the graves, bodies would float away when it rained and be lost forever. And sometimes, when you dug, the hole would fill up before you could get the coffin in." She said.

I was not too comfortable with her telling Genevieve all of this even though I found it very interesting, myself. There was something different about her, and the story coming from her made the awfulness of what she was telling, seem interesting.

"Genevieve, maybe we should be going?" I told her.

"But she hasn't finished her story." She said.

"Yes, but…"

"As I was saying," she continued without consideration of this young girl hearing her morbid story, "the city tried everything from boring holes into the caskets, to placing heavy rocks and stones on them to hold them down, but nothing worked. It was the Spaniards who taught us how to bury our dead and not have them float away."

"Are you here to see someone?" Genevieve asked her.

"I am. Would you like to go with me?" She asked her.

"Yes! Yes, I would!" Said Genevieve, and before I knew it, the shy little girl I knew had taken the hand of this strange woman and followed her to another gravesite.

I stayed on their heels hoping nothing bad would happen. We arrived at a gravesite and the woman stood right in front of it with Genevieve.

"Here we are, this is the gravesite of my daughter." She said.

"When did she pass away?" I asked.

"A very long time ago, but I come here regularly to place charms at her grave and bring potions to help her in her afterlife."

"And what does that do?" I asked her.

"It guides her through eternity, and helps her guide us through are daily life."

"And how do you know this?"

"Because I believe in Marie Laveau and her powers, she heals many and helps those that are down trodden." The woman told us.

I reached out to Genevieve to get her hand, but we both remained there looking at this woman and listening.

"What is her religion?" I asked.

"She's a very devout Catholic who has a great passion and devotion to Voodoo."

I pulled Genevieve closer to me and we both stepped back. "Voodoo? Isn't that witchcraft? Are you practicing witchcraft?"

"She does not see her belief in Catholicism and her practicing of voodoo as a conflict of interest. She sees it as an extension of charity. She uses it to help and heal, not to do bad. If you do not believe, then go away, I do not wish to have any ill thoughts surrounding my daughter. Do not close your mind to the unknown! There are things much bigger than what we can see and grasp."

She faced her daughter's grave and went in to some kind of trance. Genevieve and I stood there for a few minutes then we quietly tried to find our way out of the cemetery. We said nothing as we left, but continued to hold hands while we walked down the street.

"What did you think of that?" I asked Genevieve, thinking she would be scared to death.

"I loved it! I'm going to put something on Ma-Ma's grave just like that lady." Genevieve said.

"But your Ma-Ma is always watching over you, you don't need to place anything there."

"I know, but it would be fun. Can we think of something to put there?" She asked me.

"We'll see, but you must promise me you won't talk about his to anyone, especially your father. I would not want him upset because I took you to a place like that. Can you keep that promise?"

"I promise." She said and we walked back towards Bon Maison.

They had fixed us a picnic lunch, and Genevieve and I picked it up and headed toward the waterfront. We picked a spot in the shade near the water. I laid out the blanket and sat down as Genevieve ran around the area. I called her over when I had placed out the food, and she ran over and plopped down on the blanket, laughing.

We finished eating and then we both lied down on our backs and looked at the sky. I asked her to describe the clouds to me.

"They're white and fluffy, and move slowly in the sky." She said.

"No, no, I mean what do the shapes look like? Here's an example, do you see that one over there? It looks like a cow." I suggested.

"No it doesn't, it looks like a dog." She chortled.

"All right then, what else do you see?" We played this game for a while, and then we rolled over on our fronts and looked out over the water.

"Close your eyes, Genevieve. Do you hear the birds?" I asked her.

"Uh huh," she sounded.

"What else do you hear? Leave your eyes closed and concentrate." I did the exact same thing and listened as intently as I could.

"I hear whistles. I hear water swooshing. I hear people talking." She said.

"Me, too. Let's see if we can hear what anyone is saying." I told her.

"All right." She said, and we lied there listening for any conversation we could understand.

We must have been in this position five minutes, when I sat up straight and opened my eyes.

"What is it Cora?' Genevieve asked me.

"Shhh. Shhh!" I said. "I think I know this voice. I have to listen." I looked around while I was listening, trying my hardest to hear it and see the person who was speaking.

There was a group of men, way across the grass from where we were, standing by a ship and talking. They sounded like they were saying good-bye. I looked intently on them trying to see if I knew any of them. I closed my eyes again and tried to focus on their voices. Who was that?

"Cora, who is it?" asked Genevieve, again.

"Please, Genevieve, give me a little more time and I will tell you."

I listened, and listened, and then I slowly started to get up. Oh my goodness, I thought! Could my ears be deceiving me? I opened my eyes as the one gentleman I was thinking of turned his head slightly while saying goodbye to the men. It must be him I thought. It has to be him.

"I know him, Genevieve, I know that man!" I told her most excitedly. "Come on, let's get our things and go and tell him."

We started gathering our picnic items, when music overtook our hearing. I glanced over in the direction of the music and saw what must have been a funeral procession. Cora was excited about it and wanted to go see it down the street. I was torn, must I go her way, or might I take her with me to find the voice I recognized.

I couldn't stand it. I knew my sense of duty required me to go where she wanted, but could I pass up a chance like this? What if I never saw him again? My heart raced and pounded and my desire to see him and hug him was overwhelming. I could be free! He could clear this all up for me!

"Cora, please let us go and see the band. Listen! Doesn't it sound wonderful? Come on, let's go." She begged.

I picked up the folded blanket as Genevieve ran towards the band moving down the street. I knew I had to go with her, and so for a brief moment I stood there looking at him as he boarded a ship and walked up the ramp. I yelled at him without thinking. I had the same feeling I had the very last time I saw him.

"Brody!" I yelled, "Brody, please stop! Please!"

He stopped for a moment on the ramp, and looked my way. I waved with great enthusiasm, but he continued looking around as if he hadn't seen me or known where the voice was coming from. Curse that music, couldn't they stop, just for a moment? Couldn't he see me waving like a maniac?

"Brody! It's me, Allie!" I yelled again, but I glanced towards Genevieve trying to keep an eye on her, too. I looked back at Brody and watched him climb the top of the ramp and disappear on board. It must have been him, but he didn't hear me. Surely he wouldn't leave me here if he knew it was me? What was wrong with that man?

I looked at the ship trying to get its name, but it was facing the wrong way. My chance had passed and I was back to the reality of the moment. I ran to Genevieve and grabbed her hand. We followed the procession a little ways, and then headed back to the hotel.

We walked very slowly, not really talking to each other. Genevieve was busy talking, but I wasn't listening to what her words were. My mind was on one person, Brody. Brody

Farraday. He had turned in to a tall and handsome man. Ma was right. There he was. No longer the boy I knew, but a man in a business world.

We went upstairs, and I handed Genevieve some paper and told her to draw anything she saw today so she could show her father. She was delighted to do this, so she sat at the table with me and began to draw. I sat there, lost in the moment, not able to get what had just happened out of my mind. The image of him talking and then slowly turning his head was emblazoned in my mind.

It was unbelievable. Whether it was the actual event that amazed me, or seeing him as a man, I was unsure. What I was sure of was the hope that my letter would get to Captain, and they could come back here and get me. Captain would come and get me, I know he would.

When Mr. Patout came in, he gave Genevieve a big hug and told her how much he missed her today, and that we were going to a wonderful restaurant tonight.

"Just us?" she asked. "You, me, and Cora?"

"No, I'm afraid, not, Mrs. Clarkson will be joining us." He told her.

"No Pa-Pa, please just let it be us tonight. I have so many things to tell you about our day!" She told him excitedly.

"How about we ask Cora to join us this evening, would that make you more inclined to go?" he asked her.

"Yes." She said knowing she must give in to his request.

"Cora, will you join us this evening?" He asked me.

"I appreciate your offer, sir, but I'd rather stay here and not intrude on your dinner."

I did not feel like going out and pretending to be happy on a day that had such a loss.

"Cora, you must!" Genevieve begged.

"I agree. You must." Mr. Patout said, and so like Genevieve I acquiesced to their request.

"Fine. We shall all have a wonderful evening. Genevieve, would you like to wear your yellow dress this evening?" He asked her.

"Ooh! Yes!" She said.

"Bon! I shall wait with baited breath to hear of your day, mon plus cher." He kissed her head and headed off to his room.

Once he was out of our room, I reminded her, "Genevieve, do not forget. We must not speak of the lady in the cemetery."

"Yes, I know, but I think Pa-Pa would think it interesting."

"Maybe so, but until we understand it better, let' not share it."

She nodded and I helped her get ready for the evening, and then dressed myself in the same dress as last night. We then waited on Mr. Patout who came and retrieved us shortly. He was in a most agreeable mood.

"Did you have a successful day I asked?" As we shut the door to the carriage and headed on our way to the restaurant.

"Most assuredly. Not only am I happy with the ship's layout and plans, I am most happy with our Factor." He said.

"I've never heard of that, what is a Factor?" I asked him.

"It's an agent who transacts business for another. And this company found me the best arrangement for shipping my sugar to other places and getting the best price. It's a very nice company out of England."

My ears perked up as I sat forward on the seat. "From England did you say? What is the name of the company? Or what is the name of your agent?"

"The company's name is, Farraday, and they are transport agents."

I was stone silent with mouth gaping wide open and eyes ready to pop from my head.

"Good heavens mademoiselle, what is the matter with you?" He asked me.

"I…I…" Nothing came out of my mouth.

"Yes, go on." He prodded. "We're almost at the restaurant, can't you spit it out!"

"I…I know them. They are like family to me." I blurted

out.

"You know them? Are you sure?" He asked.

"Yes! Yes! Was one of them here today? I knew it! I saw him! Did you meet with one of them today?" I couldn't control my excitement.

"Yes, I did as a matter of fact. I even invited him to dinner tonight, but he was set on sailing this afternoon to get home as soon as possible. He said there were pressing matters at home."

"Home? Was home New York or London? Did he say?" I inquired.

"New York, I believe."

"Did you give *him* the letter? Oh, that would be perfect if he had received it and read it before he left!"

"No, I gave it to the Captain and asked him to pass it on when he arrived in New York. He said it was the owner of his ship, and he would give it to him as soon as they docked in New York.

The carriage stopped in front of the restaurant, Antoine's, the sign said.

"Here we go." Said Mr. Patout and stepped out of the carriage as if this huge revelation had not just occurred.

What an extraordinary coincidence, I thought. I was so close today to being free again and going home. I could hope the Captain gave Brody the letter and he opened it, but I knew I couldn't put all of my hopes in that thought. How was I going to sit through this dinner and not be totally consumed with the day's events and in my own life?

Mrs. Clarkson was not at the restaurant when we arrived and Mr. Patout seated us with Genevieve in between us. When she arrived, she floated in. She was wearing another beautiful dress, with her hair pulled up on the side, with the loose part lying across her shoulders and back. What man would not want this woman, I thought? She is quite a beauty.

She walked straight to Mr. Patout and held out her hand for him to kiss it. He obliged and did so, and then she greeted Genevieve, and moved to sit by me. She only nodded at me, again, and turned her attention to Mr. Patout.

She was charming and talkative, asking Mr. Patout questions about his day. She was intent on capturing his intentions and making the most of her performance. She wanted the advantage, and you could tell she was working on it. She complimented him, and enhanced his ego. She would politely ask Genevieve a question every now and then to make sure her duty was done, and then she would go back to Mr. Patout.

By the time dessert was served, Genevieve had not told her story of the day, and could barely hold it in anymore. I could see the frustration on her face and the wiggling she was doing in her chair as she spent more time looking around than listening to Mrs. Clarkson and her father. I bent over to tell her to stop fidgeting, when Mrs. Clarkson, chimed in.

"Is there something you need to say?" She asked me, "Cora, isn't it?"

"I was only asking Genevieve to sit still. She is so excited about her day, she wants to tell her father all about it, and her ability to wait has become nonexistent."

I noticed the change of face on Mrs. Clarkson, but Mr. Patout did not see it and told Genevieve we would all love to hear her story about the day.

"Yes, of course, we would," said Mrs. Clarkson with a sarcastic ring to her statement.

Genevieve sat up straight and was thrilled she was going to be able to talk. I was glad she was pleased with our day, but I was praying she wouldn't say a word about the graveyard. I was doing my best to remain attentive without speaking, and without showing my anxiety over my personal events of the day. My mind can wander, and it took everything I had to sit there myself.

Mr. Patout sat forward to pay special attention to Genevieve. I looked over at Mrs. Clarkson who was obviously trying to look attentive herself, but looked more perturbed than sincere. She caught me glancing at her and gave me a most unkindly look. I continued looking at her, watching her actions and trying to look through her eyes. I am not the best judge of character, but something just wasn't right.

Genevieve told her father of the band and how we followed it down the street. He began to tell her about such bands and what they were doing and where they were going. She said she knew. She had been there this morning. She stopped and looked at me. She knew she had said more than she was supposed to. It didn't seem to bother him, but Mrs. Clarkson picked up on it, and immediately knew she could use it.

"Did you take Genevieve to a cemetery?" She asked me. "Do you know how dangerous those places can be, and who knows what kind of people are lurking down there?"

She was pushing it, but Mr. Patout had not said anything, yet.

"I'm sorry, Cora," said Genevieve.

"It's all right, Genevieve. They should know all of the stops we made and the buildings we saw." I told her, hoping the table conversation would move on.

"Oh, yes, we saw churches and beautiful homes, and even had a picnic down by the water. Oh, and Pa-Pa?" She said, "We lied down and looked at clouds and guessed what shaped they were. Have you ever done that?"

The conversation did move on, and for right now we were all right, but I had a special inkling that Mrs. Clarkson was not finished with us, yet. She had more in store for Genevieve and me. Here Genevieve was, six years old, and she caught on before her father that there was something different about Mrs. Clarkson.

The evening finished and Mr. Patout told

George to take Genevieve and me back to the hotel, and he would walk Mrs. Clarkson home. He was to come back after dropping us off and wait at her house and bring him home later. He hugged Genevieve and said he would see us in the morning. He reminded us tomorrow was a big day, with it being the Fourth of July!

Genevieve and I prepared for bed, and I read to her tonight. She wanted to hear Peter Parley's Juvenile Tales, so I began the book but it didn't take her long to fall asleep. I brought the lantern over by my bed and lied down watching the light against the ceiling.

The light illuminating from the lamp against the dark background gave the room a mystical, but comforting feeling. I lied there thinking about the day and my vision of Brody. He was right here, in New Orleans. We were so close, and yet far away. I thought about what I hadn't done that might have helped my situation. I hadn't yelled my name. I hadn't yelled his last name. I hadn't yelled for him to look in a specific direction. I hadn't done a lot of things correctly for him to look right at me. I can be such a bumbling mess at times.

He turned out very well, I thought. Very well, indeed. I bet he has a dozen suitors or even a wife by now. I hadn't thought about that. He could be married. If he was, I bet it was to Finola. As I think back about her, she was quite a beginner in her feminine wiles compared to Mrs. Clarkson. One good thing about Finola, I believe her interest in him to have been sincere about Brody. I never felt she was trying to manipulate him or turn others away as to only get his attention. She must have adored him, and that was all right. He deserved someone to adore him and be good to him.

I wondered what Mr. Patout meant by 'pressing matters' at home for Brody. My mind went a thousand different ways…Ma, Captain, Brody's father, Patrick? What was happening in New York that would require his immediate reason to sail? I would never go to sleep if I continued to allow my mind to drift so recklessly.

I had to do something else and so I went to the pile of books we had and pulled out, *The Book of a Thousand Nights and a Night*, and began reading it. It was exciting enough in itself to take my mind off of my own concerns.

I heard Mr. Patout come in much later. He tiptoed in to kiss Genevieve good night, smile at me and say goodnight, closing the door behind him. I read late into the night and then fell asleep thinking of Persia and Shaharazad.

The morning of the fourth began like the past two

mornings, but today was to be a celebration. Mr. Patout was in another wonderful mood and he set up the day as a happy, fun day for all of us. We were to have a picnic on the lawn by the water and spend the day with music and fanfare, fireworks and food. Genevieve was delighted and was able to wear a play dress for the day.

The hotel packed another delicious picnic for us. Mr. Patout let George off for the day, and we all walked over to the water and grassy area and picked out a nice spot. I'm not sure if Mr. Patout had invited Mrs. Clarkson for the days' festivities or not, but it turned out she ended up bringing her slaves and laying her blanket out right next to us. Arthur and Delores stood there most of the day while the rest of us sat and enjoyed the food and festivities.

I felt so ill at ease. I didn't belong to Mr. Patout's society, and especially not Mrs. Clarkson's, but I didn't feel Arthur and Delores should be standing there while I sat down, either. I wondered why she hadn't let them off for the day like George. That says something about her, right there, but I had no idea if Mr. Patout noticed it or not.

I knew George did not want to be here. He told me, "Why would any black man want to be at an event that celebrated Independence, and yet those of us that are slaves, are not free."

He was right. It was quite an ironic situation. What man, or woman, would want to be held captive and not be able to live freely to learn and work for themselves? I had heard many white people talk about the Negro as if he were a different species all together. I wondered, if we were all blind, would it matter?

I guess there is always unkindness and unfairness in the world. How can I not remember Ireland and what happened to the Farradays because of their religion, only? And then in New York, the Irish were thought of as a different species, too. But, many Irish had taken jobs away from Negroes, even in New York, because their skin color was a nearer white. How does any of this make any sense?

As the day progressed, I slowly separated myself from

the blanket. Genevieve and I left for periods and played in other areas which offered activities for children. I couldn't sit there all day with Mr. Patout or with Mrs. Clarkson. It didn't feel right and I had to remove myself somehow.

The blanket stayed under the tree the entire day, until the sun set. We then moved out from under the tree so we could see the firework display. It was remarkably brilliant, and Genevieve was mesmerized by the color and splendor of the bright lights against the darkened sky. A band was playing and it was a most festive day. A most festive day for white Americans.

A great benefit from this trip is the relationship gained between Genevieve and myself. Even with Mr. Patout. I was glad I had come with them, especially since I was able to catch a glimpse of Brody. Even with me here in this situation, I was pleased with the thought of Brody being successful. I was happy for him, and glad he was not the one here. He had already been through so much, he deserved success and happiness.

The very next day, we packed and made our way back towards Belle Terre. I finished reading the book, *Notre-Dame de Paris*. Genevieve settled in to her usual position next to her father with his arm around her, and as before, it wasn't too long before she fell asleep.

Mr. Williams was not with us on our journey back, and I thought this very strange. I inquired about him, and Mr. Patout said he had sent him back yesterday to take care of some plantation business. Oh! I thought. Maybe he was going to take care of Mr. Lott and Mr. Belcher. Hah! Good riddance to both of them. Maybe now I will get a little more regard from Henrietta and some of the others.

When we arrived at the main house, it was good to see Nane, Elizabeth, and Isum waiting as they must always do each time Mr. Patout arrives or leaves. It had such a positively welcoming effect. Genevieve jumped out and ran to them. This was a family, or at least the way a family should be, but everyone should be free. No one should be forced to be waiting or at attendance. I wonder if Mr. Patout ever considers his situation as forced attention.

I could immediately tell there was something in the air. Nane was focused on getting Genevieve and Mr. Patout settled, but something was different. We couldn't speak of it, yet, but even Nane gave me some crazy eyes when no one was looking. I was dying to know what happened, and what she needed to tell me.

It would be another hour before she and I were alone, but when we did, she didn't hold her tongue.

"Girl, what were you thinking?" Nane asked me.

"What do you mean? What has happened?" I asked her.

"Mr. Williams came back and there has been all kinds of uproar over the beatin's Albert and Jim got. We tried to keep it from Elizabeth so she wouldn't get upset, but she found out last night. Somethin' terrible's gonna come from this. You just wait-n-see." She said

"But, what harm could come from Mr. Williams' making things right and getting help for Jim and Albert?" I asked her.

"You just don't know. You don't know how these things work, and they NEVER work out for us! We're all just awaitin' for the backlash. Oh, it might not come today, or tomorrow, but it's a gonna come, and when it does, you'll see."

CHAPTER 8
THE BRANDING IRON

How could I have made this situation any worse? Why did I have to mettle? I thought I had asked Mr. Patout to not make it any worse for Albert or Jim. What was I thinking? If he doesn't notice Mrs. Clarkson's manipulations, or that owning people is an immoral matter, how could he understand how one action might cause another of horrible consequence. What? I didn't even understand that my own good intentions caused this consequence. What a mess I've made!

When I returned to our shack that night, I was shunned by almost everyone except Letty and Anna, and even they didn't speak with me directly. When we woke up the next morning, I followed my house companions out the door and didn't see Mr. Belcher or Mr. Lott. I saw Mr. Williams and Mr. Dixon. I waited for everyone to head to their prospective jobs, and then I asked Letty what had happened.

"Mr. Williams let Mr. Belcher and Mr. Lott go day before yesterday, but you should have seen it. They were devils and we are all awaitin' for their wrath to be brought down on us. It's just not a good thing. I know you think you meant well, but whatever happens will be your fault. This is not over, they will be back." Letty told me.

"What should I do?" I asked her. "What can I do to undo what I've done, or make it better?"

"Nothing! Don't DO anything else!" She said. "Let's not make this any worse. You've got to live with it, and not just the outcome, but with your being snubbed by everyone. It's your payment for having brought this on us. You'll have to earn your way back, even though you hadn't earned it, yet."

She was right, I hadn't earned anything, yet, and now I had made it worse. I could take being shunned for myself, but the thought that I had made it worse for others was unbearable. Will I ever learn to keep my mouth shut? Will I ever learn that maybe my way is not the only way?

The days of the next month were spent in a very

repetitive way. I went to the main house, Genevieve and I worked on lessons, had lunch, played outside, worked again on lessons, and then I came home, ate and went to bed without much human contact. There were people everywhere, but talking or interacting with them was almost nonexistent.

To break the monotony of it, Genevieve had a birthday coming up in a month, and Mr. Patout wanted her to have a festive and lovely party. She didn't have any friends but those of us with her every day. Mr. Patout saw to it that families from neighboring plantations were invited. That included their children.

It was to be a grand event with an afternoon and evening of merriment. A daylong event, since many of the plantations were hours away. I believe he even invited friends from New Orleans, which we knew would include Mrs. Clarkson. Nane, Isum, and I worked hard to decorate and plan everything with Mr. Patout. We all wanted Genevieve to have a memorable time, but it was also a time where the entire plantation could take a day off and celebrate.

That is…if the sugar was harvested on time. If it was, then everyone could take the day off. So, some evenings were spent singing and dancing, praying the weather was good and the harvest was plentiful. As you looked out over the fields, the stalks were tall and strong, rustling when the wind blew threw them. It was to be a marvelous harvest if the weather held.

Spirits were high all around. The harvest looked good, the party sounded fun, and a day off was coming! I hadn't heard a word from Captain or Brody. I wondered if my letter had arrived in his hands safely. I knew travel had its own ups and down and that weather or port calls could delay the ship, and so I had to give it months, both ways. I had settled in to this life, and accepted it for a while.

There was no way I would allow myself to feel sorry for myself. I didn't work the backbreaking, grueling hours the Negroes did. We might all technically be considered slaves on paper, but what I did didn't compare to their lives. I knew I had a life out there and would go back to it one day. What did they have? An eternity of human bondage, with little chance of ever escaping.

Preparations for Genevieve's party were going along well, and both she and Mr. Patout delighted in discussing the boat races at the pond, and the sack races on the lawn. Mr. Patout began looking poorly the weeks before, but he was not about to slow down while his sugar was being harvested, or his daughter was having her seventh birthday party. He wasn't the only one, but everyone was on a schedule and nothing was going to stop it.

It was late in September and the chopping and the cartloads of stalks were being taken to the mill where the cane was ground and boiled. It was an amazing process Mr. Williams had a good understanding of, and Mr. Patout trusted his managerial expertise. However, Mr. Patout loved to go and see it all at work and follow the process. Sugarcane plantations are a twenty four hour operation, with people working all year long, he told me once. He acknowledged the people who worked for him worked very hard, and he knew he was very fortunate.

We were down to the last week of both the harvesting and the party preparations, and looked to be on schedule. All of the slaves were on their normal shifts, as was I. I came home this night, ate, and went to bed. The only person in the room with me was Lucy and Angus. Poor Lucy had contracted whatever that awful cough was and was running a fever. Angus was a growing baby boy now who wasn't as cooperative as he was when he was a newborn. She was exhausted and not feeling well and unable to pick him up and take care of him as easily as before. I offered to take him outside and let her sleep.

We walked around, me with Angus, bouncing him up and down and playing with him, trying to entertain him. He would laugh and smile. He wanted down on the ground, but I didn't want him filthy before he went to bed, so I carried him and walked up and down our area. I could hear poor Lucy cough as we passed our shack and knew she needed her sleep much more than I.

About the time Angus placed his head on my shoulder

and relaxed, the field bell went off and I looked out that way to see a strange glow in the sky. It looked as if a fire was burning, but how could that have happened?

Mr. Dixon came storming in on his horse, yelling. "Letty! Letty! Get up and wake everyone up! Sound the bell!"

She came running out in her gown.

"Ring the bell and get any able bodied person out to the field right away!" He shouted. "Go get Isum and tell him to go get Mr. Williams. Now!"

She did as she was told, and the place turned in to a tempestuous rally. People seemed to know exactly what to do, with the fervor and diligence of an ardent response. I stood there with Angus. He, oblivious to the moment, as a sleeping child can be, as I looked back and saw Lucy stepping out from our shack. I grabbed her and took her back in.

"You will absolutely not go out in that field!

I will make sure Letty watches over Angus, and I will take your place." I demanded.

"No, I'll be in worse trouble if I don't get out there and help." She said while coughing in between words.

"Yes, and you'll be dead if you go out there and continue working tonight, then no one will be in trouble, you'll just be dead. Which do you think they want? A dead slave or a working one? And Angus? What will he want?"

She lied back down and I stormed out the door and over to Letty. I handed off Angus, and told her I was taking Lucy's place in the field. I didn't give her time to answer, but turned and ran with the others heading towards the fire. I didn't look back because the fervor of the moment blurred every bit of thought in my head.

I followed others as we jumped on burning stalks and grabbed other stalks to beat the flames. Many of us didn't have shoes on, but that didn't matter, the crop was the most important thing right now and we had to get it out. People were screaming. They were screaming at others, giving orders and directions. The fire crackled and whipped in the wind as if it was fighting us, and the devil was winning.

Mr. Williams brought a huge metal contraption that carried water in it, and he and five other men used it to try and wet the outer edges of the fire in the hopes to keep it from spreading. It worked in some places, but not in others. People were taking their clothes off and using it to beat the fire down. Some even used their bodies to roll on the fire, thus setting their own clothes on fire and burning themselves. Everyone was trying and it was a chaotic attempt at controlling this horrible event.

It took almost the entire night to stop the flames and the devil that fought us. The hordes of people who waged war with this devil walked back towards their shelters most solemnly when they were no longer needed. We were all exhausted and tired, dirty and ragged, dragging our feet rather than walking. We knew there were only a couple of hours before the day started over, and it had to. We had to get the crop harvested and finished on time. Not just because of a day off, now, but because it had to be done.

I walked in to our shack, following Henrietta and Anna. Lucy was still coughing and I went over to feel her head. She was hot. There was a bowl of water beside her and some rags, so I dipped one of the rags in the cool water and laid it across her forehead. She moaned in acknowledgement but didn't move. Henrietta and Anna were already on their beds. None of us had the strength to do anything but drop on our beds, and fall asleep, even with our clothes on. We all fell into a deep sleep, quickly.

It was good, for in my dream, Kerry came to me. I was thrilled to see her. She looked as if it were yesterday. I was older, but she was the same girl that stayed with me on the ship. I was happy to see her, but she did not seem so happy. She was frantic and beside herself, trying to rouse me and get me up and going.

"Allie! Allie! You have to get up! You must get out of here!" She screamed at me.

I was trying to move, but I was sluggish. I didn't understand her meaning, or her urgency.

"Allie! Please! You have to try. Let's go! Come with me, now!" She grabbed me under my arms and tried to lift me. I tried as hard as I could to get up. She tried again, and then she was gone, with a jerk.

I opened my eyes expecting her, but it was Mr. Belcher lifting me under my arms and pulling me out the door. I was so groggy I couldn't comprehend what was happening, and it took me a few moments before I realized the seriousness of the situation. I tried looking around for help, but no one was awake or outside. I tried squirming and getting free, but his grasp on me was too tight. He pulled me over to the small fire that was always lit and I saw Mr. Lott standing there.

"You're not supposed to be here!" I said to him.

They both laughed, and Mr. Lott asked, "And who do you suppose is going to do anything about it at this moment? Do you see anyone coming to your rescue? Everyone's too exhausted from putting out the fire" They both cackled, and I knew I had seen the devil.

"It was you, wasn't it?" I asked them. "You started that fire! What will you get from it? Mr. Patout will never hire you again after this!"

"You think I WANT to work for him, again? He doesn't know how to keep his slaves in their place, and I won't be humiliated in front of one of them again, EVER! I think I've settled my score with Belle Terre," He said sarcastically, "but I still have something to settle with you!"

"I don't know what you're talking about!" I told him.

"Really? You don't know anything about your telling someone about my punishment of Albert and Jim? It's because of you we were fired!"

"I don't care what you do to me." I said, "Somebody should do to you what you do to them. You won't win!"

By this time a few people had come out of their shacks. Mr. Lott noticed and pulled out his pistol and pointed it in their direction, threatening them.

"Stay back! Don't you dare try to stop me!" He screamed. "If you get in my way, I'll take care of you, too!"

I knew they would stay away. It would be a futile attempt for anyone to step in and try to do something. I knew this. They just stood there and watched. They had to, they had no choice.

Mr. Lott kept the pistol in one hand and ordered Mr. Belcher to pull me closer to the fire. With his free hand, Mr. Lott ripped the top of my dress free from my shoulder and exposed the bare skin to my neck, shoulder, and arm. He then looked back at the crowd watching, and with glee picked up a burning branding iron and brought it close to my face. Mr. Belcher had my hands pulled back so tightly I could not move them, and I turned my head away from the iron to show disdain for Mr. Lott.

He took the red hot branding iron and pushed it against my naked arm. I writhed with pain, but tried my hardest not to scream and give him enjoyment from the pain he was causing. I looked at him with disgust and shed not a tear, even though I felt them welling in my eyes. He was not going to win. He was not going to shake my will. This infuriated him more.

"Get her down on her back!" He yelled, and with one fell swoop, Mr. Belcher threw me down and was pinning my shoulders to the ground. I tried kicking free, but Mr. Lott kicked my legs open and stood on my dress, as far up as he could, in between my legs.

"I'm not done with you, yet, you mixed breed. I'm going to mark you in a place no one will ever want you. You'll never be free, again!"

He tucked his gun into his pants, and then picked up my skirt bottom and pulled it up to my waist. He bent down on his knees and forced my legs open with his knees and held them there exposing me. Then, with horror, I saw him pick up another branding iron and bring it towards me. I was still writhing in pain from my shoulder and horrified at the thought of what he was about to do. I knew everyone was watching, but I cared less about people seeing me than the act that was about to take place.

"Hold her tight, Roger! She's never going to forget this!"

They both chuckled in the most sinister way, and before I knew it, he shoved the burning iron into my inner, upper thigh. He held it there getting more pleasure from the pain he was inflicting. Immediately I jolted in every muscle of my body, and I was shrieking inside with intense agony. I was writhing, and heard them both laughing their sickening cackle. I was feeling every burning, bare nerve, with shooting pain from my inner thigh. It was the last thing I remembered as I passed out.

The morning bell woke me and as I opened my eyes, I could see Letty tending to my arm. Within seconds the reality of my situation became all too real. I was in excruciating pain. My arm and groin were throbbing, and even thinking about moving caused my face to contort and my body to writhe. Letty was rubbing something on my arm when she noticed me awake.

"Lie still. You've got to be still until we finish putting this salve on your burns." She said soothingly. "It's gonna be all right, but it's gonna hurt somethin' terrible for a couple of days."

I don't think I said anything, but I must have moaned. I didn't want to be awake.

"This is arnica and lard, to promote the healin' of your wounds." She told me, "It's a salve made by heatin' an ounce of flowers and an ounce of lard, but you've got to leave it on for it to help. You can stay here with me today and rest."

Rest? My mind sprung into reality.

"Letty!" I said trying to sit up, "I can't rest, I have to check on Genevieve, and then take Lucy's place in the field. There's no time to rest." I tried my best to get up, but the pain made me dizzy.

"See? You ain't a-goin' nowhere today. Lucy's just gonna have to get out there and work. She'll be okay. You let her rest last night."

"Where's Angus? She'll want to know where Angus is."

"Angus is fine. Some of us are takin' turns with him. We'll keep him here with us so she don't have to carry him, today."

"Letty, please! This is something I have to do. Don't you see? If I rest today, I could never live with myself. Lucy doesn't get a choice, why should I? I'm going out there whether you let me or not, so please help me."

"If you're gonna be that stubborn and get out there, then I've got a dress for you to wear until we mend that one. You can keep it. But, you have to keep this salve on you, or it will get infected. Come on!"

"Thank you, but, no, I don't need it. Mine is fine." I told her. I didn't want a new dress. I wanted to wear this one, and stand proud.

"You are stubborn one, that's for sure! But, there's no need." Letty told Penelope to go tell Lucy I was going to take her place in the field today and she needed to stay in bed and rest. She then told me she was going to get me a dress and she'd be right back, but not without demanding I lie back down until she returned.

I slumped back down on the bed, grimacing as I went. How was I going to make it through today? He had branded my right arm and I was right handed. He had branded the inside of my upper thigh and walking would be an issue. The more I fretted over this and thought about it, the worse it felt. I had to move and keep moving without showing or feeling pain. I was not going to let Mr. Lott take me down, nor did I want him to turn this incident in to any reason why slaves should not stand up to their owners.

Letty came back with a dress, and helped me change. I could not see my arm completely, but I could see the brand in between my legs. I looked down at it, and then up at Letty.

"It's the initials of Belle Terre. It's to show that you are the property of this plantation." She told me.

I couldn't stand the thought of looking at it. I asked her to help me slip on the dress, but she insisted we put more salve on it before I dressed.

I was in so much pain, I had no modesty. People were coming and going for the day, and I lied back down to allow Letty to apply the salve and then wrap scraps of cloth around it to protect the salve from coming off and my rubbing it.

She then pulled my arm out to wrap the cloth around the salve. I didn't have to ask her what this brand was, for she offered, freely. "This one is a brand to show others you are a difficult slave."

I turned my head from her to cry, I tried to stop, but the tears just came.

"I told you the devil would come back, and he did. I'm sorry you had to learn this way, but now you know what we all live with. Now you know why we don't do some of the things you expect us to do. We're all just tryin' to get by."

I knew what she meant, and pulled myself back together to get up and get dressed. I was crying from pain, not from pity and I didn't want anyone to think I was worth the pity. I wasn't. They ALL were, but they didn't act that way, and I didn't want them to think I was any different.

I put on Letty's dress and she helped me fix my hair. She gave me something for pain she called Belladonna. She told me it would help some. I told her I would be back as soon as I checked on Genevieve and Mr. Patout, and then I walked out the door.

As I walked to Isum and the cart, there was a strange silence that came over the grounds. People were there and walking towards the fields, but they stopped for a moment and watched me. I inched up into the cart without Isum's help and sat there proudly. Isum cracked the whip in the air, and we were off. I looked back at everyone standing there watching. They remained until we were out of site. It was surreal.

CHAPTER 9
A VISIT FROM KERRY

Word had not made it to the main house, yet, and Nane was worried about Mr. Patout. During the night he had started to run a fever. He was bedridden today and Nane was hustling about trying to make sure he felt better. In passing she asked what was wrong with my walk today, but spent no time on it and didn't wait for an answer. They had known about the fire in the fields, of course, but not about my incident, yet. And if I had learned anything, I've learned not to bring it up and talk about it. I was not going to do it this time.

Elizabeth wasn't doing well this morning, either. Genevieve was not up, yet, so Nane asked me to go and check on her. Elizabeth was lying on her bed and mumbling something in her native tongue. I switched out her rags and put a cool one on her forehead. She looked up at me, but didn't seem to know who I was.

"Elizabeth, you should be so proud of your sons. They are such good men. They are strong and loyal." I told her.

She looked at me and smiled. "They are good boys aren't they? They will be the ruler of our tribe one day."

"And they will be good ones." I said to her as she rolled away and faced the wall. She was going to rest, which was probably the best thing for her.

I was torn. I knew Nane probably needed me up here at the main house today, but they also needed me in the field. They had to get that crop taken care of before we lost it. When Nane came back down, I spoke to her about it.

"Nane, I know you need me here, but Lucy is very sick and if someone doesn't take her place in the field, then she will have to work. If she does work, she might get sicker and die. She has Angus to think about."

"And what are you supposin'?" She asked me.

"I need to go work for her and take her place. Everything is basically done for the party, and Genevieve can take a day off from studies. If you'll let me go today, I promise to be back tomorrow and I will help you get the house prepared for whoever is arriving."

She stood there with her hands on her hips, looking at me, not saying a thing.

Finally, she said, "All right, but you have to promise me you will be back here tomorrow morning. Early!"

"Yes, I promise." I told her and hugged her. I informed her Elizabeth was fine, but was resting.

"That's probably the best thing for her today, too. Whatever this stuff is, it better not spread. We have a party and guests to entertain."

"All right, I will see you in the morning." And I turned to walk out the door.

"Oh, Mr. Williams has Isum and George working in the field, too, so you'll have to walk back." She said.

I stopped, thinking about the pain of just standing. I knew walking the entire way was something I did not relish doing. Nane saw my hesitation.

"Is there something you need to tell me?" She asked.

"No, no, of course not. I'll just walk back. Tell Genevieve I'll see her tomorrow." And I walked out and back to the fields.

My walk was painful and distorted. I walked spread legged, and had to lift the toe of the burned leg and bend my knee slightly to continue moving it. I cried. I was in such terrific pain. I stopped every now and then, leaning against the closest tree, knowing I needed to keep moving and get back to the fields. I pitied myself. I knew I shouldn't, but I couldn't help it. Oh my goodness! I was in such pain!

By the time I arrived, the rag wrapped around my thigh was loose, so I reached up under my skirt and retied it, tighter than Letty had. The wrap had to stay on my leg for I was needed in the field right away. I slipped in line with the others and began the long hard day of pulling stalks and packing carts for the plant. My arm hurt. My leg was killing me, and now my back ached beyond belief. I wasn't sure I could walk home after the long day. We were like the walking dead heading back to our graves. Moving, but motionless and worn ragged.

I looked around and watched the silent crowd walking home. Everyone was in pain and exhausted. I saw burned shirts and pants, and pink, raw skin, exposed to the air. I wasn't the only one in pain. We all were.

I returned to our shack and fell on to the bed. Henrietta came over to check on me, but I was too tired to say a thing. She slipped my arm out of my sleeve to check my wound, then stood up and left the shack. I was drifting in and out of consciousness when I realized Henrietta must have gone to get Letty. They were talking, but my mind wasn't coherently processing what they were saying.

They slipped my other arm out, and pulled the dress from my body. I felt as though I was in some strange dream. I knew they were there, but my reality was distorted. Kerry was there, too. She was guiding them and helping. Stroking my head for comfort and talking to me.

"Letty, this leg's already infected, and it's gonna get worse if we don't do something about it right now," Henrietta said.

"You're right, Henrietta. She's cold and clammy. I think she's goin' into shock. We've got to get her warm," said Letty, as I heard her yell to Penelope. "Bring me some more Arnica salve, and Henrietta, let's get her bed closer to the fire."

Kerry continued to stroke my head as they moved my bed. The women continued working on me as I listened to Kerry.

"What have you gotten yourself into?" Asked Kerry, as she lay down next to me and hugged me tightly. "This is a mess!"

"I know, but I had no other choice." I told her.

"Oh, you had a choice, but your stubborn Irish will and Catholic guilt helped you make your decision. You hurt something awful, now, but what you have done will forever change your future."

"What do you mean?"

"You have a destiny that you must fulfill. You were brought here for a much bigger reason than you think. Why do you think you are here?" She asked me.

"Because I was kidnapped. You should know that." I told her.

"Yes, but don't you think it's possible there was a reason you were kidnapped?"

"Not a good one. How could there be a good one?" I asked her.

"Well, you think about it." She told me. "You are not the only one in the world who injustice has visited, but you are determined and strong-willed enough to do something about it."

"I'm doing the best I can. I'm trying to make the best of my situation until Brody or Captain come to get me."

"You can't wait on them. You must take steps to help people on your own terms. You help yourself and others along the way."

'What do you mean?" I asked her.

"You are here to help slaves and ensure their freedom. You must make a very difficult choice in the week ahead, but I know you will make the right one. You can help the Underground Railroad from the inside, and you must."

"The Underground Railroad?" I asked.

"Yes, and the slaves you come in contact with. You must find a way to help them. You are part of their lives, now." Kerry said. "They are the hostages of this system. Remember how you felt being Irish in a British world. You were treated as paupers and vagrants on your own land. Unable to live as human beings should. We migrated to America for a better future, now why shouldn't the Negroes live in a better America? Why should only the fair skinned race be the ruling class?"

"You're right," I told her, "the Negroes should be free. I just don't know what I can do to make a difference?"

"They know what to do, you just need to help. You have the benefit of being fair skinned. Use it to their advantage and help. Remember what Nella said? Think, Allie, think! I know you can do this." Said Kerry as she stood up and leaned over me, smiling before she disappeared.

I looked up at her, and then she was gone. I glanced down towards my body, and saw Letty and Henrietta tying my legs apart on the bed. My arms were already tied down, and I tried to talk and pull, but Letty put her hand over my mouth.

"Rest," she said, "we've tied you down to keep you from rubbing your burns. You've got to allow air to get to them. If you keep rubbing them, your infection will get worse. We'll stay with you tonight. Try and go back to sleep. Rest, now."

I didn't have it in me to argue. She gave me some more medicine to swallow, and brushed my head, telling me to go to sleep. I heard other people in the room, but I didn't have the energy or the concern to open my eyes and see them. I knew I was almost naked, but I didn't care anymore. I wanted this pain to go away. The pain in my groin was so intense, I barely thought about my arm. It hurt, but my leg was unbearable.

Kerry came to me often, and we had several discussions. We talked of Ireland and of our families, and she sang to me just like she always did on the ship. I lost track of time. Time that had no measure. I was in my own world and had no idea of real time. I didn't know whether I passed out or fell asleep, but I awoke to Penelope standing over me and calling for Letty.

"Letty! Letty! She's awake! Come quick!"

I opened my eyes, trying to focus on my surroundings and get my bearings. I heard movement in the room, and then saw Letty bending down over me.

"Child, you gave us quite a scare!" Said Letty. "But I think you're gonna be all right. Your fevers down and your color is looking better. I don't think Nane would have let you die. She's been worried sick. Running back and forth between the house and here as often as she can. She even brought Genevieve this last time since your color was looking better."

"Like this?" I asked, knowing I might have been exposed inappropriately.

"No, no, no." Said Letty. "We covered you up after the second day. I think tomorrow we can put you back in your clothes."

I sighed with relief knowing Genevieve had not seen me strapped down and naked on the bed. It would have been an awful image for anyone, especially a little girl. As I took in what Letty said, I realized she said, "after the second day." Had I been out for two days?

"Letty," I asked her, "how many days have I been out?"

"Three days," she said. "You rubbed your burnt leg so badly, the skin rubbed off completely between your legs and an infection set in. The rubbing was so severe, I don't even think you'll be able to make out the branding letters. It will be an awful scar, though. I've tried to keep the salve on it, and it will help, but you've lost that skin."

"Three days?" My mind was set on the amount of time I had been out. "Then Genevieve's party is in two days? I must get up!"

"Not right now, you're not. You're gonna lie still until we tell you to get up or I'll have to tie you down again. Do you understand?"

I nodded my head knowing I did not want to be tied down. I wasn't in as much pain as I had been before, but I still felt both areas, and I remained quite stiff. I had a blanket over me and tried to move a little.

"Not very much," said Penelope, "you heard what Letty said. She doesn't want you movin' none. She's gone to get word to Nane you're awake. Nane will be very happy."

"What's happening in the fields? Are they going to be saved? Will there be much of a crop?" I asked Penelope.

"I think so. I heard the men a talkin' 'bout it, and they seem to say it is goin' to be all right. Another two days' work to be done, but they say it will get done."

"Good. And what about Mr. Lott and Mr. Belcher? Has anything happened to them?"

"I hadn't heard nothin' about them, but I know Mr. Williams and Mr. Patout have people out lookin' for 'em," said Penelope.

I nodded and lied there, looking around the room.

"Penelope," I asked her, "Do you know what time it

is?"

"All's I know it's about lunchtime." She said. "Do you think you're up to eatin' somethin'?"

"I don't' think so, not yet." I told her.

"Now that you're starting to come around, I best get back to the kitchen for Letty. You be all right?"

"Yes," I said, "You go on. I'll be fine."

Penelope left the room and I lied there silently, moving only in little bits. I was scared to death to have my legs touch one another. I had the most awful image of my thighs and the rawness that must be exposed. I didn't want to make it worse and knew I had to keep them and my arm away from anything, so I just lied there letting my mind wander. I tried not to think of the incident with Mr. Lott and Mr. Belcher. That only made my pain worse. My brain raced with hatred and anger. I knew neither would help me get well, but channeling it to prove them wrong inspired me.

I thought of Kerry and what she said. I thought of Nella, and the Captain, and for some reason, Brody. I always ended up thinking about Brody. Maybe Ma was right. Maybe Brody was more important to me than I had ever considered. He was always coming back into my life. Both in my mind and accidentally. Maybe there was more to it than I knew. Maybe Rufina was right, too, and Mr. Barnes. If I wasn't thinking about Jonathan all of the time, then who? Who, was Brody. Oh my goodness. Had everyone seen it, but me? Was I like Ma, not seeing the signs while everyone else did?

I thought about the times I was angry with him, and the time I had wasted in our letters. He was probably with Finola now, and possibly married. I wished him well, but I wished him here with me right now. We had been through so much. He could be strong for me and help me through these times. He would tell me what to do and how to go about it. Yes, I was thinking of Brody in a whole new light, and my heart yearned to hear from him and be comforted by his words.

The last time I saw him in Ireland was as
the ship pulled away from the dock. He had turned

around to wave, I think. He seemed as upset as me in our departure. If only he had seen me in New Orleans. There he was, standing in his suit, looking tall and handsome. What a fine-looking man he had become, even if I only saw him from a distance. I'm glad he is doing well. I'm glad I was able to see him. I'm glad he is all right. I am comforted thinking of him being happy and content. It pleases me in a very extraordinary way.

Letty checked on me to see if I felt like eating something. I told her I didn't, but promised I would try later. She told me Nane would check on me as soon as lunch was over for Mr. Patout and Genevieve.

"How is Mr. Patout feeling?" I asked her.

'He is better, but is still poor tired. Nane says he doesn't want to damper Genevieve's birthday party. She is very excited."

"I'm glad." I told her.

"You stay down and Nane will be along as soon as she can. I'll check on you myself a little later. I have to get Penelope back to the fields this afternoon so she can help," Letty said as she walked out.

I was there alone, again, and tired. I slipped off to asleep, hoping Kerry would visit me in my dreams. I must have rubbed my legs together because the pain of it shocked me awake. I yelped and jerked. No one was there, so I tried sitting up and letting me legs fall off the bed. I kept them apart, but I sat up. I felt a little weak, but surely that was to be expected.

Nane came in and saw me sitting up. "Well, look who's up and alive! Good thing, missy. We were all quite worried about you. This has been a mess of a week you picked to get yourself branded and sick!"

"But I…"

"I know. I'm just a playin' with you." Nane said.

I looked down and she helped me roll back over on my back and lie down.

"Now we have a party to put on for a special little girl, and she wants you to be there."

"I will, of course." I tired getting up again.

"No you don't!" Nane pushed me back down. "We want you to be there, so you have to rest the rest of today. If you feel all right, maybe you can come to the house tomorrow, but only if Letty allows says so."

"How is everyone else?" I asked her.

"Fine. Just fine. Our whole focus is having this party come off as perfect as possible."

"Have the guests responded? Are there children coming for Genevieve?" I asked.

"Yes," she said, "about twenty children should be there from the surrounding area, and even New Orleans."

"And Mrs. Clarkson, is she coming?"

"Lordy, yes, and we are expecting her tomorrow. She's to help with the party." Said Nane.

"Help? What is she supposed to do that you haven't already done?"

"Nothing! Absolutely nothing, but Mr. Patout invited her and she inserted herself in the festivities, rather than just being a guest."

"What does Mr. Patout say?"

"Humph!" Moaned Nane, "Nothing! He hasn't been feeling his best, and he lets that woman run all over him. That's one reason Genevieve wants you back quickly. She's afraid she will be stuck with her, and you know how she doesn't like that! Mrs. Clarkson is bringing her nieces who have been sent to live with her."

"Are they Genevieve's age?"

"One is fourteen, and I think Mr. Patout said the other was ten, so they are a little bit older."

"Maybe they will be good for her. Maybe they will be all right. Do you think?" I asked Nane.

"I don't know, but I don't have a good feeling about any of 'em."

I smiled at Nane, and we chatted a little longer. She didn't have too much time because she needed to get back to Genevieve. I told her I would see her at the main house tomorrow. She scolded me reminding me, only if Letty allowed me too, and then walked out the door.

Letty came in later and brought the salve and more bandages. I told her that if she would show me how to do it, I could take care of myself from now on. I told her how much I appreciated her help, truly. She wasn't one to take praise so she ignored my gratefulness and began showing me how to apply the salve.

It was my first time to actually look at my burns since I had been out for three days. My shoulder and arm were black, with crumpled skin and tender spots. Letty said the one on my shoulder should be okay, but I would have the brand scar forever. The one in between my legs was revolting. I wasn't sure I could stomach it, and it was my own leg! I turned away, but Letty said I had to watch and make sure I did the salve and wrapping carefully.

"Letty, how can you do this? It's so awful looking." I said.

"Someone's got to do it. You're not the first one who's been branded. Burns are bad, and whippings are bad. Both cut deep into the skin and you have to worry about infection settin' in. Yours coulda been worse, but you pulled through the fever and the infection. Now come on, let's show you how to do this. Give me your hand!" She said firmly.

She took my hand and stuck it in the salve. We scooped out a handful and she made me touch my burned area and myself. I closed my eyes as I rubbed, feeling the pain and knowing what I was rubbing. I think my mind made it worse. Just thinking about it made my skin crawl and my head burst. I swallowed hard trying not to cry or get sick. Enough! I thought to myself. Swallow again and stop your crying!

Letty continued to manipulate my hands as though I was unable to do it myself. I was able, but she must have intuitively realized my abhorrence of my own leg and the hesitation I had at looking at it, and more importantly, the pain I was in, still. We tied it off and she told me to lie back down.

"You'll rest here one more night, then maybe tomorrow you can go to the main house."

"Thank you, Letty" I told her and looked up at the ceiling. Just doing the salve and the wrap exhausted me. What a weakling I am, I thought to myself. Get over this! Be strong!

I was strangely happy when I heard the field hands coming back in. I should have been embarrassed at the days I had spent here not working, and causing more people to work, but I felt a closeness to them I had not felt before. People stopped by to check on me, whether I had met them or not. They didn't really talk to me, but they took the time to come in and nod, then went about their own business.

I knew they must be tired and spending time with me was not on their list of things they needed to do, but that didn't seem to matter. Anna and Henrietta brought me something to eat and sat with me as I took a little in. I sat up with them on the bed, and listened to them talk about the harvesting. I didn't ask any questions, even though I had hundreds to ask.

As I was finishing, a crowd started to gather outside the building next door. I asked Anna what was happening.

"They're almost done with the harvesting and they are gathering to ask for inspiration and destiny." Anna said.

"Destiny? But they are almost done. Why destiny?" I asked her.

"Because it will take an inner purpose for all of us to overcome our station in life, and with every harvest, we feel hope. Hope that a new beginning is available for us. One of us can make a difference. Destiny…do you see?" She said.

Letty walked in, and said, "Cora, do you know you talk in your sleep?"

"No. What did I say?"

"You spoke of the Underground Railroad, and that Negroes should be free. You must be careful what you say. You can't always be sure people will be sympathetic to your beliefs. Look what has already happened to you! We thought you might be a spy placed here on purpose, but after what you've been through, and what you've said, most of us have changed our minds about you. You should listen to these Negroes as they sing and talk. They know about destiny and fate. They know of pain and sorrow."

"I want to know and hear what they have to say. May I go and listen?"

"You'll be able to hear right here, or over in that chair. We can move it closer to the door if you want, but you can't put your legs together, understand?"

We both smiled, and Anna moved the chair over by the door opening, and Letty helped me walk. I was so very stiff and sore. It hurt to stand up straight and walk. I wanted to drag my leg, and the attempt was a pitiful one at that. I was surprised how standing up pulled at my inner thigh, and supporting myself while getting up or down pulled at my arm. I sat down and watched what I could of the people gathering next door.

Lucy and Angus came over and Lucy sat down against the outer wall next to the doorway. She let Angus go and he crawled around the area, bumping in to people as he played. We both laughed at him. He was a precious baby boy. I was glad to see Lucy looking better. I didn't ask her anything, but I could see it in her face and actions she was feeling better.

The night was absorbing. There was music and storytelling, devotionals and confessions. There wasn't a white person there, well, except me, but no master, no overseer, no one to harm them at the moment. Penelope and Isum both came to check on me, and Henrietta even came and sat by me for a while. I felt as though I was being accepted. There was no obvious acknowledgement of me, but the feeling was different.

They were a few still singing when I decided to lie down. Henrietta helped me to my bed and checked the bandage. She covered me up, looked at me for a moment, and then walked to her bed. She looked back and gave me a smile or at least I believe it was, and then she lied down on her bed.

I woke up in excruciating pain, but knew I had to get up and get moving. Anna came over to me to help, but I waved her away. I needed to

do this all by myself. I unwrapped the bandages, slowly. At the last wrap, the stickiness of the salve on the bandages pulled at the skin or tissue it was pressed on. I closed my eyes and pulled at the bandage until the last bit pulled free. I took a deep breath in and looked down. Anna was standing there watching. She gasped and turned away. I understood her horror of it, but I had to continue with my task. I reapplied the salve and took the bandage I had just taken off, turned the fold, and started wrapping again. I did my legs and my arm as Letty had shown me.

Anna brought me something to eat, and sat with me as we ate. She then helped me get into my dress. I struggled, but eventually succeeded in looking half way acceptable. My walk would still be awkward, but to all outward appearances, I was all right.

Henrietta, Anna and Lucy were walking out the door, when Henrietta came over to me.

"Don't' be so stubborn that you don't ask for some Belladonna. You'll hurt worse during your day if you don't take some." She said, and out the door she went.

Anna giggled and nodded, while Lucy rolled her eyes and pushed Anna out the door.

"Take some," Lucy said, "don't stay in pain all day long."

"Thanks." I said and gathered myself to walk out the door and try to make the best of it.

Letty saw me coming, crossed her arms in front of her and said, "Look at you! You look like a praying mantis. Stiff as a board and walkin' with a wooden leg!"

Isum shook his head and laughed as he walked towards the cart.

"Are you goin' to be all right today?" Letty asked.

I nodded in the affirmative, even though I was in too much pain to talk.

"Uh, huh," said Letty, "You come in here and take some of this Belladonna. If you're gonna make it through the day, you need some of this."

She handed me the medicine, and I swallowed it.

"Now take this with you so you can take some more after lunch. All right?"

I shook my head, yes, again and walked towards to cart.

"Isum, you go easy on the ride. I don't think it's gonna be an enjoyable one at all."

I nodded and motioned goodbye with my hand. It was more of a pitiful attempt at waving, but I was intent at holding on to the sides of the cart and remaining as still as possible. My legs were apart and spread amidst the vegetables we were taking to Nane. I tried to balance myself to minimize the bumping that occurred while riding in the cart.

With each rock and rut I grimaced and clamped my teeth so hard my jaw hurt. I spent no time looking at the scenery as it passed or the road ahead and what was coming. I didn't care. I was engrossed in pain.

As we pulled up to the main house, I sat there trying to undo myself from my clamped down hands and my stapled feet. I wasn't sure if I was going to be able to move, but Nane came out and over to me.

"You can do it!" She said. "Come on, I'll help you."

I looked at her, took a deep breath in and released my grip from the sides. Okay, I thought, now your arms are relaxed, next comes the legs. I took another breath in and scooted forward and pushed up with my thigh. My eyes were clinched closed and my jaw remained in its clamped position as I rose up on my feet. Must the whole day be like this, I thought?

"That's good," said Nane, "Now turn towards me and step."

Isum had already removed the vegetables from the cart, so I didn't have any obstacles, but myself that is! I took another breath in, closed my eyes, and turned towards her.

"Come on," she said, "You can do it. Come right over here. Isum!" She yelled, "Come over her and lift her down from this cart."

Isum came over and they both waited as I slowly drug myself over to the edge of the cart.

"Now lean over a little so he can grasp you beneath your arms." Nane said.

I leaned over and in one swoop I was down and on

solid ground again. I made some kind of grunting noise and they both laughed. I didn't laugh, but I knew it must have sounded funny. Nane placed her hand on my back and helped me towards the kitchen.

"The more you move, the better you will feel. The less stiff you'll be." Said Nane.

I looked up at her with a questionable look, and she said, "You've got to believe me. The more you move, the better you'll feel. But," she reminded me, "do not rub those legs together. We don't want them infected, again. Can't have that, now can we?"

I shook my head, no, and we walked into the kitchen. I looked around but didn't see Elizabeth.

"Nane, where's Elizabeth?"

"She's not doin' so well. She's resting in our house. She's very weak."

"May I go and check on her?" I asked

Nane nodded and went to open the back screen door for me. I walked through and out towards their house. I opened the door slowly and walked in quietly. Elizabeth acted like she heard someone, but was talking in her native language. I bent over her and reached for her hands. Her eyes were glazed over and her skin was hot.

"Elizabeth, it's Cora." I reached down for a wet rag in a bucket beside her bed and tried to lay it on her forehead.

'No, no, no" she said, and then went on saying something I couldn't understand.

"All right, it's all right Elizabeth. Would you try to eat something?" I reached for her soup, but before I could get it, she stopped my arm, and shook her head.

I sat there with her, listening to her without knowing what she was saying. She was fading in and out as I sat there, and when she eventually fell off to sleep, I just looked at her thinking about her life and her memories. Here was this woman of royalty in another land, dying as a slave in a land created for freedom. Freedom for all, but Negroes.

I heard Nane calling me from the main house. I looked

down at Elizabeth as she lay there peacefully. I touched her hand and turned around to leave. As I reached for the doorway, Elizabeth whispered something.

I turned back towards her and to her bedside. "Elizabeth? Did you say something?"

"You must do what's right. Your heart will heal. I know." She said and then drifted back to sleep.

I didn't understand what she meant, but I heard her words. I thought about it as I walked towards the main house. Genevieve was up and outside in her nightgown. She was running towards me with her arms reaching up. I knew she wanted to jump on me, and I cringed at the thought of what was about to happen.

"Genevieve!" I yelled. "I'm so glad to see you! Come here!" And up my arms went and out to catch her. I braced myself and in an instant she was in my arms and hugging me. I wasn't able to twirl around, but we shifted side-to-side, and hugged.

"I'm glad you're better, Cora." She said. "Everyone has been sick and it's almost my birthday. I was afraid you might not be able to make it!"

"Not be able to make your birthday? How could I miss it! It is going to be so much fun! I bet you can hardly wait."

"I can't, but Nane keeps telling me I must!"

We both looked at Nane in the doorway of the kitchen, and everyone smiled.

"That's right, you're going to have to wait. Now everyone come in her and let's get some breakfast into that one day away birthday girl!"

We were all happy and cheerful as we stepped into the kitchen. Even me with my awkward waddle, and slow moving motions. I tried not to make faces as I moved, but sometimes it was too difficult to keep inside. Nane and Genevieve thought I was quite funny, and Genevieve mimicked me at times making us all laugh.

The day went by with Genevieve showing me everything set up for her party. It was looking lovely, and I was amazed at the decorations and the flowers everywhere. She even showed me an original maypole Isum made for her. She said they would be playing with it tomorrow. She was so excited. As she showed me the swing we had hung up months before, her father stepped out onto the porch and asked if I would come in to see him.

I was stunned to see him looking so weak. What in the world was going around making so many people ill? He had lost weight and there were circles around his eyes. Genevieve told him she wasn't finished showing me everything, but he told her she could show me later. I took her into the kitchen to be with Nane, and then met him in the living room. He was sitting on a tall back chair with his legs crossed and his hands in his lap.

"Cora, please sit down. I'd like to talk to you." He said in a very melancholy tone. "Please sit down."

He motioned to the loveseat across from him and I went over and sat down slowly, trying not to show my pain.

"Cora, I was mortified to hear what happened to you. When I heard what had happened and that you were not doing well, I came over to see you. I know it means nothing, but I want you to know we are looking for these two awful men. They are being charged for the fire, the damage to the field, and the branding of you. I did not authorize or approve of any such action. I want you to know that."

I lowered my head and said, "I know that Mr. Patout. I never considered you or Mr. Williams as part of their evil plot. They might have had help from someone else, but I know it is not you." I looked up and right at him.

He was returning my look and conveying sincere empathy for me.

"As you walked in here, I could see the pain and difficulty in your movement. I am sorry for that. Are you going to be all right for Genevieve's party?" He asked me.

"Oh, yes. I need to keep moving, and Letty has been very good to keep me with medicine and clean wraps. So many people have been very kind to me through this. I am quite appreciative. Thank you for asking."

"Well, I wanted you to know we will hold those men and anyone else accountable for their actions."

"Thank you. Is there anything else I can do for you?" I asked as I carefully stood up from the loveseat.

"Do you remember Mrs. Clarkson? She is bringing her two nieces to the party, and they will be arriving sometime today. Please make sure Genevieve makes an honest effort to welcome them. It is going to be very hard for her. I have discussed it with her, but I believe she has grown to feel a very special connection with you, and I was hoping you could help her be more open to them."

"I am honored and will gladly talk to her about the young ladies coming. How long will they be staying?"

"As long as Mrs. Clarkson would like to stay. She is quite a determined and strong willed woman who has intentions beyond our friendship. I am considering what is best for Genevieve, and this time together will help me decide." He told me. "Cora, have you seen the invitation list?"

"No, sir, I haven't."

"I have invited our Factor to come to Genevieve's party. You know them, correct?"

I was taken aback, unable to speak.

"Cora? You know them. Is that correct?" He asked again.

I blinked and adjusted myself, trying to realize the enormity of his statement.

"Yes, sir. Yes! I do know them, your transport agents, correct? And they are coming tomorrow?"

"No, I do not believe 'they' are. I believe they only responded for one. I do not know who it is, but surely you will know whomever it is if they are the people you say they are. Oui?"

"Oui, I mean, yes, of course." I stood there, frozen, my mind racing through a thousand scenarios. Mr. Patout noticed me completely engrossed.

"Cora, are you going to be all right?" He asked, but I said nothing, again.

"Cora, do you need something? Is something wrong?" He was pushing for an answer.

"I'm sorry, I am so shocked at the possibility of seeing someone I know; someone that can clear this up for me. Forgive me, I will go and get back to Genevieve." I looked at him and remembered I needed to talk to her about Mrs. Clarkson's nieces. "I will discuss Mrs. Clarkson's nieces with her and we will welcome them with open arms and complete generosity."

"Thank you, Cora. I appreciate your help in this matter."

He stood up and smiled at me as I left the room. I wobbled back slowly to the kitchen. This time it wasn't just because of my wounds, but because of what he told me. Might I see Captain? Might I see Mr. Farraday, or Robert? Or, might I actually see Brody? Might Brody be here to take me home? My mind was still racing as I entered the kitchen.

I plopped down on the bench in the kitchen and knocked the back of my head against the wall. I stared across the way at the cabinets, stunned. I didn't notice the others in the room had stopped talking and were looking at me. The room was silent, but not my head. My head was fully occupied with thoughts and questions of what tomorrow might bring.

Nane came over to me and stood in front of me. "Girl, what has come over you?"

Genevieve ran over and sat by me, waiting for an answer, too.

Nane waved her hand in front of me and then snapped her fingers trying to get me out of my stupor.

"Can you speak? Has the cat got your tongue? What did he say to you to make you look like this?"

I still didn't know what to say, so she grabbed my cheeks with her hand and squeezed her fingers making my lips scrunch. Forcing me to answer.

"Captain, I mean Mr. Patout, has invited his transportation agents, or Factors." I spatted out.

"What does that mean? Who is Captain? What are Factors?" Asked Genevieve quite excitedly.

"I accidentally said Captain because he is the man who had taken care of me since I arrived in America." I looked up at Nane and said, "He is a stationmaster."

"What's that?" Asked Genevieve.

"She means he works at a station. Didn't you, Cora?" She asked, but actually was telling me something. I shouldn't have said what I did about Captain, and so I caught on to her hint and covered up.

"Nane's right, Cora, not a station, but a port. He is a Captain of a ship and he transports goods or cargo." I looked up at Nane, but she had absolutely no response or expression for my comment. She moved on.

"So go on, what did Mr. Patout say that got you so consumed?" Asked Nane.

"I told you, he has invited his Factor."

"But why would that matter to you?" Nane asked.

"Because I *know* them! The family he hired to transport his sugar is a family I have known my entire life. The mother, who is now deceased, God rest her soul, taught my brother and I how to read and write, and to love books and literature, and languages, and…"

"All right, so you know them and obviously like them. How does this change things for you?" Asked Nane.

"Yes, what does it mean?" Asked Genevieve.

"I'm not sure. Whoever comes can show proof I was kidnapped and I am not really a slave. I could be free tomorrow. Can you believe it? Brody might be on his way right now to prove I am not a slave. I might be able to leave with him. Don't you understand my disbelief? My total absorption in the whole situation?" I tried getting up and spinning around, but my leg stopped me in middle spin.

"A little too absorbed I would say," said Nane, "maybe we should think through this."

"Yes, Cora. Must you leave here, now? My birthday is tomorrow, and Mrs. Clarkson and those two awful nieces of hers are on their way. I don't want you to leave right now. Please say you won't go! I couldn't stand it! Not now!" begged Genevieve.

I looked down at her and realized I was being selfish at a time when she should be the center of attention. "Of course, Genevieve, I wouldn't leave you right now. I'm probably just dreaming, anyway. It will probably never come true."

I picked her up on the side of me that wasn't hurt and hugged her as we walked over to the kitchen table. She stood on the bench and faced me.

"You have other things to show me don't you? We have a party to get ready for." I looked at Nane and she told me we would talk later. She was busy spinning sugar into little baskets for Genevieve's guests. Nane was going to put candy and sweets into each as a party gift. The older guests were getting carefully formed sugar roses about the size of your palm. You could eat it or use it as decoration. Both favors took quite a bit of artistic ability. Nane said it came with being on a sugar plantation and working with sugar all of the time.

I took Genevieve's hand and helped her jump down and we walked out the kitchen, up the stairs, and towards her room. She excitedly told me about her dress and that we needed to decide how to do her hair. She had all kinds of ribbons and bows out in a mess on her dresser. We sorted through them and tried different ways of fixing her hair.

We had a red and white dotted swiss ribbon in her hair, when we heard her father beckon. We stepped out of her room and walked over to the banister and looked down at him.

"Genevieve, Mrs. Clarkson and her nieces are here. Won't you come down and make them feel welcome?" He asked.

"Yes, Pa-Pa." Said Genevieve and she turned and walked back to her room. I was still looking down at him when he gave me raised eyebrows and motioned his head towards the living room. I smiled, nodded, and turned towards Genevieve's room, knowing I had a mission to accomplish.

'Genevieve, mon enfant," I said to her, "let's make the best of this. They will only be here for a couple of days, and who knows, maybe it will be fun."

"You know it won't. I don't want them here! It is my birthday, why do they have to be here?" She asked.

"Because Mrs. Clarkson and your father are friends, and they are her nieces who are now living with her. We must be polite young ladies and welcome them into your home." I told her. "You weren't sure about me when I arrived, and look how well we get along, now."

She shrugged her shoulders and looked away.

"Genevieve, I'll be right there by your side. They might be very nice young ladies who you enjoy being with. Let's give them a chance. Que dites-vous?" That was my pitiful try at asking her 'what do you say?' in French. She laughed and gave me a hug.

"All right, but you can't leave! You HAVE to stay by me." She begged.

"Bien!" I said and she laughed again as I took her hand and we turned towards the doorways and went out to the stairs.

CHAPTER 10
FOLLOW THE DRINKING GOURD

We quietly entered the doorway of the living room without them noticing. They continued to talk as we stood there, hand in hand. Mrs. Clarkson and her nieces noticed first, then Mr. Patout.

"Genevieve! How wonderful you look in your pretty white ribbon!" said Mrs. Clarkson.

"It's red and white dotted swiss," she told her.

"Come here and let me see." Mrs. Clarkson asked.

Genevieve looked up at me and I motioned with my head for her to go over.

She stood there so I whispered, "I'll stay right here, I promise."

She slowly walked over to Mrs. Clarkson and bent her head down so she could see the ribbon.

"Well, you are right. It is red and white dotted swiss. Your father must have bought you many beautiful ribbons and bows for such a lovely young lady."

"My mother gave them to me." Genevieve told her in a very stern manner. I could tell she was not at all comfortable playing nice with Mrs. Clarkson.

"Genevieve," said her father, "Genevieve, these two young ladies are Mrs. Clarkson's nieces." Genevieve leaned into him as he introduced the girls.

"This is Molly Anne, and this is Lilly May Pagett." Mr. Patout pointed to the girls, but it must have been the wrong names for Mrs. Clarkson quickly jumped in to correct him.

"No, no, Bernard. This is Molly Anne and this is Lula May. Genevieve, Molly Anne is fourteen years old and Lula May is twelve. I think you three will get along quite well. Won't you girls?"

Mrs. Clarkson looked at her nieces who smiled broadly and nodded their heads.

I spoke up to help Genevieve. "Genevieve, how about you and I show Molly Anne and Lula May where they will be staying while they are visiting?"

"That would be wonderful!" said Mr. Patout, "Why don't you do that Genevieve? I'm sure they would also like to see the activities we have planned for the party tomorrow."

Genevieve reluctantly walked back to me and stood there without saying a thing.

"All right Molly Anne and Lula May, why don't you follow us, and we'll show you to your room. I bet Isum has already put your luggage in there and it will be waiting for you." I told them and then nodded at Mr. Patout.

The four of us went up the stairs. The girls did not say very much as we showed them around the house. Nane was in their room unpacking their things and hanging up their dresses. Molly Anne seemed quite disturbed. Nane had started putting her things away without asking her permission.

"I'm sorry, Miss," said Nane, "I just thought..."

"Well you shouldn't!" said Molly Anne. "Aunt Charlene has a particular way of wanting her things taken care of, and I do, too!"

Genevieve squeezed my hand hard. I was embarrassed for Nane being treated that way. "She's only trying to help. I'm sure she didn't mean anything by it Nane, did you Molly Anne?"

"I surely did. Was it too hard to understand? Wait for Aunt Charlene to tell you what to do." said Molly.

I was stunned, and Nane humphed and turned around to leave. Molly Anne looked as though she was going to say something else when I broke in.

"Why don't we show them the Maypole, Genevieve?"

"You have a Maypole? What fun. Where is it?" asked

Lula May.

I waited a moment for Genevieve to answer her, but she stood there silently.

"I'm surprised you didn't see it when you came towards the house. It is out front. Let's go see it." I told them and motioned for us to head out of the room.

The girls stepped out and then to the side so Genevieve and I could get in front and lead them downstairs and outside. They were whispering about something, but I couldn't hear them well enough to understand.

"Why do you walk like that?" asked Molly Anne.

"Because she's hurt!" barked Genevieve.

I squeezed her hand to stop talking like that and tried to answer the best way I could.

"I have a terrible burn on my leg, but it will get better and my walking will improve. It is an odd way to walk, isn't it?" I tried to make light of the burn and my walk, hoping they would move on.

"How could anyone burn themselves on their leg? What were you doing?" Molly Anne asked again.

"Didn't you hear her? It was an ACCIDENT!" Genevieve barked, again. I knew she was trying to help, but her attitude was not acceptable.

"Genevieve!" I said, "We must not talk to our guests in that tone. I'm sure they hear you and understand now that it was an accident. Why don't you practice on the Maypole? Since my walking is so awkward, I'll just watch the three of you."

They started out rather stiffly, but as the time went on they lightened up and all three seemed to have a pleasant time. When they looked like they had had enough, I suggested we walk around back to the swing. They liked that idea and so we headed around the side of the house and to the Pecan Tree.

"May I go first?" asked Lula May.

"Of course you can." said Molly Anne. "Here, I'll push you."

Lula May scooted in to the swing seat and Molly Anne pulled back on the ropes to get a good start. Genevieve and I didn't have to say a thing for they had assumed their positions and were entertaining themselves without our help.

Genevieve and I sat down on the ground to watch. As I awkwardly maneuvered myself down, I glanced over towards Nane and Elizabeth's house. I saw Nane scurrying out and back to the main house, and then back again carrying something, which I assumed, was for Elizabeth. She looked quite distraught and I wondered whether I should go and ask her if I could help. I knew Genevieve would not want me to leave her, but I wanted to know about Nane.

Before I knew it, Molly Anne was crying and holding her head. She had stopped pushing Lula May, and Lula May was twisted in her swing seat trying to see what had happened. I stood up as quickly as I could and went over to Molly Anne trying to see what had happened to her. Genevieve was rolling on her back laughing and Molly Anne was telling her to stop. There was quite a commotion, and I was doing my best to calm Molly Anne and find out what had happened.

Mrs. Clarkson came running out, followed by Mr. Patout. She was yelling at me and asking Molly Anne what I did. Molly Anne pointed up at the tree and we all looked quizzically, and then back down at her.

Mr. Patout raised his voice to be louder than Molly Anne and asks Genevieve what she was laughing at.

"Genevieve, what has happened? Why are you laughing at Molly Anne?" Mr. Patout asked her.

Genevieve was holding her stomach and continued to laugh.

"Genevieve, please!" He begged her.

"The pecans! As Lula May was swinging, the pecans fell on her head! It's only the pecans!" said Genevieve, in between her giggling.

Mr. Patout and I smiled realizing the situation, but Mrs. Clarkson and Molly Anne walked sternly into the house. Lula May slipped off her swing seat and followed them in. Mr. Patout came over to Genevieve and helped her up.

"Genevieve, mon amour, you must try harder. It is not

polite to laugh at another person's mishap. She was hurt and we should have helped. Let's try to do better." He said to her.

"Yes, Pa-Pa, I will try, but it will be very hard for me to do. They are not nice."

"But you have just met them. How would

you know? They seem like very nice young ladies to me, and they are our guests. You must be considerate. Oui?"

"Oui, Pa-Pa." said Genevieve, and the two of them went inside, and I followed.

"Mr. Patout, may I check on Nane for a moment? I want to make sure she doesn't need any help with dinner." I asked him.

"Of course, Cora, Genevieve will be fine with me and our guests." He said.

She looked at me with skepticism in her eyes, but she was with her father and felt safe with him. They walked into the living room as I walked towards the kitchen. I heard them talking about Margaret as I moved on. Nane was washing some rags and heading back out the screen door as I walked in.

"Nane, what's wrong? Has something happened to Elizabeth?" I asked her.

"Come on with me, I'll tell you as we walk." Nane said. "Elizabeth has Malaria, but isn't coping very well. I just don't think she's strong enough to pull through. It's the same as Mr. Patout, but he is much stronger."

"The same as Mr. Patout? What are you saying? He has Malaria?"

"Yes, but he is hanging on and struggling through it, I think he will be all right. He looks much better today. Don't you think? Oh, you haven't seen him in a couple of days, have you? Well, he is doing better." Nane continued as we walked in their house.

She was going on worry, I believe.

"Elizabeth, it's Cora and me. Are you holding on there? We're right here."

We were walking to her bedside when Nane turned to me and said, "I've sent Isum to get her sons. They should be here."

And back around she turned to tend to Elizabeth. She sent for her sons? Elizabeth must be worse off than I thought. What has happened in these last few days? I knelt down next to Elizabeth's bed, at her feet, and watched Nane take care of her. She was comforting her and talking to her.

Elizabeth was breathing heavily. I guess there was nothing we could do, but sit with her and be with her so she wouldn't be alone. As I sat there, I thought about everyone I loved that was gone. I thought about Quinlan and how I wasn't there when he died. There is so much sorrow in life. You never know when things will change, for the better or the worse.

Dan and Louis came in and walked over to their mother. "Mamangu, it's Louis and me," said Dan.

I stood up and stepped away from the bed, allowing them to get next to her. Nane stayed with both of them. They were talking in their native tongue, and I felt like I was intruding so I stepped out of the house. Isum and Mr. Williams were outside and asking about her. I wasn't sure what to say except she didn't look well. We stood there for a moment, and then I stated I should get back to Genevieve and would they let me know if something happened. Mr. Williams nodded and I headed back in to the house.

I had forgotten to take my belladonna earlier, so I poured some water and swallowed it to help with the aching. The day was almost over, but I knew it had the possibility of being a very long day. I checked the food for dinner, and then the dining room table to make sure it was set for the evening meal. Isum stepped in and told me that Letty and Penelope were gonna come and help with the meal and they would want to be with Elizabeth anyway. I thanked him and then headed back to the living room.

Mrs. Clarkson was telling some grand story and her nieces were giggling. Genevieve was sitting with her father and they were both watching her. When Mr. Patout saw me come to the doorway, he stood up from Genevieve and took me in to the hallway.

"Is it Elizabeth?" He asked.

I nodded.

"Have they called for her sons?"

I nodded.

"I'd like to keep as much of this as possible from Genevieve. I don't want to ruin her birthday. Do you agree?" He asked me.

I nodded, again

"They'll come around and sing for her tonight, so we can't keep it totally away from her, but we must remain strong. If she sees us sad and withdrawn, she might react to our sorrow. We'll be respectful and allow their mourning rituals." He said. "She deserves that."

"Thank you," I told him, and then asked, "What would you like for me to do?"

"Letty will probably come up from the fields, but you might help Nane and make sure she gets what she needs. Do you mind? I'll take care of Genevieve, and tomorrow we'll see what we need to do." He said.

"Yes, sir, of course. That will be fine." I told him and then turned back to the kitchen.

I prepared the lemonade, and then found two bottles of wine Mr. Patout liked and uncorked one to be ready for dinner. I put the cork back in the bottle so as not to allow bugs to get in. I wasn't sure which glasses needed to go with this wine, or when it was to be served, so I hoped Letty would have more knowledge of Mr. Patout's habits when she arrived.

I walked to the screened door and saw a small crowd gathering. They were singing quietly and a couple of men and women were swaying gently. I leaned against the doorway and listened to them, closing my eyes and visualizing their meaning.

The first song was *Roll Jordan Roll.* It is about wanting to go to heaven when you die. It was amazing how they would harmonize out of the blue, and their tone was deep and meaningful. They were singing *Roll Over Jordan* about basically the same thing when Dan came out. Everyone stopped singing and I looked out the door to see what he was going to say.

"Won't cha sing something joyful for Mamangu?" He asked. "She loves *Thula Baba* from home, or *I Hear the Sound, Follow the Drinking Gourd*, or even *Wade in de Water*. We don't mind you singin' the others, but I want her to hear the songs she loves before she goes."

Bay walked over and stood by him as he talked. Her head was bowed and she placed her hand on his back. Here was this big, strong man, almost brought to tears by the circumstances. Rema started singing *Thula Baba* as the others chimed in at times.

I had no idea what it was about, but the tone was more uplifting. Dan stayed to hear the song started and then he turned to go inside. Bay remained outside with the rest, and it was then I saw Letty and Penelope heading towards me. I stepped back from the opening to allow them in.

"I brought some of the salve and I need to check your burn," Said Letty, "I don't have one bit of trust you have taken care of it today. Am I right?"

I nodded. She told Penelope what to get done while she and I were out in the barn and we would be right back. She told me to follow her and we went out to the barn. She told me to draw up my dress so she could see my thigh. I looked around to see if anyone was watching.

"I know you are not lookin' for privacy! Everyone and their baby saw you these last few days so don't go supposin' they haven't seen you in all your glory." She told me.

I grimaced, but pulled my dress up for her to see. I unwrapped the bandage and we both looked at my leg. It was getting dark, and hard to see in the barn, but she knew enough to know we needed to get some air to it.

"I'm gonna put this salve on, but it's gonna need to be open. Can you keep your legs apart?" She asked me.

Lucy was holding Amos and standing in the barn doors. Lucy giggled.

"Lucy! Git on outa here! You shoulda know better!"

Letty and I both smiled as I let go of the bottom of my dress and said, "I'll try."

"Tryin' won't do it. Spread 'em and walk!" She said emphatically.

We headed back to the kitchen, walking behind the group and listening to their song.

"That's *Follow the Drinking Gourd*. Do you know it?"

I shook my head 'no'.

"You will," she said, "I'll explain it later. There's a lot you need to hear."

I had no idea what she was talking about, but our next couple of hours was spent on the dinner and getting Mr. Patout and his guests settled for the evening. He and Genevieve came out to check on Elizabeth and her sons at least two times, that I saw.

The songs went on all through dinner and

Letty told me later Mrs. Clarkson was making bad-mannered comments about the singing.

"That woman looks real pretty, but she has a mean streak in her that I don't ever want to see. I wonder what Mr. Patout sees in her?" Said Letty, and then she caught herself, "Oh, forgive me, I knows what he sees in her, like all men must see in her!"

Letty and Penelope laughed. I laughed, but only to be a part of their conversation, I didn't really understand her meaning. Letty caught on.

"Young lady, you don't know what I'm talking about, do you?" asked Letty. Penelope smiled and bowed her head. "Men can't think with their minds when a pretty woman is around. It don't matter if she's a mean one or not. Looks can get her a lot. Do you understand?"

I nodded.

"No you don't! You still don't understand. What kinda men have you been around? Well, maybe since you still have your looks, you haven't had to worry 'bout it none. Just remember what I say, looks will get you a lot more than your mind."

We were cleaning the kitchen, when Nane came back in. Letty saved her some food and tried to get her to eat. She wasn't in the mood to eat, and told us it was just a matter of time. She said Elizabeth's breathing was very labored and she was not speaking anymore. The boys were still with her.

Mr. Patout, Genevieve, and his guests were in their rooms for the night, and Nane, Letty, Penelope, and I went outside to sit vigil with the group.

They continued to sing and wait for word. The songs went on for hours it seemed, but the tone had changed back to more sorrowful ones, and Nane went back in to be with Elizabeth and hers sons.

"Do you know this song?" asked Letty. "Remember earlier when I asked you if you knew the song *Follow the Drinking Gourd*?"

"I don't know either song. Should I?" I asked her.

Penelope stood up and left us, and it was just Letty and me talking about it.

"These are Negro spirituals that help us understand one another and give strength." Letty said.

"I can imagine. I feel the heartfelt words and power of their meanings. In Ireland, lyrics and song are very important to our customs." I told her.

"No, I'm talking about the Negro, the slave." She said.

I gave her a very strange look, and she continued. "These songs link us with one another. We have songs for working, songs for church, songs for every day. Songs tie us together to share joy, pain, inspiration, and as secret messages."

"Secret messages?" I asked her.

"Yes, secret messages. As you listen to our songs, don't just listen to the words and the melody, hear the words and imagine their meaning. There's a woman by the name of Harriet Tubman.."

"I know of her. I have been told of her efforts." I said.

"It's not just her efforts, she is our guiding star. Our bodies belong to our masters, but not our souls. She understands this and has risked her own life for others she does not even know. She *is* our guiding star." Letty pointed up to the heavens and to the stars in the sky. "So you see those stars? We look towards the sky every chance we get because she has shown us how to watch and what to look for. We don't even know her, but we know she is there for us."

"I'm sure she is. Everything I've heard about her sounds that way. It's how I got caught up in all of this myself."

"It must be so. You are one of her guides. You are one of her people. Here, to help all of us."

"Wait!" I said, trying to get up, but she grabbed my arm and pulled me back down. "You don't know what you're talking about. I wouldn't know how to help anyone. I want to, but I don't know how."

"Oh, but you do. You talked more than you should when you were out with fever. You know more than you think. You can help us. All of us."

"I can't Letty! I would if I could, but I truly don't know how. Please understand, I would if I knew how!"

Mr.Patout came out of the house and stood by us.

"I can't sleep," He told us, "any word on Elizabeth?"

Letty and I stood up and by him.

"No, sir," She said, "but Nane says it's only a matter if time. Her breathing is very difficult."

"May I wait with you?" he asked.

"Yes sir, of course." Answered Letty," may I go and get you a chair?"

"No, I'll just stand and wait."

"If I may say, sir," she said, "you should be in bed yourself. We don't want you getting' sicker yourself."

"I'll be fine, Letty."

It wasn't much more time, when Dan and Nane came outside. He stepped out and shook his head. I guess it meant she was gone, for the song immediately changed, and people started weeping. I did so myself as I watched Mr. Patout go up to Dan and shake his hand. He then walked back and into the house quite solemnly. Louis came out, too, and the group continued singing as they filed by to give their condolences and regroup.

"Come on, Cora" Letty said to me, "We've got to get you home. You need your rest and you can't be any more help here. Tomorrow's gonna be a big day, and you need to rest that leg before you stand on it all day tomorrow."

"I just don't feel right leaving, now." I told her.

"There's nothin' any of us can do." She said. "The men will take care of her, and we'll make sure to have something very special for the princess as a sendoff. You go on." She motioned for Lucy and said, "Take Lucy with you and the two of you start back. We'll follow later."

Lucy, Angus, and I walked back to our house and slipped into bed. I did my best to make sure there was space in between my legs and that I didn't rub them together. I was exhausted from the day and everything that had occurred, and I knew tomorrow would be another exhausting day.

But...I thought...what if tomorrow was my last day? What if this was my last night here? I went to sleep wondering about my situation, and if Brody was coming to the party. I wish I knew.

CHAPTER 11
GENEVIEVE'S BIRTHDAY

Henrietta had to wake me up. I must have been so tired that I slept beyond everyone else moving about. I jumped up to start getting ready and rushed around. Suddenly the sharp pain of rubbing my legs together jolted me. I waddled back to my bed to clean the burn and put the salve on. I wrapped it carefully and stood back up, slowly. I laid out my dress that I came to Belle Terre in, and pulled up my petticoat and undergarments.

Lucy, Anna, and Henrietta were getting dressed themselves. I had not seen their Sunday clothes as they called it, but they looked very nice. Lucy had tight braids in little rows, while Henrietta pulled a scarf on tightly and tied it in the back. Anna smoothed her hair out and pulled it back and rolled it up at the base of her head. They all looked nice and it made me think I needed to wash my hair quickly and fix it myself.

I was short of time, but knew if I hurried I could do it. I grabbed the bucket and the washbowl and wet my hair and took some soap to it. Anna realized what I was doing and rushed over to help me. They were all scolding me for waiting to wash my hair at such a late time, but I didn't have any time earlier, and I had slept too late this morning. I had to wash my hair, even if I was running late. I couldn't let Mr. Farraday, Captain, or Brody see me this way. Not after so much time.

All of them were nice enough to help me get dressed and put on my socks and shoes. I was stiff and knew I needed to take some Belladonna before the day became too busy. I asked Anna if she would go get some from Letty, and she agreed and ran out the door. She was back in an instant with enough for the day, she told me. Henrietta was busy with my hair. She tried to dry it with a towel, and then comb through it. She told me white people's hair is much easier to handle than Negro's hair. She pulled my hair back and then twisted it up in the back and took a sharp piece of wood through it to hold it up. She pulled out two strands of hair on each side of my head and wrapped them around her finger to curl them. Then, she let go and they hung to the side of my cheeks.

They all stood there and stared at me telling me I looked very nice. They were almost mournful as they looked at me. I felt as though I was going to betray them, and they knew it. I walked over to them stiffly, and gave them each a hug.

"Thank you!" I said, "Now let's all go and have a wonderful day!"

Most of the Negroes were staying in this area and celebrating the day here. Only a few would be up at the main house. I hated leaving them down here, but knew I had to get to the main house as quickly as possible.

I stepped out of our house, and saw a wooden box out front. I stopped in my tracks remembering Elizabeth. How could I have forgotten about her this morning? I went about my shuffling, not remembering last night. What an awful person I am! She was such a special person, with so many stories about her life. The celebration today would be shadowed by her death. I walked slowly towards her wooden casket and the cart Isum had beside it.

Letty came out and spoke to me, "Don't you let Elizabeth's death bring you down. She is in a better place now. She is free. Free! I tell you. She is in a better place."

I looked at Letty not understanding how we were to celebrate, while she lied there.

"You go on to the house and have Genevieve's birthday. It's not her fault the Lord took Elizabeth last night. And you have people you know who are coming. You need to see them and decide your destiny."

I looked at her again, but made no comment.

"Yes, it is not only your destiny, but hundreds of others. We are counting on you." said Letty.

I walked over to the cart where Isum was already in his seat and waiting. Letty handed me another little doll and told me to give it to Genevieve and tell her this is a friend for the other doll she gave her. I smiled knowing Genevieve would love it. She didn't need anything fancy, just love and attention. She already had enough toys and playthings to keep her happy.

The ride was uneventful, but my mind was full of thoughts. How would I handle the day? Not the party, or the guests, or even Genevieve. But the death of Elizabeth, and heavier on my mind, the arrival of someone from the Farraday Transport Company. Please, please, let it be Brody!

Nane was already busy in the kitchen, but she was hollering to Isum to go back and get Penelope. He dropped me off and turned the cart around to go back and pick her up. Nane must have been up the entire night, for everything was out and ready to take to the tables for guests. There was food galore and beautiful flower arrangements. The party favors were all filled and laid out and Nane was busy finishing her last minute details.

"Everything looks wonderful, Nane," I told her, "What can I do to help you?"

"Let's take these arrangements out to the tables and finish setting the tables. I've got to stay her and stir the gumbo, and watch the taffy."

"I'll gladly take these out. The weather looks like it is going to be quite pleasant, with no rain." I said. "Genevieve should have a grand time, don't you think?"

"I do. I hope all of the children invited come so she can meet some new friends and play and enjoy herself today."

I took the seven sets of arrangements out

to tables and finished setting them for Nane. By the time I was done with my tasking, Penelope was in the kitchen and watching the gumbo, and taffy, and other assorted confections. Nane was putting the finishing touches on Genevieve's birthday cake. It was covered with white icing and had little yellow flowers made of sugar, bunched in the middle of the top layer. It was a lovely cake and looked delicious.

Arthur, Mrs. Clarkson's man, was standing outside the back screen and watching. I was rather alarmed, but I suppose he had nowhere else to go while his mistress was here at another man's house. I asked Nane about it, but she said he could stay out there, she didn't want him in here messin' things up. I looked at him and nodded, and then he turned and walked away. Strange, I thought.

Since there was not much more I could do at the moment, I asked Nane if she would mind if I went up and checked on Genevieve. I think she was glad to get me out of the kitchen, too, as long as I didn't wake Genevieve up, yet. She reminded me to sit down when I had the chance to allow my leg to rest and not get rubbed. I went out and up the stairs. The house was quiet, but as I stepped onto the top stair, I heard coughing coming from Mr. Patout's room.

I walked slowly towards his room, listening to see if he was all right. The door was slightly ajar and I saw him through the crack of the doorway. He was sitting at his dressing table leaning forward on his arms with his head down. I stopped, wondering if I should ask him if he was all right, or to turn and leave him alone. I backed up slowly and turned, but noticed he looked up right when I turned, and he saw me.

He slowly stood and came to the door, whispering, "Cora, it's all right," he said breathing heavily, "I'd like to talk to you, anyway."

I walked over to him and he opened the door about a foot. He stepped away from the door and went back to his dresser seat to sit down. He picked up his jacket and put it around him as though he was chilled.

"How is everyone downstairs?" He asked.

"Everything is coming along nicely," I told him, "I think you and Genevieve will be quite pleased. Nane has done an amazing job with the spun sugar gifts, and she has finished Genevieve's birthday cake, and all of the arrangements are out and on the tables. Everything looks lovely. Penelope is helping Nane in the kitchen and stirring the confections and taffy. They are focused on this day and wanting it to be successful."

"Good, I'm glad. And you, how are you feeling?"

"I am going to be fine, sir, Letty has made sure of that. I'm not sure what she gives me, but the salves and her other mixtures help tremendously."

He took a deep breath in and let it out and then leaned on his elbow against the dresser.

"I haven't heard Genevieve, yet, or our other guests.

Have you?"

"No sir, and it was Genevieve I was coming to check on when I heard you. May I get Letty to bring you something? Were you awake all night?" He was looking quite pale, but I didn't feel right telling him so.

"No, I don't believe so, I'm sure I will be just fine. It was a long night, so I am probably just tired." He said.

"Sir, if I might, you have been sick also this past week and your skin is ashen. That cannot be a good sign. Please allow me to send for Letty to help you? Or a doctor? Is there one coming to the party?"

"I do have an old friend that is coming to the party who used to be a doctor, but I won't trouble him or you. Thank you. I will be down shortly and in to check on everything."

I excused myself and turned around to see Mrs. Clarkson shutting the door to her room. She must have been watching and listening! Aaah! She must be wondering what I was doing in his room! While I know it was completely innocent, I doubt she would have the same thought about it. I couldn't do anything about it now, so I slipped into Genevieve's room and checked on her. Her eyes were open, but she was lying on her side and just staring.

I sat down next to her with one arm across her. "Well, hello birthday girl. And how are you this morning?"

"Eight. I am eight." She said quite plainly. "Eight without Ma-Ma."

"Oh, mon enfant, you're Ma-Ma is here with you in spirit. Look at the sunlight as it shines through the window. Do you see it? It is bright and glorious and shining for your special day. Look at that and see your Ma-Ma, or feel her putting her arms around you. She is here with you, but in a very different way. She will always be with you."

She turned and faced me in the bed and reached up for a neck hug. I leaned forward and we hugged.

"Well, I see mon petit précieux is awake and ready for her big day!" Said her father as he stepped into the room.

"Pa-Pa, Pa-Pa. J'ai huit ans! J'ai huit ans!" She told him

gleefully.

"Yes, and you look more like your beautiful mother today!" He told her.

She smiled. Then looked at me and said, "Let's get dressed!"

We all laughed and Mr. Patout excused himself while I helped Genevieve get dressed. She had already chosen her party dress for the day, and we had a matching yellow ribbon to go with it. I pulled her hair back, letting most of it hang below in the back. We could see her beautiful little face, and she was gleaming at the thought of her special day. We put on her shoes, and she went to look in her mirror. She twirled around once and then stopped, and turned towards me.

"I'm going to miss Elizabeth, aren't you?" She asked me.

"Very much so." I told her, "but you know she would want you to have a wonderful day today, and to make wonderful memories. She'll be here with us, too."

We both smiled and decided she was ready for her big day, so we headed down stairs for her to get something to eat. Her father and Mrs. Clarkson were already at the table and talking. As Genevieve noticed her father was not alone, she moved closer to me, almost hiding behind my skirt. She tugged on it in the back and I knew she did not want to sit with Mrs. Clarkson at the table, but I didn't know how we were to get out of it.

"Happy Birthday, or should I say, joyeux anniversaire!" Mrs. Clarkson said to Genevieve, but her try at saying 'Happy Birthday' in French was quite terrible. It sounded more like, 'joy-yucks anniversary-ree.' It was almost humorous if not such a pitiful attempt.

"It's joyeux anniversaire!" Genevieve told her, using the correct pronunciation.

Mrs. Clarkson tried not to look perturbed, but she was most uncomfortable with Genevieve correcting her. Mr. Patout smiled and ignored Genevieve's comment, asking her to join them for some petit déjeuner. I loved the French language and wanted to learn more of it. Mrs. Farraday would be proud of my interest in a foreign language.

I took Genevieve to her seat and pulled out her chair. She stood by me for a moment not wanting to sit with them, but she noticed her father looking at her above his glasses, so she sat down and I pushed her chair in. I patted her on the back and went into the kitchen.

"Ohh, that woman!" said Nane, "She is no good! I don't like her around our Genevieve, or Mr. Patout. Isum thinks Mr. Patout might marry her."

"Nane! Don't be telling people what I say. I was jes thinkin' out loud!" Isum said to Nane.

"Well, you know she's got her claws into him. She's gonna keep pushin' till she gets what she wants." Nane told us.

"That can't be true!" I said, "Genevieve would not want that. She would be miserable."

"Just wait and see, I bet she catches him any day now and announces their betrothal." said Nane.

I went back to the dining room door and peaked in on Genevieve. Then I shut the door again. "You should see her face right now. You can tell she doesn't like that woman." I told them.

"Yes, but I bet Mr. Patout believes she'll come around. He probably thinks she just doesn't want to replace her Ma-Ma." Nane said.

I opened the door again and saw Mrs. Clarkson's nieces at the table. Genevieve's face was worse.

"The nieces are at the table now, and Genevieve does not look any happier. I'm not sure she would come around to his way of thinking. Should I say something?" I asked them

"No, no," said Isum, "It's not your place.

You shouldn't be tellin' the master what he should or shouldn't do."

"Isum," said Nane, "She might be the only one. Someone's got to tell him. Someone's got to be there for Genevieve, and that's what he hired her for isn't it?"

"He didn't hire the woman to tell him what to do!"

Isum told Nane "You don't have to hire a woman. Any woman ends up tellin' ya what to do."

I went back to the door to peak on them, and Nane bumped me out of the way to take more food into the children and to check on Mr. Patout and Mrs. Clarkson. I continued watching and saw how Mrs. Clarkson looks and acts like the perfect lady around Mr. Patout. Besides being beautiful, she is charming and conversational, flirtatious and attentive. She's entertaining and trying her best to look motherly, even though it does look a bit forced. However, I don't think Mr. Patout notices that, he seems to enjoy her company and attention. She does give him that – attention!

They finished breakfast, and the girls wanted to go outside. I walked with them to the swings, and while Molly Anne and Lula May chose not to swing, I lifted Genevieve's dress up slightly so as not to get it dirty or wrinkled and she jumped up on the swing. I pushed her with my good arm and she used her legs to help get higher.

We were fortunate to not have any pecans fall on us, and Lula May remarked so as Genevieve was swinging. It seemed as though Lula May and Genevieve might get along, especially if Molly Anne wasn't there to influence Lula May.

Genevieve invited the girls up to her room, and she seemed to be all right with them for the while. I told her I was going to help Nane, but would be there for her if she needed me. They ran upstairs and I went through the hallway towards the kitchen. I passed Mr. Patout, leaning against the stairway and looking weak and flush. I asked him if I could help and he answered no saying he was fine, but I knew he wasn't. When I stepped into the kitchen, I told Nane about my two encounters with Mr. Patout, and she automatically sent Isum to get Letty and to bring something for him.

She was busy, but was talking about her worry for Mr. Patout and everyone who has been sick, especially since Elizabeth and last night. She stopped for a moment to reflect, and then turned towards me.

"Let me see your leg." She insisted. "Come on, sit right

here and pull up your skirt. We can't have you gettin' sick, too."

I sat up on the table and tried to pull the skirt up gently.

"I don't have time for your modesty." And she pulled it up and started unwrapping it faster than I could stop her. "Hmm, that is one raw spot you got there, isn't it? Don't that hurt? Penelope, bring me some of that wash water and salve Letty left for her."

She cleaned the area, took a rag to dry it, and I jumped backwards.

"Guess it does hurt! All right, Penelope, bring me that tray and I'll air dry it."

She took the tray and fanned it back and forth to force some air towards the wound. When she thought it was dry, she took the salve, and started rubbing it on. As she finished, Letty and Isum came in.

"I thought I was here for Mr. Patout? Has something happened to Cora? Let me see." Letty said as she pushed Nane aside.

"Now don't go pushin'! I'm takin' care of her, you are here for Mr. Patout. Cora said he is lookin' weak and has refused any medicine. Maybe you could make him somethin' that we could put in a tea." Nane told Letty, as she finished wrapping my thigh.

"That's exactly what I brought, something to put in his tea. See? Elder flower and peppermint. He won't even know it'll help him. You take it in to him Nane and he'll never suspect that it's from me, but I would like to get a peek at him. I thought his eyes were lookin' a little yella last night. He might have ague"

"Ague, what's that?' I asked.

"It's when you get the fever and chills and your body sweats trying to combat it. You saw it with Lucy. That's what she had. Sometimes it gets so bad it takes over." Said Letty.

"Takes over? You mean kills you?" I asked her.

"Yes. And that's not what we want to happen to Mr. Patout. Genevieve needs him." Nane said.

Mr. Williams walked in. I dropped my skirt and jumped from the table, wincing for a moment.

"Did I walk in on something?" He asked.

"No," I said, "Letty brought me some medicine for my burns, and we just finished wrapping my leg. She was going to do my arm now."

"And I'm making some tea for Mr. Patout and Mrs. Clarkson." Nane said.

"Where's her man? Arthur, isn't it? I thought I saw him around here earlier." He said.

"He's probably around back in the barn with Isum. Isum was getting' something for Dizzy before he took me back." Letty said. "Do you need somethin'?"

"Nane, what do you need Arthur to do today?" Asked Mr. Williams.

"Nothin'." She said, "He's not my property and I don't have nothin' for him to do."

"We must have something he could do, surely." Mr. Williams said. "Mrs. Clarkson will want to see him being useful. If you don't think of something he can do, I will."

"Can't he help with the horses and the carriages of the guests? I'm sure Isum could use his help." Nane said.

"Yes, but he is a house servant, and I'm not sure Mrs. Clarkson would appreciate our using him in that way." He said.

"Oh, all right, I'll think of somethin' for him to do" Nane said.

"We have about an hour before guests start arriving. Are you all ready?" He asked.

I almost fainted. People will be here in an hour? I thought it was to be late afternoon, I had no idea.

Letty looked at me and said, "Cora, are you all right. Don't you pass out on us!"

I sat back down and they continued talking. I heard noises, but wasn't listening to what they were saying. I became giddy and almost forgot we needed to check my arm.

"Whoah, girly, slow down! You go from almost fainting to being over excited. What has gotten into your head? Let me look at your arm." Letty said.

My sleeve was so that all you had to do was slip it down

slightly to see the brand burn.

"This strap is rubbing your burn. We've got to put something on it to keep it from rubbing. Nane, do you have any rags in here that we can tear apart?" Letty asked her.

Mr. Williams looked uncomfortable at the moment and said, "Everything is looking good, and I think this afternoon will be a success. I'll be back when we are warned of our guests arriving. I've got Beau and Rosa spread out on the road to relay the first sighting of a carriage or horses coming our way. I'll go and find Arthur and tell him to check in with you Nane."

Nane handed a rag to Letty who tore the rag into strips, and then began boiling some water for tea. Letty tried to keep the strips slender so you couldn't see them very well under my sleeve. She did a fine job, but the rag was thicker than my other arm and if you looked at my arm, you could see it.

"Letty, the water's boiling, so come over her and do your magic." Nane told her.

Letty took out her dried flowers and leaves and crumbled them in a silver tea infuser. I was standing right beside her watching. She placed it in a cup, and then poured the hot water over the infuser. I was getting nervous and the energy was consuming me.

"Nane, get me some sugar will you? I'd rather he be upset it's too sweet, than to realize I've put herbs in here for him. He should be all right with the peppermint tea flavor. Should we make some for Mrs. Clarkson?"

"Yes, you should," I said, "we don't want her questioning why we're giving him tea by himself. Why don't we add some little sandwiches, too, so it will be less suspicious? They didn't ask for anything, so this might be their lunch. Let's serve it under the back porch. Don't you think? That would be nice. Just the two of them"

Letty and Nane stopped and looked at me. "Well, Miss Cora, you have a streak of romance in you, don't you? Are you trying to help Mrs. Clarkson?"

"No, of course not," I said, "but it would be nice, wouldn't it?"

Something moved at the back door, and it startled me. I went over and opened the screen and there was Arthur.

"Arthur, did you need something?" I asked him.

"Yes, Nane, please." He said.

"Well, you may come in. She won't bite you, will you Nane?" I asked her as I lifted my eyebrows at the strange event of his showing up and being suspicious.

"Arthur, we're gonna serve tea to your mistress and Mr. Patout on the back porch. Why don't you set up the chairs under the fan, and then swing the fan for them as they eat and relax."

Arthur said nothing but nodded in agreement.

"Cora, you and Letty fix this tray, and I will go and tell Mr. Patout and Mrs. Clarkson about their private lunch…"

Letty laughed.

"…and bring them out on the porch. You carry it out to them after Arthur has the seats arranged." Nane told us.

The private lunch came off fine and Mr. Patout finished his tea. He asked to retire for a bit before his guests came, and Mrs. Clarkson was grateful because she said she needed to refresh herself before they arrived. We were glad he was going to rest, and I suggested Genevieve do the same.

She was not as willing today, but Mr. Patout asked her to please rest because they were to have a long afternoon and night with many fun and exciting things happening. Molly Anne and Lula May disappeared into their rooms, and Letty headed back to the field houses.

I sat nervously in the kitchen with Nane, self-absorbed and yet gleeful.

"Cora, what is it we are missing about you? There's something about you that's happenin' we don't know about? Is it just that you might be leaving us? We wouldn't blame you for wantin' to be free, but it seems to be more than that." Nane asked me.

"I really couldn't tell you Nane, because I don't know. I'm anxious about a friend coming, but I'm hesitant because of my responsibilities. I have such a connection here, and Letty said I could make a difference for many people. If I leave, if it really is coming true, then how could I let others down?"

"That's somethin' you got to figure out yourself. There's people that don't think nothin' of anyone else, just themselves. I guess there's nothin' wrong with that, because if they didn't think of themselves, might they be free? If they think of others, the consequences are severe. It's what you want to do and how you want to live your life. But I think it' more than that Cora, it's somethin' else."

I knew what she meant, but I couldn't put my finger on it either. I was anxious and I would be until I found out who was here representing the Farradays.

It wasn't long before we heard Rosa in the distance hollering for Mr. Williams. Nane and I looked at one another and scurried about, only to come full circle back to each other.

"Nane, how do I look?" I asked her.

"You look fine." She said and she licked her fingers and ran them over the edge of my hair at the front. "Now go tell Mr. Patout his guests are arriving, and then make sure everyone else knows. Here we go!"

I moved as fast as I could in my still awkward walk up the stairs and knocked on his door. He answered and I relayed the message that Nane told me to tell him. He thanked me and then asked me to tell the others. I did so and within minutes the foyer was alive and ready for the guests arriving at Genevieve's party. I thought she might be apprehensive, but she looked gay and without a worry, so it helped me feel as though she would be all right after all.

Mr. Patout and Mrs. Clarkson stepped out onto the front porch, and Genevieve ran to her father's side and held his hand, standing there proudly. Molly Anne and Lula May stepped out on the porch, but stood towards the front wall and not as one of the hostesses. I slipped back into the kitchen hoping to catch my breath.

"Now what?" Asked Nane.

"Nothing." I said, "Nothing."

"Oh yes, I can see that it is 'nothing'." She said. "So? What is it?"

"Nothing, truly." I didn't know why I was short of breath or why I was acting this way.

"Where is Arthur?" Nane asked firmly. "Arthur!" She yelled out the back door. "Arthur! Where are you?"

"Right here." He said. We both jumped at his strange ability to be listening or standing close to us without our even knowing it.

"You can just stop that nonsense. We don't need odd goin's on around here, especially today." She told him. "When the guests start arriving, you will be carrying the drink tray. Until then, why don't you go and check on your mistress to see if she needs anything right now."

"I have already checked with her." He said.

We both looked at each other and then Nane said, "Fine then, go help Isum."

"I am not your servant, I work for Mrs. Clarkson. She has not told me to do any work outside." He told us.

"All right, then wait in the foyer for our guests if they chose to come inside." Nane told him and he turned and left the kitchen heading for the foyer.

We didn't have time to talk about him because we were filling glasses and putting the finishing touches on the food trays. I was so nervous I almost dropped two glasses, so Nane told me to do something else. When she completed the trays, Nane told me to carry them out to the tables outside.

"No," she said, "you shouldn't be doing that, you might drop them all!"

I was going to disagree with her, but I knew she was right. I was so jumpy, I might trip or drop something. She took out the first tray, and I paced back and forth on the floor until she came back.

"Are there people here? Are they inside or outside? I'm scared to even look. Who has arrived?" I shot the questions at her.

Following her into the kitchen was Arthur, and she didn't answer me, but spoke to him. "Arthur, here is the tray you will carry. When you are empty, please come back to fill it." She handed the tray to him and then turned him around to show him the door.

"There are people here, but not that many. I believe the two nearest plantation owners, the ones towards New Orleans, and their three children are the only ones here. You ought to go out and check on Genevieve." She said as she changed her apron and put on a newer one for the party.

"I...I can't." I tried to speak, but was frozen in my tracks.

She continued tying her apron, but stopped and looked at me. "What do you mean you can't? You have to. That's your job. You can do it and it will help pass the time. Now go on."

"I mean it, I can't." I told her, again.

"You can!" she said more forcefully. "Genevieve will wonder why you are not checking on her."

"I can't!" I said, again!

"Cora! None of us have a choice! Until you are a free woman, you are Mr. Patout's slave and Genevieve is your concern. Today is her birthday and that is where you should be. With her!"

She turned and started back to work, not saying another thing to me.

I stood frozen. I could hear more people arriving, and sounds of laughing and children playing, but I couldn't move. I didn't know what I would do when I saw Brody. Oh, I knew it might not even be Brody, but I kept thinking how I wanted it to be him.

I turned my head towards the kitchen door and saw Isum walk a carriage past. I was standing here, scared as a child, hoping the event would go on around me and I would not be working at it, but as part of the guest list. I knew better, but that's what I wanted. I wanted to be a guest here, not a slave or a servant. Not someone's property. I wanted to do things because I wanted to, not because I had to.

Nane was getting more perturbed at me. "Cora, you have no choice! Even Arthur is doing something!"

That worked. She was right, choice or not, we had been

planning on this party, Elizabeth died and everyone else was doing their jobs when they probably didn't want to. I despised my selfish thoughts and myself sometimes.

I took the Belladonna Letty had given me, and smoothed out my dress. I walked out the kitchen door and followed Isum back to the front where the guests were arriving. I said nothing but walked with my head down, apprehensive of what I might see.

I stopped as we encountered a carriage, and decided I needed to go back to the backside of the house. I turned around and headed to the back, following the noises of the children rather than looking specifically for Genevieve. When I finally looked up, I saw them in the back swinging and playing. I dared not look around, fearing I might see someone. I wanted to see him, but I was afraid. It had been so long, and my position here was of such a different circumstance.

Genevieve was gleeful and excited as she played with the other children and moved around. It was nice to see such complete strangers playing together without a thought or worry about them. I didn't see Mr. Patout for a while, and figured he was with his guests in the front.

I couldn't see Mrs. Clarkson, but I could hear her. She was laughing and talking and being very social, acting as if this was her home and she was the hostess. She was organizing things with Arthur and with Nane, which I'm sure aggravated Nane something terrible.

As the day went on, the children became interested in the pond, and some of the boys wanted to go swimming. Mrs. Clarkson gave her approval and off went a crowd of children to play at the pond. Many parents were telling them not to get wet or dirty, but most of the children were more interested in getting wet than obeying their parents.

The other children followed to watch, including Genevieve. I stood behind her as she leaned against me, and we watched the boys as they played on the edge, having taken their shoes off to wade.

It was fun to watch them as they picked up frogs and

chased some of the girls. Molly Anne was the most silly. She played the perfect part of a flirtatious young woman. I was amazed at her adeptness of knowing how to manipulate the situation. Mrs. Clarkson had done a fine job at teaching her those skills, and the boys enjoyed her acting. She was the main attraction of their teasing and chasing.

Genevieve and Lula May loved it. They both laughed not realizing what she was doing, but enjoying the motions of everyone in this scenario. One boy, Lucas, who looked about Molly Anne's age, took a particular interest in her and went to great lengths to impress her, and she accepted his intentions. He grabbed a huge wisteria vine that once held beautiful white blossoms in the Spring, but was now the image of a strong and thick rope.

I stepped forward, away from Genevieve for a moment, not feeling comfortable with what he was about to do. He took the rope and before I knew it was swinging out beyond the edge and over the water. I looked around, hoping a parent would say something to him, but no one did, and the exciting delight he had for this action electrified the group.

I begged the boys not to swing from the rope, reminding them to obey their parents and not get wet or dirty, but no one listened. The crowd of children became more intense at everyone doing something they shouldn't be doing. Even Genevieve was squealing with pleasure, and it all seemed to be out of my hands.

I looked around again and saw people heading our way. I was glad. I would not be the only adult watching over this raucous bunch of young people, but as I looked back towards the children, I saw Lucas take a running start and grab another boy to swing with him. The boy he grabbed had a fretful look on his face, and before I knew it, Lucas dropped him in the water with everyone laughing and screaming with joy.

My eyes followed the boy in the water and I immediately realized he could not swim. I looked around for another adult, but they were still too far away. I looked back at the boy and saw him struggling mightily to stay above water. Everyone was still laughing and Lucas had jumped back onto land and was laughing himself, proud of his latest accomplishment and preening like a bird. It did not seem as though anyone felt the urgency of the situation as I did. I looked around one more time for support, but saw none.

It all seemed like slow motion as I turned towards the water, running down the side of the pond to the nearest place to enter the water. I jumped in and swam towards the boy. I lost all ability to hear sound and as I moved, my only focus was on this young boy and his not going under. When I reached him, he fought me, but I grabbed him under his arms and flipped him around and swam on my side, pulling him along.

As we fought closer to the edge, he relaxed a little and we made it back to land. I wasn't completely conscious of the moment, but another man jumped in and helped. He took him from me and carried the boy to higher ground. I stayed there in the water, my heart racing, and completely out of breath. I didn't move except for the rise and fall of my chest as I tried to catch my breath.

I began hearing noises, and time became real, again. I heard people yelling and saw a crowd gathered in front of me. Women were crying and gasping. Men were talking loudly and asking questions. I saw Mrs. Clarkson standing with her arms around Molly Anne and Lula May, and then I saw Mr. Patout running over to join the crowd and check on the boy.

Lucas was standing by himself off to the side. No one was talking to him, until his parents came and stood by him. The scene was chaotic and I slowly stood up from my drenched position and walked up the rise to dry land. I was soaking wet and my dress was stuck to me making it more difficult to move. My leg suddenly caused me great pain, and I realized I had lost my wrap in the midst of all of this and I had rubbed the burn. I must have worn off more skin because the burned spot pierced with pain.

I did my best to get out of the water, fighting my own dress and the pain of my leg and arm. I wanted to check on the boy and see if he was all right, but there was a crowd around him. I didn't have to walk towards him, because I could see him being held up and people clapping and being joyful.

I was relieved he was going to be all right, so I turned to walk back to the house and take care of my leg. I could hear people congratulating and thanking the man who took him from me in the water.

I turned to see who it was at precisely at the same moment he turned to look at me. He was staring at me. I was dripping wet with my hair loose and hanging sporadically. I stared back at him, our eyes on one another. I knew who he was, instantly.

CHAPTER 12
MOMENTS TO REMEMBER

He was Brody. Our eyes remained fixed on one another as the crowd around us continued with their joyfulness, not noticing our connection. Time stopped again and my mind raced at the thought of his being right in front of me. His handsome suit was wet, but he looked better than I could have imagined. He had a striking resemblance to his father, with a softness in his eyes that reminded me of his mother. He looked sorrowful behind his eyes, and I suddenly felt our connection without any words spoken. However, I also felt the difference in our worlds.

I was ashamed at his seeing me this way and felt as though I was not worthy of his stare. I turned and headed towards the house, crying as I went, knowing how very different our worlds were. I could hear him calling my name, using Allie as he called. His use of my name just made me cry more, and I continued across the lawn to the house.

My leg was hurting so badly, I couldn't run very fast, and he caught up to me before I reached the house. He grabbed my arm, not knowing of its burn. I cringed in agony as my sleeve pulled from my shoulder and exposed my arm, lost of its bandage, too.

He stopped and let go upon seeing my arm, and I ran into the main house and through the foyer and dining room into the kitchen. I backed up against the kitchen wall and slid down it, both in pain and in the realization of the moment. I stayed there trying to catch my breath. Trying to withstand the pain, and recover from the shock of seeing Brody. Nane came in the kitchen door and over to me.

"Are you all right? What happened out there?"

I said not a word, but pointed to my burns, and then continued crying.

"The pain? What happened?" She said as she ran to get a clean rag and salve for my burns. "I'm sending Isum to get Letty. We'll fix you right up!"

"No, please, no. I'm fine, really. I just need to catch my

breath!" I told her.

"You're anything but fine. Is it the burns?" She asked.

I shook my head from side to side, trying to stop my crying.

"All right then, what is it? You have to tell me or I can't help you."

"It's him. He's here." I spurted out.

"Who him? Who's here?"

"Brody. Brody came."

"And who is Brody?" Nane asked, totally bewildered by my statement.

"It doesn't matter," I told her as I tried to get up. "Not anymore, I can't go with him. Things have changed too much."

"I don't understand," Nane said, "why has seeing him changed the situation?"

"Seeing him made me realize how different things are. He's a gentleman, and I'm a slave. Even if he proved my kidnapping and wrongful sale as a slave, I'm here and people are expecting things from me. They expect me to be a slave and to do what I can to help."

I stood up tall and continued to lean against the wall, turning my head from Nane.

She took my face in her hand and turned my head back to her. "You must face him and see if that is what you want to do."

"But I can't! You should see him. He is smart and handsome and lives in a totally different world."

"If you were not here, where would you be? Would you be living in his world?" She asked.

"I don't know, I just don't know!" I cried. "But I do know I'm not living in that world anymore. I'm here. You said so yourself this morning. Until I'm free, I'm someone else's property."

"Yes, but you might also be free. Anyone of us would take freedom in an instant, and we would understand your wanting to be free. Don't miss your chance if it's possible. Talk to him. See what he says."

"I'm telling you I can't." I walked away from her and stood by the screen door to the back, looking for him, but not wanting to talk to him.

"Fine, then fix your wounds and get back to your job. Be someone else's property! Go or stay, but be accepting of your decision and make it wisely. Either place you can help. Decide what is best for you, and move on." She irritably said. She was obviously frustrated with me.

"May I go to your house and collect myself? I'll rebandage my wounds and pull myself together. I promise."

She pointed towards her house and I went out the door, not looking for Brody this time, just trying to walk. Her door was open and I realized it was only last night that Elizabeth and her family were in here as she passed away. It seems like a hundred years since then, but her aura was alive and I would have expected sadness about the room, but there wasn't.

The room was peaceful and the light showed through windows. I thought about what I told Genevieve earlier and how the light was love from her mother. It was a comforting thought.

I moved over to Nane's bed. I might have chosen Elizabeth's, but I didn't want to be disrespectful. Hers was an empty mattress, lying there without any sheets or covers. I sat on Nane's thinking about how we would miss Elizabeth, even if she were in a better place.

I lifted my dress to look at my burn. The skin was rubbed off again, and I knew if I didn't clean it and get the salve on it, there was a chance of it getting infected, again. I gently cleaned it, unable to do any scrubbing since the pain was so intense. I reached for the salve, dipped into it with my fingers, and began to rub it on my burn. The first touch produced a sharp pain, which then turned to comfort as the salve blended across the burn and eased the pain. I laid my head back and to the side as I rubbed gently and felt the relief.

There was a gentle knock at the opening, and as I looked up, I saw a figure in the doorway. The figure came towards me as I pushed my dress down over my legs trying to cover myself from this person. They didn't stop, but I wasn't afraid. I knew that form standing in front of me. I realized who it was - it was Brody. I tensed, and as he saw me do so, he stopped walking towards me.

"Allie, please, I don't mean to upset you. I am here to help you. What has happened to you?" He said.

I tried to get up, but he said, "Don't try, let me see what they have done. Let me help.

Please!" He beseeched.

I stood up anyway, but fell back down because of the pain in my leg and it giving away. I began to cry, not really knowing why.

"Allie, please! Don't be stubborn. I read your letter, and Captain, my father, your mother and I knew we had to come and get you. You shouldn't be here! We want you back with us."

"I can't." I told him. "Don't you see? I am here now. Things have changed. I am not from the same world as you." I continued crying.

He took a few steps closer and I held out my arm as to stop him. He did, but continued talking. "Maybe things have changed, but you are not supposed to be here. I have proof of your adoption to the Captain, and of your living and going to school in New York. I will show Mr. Patout and you will be free."

"Free? How can I be free when I know others here who are not? Am I supposed to go home with you and act as if none of this has happened, or that everything in the world is fine?"

"Of course not, but you have no idea what has been happening since you have been gone. The Captain was freed from Charleston, and he has been working faithfully to help as many Negroes as possible. He and Nella and the others work diligently to get as many people to the North as possible. Even father and I are helping in our own way. You can be a part of it, too. But you must come back to us."

"The Captain is fine? And Mother?" I asked him, pulling myself together.

"They are fine and send you their love, as does Father and of course Rufina and Angelo. She would be awfully upset with me if she thought I had not told you that!"

I smiled, and he stepped closer.

"There. That's much better. Now, will you let me see your wounds? Let me see what needs to be done."

"They are taking care of me. Letty has her own medicines to take care of all of us. She and Nane, and others, watch over me and make sure I take care of myself."

"If they can get you to do something for yourself, then I hold them in high regard." He said, and we both smiled.

"I'm not the same little girl you left on the boat in Galway."

"I know you are not, but you are the same person deep down in there somewhere. Somewhere you must still feel a connection for the past and for those of us that were in your lives."

"Of course I do, I cherish you…" I realized what I said and stopped. He turned his head ever so slightly and looked at me with a different look. "I cherish my past and those that were in it," hoping he would not catch my admission. "How could I not? It is a part of me, and helps me to this day."

"Then let me help you, again." He said.

I saw movement at the doorway, and saw Arthur. An eerie chill went up my spine. Brody saw me looking, and turned to see what was there.

"Might I help you?" Brody asked.

"No sir, Mrs. Clarkson sent me to check on Cora." Arthur said.

"She is fine, I will see to that. Please tell Mrs. Clarkson she is being taken care of." Brody said quite strongly, and then turned back to me.

I continued to look towards the door, and put my fingers up to my mouth as to motion him to be quiet.

"What are you doing Allie? He's gone." Brody said.

"Shh!" I uttered, and walked over to the door and looked out to make sure. "I don't trust that man. He shows up and listens at the most awkward moments. He makes me wary."

"Allie, don't be foolish. He's gone." Brody said as he

walked over to me and turned me around. This time he was careful not to grab my arm or my burn, but I still tensed up as if I was hurt.

He carefully turned me toward him and held both arms. "Must I force you to be open with me? I won't do that, but I wish you would trust me and allow me into your world. Let me know what has happened to you and how I can help."

"I don't know how to do that." I told him as I stepped back and he released his hold. "I've been alone for so long now, the only person I feel I can trust is myself. To trust again would show weakness which one cannot afford as a slave."

"But you are not a slave, and we can take care of this as soon as you like. I will go to Mr. Patout right now and talk to him."

"I may not be a slave legally, but I was brought here as one and have been treated as one by many. I have grown to understand the situation, and accept being a slave to Mr. Patout. I love his daughter, and I believe she loves me. I am teaching her, and being a type of governess."

"You accept being a slave?" He asked, and he gently grabbed my arm again to bring me closer to him. "How can you accept that? You should be no one's property, and I cannot believe Allie McCreary would allow anyone to treat her so."

"That's where I've changed. It's not just about me, there are others who need me."

"You can help," he said, "Allie, you can come home and help."

He drew me closer to him, and I felt my legs almost give out. Not from the pain of my burn, but from being so close to him and having him hold me. I said nothing but looked up into his face, wanting to believe every word he said. Wanting to go home with him and feel safe and be free. I thought he was going to kiss me, but instead, he turned his head and held me close to him.

My knees buckled and gave way. He dropped to his knees, holding me. I was still wet, but that did not seem to bother him. I began to cry again and feel a complete release of my pain and fear and anger. It felt right to be in his arms, and have him comfort and protect me. He lifted me up and took me to Nane's bed. He laid me on the bed and as he released me with his left arm, I grabbed his hand and brought it to my face. Closing my eyes and feeling his hand on my skin. His other arm was still caught beneath me, which caused him to lean across me on his elbow. He allowed me to cry until I had no more tears.

When I was done, he asked me, again, "Please tell me what has happened to you? Who did this?" he asked as he pulled my sleeve down slightly to look at my burn.

"Two evil men used to work here and they often tortured the slaves. I just happened to be one of them. I guess I had it coming. I was warned, and I did not heed the warning. They branded me." I told him.

"That's appalling!" He said. "Are these men still here?"

"No, no they're not! Mr. Patout has people searching for them. They tried to burn his sugar fields, but we were able to save most of the crop. It was after we put the fires out that they came in the night and pulled me from my bed. They took me out to brand me and use me as a warning to others. They were paying me back for getting them dismissed. They took a hot branding iron and branded my shoulder first, and then my inner thigh. I don't remember anything after that for I fainted."

"Allie, please come home with me!" He begged. "How am I to tell your mother and Captain this without their understanding why I did not bring you home."

He held me closer with only inches between our faces. He took one hand and gently brushed the side of my face, watching his hand, as it slid down my face, around my jaw, and then up to my lips. My heart raced as he slowly outlined his movement, and my insides tightened. We stayed in this position for a moment, staring at each other. I memorized every aspect of his face, wanting to dream about it any chance I had. I was glad the moment lasted. I was afraid I might not have another chance to appreciate him again. He took his hand back to the side of my head and he drew me closer. I tried drawing away, but released myself to him wanting to be drawn ever so much closer.

There was a knock at the doorway, but we continued looking at one another, not wanting to turn away.

Nane was outside the door, and said, "Cora, you must come back. We are about to bring out Genevieve's cake and she will want you to be there."

"I'll be right there, Nane." I told her

I had not moved from his arms. Brody and I remained spellbound in our gaze. It was a moment I never wanted to end, but I slowly moved from his arms and we both stood up knowing we had to face the real world.

"You'll see how different things are. You get to go out as a guest, and I will continue to be their slave." I told him as we stood there looking at each other.

He took my arms again, gently, and said, "I cannot leave you without at least trying to set you free."

"I know what you think you must do, but please remember, I thought I was doing the right thing by telling on the two men who were later dismissed, and look what happened to me. Nothing happens without consequences. If you care about me at all, you will respect my advice. Please believe me when I say, I want to go with you. I want to be free and see Captain, and Ma again, but my place is here. I can do more to help if I am here and working from this side. I can help guide more people to freedom than if I was in New York. Do you understand? Can you understand? It's not a matter of wanting, it's a matter of what is right and what I believe my destiny to be."

"Then I will help you with your destiny if that is what you want. I want you to be happy, and if you choose this way of life, then I must respect your choice." He said and guided me out the door. "But please, do not expect us to be happy about it."

We continued on to the kitchen, and at the door I turned to him. "I must leave you here. No one will understand if you are seen with me."

"All right, but this is not over. I will think of something. I cannot just leave you." He stepped back and away from me and the door. I turned and went inside, dying, afraid I might not ever feel the way I just felt in Nane's house. Afraid that moment was gone forever.

Nane came over to me and took my hand. "Are you gonna be all right?"

"I'm not sure." I told her.

"I hope you're not mad at me for letting him come to you. He came to the kitchen looking for you and I told him where you were."

"I'm glad you did. You were right. We needed to talk and I needed to decide what I was going to do."

"Good." She said. "Now, how about we take this cake out to Genevieve?"

"Wonderful idea," I told her as I took a deep breath and tried to change my disposition.

We took her cake out and the guests started clapping. Genevieve was out in the front yard and turned around quite excitedly clapping and jumping with joy. She ran over to her father who greeted her with open arms. He was looking rather pale, but you wouldn't know of his health by his demeanor. Mrs. Clarkson was standing by him and she grabbed his arm and stood there as he greeted Genevieve.

We put the cake down on the designated table and I had a huge knife to cut the cake. I invited Genevieve over and asked her if she wanted to cut the cake. She whispered to me she was afraid to, so I told her we could cut it together. She liked that idea so I placed her hands on the knife, and then wrapped mine around hers and we cut into the cake as everyone clapped again. She got icing on her finger, so when we let go of the knife, she licked her fingers and then smiled at her father.

As she looked at her father, I found Brody in the crowd, watching us. I continued looking at him as Genevieve grabbed me to get her presents. I could not go as fast as she because of my leg, so she let go of her grip and ran ahead, waiting for her father to tell her it was all right to open her presents.

Other children gathered around her, and Molly Anne took charge of handing each present to her. I stood back a little and watched Genevieve open her presents. She must have had fifteen presents, and they were all wondrous. Her bed will be quite full tonight if she places each of them in it with her.

While she was opening presents, the guests were taking pieces of cake as Nane and Arthur handed them out. I suggested she take her friends to the Maypole and she cheered the idea.

At the Maypole, my mind wandered and I thought about Brody and his family and the knoll. I couldn't remember the last time I thought about the knoll and I was disappointed in myself. It was so important to me, with so many wonderful, dear memories.

"And what might you be thinking of?" Asked Brody as he slipped up right behind me and stood close.

I could feel him standing behind me and I had a feeling inside I had never felt before. I could feel his breath on my neck and it took my own breath away. I had to take a step forward. I now understood what the word 'swoon' meant.

"I'm sorry, sir, did you say something?" I was trying my best to act as though he was only a guest and I was there to treat him as such.

"Yes, I did. I asked you what you were thinking." He said.

"If you must know, I was thinking about a place in my homeland of Ireland."

"And where might that place be?"

"I called it the knoll. There was a family there that would read under the tree and have picnics, and my brother and I would hide so we could listen without their knowing. I haven't thought about it in such a long time, I don't know what made me think of it right now."

"I do." He said as he leaned forward and close to me again. I closed my eyes and smiled without turning towards him. I was sure he was smiling, too. I had to lean my head back to get that strange chill from my neck and to bring myself back to reality.

I turned around to see him, and he was gone. I looked around both shoulders trying to find him, but he wasn't there. Had I imagined the moment? Surely not. I had felt his breath on my neck and heard his voice right behind me. Where could he have gone?

Genevieve called my name to watch her at the Maypole and I clapped for her to let her know I was watching. The children looked as though they were having a grand time. The adults were sitting at tables and enjoying themselves. They watched their children some, but most were engrossed in chatting with one another. I didn't see Mr. Patout, but I saw Mrs. Clarkson and she flitted between groups and made conversation with everyone.

The evening arrived and I helped Nane, Penelope, and Arthur bring out the main food to be served from the long table. There was gumbo and rice, oysters, green beans, cherries, bread and more. Nane had done a wonderful job and I knew her night was not over. She still had the taffy to contend with and I knew she wanted it to go well for Genevieve. I wasn't too worried about her tonight. She seemed very pleased with her day, so far.

As the adults ate, the children had potato sack races. The children seemed to love it and the adults laughed with glee. I remembered the boats we had for the day and wondered if the event that had occurred earlier had thwarted the children's chances of playing with the boats on the pond.

After everyone was finished eating, Mr. Patout requested one of the ladies to sing for the guests. She was shy at first, but she gave in and as they all sat out on the lawn, she sang The Lakes of Pontchartrain, Rosalie, The Prairie Flower, Buffalo Gals, and lastly Piping Tim. This was a song I knew from Ireland and as Nane, Penelope, and I sat on the grass outside, beyond the kitchen, I gleamed with happiness and tried to get them up to dance. I looked over at the guests, and many of the children were up and dancing.

I pulled on both of them to get up and dance with me. They stared at me strangely. Looking up and not moving. I did not understand until I felt a tap on my shoulder. It was Brody.

"Might I have this dance?" He asked me.

"Brody, you know I can't." I tried to sit back down, but he took my hand and pulled.

Penelope giggled, and Nane said, "Mr. Farraday, if I might, she might be more willing if you went into the kitchen."

I gave her a smirk, and then followed him into the kitchen as he held my hand. I was feeling shy for some reason, and felt my face flush. He took me in his arms, and even though the music was fast, we danced quite slowly, looking at each other once again. Even when the music stopped, he kept dancing. I didn't want him to stop, and I placed my head on his chest as we moved slowly to our own music for a little longer.

Nane knocked on the door in a bit, and said it was time for Penelope and her to get the taffy out for the children to have a taffy pull, and she needed to get it going before the fireworks. Brody asked her if he could help, but she wouldn't hear of it. She politely reminded him he needed to get back to the guests so no one would get into trouble. He bowed his head and let go of my hand, and walked out the kitchen door.

Penelope giggled again as Nane scolded her and told her to focus on this sticky taffy. I moved in to help them and take it out to the children who were waiting anxiously to pull away! Genevieve was first and she grabbed Lula May to be her partner. After they pulled, others grabbed and began doing the same thing. It looked like great fun, but messy fun at that!

As they finished, Mr. Williams had the fireworks ready and a bountiful array of light rose into the air filling the sky with sparkles. One after another went off, and all cheered with glee and clapped. I happened to look across the lawn at one time and caught Brody watching me. I smiled self-consciously, and tried to look back at the sky, but each time I looked at him, he was watching me rather than the fireworks. I wondered what he was thinking.

It was the last time I saw him this night, for we were busy cleaning the taffy and assorted dishes and glasses from the day. Isum came in later, after he had returned all of the carriages to their rightful owners.

"Everyone's gone that's supposed to be gone." He said.

"Everyone?" I asked.

"Yeh. When you're done here, I'll take you and

Penelope back."

My heart sank. Was I not to see Brody anymore? He hadn't said goodbye, and I didn't understand that? I started thinking he must have been looking at me and realized something that made him leave. What could he have seen or heard? What turned him away? Why did he leave?

I was consumed with a feeling of loss. I said nothing as we finished everything and said goodnight.

"Tomorrow you may come in later. Everyone will sleep in tonight, and I think we need it." Said Nane.

Penelope said all right, but I only nodded. I was having a twisted feeling in my stomach and my mind was heavy with thoughts of why Brody would have left without saying goodbye. Penelope talked to Isum the whole way back. That was fine with me. I didn't have it in me to make light conversation.

People were still up and singing as we pulled up to the field houses. When Isum stopped, Penelope jumped out first, and then I slid out and started walking to our house. Letty stopped me on the way.

"Are you all right Cora? Did everything go okay? Was Genevieve happy?" She asked.

"Yes." I said, and walked slowly back to the house. Letty didn't say another word, she must have known I needed to be alone.

I took my dress off and slipped into bed, staying in my underclothes. I lied on my back and stared at the ceiling. It was cool enough tonight to pull the covers up to my neck. I pulled them up and then brought my hands back down to my sides, under the covers. I lied there, stunned. Why should I be stunned? I was the one who told him I had to stay here. I was the one that asked him to respect my decision. What was I expecting? Why was I stunned?

All I could think about was Brody. How he looked. What he said. How he walked. The curve of his jaw and the feel of his heart as my head rested on his chest while we were dancing. I thought about his jumping in to help the young boy as I brought him to the shore. I had such a wonderful feeling being with him. Here we were, both adults now, sharing such a tremendous history. There was a connection, but had the separation in time separated us too much? I was the one who espoused this exact thing to him earlier, and I believed it, but I didn't want too deep down. Had he realized the truth in my theory as the night ended? I barely slept.

I woke to Henrietta heating water and starting breakfast the next morning. Letty stopped by to check on me and talk to Henrietta. I still wasn't in the mood to talk. I washed up, fixed my hair and dressed for the day. I took care of my burns and wrapped them nicely, then told Henrietta, Anna, and Lucy goodbye for the day. They had one more day off before the fields needed to be taken care of. The whole process started over for them tomorrow. Today they rested.

I walked over to the cart, but Isum wasn't standing by it at the moment. I stepped up in it and sat on the floor with my back against the sideboard. I lied my head back against the edge of the sideboard and started over with my thoughts that kept me up most of the night. Isum and Letty came out talking and walked over to the cart.

"It's just you going up to the house today." Said Letty. "We'll see you later, all right?"

I nodded and readjusted myself for the ride. Isum and I were silent as we rode along. I turned to my side and leaned into the sideboard and laid my head on my arm. I watched the trees go by and looked out onto the land as we passed. Belle Terre was a beautiful place. I could understand why they chose to live here. What a wonderful place to be in love and live. You could enjoy the trees and the flowers and each other's company. I bet that's exactly the way Mr. and Mrs. Patout were.

I heard voices as we pulled up to the house. I asked Isum if he knew what was going on, but he didn't, so I went into the kitchen to ask Nane. She was coming back from the dining room and wiping her hands on her apron and talking to herself. I knew it couldn't be too good, whatever it was.

"Nane. What is it?" I asked.

"You do not want to know! I cannot believe it. I do not

know what I am to do with Arthur!" She said.

"Why do you have to worry about him? He should be leaving today or tomorrow. Isn't that correct?"

"We all thought so, but Mrs. Clarkson has changed her plans. They won't be leaving for another week."

"What? Why is that?" I asked.

"That's not the worst of it!" She was exasperated.

"There's something worse?"

Nane began talking to herself again.

"Nane, there's something worse? What could be worse? Is Mr. Patout all right?" I asked, trying to clarify the situation.

"I don't believe he is." She said.

"Oh my goodness! What have I missed? Should I go and get Letty and tell her to bring her medicine?"

"Letty's medicine won't help, it is not his

physical health that I'm worried about at the moment." Said Nane.

"Then what? What do you mean? Japers, Nane, please!" The Irish in me swelled up.

"They're engaged! That Mrs. Clarkson has twisted him around her finger and gotten him to agree to marry her." She said.

"What? When did this happen? How did I miss it?" I asked her.

"Last night. I don't know when, or how, but she told me this morning. Gloating as she did. Even Arthur was gloating. What I am going to do with him? They are in there with some of their guests from last night who stayed the night," she said, "and your man is one of them. He is in there, too."

"Brody? Brody is still here?" My heart skipped a beat.

"Yes, Mr. Patout and he are moving to the study to talk business."

"What are they going to talk about? Did you hear what they said?" I asked her.

"No, Mrs. Clarkson has me doing things for her. Can you imagine? It hasn't been a day, and she is telling me what to do. This is not good, I'm telling you. This is not good. She is not what she seems. Oh she acts pretty and nice, but there is something to her that scares me. This is not good."

Nane continued, but was really talking to herself. I started thinking about Brody being here and what they might be talking about. I sat down at the kitchen table. Mrs. Clarkson walked in as I sat there baffled, and cleared her throat. I jumped up, and Nane turned around.

"The girls are up, won't you bring them something to eat, Nane?" She asked, "Oh, and Cora, Mr. Patout would like to see you in the study right away, dear."

"Yes, Ma'am." I told her and we both stood there until she left. We then looked at each other. Nane shrugged her shoulders, and I gave her a concerned squint. She went about preparing a tray for the girls as I collected myself to head to the study.

"You look just fine." Nane said knowing I was wondering how I looked. "If he is still interested after your pond smellin' self yesterday, I don't think you have too much to worry about."

I smiled, took a deep breath in and walked to the study. I tried not to look nervous, but my mind was full of doubt and wonder. I stood outside the doorway for a moment, and heard Brody's voice. They were talking about future shipping dates, and I was slightly relieved that their conversation was not about me. I turned past the frame of the door and Mr. Patout saw me. Brody was standing with his back to me, and he turned around to look at me.

"Bon jour, Cora. Pardonne-moi, Allie, isn't it? Mr. Farraday has explained to me your situation. It seems as though we purchased you under the most deceiving of circumstances. He has shown me your papers, and the court papers of the trial of the men that kidnapped you."

"Oh?" I said having no idea they had been arrested, or that Brody even knew about them.

"Mr. Patout, Allie has no idea what has occurred since her kidnapping. I believe her surprise is an honest one. She knows not of their arrest, or of our searching for her."

I stood their dumbfounded.

"Please, Allie, sit down. We must discuss some things." Mr. Patout said.

We all sat down and Mr. Patout and Brody discussed some of their conversation of the morning. I wasn't sure I was hearing all of it. It seemed to swirl around in my head rather than make any sense.

"Allie, are you following us?" Brody asked. They both smiled.

"Perhaps this is too much for all of us to comprehend at the moment. Why don't the two of you do what we talked about earlier, and then maybe we can have this discussion later. Would that be suitable?" Mr. Patout asked.

I had no idea what he was talking about, and my face must have betrayed me, for Brody caught on and answered him as they both smiled at my expense, again.

"That would be greatly appreciated." Said Brody.

"Bien. Then we shall talk later. Let's keep this to ourselves, until a decision has been made. Is that all right?" Asked Mr. Patout.

"Of course. That is probably best." Said Brody as I sat there not feeling as though I was really a part of any of this conversation. I was bewildered.

"If you'll excuse us, we will go and I shall try to fill in the months that we have been apart, and see what decisions shall be made." Brody reached for my arm and I stood up slowly. They both smiled as Brody and I walked out of the room.

"I'm not sure I've ever seen you so quiet, or should I say totally blarmy!" He told me as we walked toward the kitchen.

We stepped in to the kitchen and then an angry Irishman welled up inside of me as Brody began to talk.

"Mr. Patout has given you to me for the day." Said Brody.

"He's given me to you? What? Am I your property now?" I barked at him as I saw Nane turn around and stand with her hands on her hips.

"And what has gotten into you?' Nane asked.

"Please let me finish! This man thinks that I.... I don't know what he thinks, but he has discussed months of my life with Mr. Patout without telling me about it first."

"Allie, I..." Brody tried.

"I nothing. Did you not speak to him first?" I didn't wait for him to answer. We both knew the answer. "What made you think that I did not want to know about all of this, first?"

Mrs. Clarkson walked in, "What is going on in here? Oh, excuse me Mr. Farraday, I didn't realize you were in here."

I stood at attention, and Brody turned to her to respond. "I apologize if we were disturbing the household." He said while looking at me sternly. "Everything is fine. Cora was just explaining something to me."

"Are you sure?" She inquired, "It didn't sound like explaining. It sounded rather inappropriate and rude."

"Yes, but I can promise you I have it under control. Isn't that correct, Cora?" He asked me and I stood there grinding my teeth. "Cora, isn't that correct?" He took my arm and squeezed it.

"Yes, yes, Ma'am. I apologize if I was inappropriate." I had a certain amount of disgust in my response, which she must have heard.

"Well, if you are sure. I'll leave you to your business." She said. Brody nodded to her, and she closed the door.

"Under control?" I asked in a toughened whisper. "Now you are controlling me?"

"It looks like someone needs to! You are being quite unreasonable. I am going to take your demeanor as though you are so taken aback at the information you were given that you have lost your senses temporarily. What do you think, Nane?"

"Yes, sir, that's what it looks like to me." She said as I gave her an ugly scowl.

"Now why would you want to look at Nane that way? She has done nothing to you. If you want to take your anger out on anyone, it should be me, and I will listen to whatever you have to say as soon as we go to the jardin évier for our picnic." He said.

"The jardin evier? You speak French now? "I asked him.

"Yes, I do, but I am only pronouncing it that way because that is what Mr. Patout called it and it is where he suggested we go. He has ever so graciously offered this spot to us."

I was surprised. Now Brody speaks French? I had my tongue taken from me, again.

"What? No comment? Have I puzzled you again? Nane, I think I like this." She smiled as he enjoyed his repeated surprises to me and my loss of words. "Well, before I get her going again, Nane, if you will show me where the items are for our picnic, I will gladly put them together in our basket."

He stepped outside the kitchen door and picked up a basket. Nane smiled and I assumed they had known about this all along, planning it before I arrived this morning.

I looked down at my clothes and back up at his, and had a brief moment of despair. Brody saw me and read my face.

"Now don't you start that, again. You look acceptable and you have to remember that I have seen you in much worse. You were quite a ragamuffin back then."

Nane laughed, and his memory of years long gone and how I must have looked back in Ireland made me smile. He was right. I wore some awful clothes back then. He had seen me in worse, but it wasn't just the clothes, it was what they meant this time. He was trying, and I wasn't going to ruin his effort by bringing us down. I wanted to be with him and I needed to appreciate the moment.

I tried to help them pack the basket, but I enjoyed watching Nane and Brody interact. This is the way people should treat one another. People should live and work together without one group being better than another, or treating people as so.

When they were done, Brody gave Nane a kiss on her forward, and told her, "I would take you with us, Madam, but I wish to be alone with this fine, young lass. Please forgive me."

She laughed, and I thought I might have seen her blush.

"And you, will you accept my invitation? Are you ready for a picnic in the sunken garden?" He asked me.

"Yes, but I do not know where the sunken garden is? Do you?"

"No, I do not, but Mr. Patout has given me uncomplicated directions, or so he says. So, if you are willing, we shall venture out and see these sunken gardens. Oui?" He asked sarcastically.

"Oui." I told him and out the door we went.

CHAPTER 13
THE SUNKEN GARDEN

We laughed and teased, as we went, my having absolutely no idea where he was leading me. There was no rock path and he ventured the wrong way a few times, but that only added to our pleasure of being together. At one time I joked with him saying we were totally lost, but as he lead me into what looked like a wooded area, he found some steps, and as we stepped downward, we walked down into a garden. He was right. It was a sunken garden!

"Can you imagine," I asked him, "in the Spring what a beautiful place this must be?"

"Yes, it must be. I can understand why Mr. Patout said this was his wife's favorite place to be at Belle Terre."

"Did he really say that? This was her place?"

"He said this was their place, and that someone else should be appreciating it, so he offered it me so that I might bring you here."

I was so touched and humbled. He had offered a very special place to us from his heart, and what a difficult thing that must have been for him.

"I've never heard him speak of this place, nor anyone else for that matter. I understand why. I would not want to share this place with anyone. It could be your own private paradise. They must have been very much in love, don't' you think?"

"Yes, they must have been. We will let him know how much we appreciate his sharing this place with us when we get back. He'll want to know what we talked about, and what we decided. Shall we begin?"

"Not just, yet. I want to hear everything, I really do, but can we just put the blanket down under this tree over here and appreciate the moment. I don't know when I'll have another moment like this; surrounded in a private garden, hundreds of miles away from anything that is ugly or cruel."

We went over to where I asked, put down the basket,

and laid out the blanket. I awkwardly lied down as Brody reached for my hand.

"I can help you, you know." He said to me.

"I'm sorry. I'm just not used to it." I rolled down on my back and looked beyond the branches and up towards the sky.

Brody sat down across the blanket from me. We both sat there quietly for a while. I looked over at him and he was looking at me again. I blushed, and he looked up at the sky, obviously reading my face, again.

He began to recite Wordsworth's poem about clouds and I chimed in with him. We finished the poem together, and then both laughed at the thought of our saying it together.

"I read that poem to Nella once, did she tell you?"

"Yes, she did. Nella has a lot of respect for you. She says you are stronger than you think. I laughed at her when she said that, telling her you are the strongest person I know. I told her you come from good stock."

"Stock? Like cattle? Is that what you think of me?"

"No silly, stock like your upbringing. Your family, you come from a good family."

"We both do, don't we." It was a statement to him more than a question.

I reached out to his foot to touch his shoe. "We are both very lucky, aren't we, in the strangest kind of way?"

"What do you mean by that?"

"Think of all we have been through, all we have lost, and still we are so much better off than others."

"You could have it better, Allie. You don't have to live like this and be treated as a slave."

"I know, but it's really not that bad. It's very close to how we used to live in Ireland. Well, the living situation is, and I'm not on the floor. We have beds, and there is food. We are not starving."

"Yes, but if you were in New York or Ireland you would not have been branded."

"But there is the same kind of bonding, and their angst becomes mine." I sat up and leaned on one hip, towards him.

"Once you experience the abhorrent condition of slavery and the people it affects, I don't know how to turn away. We must try to eradicate it."

"That's what Captain and his group is trying to do, also. Remember, you wrote me a long time ago about his initial confrontation with the selling of slaves and how he abhorred it. He believes just as strongly as you."

"I know, but what can I do there? If I am here, I can tell slaves where to go and be a part of those that help slaves from the inside."

"Do you understand the danger involved? What if you are discovered?"

"I know, I know. They don't just put you in a workhouse, they kill you!"

His face said it all. He didn't like what I said. "Let's don't get worked up on this right now. I don't want us to be that way here in the garden."

"You're right. Tell me about Ma and your voyage from England. Tell me about New York and Captain. How did you find where I was? When was he freed?"

"He is the best one to tell you the story. When we arrived in New York, he was already there. He had returned with the Seagull and the Kate and was preparing to go back to South Carolina to follow up on the leads they had for you."

"How did they find out what had happened?"

"The sailor on the Seagull told them of the men who tricked him, and then Mr. Cotton, Mr. Marshall, and Mr. Cox talked to others who led them from one clue to another. Mr. Cotton was successful at getting the Captain released, and then he joined the investigation. Captain and his friends hunted for as much information as they could, then they successfully added cargo to the ships, and headed for New York.

"When I joined the search with the returning crew, it took us through, Georgia, Alabama, and Mississippi, before we arrived in Louisiana. It was quite an adventure finding where you'd been, and where they were taking you. We spoke to a family who thought it strange that an Irish sounding girl would be a slave. We were more than a month behind your kidnappers, but eventually it paid off and we tracked you to New Orleans. There was a young slave in New Orleans who said she had spent some time with you and dressed you the day before you were sold. Then, it was just a matter of infiltrating the area and finding you."

"What happened to Robert, Willy, and Tom? I heard you say something about their being arrested. Is it true?"

"Yes. Once we were in New Orleans and permeated the local businesses and organizations, people began to talk more freely, and one topic was the white quintroon that was sold. We knew the odds of it not being you were quite small, so finding the men who sold you was an easy matter. People had no lack of tattle, and the three men were something of an infamous trio in and about town.

"Finding them and proving their illegal activity was two different things. They touted themselves to be legal bounty hunters and you were a fair catch. Our records and the photo Captain had of you proved them wrong. Then it was a matter of who bought you and how to get into your world without your owners realizing it.

"When we found out it was Mr. Patout, it was easy to establish a relationship. Then beginning a business relationship with him followed. I was trying to manipulate the situation so we would be able to get to you. We were just fortunate Mr. Patout purchased you, and not an unpleasant landowner. Mr. Patout has been quite gracious in his business dealings and in his understanding of your predicament."

"Predicament? It sounds as though you are blaming me."

"No, forgive my wording, maybe situation would be in better use here."

"Who received my letter, and when?"

"I did. The Captain of the ship, not your Captain, but, Captain Jake, or Jacobson, handed me the letter as we arrived in Charleston."

"What? He didn't give it to you until then?"

"Don't be peevish, he didn't know of its importance, and only handed it to me to give to Captain Kiper as we landed. Captain Kiper was waiting for us in Charleston. Rest assured, I was peevish myself for a moment, but more so ecstatic that we had actually heard from you. We only spent one night in the harbor, and Captain Jake and I set sail the next day to return to New Orleans and to find a way to get to you without too much suspicion. It just so happens that young Genevieve was having a party and Mr. Patout was kind enough to invite me as a guest. Had he not, I'm not sure how I would have finagled the situation. Do you mind if I remove my coat?"

"No, of course not." I told him.

He stood up and slipped off his coat, then laid it down on the blanket. I watched him as he removed his coat and saw the change in a man who I once knew as a boy. His mother would be so proud of him. He picked up the basket and moved it nearer to us.

"Shall we have some lunch?" He asked.

"Yes, let's do, I'll help."

And as we both reached at the same time towards the basket, our eyes met. I looked down, self-conscious that he might read my face. He lifted my head and held my face close to his. He looked, as if wanting, but he took his hand and brushed back some hair that had fallen in my eyes. He then let go. I was embarrassed because I knew what I wanted him to do, but he hadn't done so. This was awkward. How do you move beyond a history of arguing and bickering, of growing up as brother and sister? Maybe it wasn't right. Maybe he didn't want me in the same way. Maybe I wanted something that couldn't or shouldn't be, but I wanted it. I wanted him.

We ate lunch and he told me about his father and his friendship with Ma's friend, Clara. He says that they miss Ma, but they are content with her happiness here in America and with Captain. I could barely stand waiting, and interrupted him asking him to tell me all about Ma and Captain. This was so new and exciting!

Brody spoke of their initial shared worry about my

situation and me. He said everyone saw that feelings existed between them, except the two of them. Rufina could barely stand it. She was the one that forced them to acknowledge their feelings, and since then they have been quite joyful. Brody seemed happy for her, too, and to have taken a liking to Captain.

Brody and Captain's relationship sounded like it had helped to make both businesses' flourish and gives the impression that it is congenial. He and Ma live at the Captain's house, and the Farraday's business is involved in England, America, and other places abroad. He didn't speak much of Patrick or his relationship to their business, so I didn't push him for information. There was so much more I wanted to hear, and Patrick could wait for another time.

I wanted to hear about Jonathan, but wasn't sure how to ask. He told me about Rufina and Angelo and how much they enjoyed their company, and Rufina's stories of me. He repeated some and I blushed at his knowing much more than I had wanted him to know. I'm happy that Ma was able to hear about our time apart and how much Rufina and Captain obviously cared for me, but stories they thought were entertaining or cute, were simply embarrassing to me.

I stood up and walked around, not only to stretch my legs but also to release some of the ire I felt building up inside. He kept going, reminding me of how we used to be. I looked back at him, seeing the pleasure in his face at relaying these stories to me. He then spoke about meeting Jonathan's family. My moment had arrived.

"You met Jonathan?" I asked him.

"Yes, and Irene, her sister and their parents. The way you described Irene is not the way she portrays herself to me. She showed me her home and remained ever the staunch advocate of moral purity. She relishes their home, helping to make it a haven for comfort and quiet."

"What an absolutely serene picture! Do you believe that? Did Rufina not tell you different?" I could feel my indignation growing. Had she won him over, too?

"I haven't finished, I…" He tried to say.

"I'm not sure I want to hear. She is up to her old ways, and I can readily see why she would want to succeed at catching your eye."

"I'm not sure you understand."

"I understand. I know how she works. A fine-looking, successful man as you would be quite a good catch for her. Is that what you want? And while we are on the subject you have not spoken of Mary or Finola."

He laughed out loud, which just made me angrier.

"Well? Might you say something about your paramours?"

He laughed again.

"You remember them? Allie, I haven't spoken to Mary in years. In fact, I believe she married Tommy Doyle and they live in Knock. As for Finola, she and I are still acquainted and I see her whenever I go to Galway. We are close friends. Why are you upset about them? What have they done?" He asked me.

I couldn't answer. I didn't know how to answer. Why was I upset? Was I actually jealous? What right did I have to be jealous, and yet, I must be. I didn't say a word, but turned away.

"What about Jonathan, Allie? How do you feel about him?"

"I don't know. What happened to him? Does he ask about me?" I asked Brody.

"I have met him, but he has never inquired about you to me. I believe Rufina was the one who told him about you, but she will not speak to him anymore."

"What?" I inquired. "Why not?"

"It was his family that turned the Captain in. They sent word to authorities in Charleston that he was carrying slaves from there to New York in his ship."

"How did they know? Who told them?"

"We're not sure. Did you tell Jonathan? Might he have known?" He asked.

"He would never have told! He wanted to marry me!" Suddenly I felt used. Were his intentions as underhanded as his sister's? Might he have been duping me all along? I wanted to know more. "What…what are you saying? You don't know him. He's not like Irene."

"I'm not accusing you, I'm just saying that somehow Jonathan and his family were involved."

"And now you are courting Irene? Does Captain know? I can't believe you would be so disloyal and unkind. Why would you do that? Is she that beautiful? Is she that appealing?"

"Do you honestly believe I would do such a thing? Is that how you see me?"

"I don't know what to believe. It's all so much at once. So much time has passed between us. So many lives are changed and new relationships have occurred. You heard about my time in school and adjusting to life in America. You know so much about my time, and me, and I barely know about you. Rufina and Captain have told you things I would not want anyone to know. I'm sure you would have your own stories, too, if you were the one living there."

"I'm not trying to say I wouldn't, or telling you these things to embarrass you." He said.

"Then why? I saw the look on your face and it reminded me of our time in Ireland and how you would enjoy being the quicker witted one or teasing me knowing I couldn't respond as quickly. I saw that glee in your face." I told him. He stood up and walked toward me.

"Allie, then you're reading me all wrong. You're not understanding why I am telling you these stories."

We stood there for what seemed to be an eternity, looking at each other until he took my arms, and held me close. I was still irritated inside and couldn't imagine why else he would be so pleased at telling me these things, and yet, he looked at me with such genuineness.

"I'm not pleased or trying to be witty. I'm not trying to be disloyal or unkind. I might not be able to show what I feel on my face correctly, but it's not what you think. I'm telling you these stories and enjoying telling them because they are about you."

He stood there looking rather uncomfortable. I stood

there stiff, feeling angst. And then, within an instant, I melted.

"I love these stories about you because they are the reason I fell in love with you."

My eyes widened and if I had not been clenching my jaws previously, they would have dropped open. Had he just said what I thought he said? My face softened and my eyes accepted his declaration. My heart melted and the ire I felt before was a hundred miles away.

"I didn't know it so immensely until I saw you jump into the water yesterday to save that young boy. As you brought him back to safety, I looked upon the lady who lived on paper and in our memories for years. She was alive and vibrant before me, awakening a feeling I did not know I had. Then as the day went on, I watched you and realized how totally unaware I was of my feelings for you.

"The stories I repeated to you are my fond remembrances of your life, without my having been a part of it. You grew up in those stories and in your letters, and my affection for you was there, but I didn't realize it. The twinge I felt as I saw your wounds, knowing I could do nothing about alleviating your pain, was too deep to explain.

"Forgive me, Allie. Forgive me for allowing you to think that I enjoyed teasing you, or you to believe you are not a part of our world. I didn't articulate well, and I..."

I couldn't wait any longer; I took his head in my hands and pulled his head down to mine to kiss him. His lips were there, but it took him a moment to encase me in his arms and totally respond. My head was arched back slightly and I felt completely enveloped by his embrace. My heart was racing and my mind lost. I was only feeling, and it felt good, it felt right. I tingled with delight as my insides rushed.

When he released me, we stood there, rendered speechless. A moment later we smiled, and he took my hand and guided me back to the blanket.

"Now might I help you to sit down?" He asked.

I nodded and he helped me down, and then lied next to me.

"Would we ever have thought about this back in Ireland? You used to make me so very mad." I said.

"Used to? I believe there are at least two times just today that I have brought out the angry Irish part of you!" He said.

We both laughed, and I raised myself slightly to look at him.

"I guess that is a part of me I can't seem to let go of." I told him.

"It's probably helped you along the way."

I propped myself up on my elbow and stayed there as we talked more about our time away from one another and everything that happened. We laughed and talked, enjoying our time together. It was enchanting. The realization of our feelings, the sunken garden and it's ideal setting. Separating us from the real world. I lied back down and we both lied there staring up at the sky beyond the branches of the tree.

"Isn't this magical? Like something in a book your mother would have read to us, or to your family." I said to him, as he then sat up on his elbow.

"You were part of our family, remember?"

"Not when Quinlan and I would hide on the side of the knoll and listen. I could never have imagined that one day my life would have had so many twists and turns, and I would be lying her with you. It really is enchanting."

"Allie, are you forgetting where we are? And why you are here?" He stood up and walked around the area. "This spot is as idyllic as you say, but beyond the trees is a world that is not as simple as you would like for it to be. Nor is the outcome as romantic. We are not in a book written by Jane Austen. We must face the world as you live in it, and decide what to do."

"I hear what you say," I sat up and looked towards him. "and I know what you say to be true. I guess I was caught up in the moment and my wanting it to be true."

He came back to me and knelt beside me.

"It can be. Why don't you come back with me? You can see your mother and Captain, Rufina and Angelo, and we can take you to a doctor to look at your burns. Let us take care of you for a while, and then you can decide. You know your mother would love to take care of you, and Rufina would fight her for your time!"

We smiled and he sat down facing me. "Come back, Allie, let us all take care of you."

"But I can't" I told him.

"You can't, or you won't?" He asked.

"Please don't make it sound as if I don't want to come back with you. I do! But how can I leave here in good conscience? You know deep down I can help from my being here."

"And how do you suppose everyone will treat you once they know you are not a slave? Won't you be questioned and mistrusted on both sides? How will that help?"

"I do not know, but we will have to think of something. Help me, Brody, please. Help me to justify my being here and making a difference."

"I can't justify your being here, but I do respect your determination and willingness to help those less fortunate. The need is there, I just wish it wasn't you who felt so strongly about making a difference on your own. I suppose I will not be able to change your mind, thus I want to make it the best for you."

I looked at him, knowing the only answer was to be separated again. I wouldn't be going home, and he would have to leave. He stood up again, thinking.

"What if I spoke to Mr. Patout about your being Genevieve's governess officially? Not slave, but her governess. Then he would be the person over you and not Mr. Williams."

"I'm not sure. I would then be separated from everyone, and like any other free white person. I have to remain a trusted ally somehow. I need to be trusted by both whites and slaves."

"I believe that is where your own intuition and ability must be different than others. You must earn the respect of both and play a very careful game with all parties. We both know being caught as a collaborator can have dire consequences. You might be willing to take these risks, but to those of us who care about you, it is a steep price to wager."

"Yes, you're right, but think of the payoff? We will be able to sleep at night knowing we are making a difference for so many. It excites me to think I could actually save someone and get them to freedom."

"I can understand your enthusiasm, but what of the down side? Have you thought through all of it? What if the person you are trying to free is caught? What might happen to them? What if someone you have tried to help is hung? What if anyone that helps you gets into trouble? Can you live with the harmful aspects of this humanitarian effort you are trying to portray? Can you sleep at night knowing someone has died or was punished because of your actions?"

My head was spinning. He was right, I had not thought through all of it. I knew the consequences, but I had not actualized them against my own actions. Would I be able to accept something as he describes? I went back to the blanket and dropped down, falling back on my back. I bent my knees and placed an arm across my forehead. Brody walked over to me and sat next to me.

"Allie, if your heart is set on this, I know I cannot persuade you differently. If you have any bit of the old Allie in you, then you are too stubborn to be dissuaded, but surely you will allow us to think through the best situation for you to make your desire successful. I believe you must remain in the same house as you have been, and continue to live with the people you have been living with. Do you sew?" He asked me and I looked at him ever so strangely.

What a question to ask in the middle of all of this serious conversation? I shook my head 'no.'

"Then you must learn." He stood up and began walking around again, talking through his thoughts. "You must learn to quilt and to learn the signs and signals of the Underground Railroad. You must use the quilts you make as instructions for those who want to be free. I must explain to you our connections along the way so you will know what to tell those people. You must learn them and never write them down. We must have our own code for you so you will understand it in our correspondence. Never right down anything directly, in case the correspondence is confiscated. It must all be in code."

His methodical thought process captivated me, and I sat there quietly listening to him, trying to remember all of it. He came back and sat across from me on the blanket once again, and listed off the places that were friendly and how slaves could get to them. He would ask me if I understood or to repeat what he said, then he would move on. He never used names, except for the ones I already knew. He explained what friendly signals were and how slaves were to look for them. He also explained about those people who try and trick friends of the Underground Railroad or slaves and that we always have to be diligent. He spoke of the vow of silence we must all keep. Understanding that giving up names, secrets, or places meant someone might die because of our inability to keep that vow.

He knew so much, and I felt a deeper connection to him knowing we shared the same conviction for this cause. My mind went back and forth between being amazed at how much he knew, looking at him talking, and listening to his words. I had no idea he had so totally consumed this cause, as Captain and I had.

"Allie, are you listening to every word? You must! If not, someone will get hurt, and I cannot have it on my conscience for that person to be you."

I tried my best to hear everything, but there was so much. I knew I needed to listen because my conscience could not handle someone being hurt on my account. He was right, and I knew my tendency for romanticizing things. I did my best to focus on hearing his words, not just listening to them. It took a long time to go through everything, and before I knew it our day had passed.

We packed up our things, and started to walk back. Before leaving the garden, I stopped and turned around, trying to remember it. Brody stopped, too, and didn't say a thing as I stood there. Eventually, he came over to me and took my hand.

"Allie, we'll be back. If not, we'll have our own secret

garden somewhere else, just like the knoll."

He pulled slightly and I smiled at him and followed him out of the garden.

CHAPTER 14
MY DESTINY

We walked without saying a word for a while, very different from our walk to the garden. We were both solemn, and walked this way until we could see the house at a distance.

Brody turned to me and said, "I will talk to Mr. Patout and discuss our arrangements. You will no longer be a slave, but you will be Genevieve's Governess and I will expect you to be treated as such. You should probably remain as Cora, for your protection and for a better association from whence you began here. It will be up to you to set in motion the groundwork for helping those you wish to, but remember to be careful and to not be too trusting. I will contact you as often as possible, and hope that one day you will want to come home with me."

I squeezed his hand in acknowledgement, and before I could say anything, we heard Isum. He was coming our way.

"Mr. Farraday! Cora! Nane wants you to come quick! Mr. Patout has taken ill and he would like to see you."

We looked at each other in astonishment, and ran towards the house. We dropped our picnic things as soon as we arrived and headed towards the stairs. Nane was at the top of the stairs and motioned for us to come up. She met us at the top landing.

"Mr. Patout's fever went up while you were gone this afternoon and we put him to bed. Mrs. Clarkson is in there with him now. He asked to see you both when you returned." Nane said in a whisper.

"And Genevieve? Where is she?" I asked

"I had Isum bring Penelope to be with her and the other girls. She is fine, but worried about her Pa-Pa." Said Nane. "Let me tell him you are here. He won't rest well, until he talks to you both. Just a minute…"

We stood there looking at each other. Nane went in to his room and then came back to the door and waved for us to come in. I went in first, walking towards Mr. Patout's bed. Mrs. Clarkson acknowledged us and stepped back away from the bed to allow us closer access to Mr. Patout. We stood beside one another at his bedside. He looked weak and pale, and I saw that yellow tinge in his eyes, which worried me.

"Were you able to enjoy yourselves?" He asked. "Mrs. Patout always believed it to be a magical place."

"It is magical. Thank you for allowing us to go there." I told him.

"I can see why Mrs. Patout would cherish your property. Belle Terre is truly a remarkable place. I am grateful for your consideration and hospitality." Brody said.

"And were you able to come to any agreements? Are we to lose Cora?" Mr. Patout asked.

"We have discussed the situation thoroughly, and Cora would like to stay. She says she has a very special relationship with Genevieve and would like to remain. If we could," Brody glanced towards Mrs. Clarkson, "I would like to discuss the rest of our agreement in private."

"D'accord. Charlene, would you and Nane please excuse us for a moment?" Mrs. Clarkson nodded, and she and Nane stepped out the door. I noticed Mrs. Clarkson did not close the door entirely but left it slightly open. I wondered why.

"Now, what is it you would like to tell me?" He said to Brody.

"Allie should never have been sold to you as a slave, and you have so graciously acknowledged the wrongful action that occurred. We both appreciate that. While it was a criminal act, I acknowledge your loss of monetary value in the situation and have the money to pay your losses and correct the injustice." I looked at him, having no knowledge of this transaction. "However, as part of this arrangement, I expect her to no longer be a slave and to be an acknowledged governess for Genevieve. She is not to be treated as a slave, and is to be considered as free as you and me."

I looked back at Mr. Patout, waiting for his response.

"And is that what you want?" He looked at me and inquired.

"Yes, but I would like to stay where I am in the field

houses. I am already settled there and I would still be available whenever you or Genevieve needed me." I told him.

Brody continued, "She should be paid four to five dollars a week for her services, plus, she should be allowed to learn French from you."

I stared back at Brody, stunned at his forwardness with Mr. Patout. My eyes darted back to Mr. Patout, waiting for an overwhelming difference of opinion from him.

"That sounds very reasonable." He said, as I looked back and forth between them. "Genevieve will be glad she is not to lose Cora. What shall we call you, Cora or Allie?" He asked me.

"I would prefer to remain as Cora." I told him. "No one would understand my change in name. So, Cora, please."

"If I might remind you, she is to be free. She may come and go as she pleases. I will give you a signed paper stating so in the chance someone would challenge her status." Brody told him.

"It sounds as though you have thought through this quite comprehensively. Cora has very good friends and family, to have you go to so much trouble to find her and set right her situation. I suppose I would hope to do the same for Genevieve. Mrs. Patout always believed in providence and I believe this to be one of those times. She would say it is not always the desired outcome or good fortune as wished, but the embodiment of the final design as laid out by God. Sometimes it is hard for me to believe that, but as I think through things as they happen, it is most always true." He told us.

"I would have enjoyed knowing Mrs. Patout." I told him. "I could have learned much from her wisdom, experience, and outlook on life."

He smiled, but there was tiredness in his eyes with a feint hint of sweat around his hairline.

Brody picked up on it and said, "We will leave you now. I will be leaving tomorrow morning and sailing back to New York the following day. We will stay in contact and I am to assume that business will stay as it has been?"

"Yes, yes, of course. I will see you before you leave in the morning." Mr. Patout said. "Cora, would you please tell Mrs. Clarkson and Nane that I will be resting for the evening and they are not to worry. Tell Nane I am not hungry. She shouldn't worry about bringing me anything"

"Yes, sir, but I'm sure Nane will want to make sure you get something to eat or drink. I bet even Letty has something for you to help you." I told him.

"I'm sure you are right." Mr. Patout and I smiled, and Brody and I stepped out of his room.

As we opened the door, Mrs. Clarkson was standing on the landing outside. She acted as though she had not been listening, but I do not know how she could not have heard. I told her what Mr. Patout had said, but she said she wanted to sit with him anyway. We went to the kitchen to tell Nane.

"Did that woman go back in with him?" Nane asked us.

"Yes, she did Nane, but she said she was only going to sit with him and let him rest." I told her.

"Humph! I don't know what it is, but there is something about that woman I am not comfortable with. Did you see Arthur anywhere up there? I cannot keep up with that man and he shows up at the strangest times." Nane said. "You should probably see Genevieve. She is fine with Penelope, but those nieces of Mrs. Clarkson are with her and who knows what they are up to!"

I suggested Brody stay in the house while I checked on Genevieve, but he insisted on going with me and promised he would stand back and watch without interfering. Nane reminded us it was almost their dinnertime, and they should be coming in shortly.

We walked out and found them in the front on the maypole. They were all playing nicely and it looked like Penelope was enjoying herself with them. When Genevieve saw me she let go of her ribbon and ran towards me. She hugged me and told me about her day and asked if I had seen her Pa-Pa. I told her I had and he was resting. She looked at Brody very cautiously and stood right by me. I looked at Brody and then bent down to talk to Genevieve.

"Genevieve, this is my good friend, Mr. Farraday. I have known him for a very long time. He and I grew up together in Ireland." I told her.

She was curious now and asked him some questions. He interacted with her very well and even offered to tell her some stories about me as a little girl. Genevieve loved the thought of that, but I was saved by Nane calling them to dinner.

"Must you bring up those stories?" I asked him. "They were so long ago."

"But they are a part of you, and I'm sure Genevieve would love to hear how you were a little girl, once." He said.

We went back to the kitchen and Nane had made us both a plate to take on the back porch. She gave me a wry smile as she told us where to go and have dinner. I was sure she was thinking about my setting the same stage for Mr. Patout and Mrs. Clarkson just a day ago.

"You don't have much time the two of ya'." Nane said. "Go on and enjoy yourself.

Penelope and I will take care of tonight."

Brody and I went to the back porch and sat. We didn't say very much. It wasn't that we didn't have anything to say, we did. It felt as though we didn't say anything because we didn't want this time to end. We knew it was going to and I was melancholy.

"You haven't told me anything to tell your mother or Captain. If I don't go back with something, even Rufina, everyone will be upset." He said.

"I know Rufina will. She probably would not let you hear the end of it." I said. "I know they'll think I'm blarmey, except for Captain. I think he feels strongly enough to know my intentions are honorable, but worrying about me will be a whole different situation."

"You are different, Allie. You are not the little girl your Ma hugged goodbye in Knock, or the little girl I waved goodbye to on the docks in Galway. Even Rufina and Nella, why even Skully, talk about your innocence and naivety. I do believe you are still quite the romantic and life is part of some wildly adventuress storyline, but I don't believe you to be naïve anymore."

"Thanks to your mother, I can make my imagination become part of my reality." I told him.

"She would only want you to enjoy the escape of reality literature gives you, not make it part of your reality." He said.

"You are not the only person to have told me so, but how do I change the thoughts that my mind processes or my natural instincts as I look at life. Even with some of the horrible things that have happened, I think I understand and believe what Mr. Patout said Mrs. Patout believed about providence. What do you think?"

"I believe in it some, but I also believe we can make our destiny, or our destiny is what we make of it. Maybe that is what I am supposed to tell everyone at home. You have elected to shape your destiny."

"Yes, Brody, tell them that. You always say things so eloquently. You can make them understand. Do try."

"I'll try, but how do I make them believe when I am not sure myself?" He asked me.

I did not have an answer, but I put my plate down and stood up from my chair. I sat next to him on the wooden porch and wrapped my arm around his leg and laid my head on his knee. He placed his hand on my head and stroked the hair from my face. We sat there for some time, talking about nothing, but sharing an immeasurable awareness of our bond.

I must have fallen asleep, for I only remember his placing me in the cart and kissing my forehead. I was too groggy to say anything but I could see him standing there as Isum snapped the reigns and Dizzy took off in a trot. I turned on my side and watched him standing there until I could no longer see him. It was a site I had remembered, and one I realized would happen many more times in my life.

I rose early the next morning to rush back to the main house and see him before he left. I helped Letty put some things in the cart for Nane to give to Mr. Patout. Letty took her time telling me what Nane should do with each of these herbs. I tried my best to concentrate on what she was saying because I knew it to be important, but I just couldn't. My mind was on getting to Brody and seeing him before he left.

"Are you paying attention to this, Cora?" She asked me. "You have to get it right. If not, it could have dreadful consequences, and we don't want to do anything to hurt Mr. Patout. Cora? Are you listening?"

"Yes, yes! I have it." I tried repeating it back to her, but it took her explaining it to me two more times before I had the right combinations and mixtures to give to Nane.

When she thought I had it memorized correctly, she allowed me to get into the cart and leave with Isum, but she was reiterating her procedures until we were out of site. I heard her yelling them at me in the distance, but my mind was only focused on one thing, and that was getting back to the main house and seeing Brody. I anxiously sat towards the front of the cart, urging Isum to hurry Dizzy along.

When we saw the house in sight, I noticed Nane outside waiting for us.

"Is Mr. Patout all right? Has something happened to him?" I asked, assuming he must have taken a turn for the worse.

"No, no, it's not Mr. Patout, Cora, he's fine. He had a good night, and he is up and moving about this morning, or at least looking that way."

"Then what is it? Why do you have that look of concern on your face? Is it Genevieve?"

"No, it is not Genevieve, either." She said, and with that I had the most ominous feeling. I knew instinctively why she looked that way.

"It is your friend, Mr. Farraday. He left very early this morning. He left you a letter and said to tell you goodbye." Nane said.

"What?" I asked her incredulously. "What do you mean he left? He left me without saying goodbye? This is a cruel joke. Isn't it? He would not leave me without saying goodbye! Nane!

Please tell me he did not leave and you are coddin' me!"

Nane stared at me with a most solemn face. I looked at Isum, and he looked down. Neither said a word, and the shock of the moment had me taken aback. I plopped down on the ground, stiff-arming myself to hold me up, but bowing my head as in some surreal moment. My heart was pounding and my head swirled. Nane reached into her pocket and pulled the letter from it and held it out for me to take. I shook my head, but she bent down in front of me and urged me to take it.

"Cora, he didn't want to hurt you. Read it, maybe his words will explain it better than I can why he had to leave. Men don't always do well with emotion, and maybe he thought this would be better. Read the letter, see what he says." She urged.

I grabbed at it and pulled it into my lap, crumbling it slightly as I held it tightly in my hand. I was angry. I was hurt. I was sad. Ugh! I had been this way with him so many times before, but the feelings had a different meaning this time. They had a different association. I knew it was not only in my head, but my heart.

Nane and Isum helped me up and Nane held my arm as we walked into the kitchen. I sat down on the bench of the table, with the crumpled letter still held tightly in my fist. My head was resting on my arm, and my eyes were closed with my head tilted down toward the table.

"Cora, why don't you go out to my house and read your letter. Go do it in private. I bet you'll feel better once you've read it. He's too nice a young man to hurt you the way you think he has. Go on, now, get out there and read it." Nane insisted.

I didn't move until she came over and tried to lift my shoulders and physically get me to get up. I resisted momentarily, but then begrudgingly stood up and walked out the door; the letter still crumpled in my angry fist. I walked across the way and into the room that carried a memory of Brody. I lay down on Nane's bed, on my side, and tried to think of our time together. I couldn't believe he left without telling me goodbye. I was devastated. I wanted to read his letter, but I hadn't let go of it in my hand, and was almost afraid of what it might say. What could he say that would ease my discontent at this time?

I rolled back and looked at my fist, releasing the letter from my tight grip. I slowly smoothed out its wrinkles and flattened it the best I could. I looked at this folded letter, knowing the words inside were from someone I cared deeply about. He was my connection to a world I cherished and loved. He was my past, and the love he expressed to me was accepted in my heart and I yearned for it to be a part of my future. I rolled back on my side and unfolded the letter. I smiled at his handwriting having memories of his penmanship and words as they flashed through my mind.

October 8, 1953

Dear Allena,

I know as you read this letter you are a mix of emotions. No doubt angry, confused, disappointed and possibly feeling rejected and lost. Please do not take my leaving you before we said goodbye as anything but what it truly is. As I carried you to the cart last night and watched you ride away, I realized I could think of no easy way for us to separate, again.

You believe in the most idealistic of worlds and while that might be impractical at times, it is a strength you have that leads others to feel there is hope. In the middle of my very ordinary life, you have given me direction and hope and have made me realize love can be attained in the twists and tales of our own lives. I believe William Shakespeare when he wrote, "The course of true love never did run smooth."

I can't imagine a life with you would ever be smooth, and I would never want it to be that way. You are adventurous and strong, and at the same time kind and selfless. Whether my feelings are to be reciprocated or not, I want to support and love the spirit that drives you and to be the one that reminds you of that spirit if you are ever to doubt it.

I will remain in touch with you and ask to see you when we come to New Orleans. I have faith in Mr. Patout, and in your ability to handle yourself. Your desires for fairness are admirable and worthy, and I shall do all I can to be of assistance to ensure our common goals are achieved.

Please remember to be vigilant and cautious in your dealings, and to remain strong. You, and you alone, have the ability to keep within your own mind and heart a place where your imagination can take you and your vision encourage you. That power is yours.

I shall think of you with each breath I take, and shall cherish the memory of our last two days until we see each other again. Please destroy this letter knowing if it were to get into the wrong hands, it could be misunderstood and used against you.

With deep affection,
Brody

I lied there reading back through the letter, at least five times. I could not remember the last time anyone had called me Allena. Not even Ma. It made it special he had remembered it and used it. I no longer felt the myriad of emotions I felt as I arrived this morning to find out he was gone. He knew me. He was right. He had listed the emotions he knew I would be going through, and while his explanation for leaving was not as strong as I had wanted, his letter in general was more than I could have expected.

I was relieved of the angst I had felt before. It had slipped away like a ribbon in a stream.

Lightly floating and moving away, balanced and calm. How could he do this so precisely, so specifically, so individually? He had done it. He had taken me through my emotional spectrum and brought me back to my destiny and filled me with determination.

I would go on with my responsibility as I saw it and be a part of my vision for others to be free. I had so many things to work on. I had Mr. Patout and Genevieve. I had Nane and Isum and Letty and the others, and their continued trust of me. I had connections to make, and quilts to design. If this was to come to fruition, then it was going to be my own determination and will power that fulfilled this vision.

I had made this choice, and I was to live in it and make the best of it. Brody was right. The power was mine to dream and make my vision come true. I owed it to him and his belief in me. I owed it the many echelons of people who made the Underground Railroad possible. I owed it to slaves who want their souls to be free. I owed it to myself and my conviction that what I was doing was right.

I folded the letter, put it in my pocket, and stood up from Nane's bed. My leg no longer hurt, but my heart did. I would miss Brody and the moments we had, and the ones that could have been, but I knew I must bare that pain just as I bared the pain of my burns. This one might not go away, and my heart shared a love that consoled the pain at the same time. I was going to make it. I would see him again, and I would write to him and continue to correspond.

I loved Genevieve and would enjoy being her governess. I enjoyed the people here at Belle Terre, and I was going to help them. My future was promising, and I felt assured and confident.

I walked into the kitchen and surprised Nane by my resounding manner. I was cheerful and poised, ready to begin my life again as part of this household.

I had to put aside my doubts and personal wants. The risks I would face would change my life forever, and those I loved. Not truly knowing what my future held, I had a destiny and it was time for me to begin it.

THE END

The Second Book
of
The Knoll Trilogy Series
By Ginger Cucolo

Book One - <u>The Knoll</u>

The potato plants are turning black, their leaves curling and crumbling. No one understands the reason why, especially Allie McCreary. But the potatoes are just the beginning. Widespread starvation is followed by social upheaval. When the McCreary's landowners, the Farradays, find their property and possessions stripped away, Allie's life becomes entangled with them as both families fight to survive in the same world. Her stubbornness is both a blessing and a curse. She and the Farraday boys must find a better way to live. Looking to the opportunity of America, Allie embarks on a journey for a better life, a journey she may not survive.

Book Two - <u>Beyond the Knoll</u>

Allie McCreary embraces her new life in America with the Captain and Rufina, and goes to school in New York City. Her life seems perfect. The Captain purchases a new ship and uses it to stowaway slaves and bring them North to freedom. Allie is independent and strong-willed. She finds herself in a relationship with a wealthy, young man who is the brother of one of her schoolmates whom she does not like. She also chooses to get involved with abolitionists only to find herself in a new adventure that changes her life, again.

Book Three - <u>Return to the Knoll</u>

Allie escapes from slavery and the brutal new land owners who followed no law. Following the Underground Railroad, she finds her way back to New York, and then to Ireland to find what she loves the most.

Made in the USA
Charleston, SC
31 January 2015